An instant reader favorite!

FIND YOU IN THE DARK

Picked for the "What to Read After *Hopeless*" List
by *Maryse's Book Blog*

"Emotional, turbulent, and honest."

—*Heroes and Heartbreakers*

"I can't recommend A. Meredith Walters's books enough. . . . You don't leave her books behind after the story has ended. These are the kinds of books you carry with you."

—*In the Best Worlds*

"There is no question that A. Meredith Walters is one of my favorite authors. She always writes her stories so that we can relate to the characters; they jump out of the books and into our hearts each and every time. Her books have deep meaning to them but are also sweet and sassy with some sexy to steam up the pages."

—*Book Addict Mumma*

"Brilliant, amazing, gut-wrenching."

—*Shh Mom's Reading*

"One wildly bumpy ride. . . . Emotional doesn't even begin to cover it. The feelings were so raw and vivid that it seemed so real. . . . This is one story that I plan to follow to the end. It's going to be me and my t

Bookish Brunette

ALSO BY A. MEREDITH WALTERS

light in the shadows

find you in the dark

in the dark

find you

dark

A. MEREDITH WALTERS

G

GALLERY BOOKS

NEW YORK   LONDON   TORONTO   SYDNEY   NEW DELHI

Gallery Books
A Division of Simon & Schuster, Inc.
1230 Avenue of the Americas
New York, NY 10020

First Gallery Books trade paperback edition June 2014

GALLERY BOOKS and colophon are registered trademarks
of Simon & Schuster, Inc.

For information about special discounts for bulk purchases,
please contact Simon & Schuster Special Sales at 1-866-506-1949
or business@simonandschuster.com.

The Simon & Schuster Speakers Bureau can bring authors
to your live event. For more information or to book an event,
contact the Simon & Schuster Speakers Bureau at 1-866-248-3049
or visit our website at www.simonspeakers.com.

Interior design by Jaime Putorti

Manufactured in the United States of America

10 9 8 7 6 5 4 3 2 1

ISBN 978-1-4767-8231-7
ISBN 978-1-4767-8228-7 (ebook)

For Ian . . . they're all for you.

find you
in
the dark

prologue

how did I get here? When was it that my life took this insane detour into the gigantic mess that I now saw when I looked in the mirror? Sure, everything had started so simply. A look, a touch, a kiss. Your first love is supposed to be beautiful, right?

And maybe it still is. I don't know. All I do know is that I'm kneeling on this nasty bathroom floor in a dingy motel room in the middle of nowhere, wiping my boyfriend's blood off the gritty tiles, the skin of my knees raw from my morbidly methodical task. The sting of tears burns my vision and I feel like I'm about to follow him off the edge.

Wipe, scrub, sweep. That's what I'm doing. Wiping up the turmoil of our relationship. Sweeping away the anger, the hurt, the fear. Scrubbing it all away as I try to figure out how to piece myself back together.

But then I remember those elusive moments. The tiny slivers of time that help me recognize that it wasn't all bad. Because I love him. And he loves me, in the only way he can. Perhaps my only failing was not seeing that I wasn't able to hold it together on my own.

But I'm not one to give up—or forget. No matter how much *they* wanted me to. Because he had, for a moment in time, been my world. My focus, my entire being. And it's hard to think I'm now without that. And maybe what we had, for those few blissful months, had truly been beautiful. Crazy beautiful. Or maybe just crazy.

Who knows? I was scared, tired, and alone, and missing that vital part of myself that had once felt whole and complete and now felt sad and empty. Wipe, scrub, sweep.

The holes would close up. The torn seams would come together. But I would never be as I was before. Before him. My crazy beautiful love.

chapter
one

"You have got to be kidding me."
I groaned, kicking the tire of my piece-of-crap Toyota Corolla that
had refused to start. Standing in my driveway, I unleashed every
curse word imaginable as the minutes slowly ticked toward my inevitable tardiness. "Won't start again, Maggie-Girl?" My father
had poked his head out of the screen door. He had most likely
been made aware of my predicament by my sailor-worthy tirade.

Sighing, I slammed my car door shut and picked up my messenger bag. "Nooo . . ." I dragged out the word in tired defeat. My
dad held the door open for me as I made my way back into the
house. "Didn't you just have it in the shop two weeks ago?" he
asked as I slammed my bag down on the kitchen table and threw
myself into a chair.

I blew my bangs out of my eyes in frustration and didn't bother
answering. Everything was going so spectacularly wrong today. I
shouldn't have bothered to get out of bed. Maybe I should fake a
cough or something and try to convince him to let me stay home.

My father took a bite of toast, crumbs falling into his neatly
trimmed beard. "Well, I'll drive you to school. Can't have you

missing that big chemistry test." He smirked at me, as if reading my ulterior plot to skip school.

I groaned for the millionth time that morning. I'd completely forgotten about the test, but of course my dad, with his iron-trap brain, remembered. Well, that thoroughly screwed up any chance of a good day. Merry freaking Monday.

"Maggie May, what are you still doing here? The tardy bell rings in T-minus-ten minutes." My mother breezed into the kitchen, pouring herself a cup of coffee and conferring with her watch to make sure she wasn't mistaken about the time. Looking at my superserious, all-business, pretty fantastic-looking mother, I wondered, and not for the first time, how I could have come from her DNA. She was my opposite in every possible way: where her hair was blond and shampoo-commercial perfect, mine was a dull, mousy brown that refused to be managed into anything resembling a fashionable style. My mom had a perfect figure. She didn't look anywhere near her age, whereas I had the misfortune of being dubbed a "late bloomer." My underwhelming cup size and nonexistent hips were hardly anything to write home about.

But I did have her eyes. And I will say, allowing myself zero modesty, that they were pretty awesome. I loved that I shared the same dark-brown eyes and thick lashes. They were my best trait (well, aside from my astounding wit and amazing personality, of course), and I received my fair share of compliments because of them. So, no, you couldn't compare me to the back end of a dog or anything, but, like most teenagers, I was anything but pleased with myself.

"Her car wouldn't start. I'm just getting ready to take her to school." My dad filled her in before I could answer. My mom gave me a sympathetic smile before giving her husband a rather obnoxiously sweet kiss good morning. They were really nauseating at times, the way they were still so in love with each other. However, deep down, I just wanted the same thing and I spent a lot of time freaking out that I would never find it. But that was a panic attack for another time.

"We can help you with it this time, you know. You worked really hard over the summer to buy it and it's been nothing but trouble since you parked it in the driveway." My mom, despite her Barbie-perfect appearance and a no-nonsense accountant's personality, was pretty amazing. I took the bagel she handed to me and licked the cream cheese from the top.

"Thanks. But I still have money saved up. Let's just hope I don't need a whole new flipping engine or something," I muttered. My mom ruffled my hair as if I were still five and picked up her briefcase. "Well, Marty, if you've got this under control, I've got to get to the office. I'll probably be late tonight." My mom ran her own accounting firm in the city—and worked a lot.

She leaned down and gave me a quick kiss on the forehead and my dad another loud smack and left. I shoved the rest of my bagel into my mouth and wiped my lips with the back of my hand. A napkin appeared under my nose. "I don't think you were raised in a barn, Maggie," my dad joked. I lightly touched the napkin to my now-clean mouth, just to make him happy.

"You can head on out to the car. I'll meet you there. Call Burt's garage today; they'll come and tow the car. Mom and I will pay for the towing, you pay for the repairs. Deal?" My dad put his tea mug in the sink and filled it with water. I felt guilty having my parents pay for my car in any way, shape, or form.

I had been the one who insisted on buying the shitmobile outside. My dad wanted me to shop around more, to get a CARFAX report; all that rational stuff that I, of course, wouldn't listen to because I was seventeen years old and I knew way more than my parents. Well, I learned that lesson the hard way.

But I knew I most likely wouldn't have enough money to pay for the tow *and* the repairs. My savings from my job at the ice-cream stand over the summer were almost depleted and I would be firmly in mooch territory soon if I didn't find another way to earn money.

I mumbled something unintelligible, not bothering to formulate words. Dad only chuckled. "I'll interpret that as a thank-you," he said, shooing me out of the kitchen. I walked out to the family minivan, not focusing too much on the public mortification of my librarian father taking me to school. If I hadn't been feeling so negative, I'd have appreciated how considerate he was.

I really was lucky in the parental department. My mom and dad always seemed to take my teenage moods in stride. Not much ruffled their feathers. Not that I'd done much ruffling in my seventeen years.

So here comes the obligatory life rundown: I was your typical teenage girl, living in small-town America (Davidson, Virginia, if you really wanted to know), on the corner of Cliché and Stereotype. My life had been conventional and uneventful. I grew up the only child of the local beauty queen and the bookish guy she fell in love with. We had an apple-pie life of family dinners and games of Monopoly on Thursdays (Wednesdays if it was Mom's week for Bunco).

My best friends, Rachel Bradfield and Daniel Lowe, had been my partners in nonexistent crime since the womb. Our mothers had grown up together and it was predetermined that we would be as close as they had been.

I was suitably smart, sporting a solid B-plus average, and had aspirations toward college, just like my friends. I did my homework, followed the rules, and basically bored myself to death. I also was in a very deep, crater-sized rut. How sad to be a senior in high school and already done with it all. And the year had only just begun! It was the first week of September.

My car's refusal to cooperate this morning only added to my overall malaise. I waited less than patiently in the passenger seat, tapping my fingers on the dashboard in an imperfect rhythm. "All right, Maggie-Girl, buckle up." My dad's persistent use of my childhood pet name (only mildly less obnoxious than the fact that I was named after some '70s rock song by a guy with really bad hair and a penchant for supermodels) was sort of grating this morning. I wasn't sure if Dad had yet realized that I wasn't ten anymore. My parents had a really hard time accepting that I was—*gasp*—almost an adult. Although, to be fair, most days (this morning included) I didn't necessarily act the part.

I pulled out my phone and sent a quick text to Rachel and Daniel, letting them know I was running late. Judging by the time, I was at least missing the painful drone of our assistant principal, Mr. Kane, as he read the morning announcements. He always sounded as if he needed to blow his nose.

So maybe the day was still salvageable. I tried to minimize conversation as Dad drifted lazily through our tiny town toward the high school. He sang along, rather badly, to the Righteous Brothers, his voice an alarming falsetto. His shoulders swayed with the beat.

Dad was being so over the top that I couldn't help but crack the barest hint of a smile. He caught me, of course, my emo facade at an effective end. He let out a whoop. "There's my girl's smile! I knew it was hiding somewhere." He reached over and poked me in the side, causing me to squirm and laugh grudgingly.

"You are such a dork, Dad," I told him, not unkindly. He only grinned and turned up the radio. The auditory torture didn't last much longer before we pulled up in front of Jackson High School. I barely gave my dad time to slow down before I propelled myself from the still-moving vehicle.

"Don't forget to call the garage at lunch," Dad reminded me again. I gave him an ironic salute and turned to walk toward the school. I was glad to see I wasn't the only straggler this morning. A few other kids were hurrying from the parking lot.

I fumbled to get my phone out of my jacket pocket, wanting to send a last text to my friends to let them know I was there. I was having a lot of trouble getting it out; thus I was less than attentive as I slammed into the back of someone who had stopped in the middle of the sidewalk.

"Hey!" I yelled as I collided with the very solid body. I dropped my phone, the back popping off and the battery skittering across the concrete. The guy dropped the papers he was holding and they scattered at his feet.

We simultaneously let loose a string of expletives that would have earned me a mouth full of soap had my mother heard. "What the hell?" the guy growled, stooping to pick up the items he had dropped in our human fender bender. Okay, I was already in a craptastic mood and his snotty tone was just the icing on an already pissy cake. So, maybe I was being clumsy and all, but I didn't need some random guy giving me grief. "Oh, I'm sorry; did I miss the Stop sign?" I fired back, not bothering to look at the jackass as I tried to fit the broken metal onto the back of my phone.

I heard what sounded like a gritting of teeth. "Guess it's too much to expect an apology." His sarcasm was thick, his words ground out through an obvious grimace.

"Probably," I quipped, finally looking up into the most amazing pair of brown eyes that I had ever seen.

Hot damn. Cue the violins and happy cartoon bunnies; I was in the middle of a Disney moment. Because this guy was gorgeous. And we were standing so close to each other. If he hadn't been holding on to a barely contained rage directed at yours truly, it could have almost been construed as romantic.

Just add delusions to my growing list of issues.

Mr. Cutie stood there in all his infuriated glory—and he was seriously angry. His perfectly symmetrical face (covered with a fine dusting of adorable freckles, I might add) was flushed a rather alarming shade of red. Those awesome brown eyes flashed murder. He was quite a bit taller than I, with dark hair that curled around his forehead and ears as if he hadn't bothered with a haircut in a while. He had a cleft in his chin and a tiny scar under his right eye. And, despite his obvious good looks, he appeared decidedly unhinged. Wow, they were only papers.

Cute Boy took a deep breath and closed his eyes. I jammed my hands into my pockets and made the decision to get the hell out of there. I started to move around him, making sure to give him a wide berth. His voice, much calmer now, stopped me. "Well, you could at least tell me where the main office is. You know, after practically running me over and all."

If his tone had been playful, I would have been able to pretend he was flirting with me. But nope, he was terse and irritated and in a very bad mood. And I had had enough of it for one morning. So, his cuteness aside, this guy could go take a flying leap somewhere.

"You're a big boy; I'm sure you can handle this one on your own." I turned and quickly walked away.

"Thanks for nothing!" he yelled after me. Yep, Hot Boy came with a bad attitude. Not really my idea of a good time, thank you very much. I couldn't get away fast enough.

chapter
two

"That's it! I'm swearing off every member of the female population. Do they still have monasteries? 'Cause a lifetime of praying and bad haircuts sure as hell beats chicks and their freaking drama." Daniel's lunch tray came down with a loud clang on the table.

Rachel and I rolled our eyes in unison and turned to the third member of our trio with what we hoped were supportive expressions. "What did Kylie do this time?" Rachel asked, popping a Cheeto into her mouth. Daniel ran his hand over his buzzed blond head. He was clearly very agitated. But, honestly, when wasn't he agitated? Daniel was as big a drama queen (or king, or whatever) as any girl.

He let out a long, tortured sigh and propped his chin on his hand. Rachel's eyes went all gooey and I saw the telltale signs of her unrequited crush rearing its ugly head. Looking at our best friend, it was easy for me to understand why she felt the way she did. Daniel was easily one of the best-looking guys at Jackson High School. If he weren't the closest thing I had to a brother, I would have joined Rachel in Crushland. His puppy-dog eyes and perfect lips were many a girl's dream and definitely helped in the popularity department. Rachel and I, being his best friends, gained popularity by association. Not that I cared much about all that.

Daniel's on-and-off relationship with Kylie Good, a perky junior who happened to be co-captain of the girls' field-hockey team and was so cute you wanted to slap her, was the source of a lot of drama. Honestly, it was exhausting, even as a spectator. Kylie was nice in a fake kind of way but, in my opinion, her insane insecurities and even more insane jealousy made her truly insufferable and a really shitty girlfriend.

Personally, I thought Daniel got off on the craziness of their relationship. Some people were like that—getting some sort of thrill out of constant turmoil. Otherwise I couldn't wrap my mind around why Daniel had put up with all of that nonsense for the past year and a half.

"I've been staying after school getting help in trig from Laura Johnson. Shit, it's just schoolwork. And it's fucking Laura 'Granny Panties' Johnson! It's not like I've been secretly banging her as she whispers math problems in my ear or something." Rachel and I each stifled a giggle. Daniel shook his bottle of chocolate milk, his admitted weakness, and opened it roughly. He raised his eyebrows as we tried to stop laughing. I schooled my face into blank attentiveness.

"So Kylie thinks you're getting it on with Laura? Really? Has she lost what few brains haven't already gone missing from one too many hockey sticks to the head?" I asked, popping open my can of soda. Daniel frowned and chose to ignore my comment. Rachel jumped in, the epitome of understanding and support.

"So, what happened, Danny? Did you guys have a fight?" Daniel's expression smoothed out and he sighed again. Yep, total drama queen.

"Yeah, Kylie just went off on me. She says I shouldn't be spending so much time alone with girls that weren't her. She is just completely irrational."

"What about us? You spend tons of time with us. Last time I checked, we fit in the vagina column," I remarked. Daniel choked on his milk. Rachel snorted.

Daniel cleared his throat. "You guys don't really count. I mean, you're Rachel and Mags. Kylie knows that you guys might as well have a penis." Well, that was more than bordering on offensive. Rachel moved her hands into her lap, clearly hurt by Daniel's words. He was so dense. How could he not know that saying something like that could hurt someone's feelings?

When he saw the looks on our faces, his cheeks went red. "No, I didn't mean it like that. Of course I know you're girls . . . it's just you're my friends and everything . . . and . . . oh, hell, I didn't mean to be a dick." Okay, maybe he wasn't a complete dolt. I shrugged, letting him know he was cool—with me, at least. Rachel wouldn't look at him. "Rachel, I'm sorry. Don't be mad at me. You know it's just my verbal diarrhea brought on by a bad case of Kylie angst. Forgive me, darlin'." Daniel was laying it on thick and Rachel was defenseless against his evil attack of charm.

Rachel smiled at him. "I understand," she told him, and I thought I would gag at her simpering. I loved Rachel, don't get me wrong. But I wished she would grow a pair when it came to Daniel. He unknowingly walked all over her. Daniel was not an asshole by nature, just really self-centered and egocentric. He was a good friend, though, and fiercely protective of Rachel and me, which is why it was so easy to dismiss his moments of jerkiness.

But Rachel had it so bad that I felt horrible for her. She had loved Daniel pretty much since we could formulate words. She held him up as some sort of perfect specimen of man. She never dated, holding out hope for her fairy-tale ending. Poor girl. And Daniel had no flipping clue. Okay, he *was* a dolt. Because Rachel was stunning. Her brown hair wasn't mousy like mine; it was lovely and curly in a way I always envied. She was shorter than I but possessed curves that clearly stated "I am Girl, hear me roar." She and Daniel would have made the most gorgeous couple, if only he could see past his own idiocy.

"I just can't take her crap anymore," Daniel moaned, bringing the conversation back to him and Kylie. Rachel, being the total nurturer, rubbed the back of his hand.

"Danny, you are only seventeen. You really don't need all the hassle." As if I couldn't see the true motive behind her words.

Well, I was less diplomatic. I leaned over and grabbed a fry from Daniel's tray. "Just dump her, Danny. She's a serious wack job. One day you'll come home and she'll have boiled your guinea pig." Daniel arched that annoying eyebrow in my direction and started eating his less-than-edible hamburger.

Rachel frowned at me, clearly irritated by my lack of sensitivity. Excuse me if I didn't understand why people wasted so much energy on relationships that made them miserable. I had an awesome example of what functional love was supposed to look like and so much of what I saw around me was anything but that—which, I guess, is why I never bothered with the whole dating thing. Nothing lived up to the standards that I had set for myself.

Sure, kissing was fun, but it was all that other messy stuff that seemed to come with teenage dating that I could do without.

I'd never had a "boyfriend" per se. I'd gone on a handful of dates, made out some, feinted going to second base at the occasional party after a football game (though I was by no means a slut or a tease; my boundaries were firmly in place). That was all fine and dandy, but I just didn't see the need to pair off with some random the way Daniel and Rachel did.

Rachel was a hopeless romantic, her crush on Daniel a case in point. She longed for her one great love and all that Romeo and Juliet junk. She had told me more than once that my double-X chromosome must be on the fritz because I was unconcerned with all those female trappings. Not that I was a tomboy or anything; I just had a more masculine approach to hooking up and dating.

"You make it sound so easy, Maggie. One day you'll get it," Daniel muttered. I just shrugged and focused on my lunch, letting Rachel do the whole advice-and-consoling thing. She was much better at it, anyway.

While my friends ruminated on the disastrous state of Daniel's love life, my eyes flitted around the cafeteria. Everyone and everything was just as it should be. The population of Jackson High School existed in their perfectly predestined circles. The jocks ate at their table in the middle of the room, making suggestive comments to the cheerleaders and tripping the A/V geeks as they scuttled by. The goth kids sat in the back, writing bad poetry, or applying more eyeliner, or whatever it was they did. The social outcasts sat on the fringes, not making eye contact. Nothing changed. Everything was so predictable and boring I wanted to gouge my eyes out.

Then my eyes landed on *him*. That familiar black hair and beat-up army jacket. It was the not-so-pleasant guy from this morning. Now, there was someone who was anything but boring, even if he seemed a bit psychotically temperamental.

He was making his way through the lunch line, haphazardly dropping food items on his tray. He obviously couldn't care less about what he was going to eat and seemed to be doing nothing more than going through the motions.

Even from here, his good looks were startling. He definitely had the attention of most of the kids in the room. The girls whispered to each other as they batted their Maybelline-mascaraed eyes in his direction. The jocks stared him down, feeling the threat of encroaching testosterone in their territory.

What was interesting to watch was this guy clearly not giving a shit about any of it. In fact, his body language practically screamed "Leave me alone!" He stood with his shoulders hunched forward, his chin pointed down toward his chest. His shaggy hair hung in his face, obscuring his eyes. He shuffled along as if he were trying not to draw attention to himself.

Good luck there, buddy. Davidson was a small town, and the arrival of a new student was like a bloody steak dropped into a tank full of sharks. He'd be devoured in no time.

I watched him pay for his food without saying a word to the lunch lady. He picked up his tray and moved quickly toward a table near the back. Into the outcast zone. Interesting. This guy could easily have sat anywhere. He could have carved out any place within the social hierarchy that he wanted. But instead he sat at a table by himself without once making eye contact with anyone. He pulled an MP3 player out of his tattered army-jacket pocket and put the earbuds in. His vibe was loud and clear: don't approach under fear of death!

"Hello! Earth to Maggie!" Rachel wiggled her fingers in my face, breaking my single-minded focus on Mr. Cute and Gloomy. Rachel followed my line of vision and smirked. "Ah, checking out the new kid, huh?" I grunted noncommittally and turned my back on the lonely boy at the rear of the cafeteria. I looked at Rachel and Daniel, who wore identical grins.

"What?" I asked defensively.

"Aw. Mags has a whittle ol' cwush." Daniel obnoxiously ruffled my hair. I swatted his hand away and smoothed the flyaway strands.

"You're as crazy as your Glenn Close psycho girlfriend. I met him this morning and he's a total ass. Not remotely crush-worthy," I lied, stuffing a Snickers bar into my mouth in an attempt to limit conversation.

Rachel laughed. "Well, whatever he is, he is smokin' hot with a capital *H*. Though he's kind of an oddball. He was in my creative-writing class this morning. His name is Clayton Reed and he just moved here last week from Florida. But he's some kind of socialphobe or something. He wouldn't talk to anyone and pretty much ignored everyone who tried to talk to him. And Lord knows the girls were trying."

"Well, he certainly didn't have any trouble talking when he was chewing me a new one this morning," I said, glancing over my shoulder at Clayton again.

"What is this? Was he mean to you? Do I need to have a talk with this guy?" Daniel asked, jumping into protective-brother mode. Daniel took his role as pseudosibling very seriously. No one messed with Rachel or me without making a very serious enemy. It was nice to know someone like Daniel had your back. The boy had clout in our little ecosystem and I felt pleasantly protected by Daniel's friendship. But I recognized the mama-bear glint in his eyes and I had to neutralize it before it led to a confrontation and further humiliation and embarrassment.

"Heel, Danny. I'm a big girl and can fight my own battles. I wasn't Miss Suzy Sunshine either," I conceded.

Rachel chuckled. "Now, that sounds more like it. Our Maggie doesn't take being verbally berated without giving as good as she gets." I tossed my straw wrapper at my best friend.

"Shut up, Rachel. I'm the nicest person you know," I told her with mock indignation. Rachel balled up the paper and flicked it back in my direction.

"Yeah, right, Mags. It's not like you don't have a reputation for taking people out at the knees or anything," Daniel joked, jabbing his fork into his fruit cup. Okay, I admit it: I'm not the easiest person to be around sometimes—or maybe even most of the time. I had a habit of speaking my mind without thinking, of telling the absolute truth without any thought of the possible consequences. I had no time for fluff, so I simply didn't bother.

"I just have a low bullshit tolerance, and I, for one, think that is an admirable trait," I bit out, a little annoyed with my friends for

painting me in such a negative light. Daniel patted my arm, noticing my dark look.

"You're right. I'd rather be around someone who tells it like it is
than have to second-guess everything coming out of their mouth.
I think you are a refreshing change from the rest of the sheep at
this school."

Rachel smiled at me. "Ditto," she said, reaching over and giving
me a one-armed hug.

My friends were so cool and great for that needed self-esteem
boost. There was a reason I kept them around.

My attention was suddenly pulled back to the table occupied
by Clayton Reed. I heard a raised voice and groaned at seeing
meathead Paul Delawder holding Clayton's MP3 player. Paul was a
raging douche bag. He made it his mission in life to taunt, terrorize, and humiliate most of the student body. He skipped school at
least three days each week and failed most of his classes. He had
already been kept back twice and he was the oldest senior in our
class, being nineteen and all. He had a designated desk in the de-
tention room and bragged about getting a plaque for it. He was a
nasty moron with a taste for abuse and definitely not my favorite
person. He and I had had multiple run-ins over the years and I
also had been on the receiving end of his harassment a time or
two. My hands clenched as I watched the school bully zero in on
his new target.

Paul leaned across the table and got in Clayton's face. Clayton
wouldn't look up, his hair still in his eyes, but I could see the tension in his shoulders. Clayton was not a small guy: his chest was
wide and his arms were thick. I bet he could have taken Paul if
he'd wanted to. But instead all he did was sit there and seem to
shut down, refusing to engage.

"One day someone is going to punch that loser right in the
face," Rachel muttered, looking away from the scene. I wanted
that person to be Clayton. I don't know why I felt such a weird

protectiveness for this guy who had been a total jerk to me. Maybe it was because there was something about Clayton Reed that seemed to broadcast vulnerability. The hunch in his shoulders, the refusal to look at anyone. It was as if he didn't want anyone to see him, and that made me want to do just that.

I had never been drawn to someone the way I was finding myself drawn to Clayton. I didn't even know him, had only shared a mouthful of words (and they weren't nice), but I wanted to say more, to hear more. So seeing Paul make Clayton his new verbal punching bag set off my once-thought-nonexistent nurturing side.

When Paul threw the MP3 player on the floor and stomped on it, I couldn't take it anymore. Without thinking, I got out of my seat and started moving toward the pair. I barely registered the "oh, crap" looks on my friends' faces before I found myself behind Paul. The bully didn't hear me approach; he was much too focused on his prey.

"Look at me, you little faggot. You are such a fucking pussy, can't even say anything. Are you fucking retarded?" Paul snarled. Clayton continued to stare at the tabletop, but I noticed the fine tremors in his hands. I wasn't sure how he could sit there and take this crap. But I, for one, wasn't going to.

"Shut up, Paul. Don't you have a toilet somewhere that you should be drinking out of?" I said, shoving the much bigger senior out of my way. Paul looked down at me in surprise. Then he laughed.

"You want some of this, bitch?" Paul made a threatening move toward me. I caught a movement out of the corner of my eye and saw Clayton get to his feet, his face red. He looked like he was about to kill someone. I shivered at his expression. Paul stepped forward and I instinctively kneed him in the groin, sending him to the floor like a bag of rocks.

I heard a collective gasp from the kids sitting at the tables around us. Typical sheep mentality. They will sit there and watch it all go down but won't lift a finger to help. Refusing to rock the proverbial boat. Jerks.

Then I heard the sound of the assistant principal, Mr. Kane, approaching quickly. "What's going on here?" Dear God, someone give this guy a tissue already! He was always stuffed up. Mr. Kane frowned at me and then at Paul, who was still on the floor with his hands cupped around a very specific part of his anatomy.

Paul struggled to his feet, his face purple with a barely suppressed rage. I gave my best innocent smile. "Nothing, Mr. Kane. I think Paul was about to get sick or something. I was just making sure he was all right."

Paul gave me a look that could have knocked me dead. But he proved he wasn't a complete moron by giving a tight nod and an even tighter smile. "I'm fine. This girl here"—he couldn't even remember my name, asswipe—"was just making sure I was okay. It's nothing." Mr. Kane gave him a sharp look, and I was sure he wasn't fooled by our barely concealed lie. "Well, if you're sick, you'd best get checked out by the nurse." Paul didn't move right away, not wanting to leave the scene of his attempted crime.

Mr. Kane shooed him with his hands. "Go on, Mr. Delawder. I'll walk you there, to make sure you get to where you are supposed to be." The assistant principal turned back to me. "And you can get to class." Paul met my eyes as he was being herded out of the cafeteria and mouthed a really nasty word. One for a female body part.

Finally, when things had settled and conversations around us had resumed, I turned to look at Clayton. I had fully intended to ask him if he was okay but was surprised to find him looking at me with full-on anger.

He picked up his ruined MP3 player and shoved it into his pocket. He slowly slung his bag over his shoulder and met my eyes with a gaze as cold as ice. "In the future, mind your own business," he told me. I stared at him with my mouth hanging open; for once I had no comeback readily available.

Seriously? I had just stopped him from being bullied by the resident jerkwad, and this was the thanks I got? Before I could find my voice, Clayton Reed turned and walked away, leaving me dumbstruck and strangely intrigued by this mysterious new student. It was official: I had lost my flipping mind.

chapter
three

"You stepped all over his manhood with your sparkly flip-flops, Mags. No guy likes to be saved by a chick. It's *our* job to do the saving. It's in the man code or something," Daniel told me after school, four days after my disastrous run-in with Clayton Reed. Four days, and I was still venting about his attitude and lack of gratitude.

Okay, to be honest, I wasn't really irritated by that anymore. I was more irritated by the fact that I hadn't crossed paths with him since. Clayton seemed to be making it his mission to stay out of my and everyone else's way. So I was still talking about our exchange in a desperate attempt to keep it all relevant, mostly because I couldn't stop talking about him. *Or* thinking about him.

But Daniel's words were just completely asinine. I frowned at best friend number 2. "That is so dumb. What was with the whole suffrage thing and the entire push for gender equality if we still have to bow down to gender stereotypes?" I asked in my best haughty tone.

Rachel, who stood beside me rummaging through her purse for her car keys, lifted a hand to pat me on the back.

"I know it's stupid, but guys are still just cavemen deep down," she mused as the three of us made our way toward the parking lot.

"Please don't tell me you buy into this macho BS, Rache. My inner feminist can't handle it," I muttered, pulling my hair tie from my wrist and scraping my hair into a tight ponytail. Rachel only smiled and pulled on the hair tie, loosening it.

"You're going to cut off the blood flow to your brain if you keep wearing your hair that tight," she said. Rachel had been after me to let her cut my hair for years. But I liked it long. It was like my security blanket.

I grumbled under my breath, although I gave up on my irritation. It wasn't directed at my friends anyway and they didn't deserve my foul mood. Rachel, in her Psychic Friends Network way, nudged my shoulder with hers.

"I haven't seen much of him either, you know. He sits in the back of class and doesn't talk to a soul. So it's not just you he's rude to."

I wouldn't meet her eyes, couldn't let her know that her words comforted me in some strange way. I needed to let this go. It was painfully obvious Clayton Reed and I were not destined to be BFFs anytime soon. He was a social misfit, a pariah, and apparently had no desire to interact with the world in general. And while I wasn't always the most likable person out there, even I couldn't get to know someone who wanted nothing to do with me.

Daniel jumped down the last three steps outside the school, landing on his feet with a dramatic flourish. Rachel and I gave him an obligatory round of applause. He was such a show-off sometimes. "Seriously, though, Mags, that dude is super-odd anyway. It's probably best you steer clear of him. Rumor has it he was shipped here because he had been expelled from his last school for calling in a bomb threat or something. Guy seems unhinged, if you ask me," Daniel remarked, walking backward down the side-walk.

"You're going to fall on your ass, Danny." I laughed as he came off the curb and stumbled into the street. Daniel straightened himself and gave a quick look around to see if anyone had witnessed his moment of uncoolness.

But my friend's words interested me. Bomb threat, huh? Yet I wasn't one to put much stock in rumors. Last year I had broken my arm after lamely falling down the stairs at home in the middle of the night when I wanted a snack. I never told anyone but Rachel and Daniel how it happened, but somehow a story started circulating that I had broken my arm after a confrontation with a mugger in the city. I had apparently fought back and slammed my arm into a parked car as the villain tried to take off with my purse. The story was so detailed, I almost believed it myself. Where do people come up with this stuff? However, I never corrected anyone because the made-up story was way better than the truth.

We reached Daniel's overly masculine diesel truck and he gave me a quick hug. "Like I said, don't worry about some dude ignoring you. You always have my full attention." He gave me a sloppy kiss on the forehead, laughed, and jumped into the driver's seat before I could smack him. He gave Rachel and me a wave and then pulled out of the parking lot. Rachel sighed as he drove away.

I gave her a gentle nudge. "He's a goob, Rache. Sure, we love him, but he's Daniel and he won't ever change," I tried to tell her supportively. Rachel gave me a shaky smile. Her unrequited crush was becoming harder and harder to watch. And she was having a harder and harder time pretending that Daniel's blasé attitude toward her didn't hurt.

"You heading home?" I asked her, trying to change the subject. Rachel shook her head.

"Nope. I've got to be at work in fifteen minutes. I'm going to have to change when I get there. Sorry. You staying for cross-country?" she asked me, pulling her keys out of the front pocket of her book bag.

"No, practice was canceled. I was hoping you'd keep me from feeling like an unsociable loser and give me something to do." I pouted playfully. Rachel laughed.

"You want to get together over the weekend? Maybe see a movie or something?" she asked me. Then she looked down at her shoes, suddenly finding them really interesting. "I'm sure Daniel will be with Kylie, so let's not bother asking him to come," she added, her voice getting all wobbly when she said our friend's name. I didn't address the issue again and instead smiled brightly at her.

"Sounds good. Call me when you get home tonight and we'll make plans."

Rachel nodded and we parted ways, each going toward our respective cars. It was nice having my wheels back. The two days of being without them had been torture. I was lucky that I'd needed only a new battery, so I was able to pay for it and the towing without having to bum money off my parents. Though that didn't change my desperate need for a job ASAP.

I was thinking about going home to look online for gainful employment when I saw him. Clayton Reed. By now the school parking lot was pretty much cleared out and it almost seemed as if he had been waiting until he could sneak out without anyone noticing. But of course I noticed.

One thing was certain. Clayton seemed to be making a supreme effort to avoid contact with the rest of the human species. So it wasn't surprising that rumors were flying like crazy about him. Aside from the one that Daniel had told me, I had heard that he was in the witness-protection program. I had also overheard some girls in my English lit class saying in breathy whispers that they'd been told he had a terminal brain tumor and had come to Davidson so he could get treatment at the hospital at the University of Virginia, which was twenty minutes away. I had rolled my eyes at that one. Then there was the rumor that he was actually an indie-rock star and was lying low to get some downtime from the craziness of fame. It really depended on whom you talked to as to what story you heard. I was certain that none of these scenarios were remotely accurate, but there was something very mysterious about Clayton, that was for sure.

Why did I feel this persistent need to see him? To talk to him and figure him out? Maybe I felt a sense of kinship at the way he shunned everything high school. Maybe it was the way he was shut down with everyone else but would breathe fire when he spoke to me. Yeah, he had been a dick during our two interactions, but passionate and furious—so different from the closed-off persona he exhibited the other 99 percent of the time.

So when I saw him walking across the parking lot, I followed some half-cocked instinct and made my way toward him. His head was down and his hands in the pockets of his signature green army jacket. He must have gotten a new MP3 player, because I could see the wire of the earbuds peeking out from his collar.

He was oblivious to everything around him, so he didn't notice me until I was standing right beside him.

"Whoa. Stalk much?" he asked, yanking the earbuds out in irritation. What was it about me that coaxed this reaction from him? He never ignored *me.* No, he acted as if my one purpose on this planet were to annoy the shit out of him. He was testy and terse and not displaying any of the social aversion he showed at school. And I loved it. I was such a weirdo.

But I figured it was time to call him on his attitude. No sense in letting him think he could treat me like that and get away with it, no matter how much I dug his James Dean *Rebel Without a Cause* shtick. "What is your problem? Have I unknowingly run over your puppy or something?" I bit back, crossing my arms over my chest, doing my best to act unaffected and maybe even mildly intimidating.

Yeah, that didn't work. Clayton snorted, and I swear I saw a hint of a smile. I held my hands up, palms out. "Stop the presses! Was that a facial expression other than annoyance and disdain?" I asked sarcastically. Clayton smirked at me, his lips turning up slightly. He actually seemed amused, for once.

"Are you trying to tell me that my reigning title of Mr. Congeniality is in jeopardy?" he asked, openly smiling at me now. His face seemed to light up when he did that, and my throat constricted painfully. If I thought he was hot before, that was *nothing* compared to the way he looked when he smiled. I was a goner.

I relaxed a bit, taking a cue from his change in demeanor. Nice to feel like we weren't going to war at any moment, as much as I got into the verbal-sparring thing. I flipped my bangs out of my eyes, trying to get a better look at him. He had gotten a haircut, much to my disappointment. His shaggy hair was much more manageable now, and I found that I missed the curls around his ears and at the base of his neck. Maybe I *was* a stalker.

"Well, you aren't earning a reputation for your witty banter, Mr. Chatterbox," I volleyed back. I hadn't realized we had stopped walking until I heard the chirp of a car lock being opened. We were standing at a black BMW. My eyes widened some. "Your car?" I asked, looking through the window at the sleek, leather interior. Clayton nodded, opening the door and tossing his bag onto the passenger seat.

"Nice wheels," I commented, not wanting to draw any attention to my crapmobile, two rows over.

We fell into an uncomfortable silence. Obviously he wasn't interested in discussing his car. So I had no idea what to say next. I kicked a piece of gravel and dragged my toe through the dust of the parking lot, making patterns with my shoe. "So, did I kill your dog or what?" I asked, trying to continue our struggling conversation. I didn't want him to go. I wanted to keep him here, looking like that—you know, without the cold anger in his eyes.

"No pet-icide that I know of," he answered shortly, leaning against the BMW. I was relieved to see he wasn't making any moves to leave. So maybe he didn't hate my guts after all.

"So why the attitude when I talk to you? I mean, I get that I stole your guy card the other day, but I honestly didn't mean to. But Paul is such a dickface and I hate how he mouths off like that. I was seriously only trying to help . . ." My voice tapered off and I realized I was majorly rambling.

I looked at Clayton, who was staring straight ahead of him. That tightness had returned to his shoulders and, inexplicably, I wanted to rub them for him. After a few seconds, he finally spoke up. "I know you were just trying to be nice. I get what you were doing. I was just pissed, I guess. Or maybe 'embarrassed' is more like it. You were there, I was mad, so I shot my mouth off at you. You didn't deserve that. I'm sorry." He finally looked at me, and I was taken under by the intensity of his brown eyes. He looked at me like I was the only person in the world. It was a heady feeling.

I had to break the moment. I was scared my mouth was hanging open. And it felt like things were building to a point that I wasn't ready for.

"Well, what about that morning? You sorry for that, too?" I asked jokingly. Clayton cocked his eyebrow at me. Damn, he was sexy.

"Um, no. You were the one who resembled a human wrecking ball. I didn't have a chance."

I chuckled. It was nice to know that Mr. Grumpy actually had a sense of humor. I stuck out my hand and he looked at me as if I had grown three heads. "Let's start over. Hello, my name is Maggie Young. Seventeen-year-old self-confessed chocoholic and overall fabulous human being. Pleased to meet you."

Clayton slowly reached out and clasped my hand in his. His handshake was firm and made those obnoxious butterflies in my stomach take flight at the feel of his warm skin against mine. His smile was wide and genuine, making his brown eyes sparkle. "Clayton Reed, though you can call me Clay. Seventeen-year-old senior and unabashed misanthrope." He dropped my hand and stood there awkwardly.

"Misanthrope, huh? So you're a people hater? Well, aren't you a barrel of fun?" I leaned against his car beside him. We were standing so close that our shoulders brushed against each other. I couldn't help but notice the tantalizing smell of his cologne, something citrusy and musky all at once. Clay moved marginally so that no part of our bodies touched. I tried to squelch my disappointment. I secretly—and, I hoped, imperceptibly—sniffed myself. All clear: deodorant was still working.

"Can't say that *fun* is a word I would use to describe myself lately. Maybe at one time . . ." Clayton's words trailed off and he peeked at me through his lashes as if he were embarrassed at revealing anything remotely personal about himself.

"It must have been hard to have to transfer your senior year of high school. I mean, leaving your friends, girlfriend, whatever." Wow, I wasn't subtle at all. I cringed at my obvious dig for information. I didn't want to seem so blatantly eager, but I just couldn't help myself.

Clayton's small smile appeared again, letting me know he wasn't fooled by my conspicuous line of questioning. "It wasn't that big of a deal. No real friends to speak of. No girlfriend." He smirked and then looked away. His answer made me sad, though. How depressing to not have any friends, nothing to really tie you to a particular place.

"Well, maybe that will change here," I said. Clayton looked at me questioningly and I realized that the statement sounded more like a coy invitation. I coughed uncomfortably and cleared my throat. "I mean, making friends and all," I covered lamely.

Clay nodded. "Maybe." He didn't sound at all convinced.

"Did your parents get new jobs or something? Is that why you moved?" I asked. Clayton's discomfort seemed magnified with my question. I thought it was innocent enough, nothing to incite the reaction I got. Clayton moved a good foot away from me and shoved his hands deep into the pockets of his jacket. He turned his head away.

"Uh, no. There were just . . . um . . . circumstances that required me to move." The tone of his voice let me know that that particular subject was closed.

"You're not in the witness-protection program, are you?" I kidded, not wanting to drop the conversation. I wanted to know everything about Clayton Reed. He was going to be my friend, whether he wanted to be or not.

Clay laughed. "Nope. Can't say that I am."

"Rock star, then."

He shook his head.

"Please tell me you don't have a brain tumor." By this point Clayton's laugh was deep. His eyes crinkled at the corners and he seemed genuinely tickled by my questions.

"Brain tumor? Really? Where the hell did you get that one?" he asked, wiping the tears from his eyes after he had finally stopped laughing.

I shrugged. "You should hear the rumors going around about you." Clay groaned. I playfully nudged his arm. He seemed startled by the physical contact but, for the first time, didn't pull away.

"That's what you get for your International Man of Mystery persona, buddy," I told him.

"Well, I just don't want people all up in my business, is all. I'm not exactly outgoing, if you couldn't tell," Clay conceded, looking at me for a moment as if I were one of those people he didn't want "up in his business."

Well, too bad, Clayton Reed, I *was* going to be *all* up in your business. This guy was way too closed off and more than a little sad. I didn't think anyone could survive on so little personal interaction. Maybe I was being pushy, but something told me that there was a part of Clay that needed this. Someone taking the time to get to know him, and to give a shit.

After a few more minutes of less-awkward silence, Clay turned toward his Beamer. "Well, I'd better head home. Nice meeting you, Maggie." He pulled open the door and stood there for a moment, as if trying to decide whether he really wanted to leave or not.

I moved away from his car, pulling my book bag onto my shoulder. I gave him a small wave. "Sure. It was nice meeting you, too. Maybe I'll see you around," I said noncommittally, although I knew I'd be hunting him down in the hallways first thing Monday morning. Clay smirked at me again, as if he could read my thoughts.

"I'm sure you will." He started the engine and pulled out of his parking space. He gave a small salute and headed out of the parking lot. I stood there, mute, watching him go. I really hoped he didn't look in his rearview mirror and see me staring after him like that, but I just couldn't make myself move. Not until he was long gone.

✦

"Wait! You actually spoke to him? Why did it take you this long to tell me? You should have said something immediately! This is major! What's he like?" Rachel shot off her questions at a rapid-fire pace as we sat in my kitchen Saturday afternoon. We had just returned from seeing a really horrible romantic comedy, and we were trying to figure out what to do with the rest of our day. I had casually mentioned my conversation with Clay and she had jumped all over it.

I went to the refrigerator and got a soda, tossing Rachel a bottle of water, which she missed and which hit the tile floor with a loud thud. "Nice catch, DiMaggio," I said sarcastically. Rachel flipped me her middle finger and leaned down to pick up the bottle. Once upright, she pushed it onto the counter and gave me the look that let me know I had a lot of explaining to do.

"Do not evade, Maggie May Young! Answer my questions! I need to know everything about your exchange with Mr. Clayton Reed."

I perched on the stool beside my friend and slowly popped open my soda can. Then I took my time taking a long drink before setting it down on the counter. Rachel was ready to pop. "C'mon! Stop stalling! Tell me about him!"

It was at that moment that my mother decided to make an appearance. "Tell you about who?" she asked breezily as she took a glass from the cabinet. My face flamed red. I absolutely *did not* want to discuss Clayton Reed in front of my mom. As much as I loved my parents, there were limits to what I wanted them to know. I had stopped talking to my parents about my crushes around the time I had started shaving my legs. It's not as if they would be weird or overly protective or anything; it was just too embarrassing.

"Claay-ton Reee-eed," Rachel told her in a singsong voice. I shot her a dark look and she stuck her tongue out at me, whispering, "That's what you get."

I rolled my eyes and sighed. My mom came over with a glass of some gross mixture of herbs that she swore kept her healthy.

"Clayton Reed? Who is that?" my mom asked, sitting on the stool to the other side of me. Great, she was preparing for a full-on gossip fest. This would take a while. I wanted to throttle Rachel.

"Nobody," I evaded, drinking the last of my soda and getting up to throw the can into the recycling bin.

"Nobody, my butt! The new hot guy at school is who," Rachel eagerly volunteered, giving my mom a dramatic raise of her eyebrows.

"Oh! Do tell, Maggie May! I want to hear all about him!" My mom was enthusiastic and really getting into the girl talk.

"Yes, do tell, Mags," Rachel agreed, grinning at me. I turned my back on them as I rummaged through the pantry, trying to find something to snack on. I wasn't really hungry; I just didn't want to look at them. No sense in getting ragged about the bright pink blush I could feel on my face.

"Nothing really to tell. I spoke with him yesterday before leaving school. He's pretty funny, though he didn't have a whole lot to say," I said, pulling out a package of Oreos and cramming one into my mouth. Yeah, it was my age-old defense mechanism. Eating so I didn't have to talk. Amazing that I didn't weigh two hundred pounds by now.

"That's it? Come on, Maggie, what did you talk about? What does he look like?" my mom asked.

"Oh, he is really good-looking, Mrs. Young. He has dark hair and dark eyes. He's pretty tall and has these awesome broad shoulders and cute-as-hell freckles on his nose and cheeks." I was a little surprised at how much Rachel had noticed about Clayton. Considering he wasn't Daniel Lowe, I didn't think she'd pay him any attention.

"He sounds dreamy," my mom said. I choked on my cookie.

I cleared my throat. "'Dreamy'? Really, Mom? Did we enter a time warp and end up in 1950?" I asked her sarcastically. My mom rolled her eyes. Hmm, wonder where I got that particular facial expression from.

"Well, did he ask you out? Is he going to be your boyfriend?" my mom joked, getting up and throwing her arm around my shoulders, squeezing.

I squirmed. "Uh, no. I'm not even sure I'm going to be his friend. He's pretty standoffish."

"Maggie has a boyfriend," Rachel teased. I threw my balled-up napkin at her.

"You are not helping here, Rache," I muttered.

My mom laughed. "I'm just teasing, Maggie. But if this boy ever becomes something, you know we'd want to meet him," she said seriously. I clenched my teeth. Yeah, I knew that. As much as I would love for Clayton to be something more, I didn't want to go through that mortally humiliating rite of passage, otherwise known as "meeting the parents."

"Sure," I said dismissively. Rachel was trying really hard not to laugh at my discomfort. She would be getting an earful as soon as my mom decided to leave the kitchen.

"Well, you girls enjoy your afternoon. Dad and I are going to the farmers' market in Charlottesville. If you go out, don't forget your house key." I nodded and was relieved when she left.

I whipped around to face Rachel, who had already put her hands up in surrender. "Don't say it. You deserved it, stringing me along with the details like that," she said. I frowned at her.

"Using my mother as your weapon was a low blow, and you know it," I retorted. Rachel only grinned, not concerned by my irritation.

At that moment her phone went off. It vibrated across the countertop and she had to grab it before it fell off the edge. "What's up, Mom?" she asked after answering it. I resumed my seat on the stool and picked at my bright-blue nail polish as I waited for her to get off the phone.

"Seriously? Do I have to?" I looked up, and Rachel did not look happy. She sighed heavily. "Fine, I'll be there in ten." She hung up and looked at me apologetically.

"You're bailing on me?" I whined. Rachel got up and grabbed her purse.

"Sorry, Mags, but my mom needs me to take Caitlyn to some stupid birthday party. She was called in to work. Duty calls." Caitlyn was Rachel's eight-year-old half sister and permanent pain in the butt. Rachel lived with her mom and Caitlyn. Rachel's dad had been out of the picture since Rachel was five, and Caitlyn's dad had left a few years back. Her mom worked as a nurse over at County General and often got called in, leaving Rachel to play Mommy.

"That's cool. Just call me later," I told her, not wanting her to feel guilty for having to cancel our afternoon. She gave me a hug.

"I still want to hear all about your run-in with Clayton. I know there was more to that conversation than you're telling me." She wagged her finger at me and I chuckled.

"Sure, whatever you say," I said, following her to her car.

I waved as she pulled out of my driveway. Mom and Dad had already left and I was stuck in the quiet house alone. I really didn't feel like being by myself so I tried calling Daniel. I got his voice mail and didn't bother leaving a message. Well, that exhausted my entire social circle; how sad. I was then faced with an endless afternoon with nothing to do.

Grabbing my keys, making sure my house key was on the ring to appease my mother, I got in my car with no real agenda. I headed over to Fayetteville, the next town over. Once there, I made my way toward the older part of town and pulled into a small parking lot. I looked at the beat-up sign in front of the tiny brick building and smiled. Ruby's Bookshelf was my favorite store. I hadn't been here in months and it seemed a great way to pass the afternoon.

The door chimed as I went through it and I breathed in the familiar smell of old books and incense. The owner had the best collection of eclectic and used books. At the front of the store were glass cases full of crystals and New Age jewelry. The shelves on the walls were lined with tarot-card decks and rune sets.

I made my way to the back of the store, where it opened into a separate space for the used books. I stopped first at the small cart just inside the room, looking through the "new" items Ruby had brought in. I picked up a collection of essays by William Faulkner and went to a worn armchair in the corner.

I was so engrossed that I didn't know *he* was there until I felt someone beside me. I looked up to see Clayton Reed standing beside my chair, his arms loaded down with books. He turned up one side of his mouth in a half smile.

"Hey, Maggie," he said quietly, not looking away from me. I felt the insane urge to smooth my hair, but I resisted, not wanting to come across as a moron.

"Hey," I said back, closing the Faulkner book and getting up so I could return it to the stack.

"So, what are you doing here?" he asked, shifting the books in his arms. I looked around and lifted my hands.

"Oh, I don't know, baking a cake. Learning CPR. Take your pick," I remarked sarcastically. Clay smiled, apparently appreciating my dry humor. He dropped his armful of books on a nearby table and started going through them, checking them over carefully, selecting one and then disappearing down an aisle to place it on a shelf.

I walked over and picked up a beat-up copy of Kurt Vonnegut's *Deadeye Dick*. Clay appeared at my side and looked over my shoulder at the book. "You ever read it?" he asked. I shook my head and looked at him. Wish I hadn't done that. Because being that close to him literally took my breath away. Why did he have to be so cute? And smell so good? It was almost disconcerting and more than a little hard to deal with when I was trying to be all normal and stuff.

"You should. It's one of my favorites." I started to hand it to him, but he gently pushed it back into my hands. "No, you take it. Read it when you've got time."

"Uh, thanks," I murmured, tucking the book into my bag.

I followed Clay down another aisle as he put more books on the shelves. "So, you work here or something?" I asked him.

Clay arched his eyebrow at me. "Nah, I'm here to go fishing, or learn tightrope walking. Take your pick." He parlayed my sarcasm back at me and I grinned.

"Touché, Mr. Reed. Touché." He chuckled and handed me a pile of books to hold as he carefully put each in its proper place.

After a few minutes, Clayton finally answered. "I started working here last week. You know, after I moved here. My aunt Ruby owns the place," he said shyly. Again, he seemed uncomfortable with revealing anything personal.

"Really, your aunt owns this place? It's seriously my favorite store. I try to come in here at least once a month," I told him, genuinely enthusiastic.

Clay smiled. "I'll tell her you said that. She'll be pleased."

"So your aunt . . . do you live with her?" I asked, digging again for any little bit of elusive information. Clay turned back to the books he was putting away, his shoulders suddenly very tense.

"Yeah," he said shortly.

He was definitely communicating loudly and clearly that he did not want to talk about this topic. Too bad for him, because I wasn't listening. "So, where are your parents, then?" I asked, following him again as he moved down the rows of books.

"They're in Florida. Where I'm from," he answered. Okay, he was not very good with the details.

"So, you're not living with them because . . . ?" I trailed off.

Clay turned around and looked at me. His cheeks were two bright blotches of red and he looked annoyed. "Look, I'm not trying to be rude or anything. But I don't really know you. I'm not one to vomit up my life story to random people." I felt my gut twist. I tried not to be hurt by his words. He was right, after all. He didn't know me from Adam and here I was, grilling him about his life. I was the one being rude and invasive.

"Sorry, Clay. I'm not trying to be nosy. I'm just interested in getting to know you, is all," I told him sincerely. The tension left Clayton's shoulders and he seemed to relax. He turned back to shelving the books.

"Why are you so interested in me?" he asked quietly. Hmm. How to answer that one? I didn't want to tell him that I thought he was the most gorgeous creature I had ever seen and wanted to have his babies. That might be a little much. So I gave him the next true statement that came to mind.

"I would like to be your friend. If that's all right."

Clay looked at me strangely. I couldn't read his expression at all, and he stood quietly for a moment, studying me. "Yeah. That would be cool," he said. I smiled tentatively at him, and he returned my smile with one of his own.

After following him around the back of the store for another fifteen minutes, engaging in casual chitchat, I finally got up the nerve to ask him the question I really wanted answered. "So, when do you get off work? Do you want to go grab a cup of coffee or something?" I braced myself for his rejection. I was being really ballsy today.

Clayton looked up at the clock on the wall. "Actually, I'm not technically working today. I just came in to help Tilly with stocking the shelves." Clay indicated the twenty-something girl who manned the cash register. The girl looked up when she heard her name. She was pretty, in that hippie sort of way, with long blond hair and a colorful gypsy skirt.

I tried not to be eaten alive with jealousy when she gave Clay a full-toothed smile that clearly said she liked hearing him say her name. "Tilly, I'm gonna take off now. You cool?" he asked, walking behind her to grab his jacket. Tilly flicked her hair over her shoulder and straightened her loose blouse that was covered in tiny bells.

"Sure, Clay. You going to be in tomorrow?" she asked with barely concealed hope in her voice. Clayton bestowed a beautiful smile on her. I wanted that smile directed at me, damn it!

"Nope, I'm off until Tuesday."

Tilly's smile fell. "Oh, well; I guess I'll see you next week," she said with disappointment. She finally looked at me, and I could see jealousy flash in her eyes when she realized Clayton was leaving with me. Take that, bitch! I thought unkindly. Wow, where did this harpy come from? I was becoming a possessive shrew and he wasn't even my boyfriend.

Clay gave Tilly a final wave and ushered me through the door of the shop. Once we were outside, I took off my fleece and tied it around my waist. The sun had come out and it had warmed up while I had been inside. We stood on the sidewalk looking at each other.

"So, coffee?" Clay asked.

I nodded. "Yeah, let's do that. There's a great place down the street. They have the best biscotti," I suggested.

Clay rubbed his stomach. "Mmmm. Biscotti. My favorite." He licked his lips and I suppressed a groan. This guy was going to kill me.

As we walked down the sidewalk, not saying much, my heart beat a mile a minute and my palms were sweaty. I discreetly wiped them on my blue jeans. Clayton made me feel nervous and giddy all at once. I liked it.

When we got to the coffee shop we both headed for the back. It was dimly lit, with an overstuffed couch, and it felt cozy and intimate. "What would you like?" I asked him.

Clay shook his head. "No way, I'll get this. You just grab us a seat."

I thrilled at his words. He was buying me coffee! It almost felt like a date.

I was proud of how steady my voice was when I gave him my usual order of a medium mocha latte with extra whipped cream and a vanilla biscotti. I watched Clay walk to the counter and couldn't take my eyes away from his massive shoulders. He really was a big guy. He could easily have been mistaken for a football player or something. I also noticed the way others watched him, as if they were just as aware of how special he was. His shoulders were less slouched today and he was carrying himself with a bit more confidence than I saw at school.

He returned a short time later with my order. "I see you took my word on the biscotti," I said, indicating the three pieces on his plate. Clay smiled shyly.

"Yeah, I'm a little hungry." He sat beside me on the couch and sipped his own drink. I picked up my mocha and took a sip, careful to make sure my lips were free of whipped cream when I was done.

Our silence was becoming more companionable than before. There was still that little bit of awkwardness laced through it, but it was less noticeable. "So, what do you think of Jackson so far? Does it live up to all of your high-school fantasies?" I asked as I swirled my biscotti in my drink.

Clay gave an adorable snort and put down his mug, reaching for his own biscotti. "I'm still waiting for the flash mobs, but other than that, it has been just fine," he replied. I sipped my mocha again, taking time to watch him hold his food with long, careful fingers.

"'Fine'? That's it? No stronger adjectives to use?" I asked. Clay met my eyes and I was once again taken aback by how dark his were. So brown they were almost black.

He shrugged. "All schools are really the same. This one is no better or worse than the others I've been to."

His answers always gave just enough information to tantalize me, yet never actually revealed anything. I was a little hesitant to broach any subject that he deemed too personal after having been abruptly shut down before. But I had told him I wanted to be his friend. He came here with me, right? So that showed he wanted to be my friend too, I thought. And friends got to know each other. That was the whole point of friendship. So, without giving myself time to ruminate more, I plunged right in.

"So, you live with your aunt Ruby. Do you . . . um . . . like living with her? What's she like?" I waited for his anger and was relieved when none came.

"You just don't give up, do you? We can't just sit here and talk about the weather?" he asked lightly.

I shook my head. "Nope, I want to know about you. That's what friends do."

"And we're friends?" he asked me. His eyes seemed to be asking something else, but I didn't know what.

So I nodded. "I'd like to be, anyway," I said.

Clay smiled. "Friends, then."

I smiled back. "So, your aunt?" I prompted.

"Yes, my aunt. Well, Ruby is pretty awesome. She's my mom's older sister and they don't exactly get along. Lifestyle differences and all that. Mom doesn't approve of Ruby's partner, Lisa."

"Ah," I said knowingly. Clay dunked his biscotti in the hot drink and nibbled.

"But Ruby has always been there for me. She's always helped out when I needed her. So I'm thankful she let me come stay with her and Lisa. It was a lifesaver, really." The way he spoke about his aunt made it clear how much he loved her. My heart clenched at the raw vulnerability I heard.

"She sounds like an amazing person," I told him quietly, not wanting to mess with the intimate mood that had encircled us. Clay shook himself slightly, as if realizing how much he was actually revealing.

"Yeah, she's pretty fantastic," he said wistfully. "And Lisa is a hoot. She's this hardcore biker chick and she could definitely kick my ass if I got out of line." He laughed. I laughed with him, picturing his aunt's girlfriend, the biker lady.

We finished our drinks and took the empty mugs up to the counter. We left the shop and stood on the sidewalk, neither of us wanting to go our separate ways.

"So," I remarked at the same moment that he said, "Well." We laughed awkwardly.

"Thanks for the coffee," I said, putting my hands into my jeans pockets.

"Sure, anytime. I enjoyed myself. I'd like to do this again some-time," he admitted, looking at me through his thick lashes.

I relished his words, feeling happy that he liked spending time with me. "Yeah. Me, too," I told him. We walked back to Ruby's Bookshelf and I noticed his car was parked next to mine. How did I not notice it there when I pulled in?

"So, I'll see you on Monday?" His words came out as a question.

"Definitely," I answered as I got in my car. He rested his hands on the door and leaned into my open window, and for a moment I imagined his beautiful lips on mine.

"'Bye, Maggie," he said softly before stepping away. I put my car in reverse and backed out of the parking lot.

This time it was me looking in my rearview mirror. And I de-lighted in seeing him standing there watching me leave.

chapter
four

"damn it!" I grumbled as I realized I had left my gym bag in my locker. It was after school and I was on my way to cross-country practice. This was my third year on the team and I was proud of the fact that I was in a prime position to lead us to state this year. Coach Kline was convinced that I would break some records during the season.

Yeah, I was pretty good. And modest, too.

And running really, really late. Coach Kline would make me run extra time if I didn't pull my finger out. I jogged back down the hallway toward my locker and collided with someone coming from the opposite direction.

I reached out to grab hold of the other person's arms to steady myself.

"I'm so sorry," I breathed out, feeling embarrassed.

My head shot up at the throaty laugh. Clay's eyes twinkled at me as he held on to my wrist. "We've got to stop meeting like this," he said with amusement. I swallowed hard and felt my heart thud against my chest.

I had looked for him at school today. It had been only two days since our impromptu coffee date on Saturday but, strangely, I missed him. I mean, I didn't even know the guy, but I wanted to be around him way more than was normal.

But he had been elusive. He hadn't come into the cafeteria and I never saw him in the hallway. I even made a point of waiting outside the creative-writing class I knew he had with Rachel, but he somehow snuck out without me seeing him. Okay, I admit, I was becoming a bit obsessed.

So seeing him here after searching for him for the past eight hours was a bit of a shock.

"I think we need to start wearing neon safety vests or something," I joked, righting myself. I realized we still held each other's arms. I felt all tingly when I realized how close we were. I unceremoniously dropped my hands to my sides, feeling awkward.

Clay released me from his hold and hefted his book bag up on his shoulder. "Probably not a bad idea; you're kind of lethal. It would give me a bit of warning the next time you come careening at me." His smile made me tremble. It was crazy, this effect he had on me.

We stood in silence for a moment. I was suddenly tongue-tied, which was definitely not my norm. "You heading home?" I asked him lamely. It was 3:30; of course he was leaving. What a dumb question. If I could have smacked my forehead, I would have.

"Uh, well, I was thinking of taking a drive, doing a bit of exploring. I still don't know my way around very well." He looked at me and raised an eyebrow. "Wanna come with me? I could use a local's expertise."

Oh, shit. Clay and me in a car together. Alone. That sounded like heaven. Or the source of some very serious anxiety. I opened my mouth, not sure what to say. I looked at the clock. I was already late for cross-country.

I looked at Clay again as he waited expectantly for an answer. "Come on, Maggie. Please. Take pity on the new kid," he teased.

Without waiting for me to say anything, he took my book bag from my shoulder. "Come on." He cocked his head in the direction of the door.

Glancing at the clock again, I shrugged. Screw it. Missing one practice wouldn't kill me.

"Sure, why not? Can't have you wandering around lost in the middle of nowhere. The natives could eat you." Clay laughed. I followed him out of the school, trying not to feel guilty for blowing off practice. But as I watched his fantastic ass in his dark jeans, I forgot about guilt and was overcome by unbridled hormones.

Clay put his hand on the small of my back and steered me toward his car. I tried not to sigh at his touch. His fingers felt warm through my shirt and my mind drifted to some very dirty thoughts of his fingers touching me in other places. Wow, I was turning into a tart.

He clicked open the locks and opened the door for me. I looked up at him and beamed simperingly. "Such a gentleman." I batted my eyelashes. Clay laughed again and shook his head after I got inside.

"Well, I try. No sense in revealing my evil intentions right away." His eyes smoldered as he looked at me, and I tried not to gulp.

Clay closed my door and quickly got into the driver's seat. He started up the BMW and I delighted in the smooth purr of the engine. "This is some car. I'll try not to hate you the next time I try to get my junk pile to start."

Clay smiled tightly but didn't respond. For some reason, his car was a touchy subject. He pulled out of the parking lot and onto the main road.

"Do you mind?" I asked, indicating the radio.

"Go ahead. There are some CDs in the glove compartment there."

I pulled out a handful of CDs and was surprised to see several of my favorites. "You like Placebo?" I asked, holding up *Sleeping With Ghosts.*

"Hell, yeah. I saw them live in Miami a few years ago. They're amazing."

"Lucky," I grumbled with good-natured jealousy. I popped open the CD jewel case and put the disc into the player.

We sat quietly for a few minutes as the alternative-rock music filled the interior of the car. I was mesmerized as I watched Clay's long fingers drum along to the beat on the steering wheel. Why was it that he could make such mundane actions so interesting? It was official: I was pathetic.

"So, where to, O wonderful tour guide?" Clay asked. I thought for a moment, but ultimately my growling stomach made my decision for me. I pointed to a street sign a few feet ahead.

"Turn right onto Crane Avenue and take the first left," I instructed.

Clay followed my directions. "Now pull into the parking lot," I told him, indicating the car lot to the left.

"Bubbles Ice Cream?" Clay scoffed. He looked incredulously at the huge pink giraffe that graced the front of the bright-yellow building. "Seriously? This place looks like it was built by a five-year-old," he said as we got out of the car.

I playfully punched his arm. "Don't be so judgy. Just wait until you have Bubbles banana splits. You will die a happy man for having had one," I assured him, tugging on his hand. To my absolute delight, Clay laced his fingers through mine and squeezed. My heart fluttered painfully in my chest.

"I'll take your word for it, Mags." I looked at him in surprise as he so naturally used the nickname reserved for my closest friends and family. The sound of my name on his lips was downright sensual. Like a promise.

We walked into the ice-cream parlor, the bell dinging as we went through the door. Clay never dropped my hand as we walked to the only empty booth in the place. Sliding onto a cracked vinyl seat, Clay looked around. "This place is packed," he remarked.

I grabbed two menus from behind the plastic bottles of ketchup and mustard. "Bubbles is an institution. They have the best ice cream and hamburgers in the county. You have to get past the cheesy decor," I insisted.

Clay picked up a ceramic penguin saltshaker and looked at it like it would bite him. "Ooo-kay," he said slowly, putting it back down. We looked at our menus. There was a lot to choose from. Clay seemed to be struggling with his order.

"Trust me, just get the banana split. You'll thank me," I told him when the waitress arrived.

"Sure, why not? You only live once. Two banana splits and two Cokes, please," he told the waitress. She jotted down our order and left the table. "So, you never said where you were off to in such a rush earlier," Clay said conversationally.

"Uh, nowhere; I'm just a perpetually busy person," I lied, not wanting to admit I had blown off cross-country practice to hang out with him. That would have seemed too desperate. "So, where have you been hiding yourself today? I haven't seen you around," I remarked, shredding my napkin into tiny strips. Boy, I was nervous.

Clay smirked. "Why? Were you looking for me?" he teased. If he only knew. I stuck my chin out and met his eyes.

"No way. I just happened to notice that the jerk level was re-markably low today," I said. Clay laughed.

"I had a lunch tutorial for physics. It's kicking my ass. I didn't realize how behind I was in so many subjects when I moved here," he said, drinking the Coke that the waitress had just brought over. I dropped my napkin and put my fidgety hands in my lap.

"Why are you so behind? You seem like a smart guy," I commented. Clay's expression darkened and he looked out the window. He cleared his throat.

"School got a little . . . uh . . . disrupted for a while. Not a big deal. I'm just busting butt now to get where I need to be." I noticed he wouldn't look at me.

He must have been out of school for a while. I wondered why. But I knew that if I asked, he wouldn't tell me. Clayton Reed was a closed book. At least for now.

"So, have you met many people yet?" I asked, moving on to another subject. Clay's eyes turned back to me and I felt a little jolt. There was just something about him. I really wished I could get a handle on what it was that made me feel like I would dissolve into a puddle at his feet.

"A few. Not many. I'm not what you would call a 'people person.'" He used air quotes and I laughed.

"Yeah, I'm getting that impression. But not all of us are bad, you know. You should give 'people'"—I mimicked him by using quotes—"a chance; you never know, it might not be a bad thing," I remarked half-jokingly.

Clay looked at me, his expression intense yet unreadable. What I wouldn't give to know what was going on in that head of his. "There are some people I'd like to get to know," he said softly, never taking his eyes off me. I suddenly felt hot and I took a long drink of my soda.

I was saved from saying something ridiculous by the arrival of our sundaes. "Jesus. I can't eat all of this. Are you trying to kill me, woman?" Clay gaped at the huge pile of ice cream, whipped cream, and bananas in front of him. I handed him a spoon.

"Dig in," I prompted, taking a mouthful myself. The next ten minutes were silent, punctuated by the clink of spoons as we ate our weight in ice cream.

Finally, Clay pushed the bowl away from him. "If I eat any more, you'll have to roll me out of here," he groaned, but I was happy to see him smile. His entire face transformed when he smiled like that. He was normally so moody that he looked much younger when he was happy.

"Wow, no wonder. I wasn't expecting you to eat all of that. I'm impressed." I indicated his nearly empty bowl. I had only gotten through a third of mine and I was full. "So, what's the consensus?" I asked, pointing to his decimated sundae.

"Well, I think I can definitely die a happy man," he conceded, looking at me.

There went those stupid butterflies in my stomach again. I wished I could squash them.

I coughed pointedly and moved to get out of the booth. Clay held out his hand. "I think you might have to help me," he joked. I laughed and pulled him to his feet. He wrapped his arm around my waist and hugged me to his side. "Thanks, Mags," he said softly into my ear, and dropped his arm.

I stumbled a bit after he let me go. I felt completely flustered. Clay insisted on paying again and I argued. "No way. You paid last time!" I tried pushing cash into his hand. Clay took the bills and tucked them into my front pocket. It felt like such an intimate thing to do. I tried not to focus too much on the feel of his fingers so close to such sensitive parts of my body.

"You pay next time," he said, looking down at me. Next time? There would be a next time? I couldn't stop the happy little dance that was unleashed in my stomach.

"Hi, Maggie," a voice said from behind me as Clay paid at the cash register. I turned around to see Daniel's on-again girl-friend, Kylie. She was with her friends Dana Welsh and Mc-Kenna Riley.

"Hey, Kylie. Dana, McKenna," I acknowledged the other girls grudgingly. I really disliked Kylie's friends. They were snotty and obnoxious. I had always hated it when we were forced into the same social circles. They just weren't my type of people.

McKenna gave me a fake smile but Dana didn't bother to look at me. She was too busy checking out Clay's backside. I felt myself bristle. Dana was beautiful in that typical blond-bombshell sort of way. And, trust me, she knew it.

Clay turned around and blinked in surprise at our sudden company. "Hello?" he said questioningly to Kylie and her friends.

I watched the Clayton Reed effect in full force. Kylie's smile widened and I swear she licked her lips, seeming to forget the fact that she was currently involved with Danny. Great girlfriend, there. Dana stuck her chest out and McKenna flipped her hair.

Oh, God. It was like watching a mating ritual on the Discovery Channel. The pheromones these girls were throwing off could choke a donkey. I realized I was being rude but I really didn't want to introduce them.

Clay looked down at me quizzically and finally stuck out his hand. "Hi, I'm Clay," he said tightly. I could tell he was uncomfortable and I felt like an ass for not stepping in to make it easier for him. But I was trying to suppress the urge to inflict bodily harm on the dumb bimbos standing in front of us.

Dana jumped in first and wrapped her hand around his, pressing closer to him than was socially acceptable. "I'm Dana. You're the new guy, aren't you?" Her voice had dropped a few octaves and I knew she was trying really hard to be seductive.

I watched Clay's mouth fall open as she held on to his hand. He seemed a little at a loss. If he fell for this bitch's bullshit, I vowed to make him take me home.

Finally he extracted his hand from her ironclad grip. "Uh, yeah. That's me." He put his hand through his hair.

"I'm Kylie and this is McKenna. We're just so excited to meet you." Kylie elbowed her way in front of Dana so that she was now standing absurdly close to Clay.

I didn't even try to hide the fact that I was rolling my eyes. Were these girls for real? Clay seemed a little weirded out. "Excited to meet me? Why?" His eyes darted to me and I only shrugged. Kylie put her hand on his arm. Did this girl have no shame? She was currently dating my best friend, and here she was hanging all over someone else. Right in front of me!

"You're all anyone is talking about. You're very mysterious," she purred. Oh, gag. Enough was enough!

I positioned myself between Clay and Kylie and gently pushed Clay toward the door. "Well, it was fantastic seeing you gals, but we have to run. Later!" I called over my shoulder as I herded Clay out of the ice-cream parlor.

"Those girls were . . . um . . ." Clay started.

"Overbearing? Trashy? Walking STDs?" I finished, getting into his car. Clay shot me a look. Okay, I had to get my raging jealousy in check.

"I was going to say they seemed nice."

I rolled my eyes again. "I guess it depends on your definition of 'nice,'" I muttered, fastening my seat belt.

Clay turned in his seat and looked at me. I stared straight ahead. I was being really juvenile and I was probably ruining any chance I had with this amazing guy who sat beside me. But Clay made me feel sort of out of control and it was more than a little disconcerting.

"Well, I think you're nicer" was all Clay said, and he turned the key in the ignition. I couldn't stop the smile that spread over my face. "Where to next on our grand tour of Davidson?" he asked, before leaving the parking lot.

It was really warm in the car. The day was hotter than average for September. I grinned over at him. "Wanna go swimming?" I don't know what came over me. I was feeling spontaneous, which was so unlike me.

Clay grinned back. "Hell, yeah! Lead the way!"

I laughed and gave him directions to the local swimming hole.

We turned on to a dirt road outside of town that ended in a big field. Clay got out of the car and looked around.

"Mags, I don't see any water," he said. I started walking through the tall grass. Clay easily caught up with me. Finally we broke through some trees and found ourselves by the river. It was really pretty. I used to love coming to that particular spot with my parents when I was younger. "Now, this is awesome!" Clay enthused from beside me.

I looked at him. He had pulled his shirt over his head. My mouth went dry as I took in his perfectly chiseled abs. Oh, crap. I hadn't thought about *what* we'd be swimming in. I looked down at my denim skirt and blue short-sleeved top, feeling like I was frozen in place. Do I just jump in with my clothes on? I hadn't thought this through very well.

Clay dropped his pants and stood before me in his boxers. Fuck! He was mouthwatering. I tried not to stare, but it was really hard. He was too perfect. Clay noticed I hadn't moved. "I thought you wanted to go swimming." He frowned.

"Well, I don't have anything . . . you know . . . to swim in." I indicated my clothes.

Clay laughed. He seemed so different than he had at school. Like he was two people. This Clay was carefree and fun. I liked him a lot. Not that brooding, angsty Clay wasn't hot. But this side of him was so easy to be around.

"Well, you've seen me in my Skivvies. I think it's your turn."

My jaw dropped. "I'm not stripping in front of you!" I gasped. I knew I sounded like a prude. But I just couldn't do it. I barely knew him. Hell, even Daniel had never seen me in that state of undress.

If I was honest with myself, though, the thought of the two of us in so little clothing made my blood boil. Clay raised his eyebrow at me in what I was learning was a characteristic expression. "I promise I won't look. I'll get in the water and wait for you." I looked at him in disbelief. He held his hands up. "I promise."

And, like that, he turned and made his way into the river. "Fuck me, it's cold!" he yelled as he plunged in. I stood there for another minute, not sure what to do.

"Screw it," I muttered (that seemed to be my mantra for the day), and I dropped my skirt onto the ground. I then pulled my shirt over my head. I was glad I had decided to wear my cute navy-blue bra and matching underwear.

I ran to the riverbank. I squealed when I stuck my toes into the frigid water. Clay still had his back turned. "Come on; if I can do it, so can you," he called to me. I sucked in a breath and jumped in. The cold of the water shocked the air right out of my lungs and I kicked to the surface. The water was really deep. A few feet from the shore, you couldn't feel the bottom anymore.

"Is it safe to look?" Clay asked. I treaded water, keeping most of my body submerged.

"All clear," I said. Clay turned around and I splashed him in the face. He sputtered and wiped water from his eyes.

"Oh, that's it. Payback's a bitch," he growled, and lunged for me. I yelped and swam away from him, laughing so hard that I drank a mouthful of nasty river water.

Clay finally caught me, his arms going around my waist. Before I could relish the feeling of his naked skin against mine, he hefted me out of the water and threw me. I landed with a huge splash. "You suck!" I yelled, and went after him.

I dunked him, he threw me. I splashed him, he pulled me under. I felt like a little kid. I couldn't remember the last time I had had that much fun. And Clay laughed and smiled the entire time.

After calling a truce in our ongoing water battle, Clay and I floated for a bit in the river. "This is so much fun, Clay. Thank you for hanging out with me." I looked over at him. He smiled, but continued to look up at the sky.

"So spontaneous swimming isn't something you usually do?" he joked.

I snorted. "No way. The most spontaneous thing I've ever done is wear my hair down instead of in a ponytail." I couldn't help the tiny bit of bitterness that seeped into my voice. Clay finally looked at me.

"Well, maybe we need to fix that," he suggested with a small smile.

My stomach buzzed again. "I'm just . . . I don't know . . . bored, I guess. Everything, every day, is the same. It gets tedious." I made a face and Clay laughed.

"I don't know. I could use a little monotony in my life. Spontaneity is exhausting." He gave me another little splash and I looked at him in warning.

He laughed, a deep sound that made my breath hitch. "You don't have fun with your friends? I mean, I see you hanging around with some people. You always seem to be laughing and having a good time when you're with them," Clay said.

He had just admitted that he watched me. *Oh, my God!* I wanted to do a little tap dance, I was so happy. I looked at him and he ducked his head shyly, as if he realized what he had just admitted. God, I wanted to touch him so badly but didn't know if I should.

"I love my friends. I've known Danny and Rachel my entire life. Our mothers were best friends growing up. But even that seems a little trite."

Clay raised his eyebrow at me. "Trite?"

I nodded, swimming closer to the shore so I could sit down on the river bottom, the water lapping at my chin and keeping me insulated from the afternoon breeze.

"Well, you know: our parents were best friends, so of course we're best friends. And we have this vanilla life with vanilla conversations and the occasional vanilla party on the weekends. Nothing crazy. Nothing to rock the boat. I feel like I've been doing the same thing for so long I don't know how to be anything different. Like I said, I'm just so bored. And any time I try to talk to Rache or Danny about it, I just don't think they hear me. I mean, I feel almost . . . depressed with it all. I want to feel energized, *passionate* about something. Anything."

Or *someone*, I thought to myself, looking at Clay, who still treaded water a few feet away from me. I had said more to him about my feelings than I had to anyone in a very long time. And Clay didn't look at me like I was crazy. In fact, he seemed to take my words very seriously. And I swear it was in that moment that I began to fall in love with him.

The way he listened to me and actually heard me. And as if what I was saying wasn't stupid. At least not to him. He only nodded. "I understand. I do. But trust me, you are anything but boring."

I harrumphed, not believing him. "Yeah, I'm so interesting. Maggie Young, with her happily married parents and her B+ GPA, ordinary after-school activities, talking about average topics every day with her average friends. How can that *not* be boring?" I exhaled through my nose in frustration. How could I have thought I had anything to offer this interesting and amazing guy? I was seriously deluded.

Clay swam over to me and sat beside me. Our arms brushed under the water and then stayed like that, touching, like even our skin couldn't get enough of each other.

"Maggie. What you just described to me sounds perfect." I rolled my eyes and Clay grabbed my hand. "No, listen to me. You are beautiful and smart and you have this fantastic life all laid out in front of you. You are kind and open-minded, plus you're sarcastic and sexy as hell."

I couldn't help but smile at the girl he was describing. Me, sexy? I had never thought of myself that way.

"I would give anything to have what you have. Parents and friends who love you. Knowing you have that kind of unconditional love is unbelievable. You don't understand how lucky you are." He sounded sad and I leaned into his shoulder.

"And you don't have that, Clay?" I asked him softly.

Clay looked down at me with his deep, dark eyes and all I saw was this aching loneliness that tore at my heart. I knew without his having to answer me that his life had been a hard one. And that whatever was going on with him had forced him to create this giant wall that effectively kept everyone at a distance. As if he couldn't handle any more personal admissions, Clay suddenly dove back into the water, shutting the door on our confidences.

I was more than a little disappointed. I felt like I was just starting to understand him a little bit and then he had to go and throw the wall back up. But before I could pout or get in a huff, Clay pulled me by my ankle back into the water, starting our water fight all over again. And, after a few moments of his playfulness, I had forgotten why I was irritated.

We must have been there for a while, because I suddenly realized it was getting dark and the air had started to cool. Without thinking about the fact that I was only in my bra and panties, I got out of the water and went to the tree stump where I had left my cell phone. "Crap, it's six thirty. I've got to get home."

Now that I was out of the water, I was freezing. And, like idiots, we'd gone swimming without towels. I heard Clay get out of the water. I didn't want to look at him, feeling suddenly embarrassed by the fact that I was practically naked in front of him. I gathered my clothes and held them to my chest.

Suddenly I felt Clay's hands on my arms, as he rubbed them up and down to try to generate some warmth. I turned and looked up at him. Something flashed in his eyes and I felt like there was a definite moment going on. We had been slowly building toward this all day and I knew that something was about to happen.

He came closer to me and his hands stopped moving but stayed on my bare skin. Slowly he pushed my wet bangs out of my face and looked at me with the most intense expression I had ever seen. I felt rooted to the spot, thinking only of how close our bodies were. He wanted to kiss me, I could tell. His eyes fell to my mouth as I nervously licked my lips.

His expression seemed to heat up and he ran the ball of his thumb along the curve of my bottom lip. The pull between us was tightening and I felt sucked into his orbit.

Then my phone rang.

Talk about a mood killer.

"Sorry," I murmured, looking down at the display and seeing my mom's number. I hurriedly answered it. "Hey, Mom." I looked at Clay, but he had moved away and was putting on his jeans.

"Where are you, Maggie? We've had dinner waiting for almost forty-five minutes."

I couldn't help but stare as Clay pulled his shirt over his head, his stomach muscles taut. My mouth went dry and I had a hard time swallowing.

"Maggie!" my mom said tersely on the other end, and I realized I hadn't answered her.

"Sorry, Mom. I met up with a friend. I have to get my car from the school and then I'll be home," I told her. I prayed my mom would be cool and save the thousand questions for when I got home.

No such luck. "Friend? What friend?" she asked. I walked a bit away and dropped my voice.

"Clay Reed. I was just showing him around town," I said quietly into the phone. I heard my mom tapping her fingers on something on the other end. Great, she was pissed.

"I don't like the idea of you out with some boy we don't know. I'd like to meet him. Particularly if you're going to be going out with him."

I tried not to groan into the phone. "We're just friends, Mom. Not a big deal." I tried placating. Well, my mom wasn't having it.

"Well, regardless. You know how we feel about you getting into cars with boys we don't know. I want to meet him." She was going to be unyielding about this. Just fan-fucking-tastic.

"Fine," I said curtly. I heard my mom sigh. She knew she had made me mad.

"We just worry. It's a scary, scary world out there for a girl." I didn't say anything. "Just get home. But be safe. We'll talk when you get here," my mom said, and then hung up.

I turned and saw Clay standing there, looking at me. "Your mom?" he asked. I nodded and realized I was still in my bra and panties. If my mom could see me now, she'd have a heart attack. I tried to discreetly slide into my skirt and I noticed Clay respectfully look away.

After I was dressed, he and I walked back to his car. I wrung my hair out but shivered as the water made its way down my back. Clay reached over and pulled my heavy, wet hair over my shoulder, his fingers skimming the back of my neck.

"Was she mad you weren't home yet?" he asked after we had gotten in and were backing out of the field.

"She's just majorly overprotective," I said, watching him shift gears. There was something seriously sexy about his hands.

"Understandable. I'd be overprotective too if you were my daughter." He smirked at me and I smirked back. Okay, how to broach the subject that they wanted to meet him, without sounding incredibly lame?

"Well, um . . . Clay. They sort of want to meet you."

Clay cocked his eyebrow and gave me a quick look. "Okay," he said slowly.

I hurried on. "It's just they're weird about me being in cars with guys. And I told her we're just friends, but she still wants to meet you and I promise you it'll be cool. It's just that they want to make sure you're not a serial killer or anything." I was rambling to try to cover my complete mortification.

Clay reached over and squeezed the hand that sat clenched in my lap. "Mags. It's okay. I understand. I want them to be cool with us hanging out. I'll meet them," he assured me. I let out a breath and sighed with relief. He made me feel like less of a tool, and I appreciated that.

"Thanks," I said quietly. He smiled.

"No, thank you, Maggie. For today. I can't remember the last time I had so much fun." I felt warm at his compliment. He took a deep breath. "The last few months have been really tough and sometimes I forget that it's okay to let loose and just live life, you know? I have a feeling you'll be really good for me." The look he gave me made me tingle to my toes.

"I hope so," I said.

Clay smiled coyly. "Oh, I *know* so."

chapter
five

If I could have cut off my legs, I would have. Every muscle from the waist down ached and I couldn't suppress a groan as I sat down at my usual lunch table. Rachel looked up from her phone and tried to hide the smile on her face.

"What?" I growled, slowly swinging my legs around as I situated myself oh-so-carefully. Rachel spooned some pudding into her mouth and shook her head.

"Nothing," she mumbled around her food. I glared at her.

Daniel wasn't so discreet. "Why are you moving like an old lady, Mags? You look ridiculous." I picked up a potato chip and chucked it at him.

"Coach Kline made me run this morning because I didn't show up for practice a couple of days this week. He was kind of pissed." I leaned down and rubbed my calf muscles, trying to alleviate the burning sensation.

I understood why Coach was mad. I was his star runner and I had disappointed him. We had our first meet coming up on Friday and I had blown off practice three times this week. I felt guilty for shirking my responsibility. But I couldn't regret using the time to get to know Clay instead.

We had gone "exploring" a few more times. We went hiking at Crooked Run National Park, played minigolf in Warminster, and saw a movie at the IMAX theater in Charlottesville. I loved spending time with Clay. For the first time, my life felt interesting; exhilarating, even.

I found myself doing things and trying things that I never would have before. Like eating Thai food and watching a foreign movie with subtitles. Okay, that might not seem like a lot . . . but I would never have thought to do any of that stuff until Clay came along.

"You blew off practice? Seriously?" Daniel asked incredulously. Rachel looked out the window behind her.

"Is it snowing?" she asked in mock surprise.

"Hardee-har-har, you two." I got what they were saying. My doing something outside of my norm was unheard of. I went along, doing my thing, not deviating. Which is why, until three weeks ago, I had been hopelessly and utterly bored.

Now, well . . . I looked forward to getting out of bed.

"Where the heck have you been slinking off to, then?" Daniel seemed really confused by this. I understood his surprise. Typically if I wasn't at (a) school or (b) home, I was with him and Rachel. My developing a life outside of them was just weird. Like the earth had been thrown off its axis.

"Well, I—" I started, but was cut off by a voice behind me.

"Mind if I sit with you guys?" I turned (very carefully, of course; sore muscles, here) and saw Clay standing there with his lunch tray. He gave me a small smile, his eyes flicking to Rachel and Daniel.

This was the first time I had seen him in the cafeteria since the Paul Delawder incident. I quickly looked at my friends. Rachel had her mouth hanging open and Daniel was frowning. Neither of them spoke. Sheesh. Rude, much?

I pulled out the chair beside me. "Have a seat." Clay sat down and put his tray on the table. He looked at me. Just like every other time our eyes had met, I felt my face flush. I swallowed and then turned to Rachel and Daniel. "Rachel, Daniel, this is Clay. Clay, these are my friends Rachel Bradfield and Daniel Lowe." Clay gave them a shy smile. "Hey."

Neither of my friends said anything. They seemed to be a bit taken aback by Clay's appearance at our table. How humiliating! "Say hi, you two. Or he'll think you never learned to talk." I rolled my eyes and Clay smiled tightly. I could tell he was uncomfortable.

Rachel blinked rapidly, the way she did when she was caught doing something embarrassing. "Sorry, Clay. Nice to meet you." She gave him an overly bright smile. I frowned at her and silently communicated to her to stop trying so hard.

Daniel looked at Clay almost as if he were examining him. "Hey," he replied back.

Okay, well, it looked as if Daniel would be a hard sell. He was so territorial sometimes. Clay cleared his throat and started eating his lunch. The vibe around our table became really tense.

"So, how's your day so far?" I asked Clay, trying to cut through the thickening silence.

Clay shrugged, not looking at me. "Just another day," he said before returning to his lunch.

Wow, this was getting bad, and fast. If he didn't want to talk, why the hell did he sit down? Of course it didn't help that Daniel was watching him while he ate. I shot daggers at my best friends, urging them with my eyes to snap out of it.

Rachel sat up straighter and opened her eyes dramatically at me. "Sorry," she mouthed. I pointedly looked at Clay, who was shoveling Salisbury steak into his mouth. "So, Clay. Did you finish that assignment for creative writing? I'm having a hell of a time writing my short story. I think I got a whole paragraph before I gave up," Rachel said, laughing in that really fake way of hers. At least she was trying.

Clay shrugged again. Was that his only reply? He was being really rude. Not at all like the Clay I had come to know over the past two weeks. I felt a knot in my stomach from his attitude. He was so rigid in his seat, as if he wanted to be anywhere but at our table. I just didn't get what he was trying to do. I mean, *he* was the one who had approached *us*. But now he looked as if he couldn't be finished with his food fast enough.

Was it me? Had I done something wrong? Should I have been more vocal to my friends when they were being so weird toward him? Why was I obsessing over what I did? But *did* I do something?

Then, after a few minutes of complete silence, Clay stood up. I looked up at him in surprise. What the heck was going on?

He finally looked down at me and I saw his face soften a bit. "Thanks for letting me sit with you. I'll see you later." He gave me a half smile and then turned and left.

"What the fuck was that?" Daniel asked after Clay was gone. I was still watching him make his way through the cafeteria, his shoulders slumped and his head down. I had no idea how to answer Daniel's question. Because I didn't know what *that* was.

"Maybe he's just shy," Rachel volunteered.

Daniel snorted. "Or a wack job. He has that whole school-shooter thing going on, you know?" Okay, that made me lose it.

"You don't even know him, Daniel! So stop being so goddamn judgmental! Maybe he was acting strange because you were being an ass! Did you ever think about that?" My voice was loud and I had to struggle to calm myself down.

Daniel looked at me like I had grown a second head. I never yelled at him. Ever. "What is your problem, Mags?" he asked me.

"Ugh!" I gathered up my trash. "My problem is that Clay is my friend. And you are my friend. So you need to start learning to get along with him. And maybe next time engage in a little conversation. Show people you have the social skills of more than a fucking first grader!"

"Maggie! Chill out!" Rachel urged, trying to smooth over a situation that had started to escalate. I just shook my head and got up to leave. Forgetting that I was really sore, I groaned as I moved too quickly.

Rachel was on her feet and moved to stop me from leaving. "We're sorry, okay? We didn't mean to make him feel uncomfortable. The whole thing just threw us, all right?" She was using the placating tone she usually reserved for Daniel.

What was my problem? Why was I so upset with them? It wasn't like me to fly off the handle like that. I needed to get myself in check.

Sighing, I gave Rachel a quick hug. "I know. Thanks. But I better go catch up with Clay, make sure he's cool." I gave my friends a smile and took off out of the cafeteria.

Looking down the hallway, I saw Clay at the other end. "Clay!" I called out, moving quickly toward him. He didn't turn around. Did he not hear me, or was he ignoring me?

I caught up with him and grabbed his arm to stop him from walking. I felt his muscles tense under my hand. I moved so that I was standing in front of him. His jaw was clenched and he wouldn't look at me. "Why did you leave so quickly?" I asked him. He shrugged (I was starting to really hate it when he did that).

"Didn't really want to hang out with people who didn't want to hang out with me," he said coldly as he stepped around me to move down the hallway.

"Hold on a sec, Clay. You're being ridiculous." I let out an incredulous laugh. Okay, so maybe my friends were less than welcoming at first. But I thought his reaction to the whole thing was a bit over the top.

The look Clay leveled at me froze my blood. Clearly, he didn't think he was being ridiculous. Without saying another word, he left me standing alone in the hallway. This time, I didn't go after him. There was only so much rejection a gal could take.

I stomped back to my locker, throwing the door open so that it bounced off the locker next to mine. "Seeing as you're in a seriously shitty mood, I'm assuming Lover Boy was still an ass when you chased him down like a lovesick puppy?" Daniel snarked, leaning on the locker beside mine.

I yanked my books for the afternoon from the top shelf and glared at my friend. "What is your problem with him anyway, Daniel? It's not like you to be such a dick to someone you don't even know." I couldn't help the hurt that bled through my voice. I tried to stay indignant and self-righteous but I could hear the vulnerability in my words.

Daniel softened immediately and put a hand on my shoulder, squeezing slightly. "Sorry, Mags. I know you want to be friends with this dude. But there's just something about him that rubs me the wrong way. Though I'll put on the happy face, just for you." I smiled at him and leaned in to give him a hug. Daniel patted my back awkwardly, unaccustomed to such a show of affection from me.

He pulled back and looked at me, a strange look on his face. "What?" I asked him, frowning.

Daniel only shook his head. "You really like this guy? I mean, really?" He seemed to be in a state of disbelief. Why was that such a strange concept for Daniel to get?

"Yeah, Danny. I really, really like him." I couldn't help my dreamy tone and I tried to ignore the eye roll Daniel gave me.

"Why? He has the personality of a rock. I don't get it." Daniel seemed genuinely perplexed. And I guess I didn't blame him. It wasn't as if he had seen the same Clay that I had. The Clay that made me forget everyone and everything else.

"No, he doesn't. He's a lot of fun. I can talk to him about stuff that I can't talk about with anyone else. He has this crazy spontaneous side that makes everything we do so much fun. He's cute and smart and . . ." Daniel held up his hand.

"Okay, enough already. I think I vomited in my mouth a little. Whatever. Just be careful. I worry, is all." It was my turn to roll my eyes. How many times had I told him the exact same thing when it came to Kylie or some other girl he was drooling over? I thought, of anyone, he would understand how I was feeling.

Maybe not.

"And I'll be nice. For your sake. But that doesn't mean I trust him . . . or like him." Daniel gave me a hard look and I tried not to yell at him again. I wanted to shake my best friend.

Not wanting to start another argument, I opted to stay silent. I threw a smile in Danny's direction, left him, and headed to class.

◆

I hated to admit that I'd looked for Clay all day but he'd successfully avoided me. Had I unwittingly ruined our friendship? Was I trying too hard to hold on to something that had barely begun? I was the worst kind of pathetic. I should have been focused on kicking ass in my last year of school. Thinking of where I'd go to college. Working my butt off to get the cross-country team to state. I had a million and one other things going on in my life but the only thing I could think about was him.

Clay fucking Reed.

He had royally screwed up my head in the short time that I'd known him. And I couldn't even claim to know him that well. I had really thought we had the beginnings of something. But I'd be damned if I would invest energy into something that wasn't reciprocal.

I had worked myself up into a ball of determination. I would not allow myself to obsess over some boy. I was better than that. I had more going for me than being some stupid girl who fixated on whether a guy would give her the time of day. That was not the person I was.

My internal monologue had me fired up. I could practically hear my own personal soundtrack. I hummed a tune with an angry beat the whole way to my locker. I was feeling strong and untouchable.

And then a piece of paper fluttered to my feet. It had been shoved between the slats of my locker and had fallen out when I opened it. Probably some stupid flyer for the pep rally. I started to ball it up and throw it away when my name caught my eye.

Maggie.

The handwriting wasn't familiar to me but somehow I knew it was his. So, just like that, all my newfound strength went straight to hell.

I opened the folded paper and smoothed it out. It was an amazingly intricate charcoal drawing of a gothic-looking butterfly. The detail was unbelievable. It looked like one of those cool tribal-art tattoos. It was edgy yet delicate at the same time. I couldn't quite believe that Clay could be capable of such beautiful artwork. His aloof coldness belied the sensitive soul who was able to communicate so much through a drawing. Then I noticed some writing at the bottom.

In thin, sloping script it read, *Goodness is your virtue. Quiet beauty your weapon.* I almost stopped breathing. The words sounded like some sort of love poem. What did he mean by them? And why could he act like he wanted nothing to do with me one minute and then practically lay his heart out on the table the next? It made no sense.

I looked up and found Clay standing a little way down the hallway, watching me. Our eyes met and an undeniable electricity passed between us. Did he feel like I did? What did this drawing mean? Was he trying to tell me something? I gathered up my book bag and shoes for cross-country and walked toward him.

He watched me the entire time with a hesitant look on his face. I stopped in front of him and held up the drawing. "You did this?" I asked him, although I already knew the answer. Clay nodded.

"I didn't know you were an artist. This is . . . just . . . wow." God, why did I have to be such a moron?

Clay's lips twitched in the beginnings of a smile. "Thanks," he said simply, still watching me in that intense way of his.

"And the words at the bottom? Did you write them?" I asked, trying to pull something out of him that would get him to open up. To tell me what he was thinking.

Clay pushed himself off the locker and started walking with me down the hallway. "No. It's a Japanese poet I really love. That particular poem made me think of you. You should read it." Japanese poetry, huh? Deep stuff.

He was reciting pretty Japanese poetry to me. A guy didn't do that sort of thing unless he liked the girl, right? I mean, that was the only thing that made sense. But then, what was with the arctic freeze-out earlier?

Ugh! There was that obsessive self-doubt again. It had to stop!

"Well, thanks," I forced myself to say coolly. There was no way I would let Clay know what he did to me. It was becoming a bit embarrassing. Clay took hold of my hand and pulled me to a stop. I should probably have moved out of his grasp. That would have been the smart thing to do. Not throwing myself headfirst into this crazy whirlwind that seemed to suck me in and refused to let go. But I liked how his hand felt around mine way too much to do that. So I looked at my shoes, finding them suddenly very interesting.

"Mags. Look at me," Clay said softly. The way he said my name made me feel fluttery inside. Like that beautiful butterfly he had drawn for me. Damn him. I looked up at Clay. His dark brown eyes were full of contrition and I found it impossible to stay distant and closed off.

"I'm really sorry for how I acted earlier. I was an ass. Do you forgive me?" Did I forgive him? Um, yeah, of course I did. But I had to play it cool.

"What was your deal? I mean, why did you storm out of the cafeteria like that?" Clay sighed and dropped my hand. I felt the loss of his warmth immediately.

"I was feeling uncomfortable and insecure. I know your friends didn't want me there. And it came out as anger instead. I have a bad habit of taking it out on whoever's closest to me. I'm not always the nicest guy, Maggie. I have a lot of crazy baggage that you don't need or deserve."

There it was again, a somewhat personal admission. One that gave me only the teensiest idea of what was going on behind his hard exterior. But not enough for me to understand him. I did know that his words were meant to give me pause. For me to think about what it meant to be close to him. I looked down at the beautiful picture he had given me and I didn't want to think about his baggage or his insane mood swings. I just wanted to be around him.

"Just promise to talk to me when you're feeling that way. I can help you with that baggage, you know." What was I saying? I had never dealt with anyone's baggage! I didn't even know what it was! My life and my friends' lives were predictable and boring. I couldn't imagine what it was he was alluding to. But I needed him to know I was there for him. No matter what.

Clay looked at me again and I felt my stomach turn to jelly. "You're pretty amazing. You know that?" he asked me with a smile in his eyes. I puffed up at his compliment.

"Thanks. I think so, too," I joked. Clay finally laughed, the seriousness of our conversation lightening a bit.

"Where you off to? Do you wanna go grab something to eat?" Clay asked, looking down at the running shoes in my hands.

Crap. I had cross-country. I couldn't miss another practice or I would be suspended from the meet for sure. Coach Kline would kill me!

So what did I say?

"That sounds great."

chapter
six

"What do you think about going to Melissa James's party tonight? It would be a great way for you to meet people and to have a good time," I told Clay while he loaded one of the glass cases in his aunt's shop with merchandise.

Clay frowned as he placed chunks of amethyst and quartz on the shelves. "A party? I'm not sure about that," he answered hesitantly.

Clay and I now spent most evenings together. I would come see him at work after cross-country practice. I was making an effort to get my act together. After I missed practice last week, Coach Kline had followed through on his threat and suspended me from that Friday's meet. And that did not feel good. I hated disappointing him. Even worse, I knew I was letting myself down, too.

Coach had pulled me into his office after lunch on Monday. I knew what was coming. I had been dreading this conversation for weeks. Coach Kline was like a big teddy bear. He was popular with the kids because he was approachable and easygoing. His faith in his students was unwavering. But I knew I had broken his trust. And that hurt.

"Close the door, Maggie, and have a seat," Coach directed after I followed him into his office. I felt my hands start to sweat. I hated confrontation on any level. Coach Kline sat down behind his desk and looked at me. "Is there something going on with you that I need to know about?"

I didn't know what to say, so I decided playing ignorant was a good place to start. "Uh, not that I know of." I couldn't look at Coach. I felt too guilty. I heard him sigh.

"Maggie, you are the best runner on the team. I really thought this was your year. But I feel like your heart just isn't in it anymore. You know, if there is anything you ever need to talk about, I'm here. My door is always open and what we discuss is confidential."

I wanted to cover my face with my hands. God, what did he think was going on? It was my own fault, though. My unprecedented flakiness raised a million red flags. But I couldn't admit that it was nothing more dramatic than me spending my afternoons lusting after the new guy. That probably wouldn't go over too well.

"Everything's cool, Coach. I guess I just have other stuff going on right now." Well, that was sort of the truth. I heard Coach click his pen over and over again. I looked at him and knew that I couldn't keep shirking my responsibilities. It wasn't fair to Coach or the team.

Coach Kline looked at me and frowned. "Well, I don't need to tell you that you miss one more practice and I have no choice but to suspend you for the rest of the season. It's the school policy. And I would hate to lose you. You have scholarships out there waiting for you. With your record, you'd be a shoo-in. Don't throw it all away. You'd regret it down the road." I knew he was right.

"I won't, Coach. I promise." At the time, I really meant those words. I wanted the scholarships and the sparkling, pretty future.

I wanted to make my family and school proud. These were all rational thoughts.

But when I saw Clay waiting for me after school, all rational thought went right out the window. It was too easy to lose myself in his company. He was like a drug and I was hopelessly addicted.

So cutting out our afternoon rendezvous was like going cold turkey. It seriously sucked. Instead, I had started stalking him at Ruby's Bookshelf. I knew he helped out there after school. I just couldn't go an entire day without having that alone time with him that I had come to crave. I also hated to admit that I was driven by my horrible jealousy over the too-pretty-for-comfort Tilly— whose crush on Clay was becoming more and more obvious. Luckily, Clay was oblivious, otherwise I would have had a serious catfight on my hands.

Clay always seemed happy to see me, and so it had become our thing. He got help at the shop and I got my Clayton Reed fix. Of course, now, instead of pissing off my coach, I was pissing off my parents by missing dinner most nights of the week.

But I needed this time with Clay. When we were by ourselves, I saw a side of him that was so different from the image he projected at school. After our disastrous lunch together, Clay had joined us a few other times. Rachel tried really hard to be nice to Clay and there were times when I thought maybe these two parts of my life might be able to coexist. Clay could be talkative and polite with my friends when the mood suited him. I loved seeing him banter with Rachel and talk to Daniel (who was making an effort, at least) about soccer. Clay made me feel so endlessly happy when he was like that.

But then there were the days when Clay would disappear, not showing up for lunch and becoming again the shadow in the hallways. If I approached him, he would either blow me off or act like he was angry with me. His moods were mercurial. He seemed to close in on himself at times and it made me sick to my stomach. I asked him about it once and he pretended that he didn't know what I was talking about, that I was imagining things.

But when things were good they were fantastic. He was so much fun to be around. He made me laugh and let loose in a way that I never had before. He made the most mundane things exciting and interesting. There was something magnetic about Clayton Reed that made it almost impossible for me to stay away from him.

We were still technically "friends." However, we danced on a very fine line between friendship and something else. I could feel it. I knew Clay could feel it. But I also knew Clay held back for some reason, and right now I was okay with letting us go at his pace. Because I knew it would lead to something life altering. Even though it drove me nuts.

Clay continued to garner a lot of attention from the girls at Jackson High School. I hated the painful jealousy I'd feel whenever I watched some stupid cheerleader or other annoying flirty girl try to get his attention. I was possessive of my relationship with Clay in a way that surprised me. But I found, to my intense relief, that he seemed content with spending time within my small circle.

I had come to realize how amazing Clayton Reed was and I didn't want to share him.

"What's wrong with going to a party?" I asked innocently, deliberately not acknowledging his wariness. I passed him a handful of pewter figurines and he carefully placed them on top of the case. I watched his purposeful yet delicate movements and thought about those hands touching me with the same gentleness.

Clayton seemed to be weighing his words before he answered me. "I'm just not really a party person anymore."

"Anymore? Were you a party person before?" I asked him.

Clayton sat back on the chair behind him and started digging through the box on the floor at his feet. He was still so choosy in the information he revealed about himself. I had learned in the past few weeks that he felt his parents could no longer "deal" with him and that's why he was now living with his aunt. He admitted to having a lot of "problems" and it had become too much for his mom and dad to "handle." His aunt was apparently much more patient and supportive of him, and he felt more relaxed in her home than he ever did with his parents.

"Yeah, partying was part of my issue in Florida," he said, getting up and carrying the box to the back room. Tilly gave him a smile as he passed. Her smile at me was much tighter and I knew it bothered the older girl that I hung out with Clayton in the store, which she must have viewed as her territory.

Okay, so maybe my smile was a little smug as I followed Clayton with another box. But I couldn't help it. "Do you need any help, Clay?" Tilly called out. She was tenacious, I'd give her that.

"We're good, Tilly. Thanks, though," Clay replied over his shoulder without looking in her direction (earning Tilly another smug smile from yours truly).

I dropped my box on the floor inside the dark storage room. "Be careful, Mags. Ruby will have my head if you break the crystal balls in there," he said sharply, quickly looking through the box to make sure everything was still in one piece. Despite his terse tone, I thrilled at his use of my nickname. I loved it when he called me Mags instead of Maggie, thinking it hinted at an intimacy that I desperately longed for.

"Sorry, Clay," I said, sitting down in a metal chair. I stretched my back after carrying the heavy box. "So, you had a problem with partying in Florida? What kind of problem?" I asked as he sorted through the greeting cards inside his box. Clay looked up at me with that unreadable expression he was prone to displaying.

"Well, I got in heavy with drugs and stuff. Hanging with the wrong crowd and all. Things got a little out of control for a while.

But that was only a symptom of everything else, I guess." His voice was cagey, always aware of how much he was revealing about himself.

"Wow, Clay—you just don't seem like that kind of guy. I'm a bit surprised," I said, watching him closely.

Clayton sighed. "I'm definitely that kind of guy. You have no idea," he muttered. I wanted to ask him more. To find out how "out of control" he had been. I wanted to know everything about my mysterious friend, but he remained hesitant and wary. Despite how close we were becoming, there was a very significant line that I just couldn't cross. Yet.

"So, no party, then?" I asked him. Clay's shoulders dropped as he stood up. He seemed unsure of himself and it made me want to hug him.

"Would we go there together?" he asked me. Would we ever! I wouldn't let him out of my sight if I could help it.

But I responded with an airy "Of course, if you want to."

Clay seemed to be ruminating over his response. How a high-school party could be such a matter of life and death was beyond me. "And Rachel and Daniel are going?" Clearly he needed strength in numbers or something. I nodded. "Okay, then. I guess I'll go. If you want me to." He looked at me, waiting for my affirmation.

"I'd love for you to go," I said, relieved that he would be with me in a social setting. I had this primal need to mark him as mine. To make it clear to all the idiots at school that he belonged to me. Wow, had I gone all alpha?

"Will there be, you know, drinking and stuff? Because that's kind of hard for me," he admitted softly. He seemed sad all of a sudden, the change in him catching me by surprise. His moods were so up and down; he was hard to keep up with.

"Melissa's parties aren't like that. Her parents are usually there somewhere. It's typically a bonfire in her back field with music and people just hanging out. It's a good time." Clay still seemed a bit unsure but took me at my word.

"Okay, then; sounds good," he said, giving his first real smile since I had brought the whole party thing up.

"Great!" I said a little too loudly, and I winced at my overt display of enthusiasm. Clay reached over and squeezed my hand. I startled at the physical contact. He wasn't a touchy-feely kind of guy, so I was taken aback by it.

"You're so cute when you get excited," he said, looking at me with something that could only be described as tenderness.

I know I stopped breathing. He thought I was cute? Our eyes held each other's, not moving away. A moment began to build and Clay took in a sharp breath. His eyes dropped to my lips and I could have sworn he wanted to kiss me. My tongue darted out and wet my suddenly dry lips, and I watched his eyes follow the movement.

The air crackled with the tension. Clayton's eyes burned with intensity. I felt like we were trapped in slow motion. His hand came up and lightly touched my face. I angled my cheek toward his palm and I closed my eyes.

"Maggie," he whispered, his breath on my face as he moved closer.

And my phone started buzzing in my pocket. Why did this always happen?! Clay immediately jumped back, putting space between us. He was suddenly focused on finishing his task of unloading the boxes on the floor. Crap! Someone had better be dying! I glanced at the screen on my phone and saw Rachel's name.

"What?" I barked after I answered.

"Jeez. Who pissed in your cornflakes?" Rachel's testy voice asked on the other end. I took a steadying breath and tried to calm the frantic beat of my heart. I looked back over at Clay but he had turned away from me.

"Sorry, Rache. What do you need?" I tried to not sound as agitated as I felt.

"I was just calling to see what time you wanted me to pick you up tonight," she said, still sounding miffed at my earlier attitude.

"You're not going with Daniel? I thought you guys were riding over together," I asked, already fearing the answer. Daniel must have bailed on her, hence her prickliness. Confirming my thoughts, Rachel told me that he had called an hour ago and said he'd be taking Kylie to the party. Rachel sounded so dejected that I wanted to call Daniel and ream him out. I was sick of him doing this to her. Even if he was my other best friend, it didn't mean I had to sit by and watch him be so thoughtless all the time.

I didn't comment on Daniel's ass-itude, knowing that it wouldn't help Rachel feel better. "Hold on," I told her, covering the mouthpiece with my hand.

"Hey, Clay," I whispered. Clay turned around, not really meeting my eyes. His expression was cold. Great, he was totally regretting our little moment earlier. Whatever—I could play the I-don't-care game with the best of them.

"Do you want to ride with me and Rachel?"

Clay shrugged. "I can just meet you guys there. Don't worry about me," he said, turning back around, walls firmly in place. His earlier nerve seemed to have taken a backseat to his need to stay away from me. I suppressed a sigh and returned to my conversation with Rachel.

"Eight thirty good for you?" I asked her, trying to sound more upbeat. The truth was I was bummed that Clay wouldn't be going to the party with me. Sure, he'd said he'd meet us there, but that's not the same as actually arriving together.

"Sounds fab. I'll see you then." And, with that, Rachel hung up. I put my phone on the table and picked up my jacket. Jamming my arms through the sleeves, I roughly zipped it up with an annoyed huff. Clay turned at the noise and looked surprised.

"You leaving already?" he asked me. I met his eyes defiantly. I was hurt by his attitude after our near kiss minutes earlier. Maybe I was setting all my hopes on something that most certainly wouldn't happen. But it didn't stop the sting. I just wanted to get out of there, put some space between me and this moody boy whom I felt I would never understand.

Clay's face softened, as if he were reading my thoughts. "Okay, then," he said quietly, taking a small step toward me. I stood my ground, not moving toward or away from him.

"Guess I'll see you tonight. You're not going to bail at the last minute, are you?" I asked him, frustrated by the needy note in my voice.

"No, I'll be there. Wild horses couldn't keep me away," he said with his ironic smile. I didn't smile back, my feelings still hurt too much.

I turned away and walked toward the door. "See you then," I called over my shoulder, refusing to show how badly I wanted *that* moment to happen. How much I wanted him to call me back, pull me into his arms, and kiss me senseless. When did I become this gooey romantic? When did I become freaking Rachel? I shuddered.

"Maggie." He stopped me with the sound of my name on his lips. I didn't turn around and he made no move to come any closer. Every second that passed amped up the angst level to an unbearable degree. Did he realize how much I wanted him? Needed him with a passion that scared me? Or was he a dolt just like Daniel?

Clay cleared his throat. "I can't wait to see you tonight," he said, almost strangling on his words. My cheeks flushed hot. I nodded again with my back to him, and left.

Dolt it was.

Once outside with the door firmly closed behind me, I sagged. I wasn't sure how long I could keep up this "friendship." Not when

I wanted so much more. I'd never experienced anything like the crazy feelings that Clayton stirred up inside of me and I didn't know what to do about it. There had been about thirty seconds there when I just knew he wanted the same thing I did, before the window slammed shut.

Was I expecting too much too fast? Maybe I was being pushy and inconsiderate about Clay's feelings and needs. Should I back off and let him come to me when he was ready? As great and thoughtful as that all sounded, it so wasn't me. I wasn't one to sit back and wait for shit to happen. So that's why this whole will-they/won't-they thing was exhausting. But I didn't want to give up. Clay was worth more than that. Our friendship was something special and I couldn't ruin it.

I chuckled to myself and I headed home. Damn it if Daniel hadn't been right (not that I would *ever* tell him that). He had told me that one day I would get what all the fuss was about, and that day had just arrived.

chapter
seven

"It's packed! I don't even recognize half of these people," I whined as Rachel and I parked my Corolla in the field behind Melissa James's house. Rachel pulled the visor down and touched up her lip gloss and fluffed her hair.

"Awesome! I'm down with meeting some new people tonight," she said, pulling on her pink cardigan.

I was less enthusiastic about getting out of the car. The thing I had always liked about Melissa's parties was that they were usually tame and relatively controlled, with no more than eighty or so people. I could relax and hang out without dealing with drunken idiots trying to cop a feel. If I was going to be groped, it would be on my terms only.

But this party was heaving. There were at least a hundred cars parked in the field and crowds of people dancing and drinking out of Solo cups around the humongous bonfire. "Get out of the car, Mags. Let's go mingle." I ran a brush through my limp hair and finally gave up and pulled it back in a ponytail.

"Uh-uh," Rachel said, pulling the tie out. She hated it when I wore my hair back, telling me I was so much prettier with it down. She threw the hair tie out the window.

"Rachel!" I yelled. But she was already moving away, toward the huge fire leaping against the dark sky.

I looked around quickly, trying to spot Clay's BMW in the throng of cars. I couldn't find it, so I grudgingly followed my friend. "Hey, Maggie," a guy slurred as I approached the crowd. I squinted in the darkness and made out Raymond Lewis, a kid in my year who was friends with Daniel and often hung in our circle. I was also friends with his girlfriend, Clare, who had been in French Club with me our freshman year.

It was obvious Ray had already had a lot to drink, as he hung on to me for support. Damn it, I had told Clay this wouldn't be that kind of party. I had just been made a liar, and that pissed me off.

"Get off, Ray." I shook my arm, trying to get loose. Raymond awkwardly slung his arm around my waist; more in an effort to stay upright, it seemed, than with any kind of friendly affection.

"I think you need a drink, Maggie. Come on." I wiggled out of his grasp and didn't follow as he tottered off in the direction of Melissa's house.

I found Rachel, red cup already in hand, who had been intercepted by Jeremiah Higgins and Lila Casteel. Rachel gave me a smile as I approached before turning back to her conversation with Jeremiah and Lila. They were apparently trying to recruit her for the Humanitarian Club or something equally boring. I stood there not really listening, tapping my foot, and scoping out the party.

People were really drunk. I could see a few girls throwing up in the bushes already. Couples were grinding against each other as they danced badly to the techno music blaring from the house, and people were sneaking off to do God knows what in the woods. Wow, this was seriously awful and I couldn't believe I had actually wanted to come. I just hoped Clayton had decided to bail, even though I had asked him not to.

No such luck. Just as the thought crossed my mind, there he was. He had just started toward the bonfire when Kylie (Daniel's now on-again girlfriend) and her bitch posse stopped him. I wasn't sure whether Clay had spoken with any of them since their awkward introduction at Bubbles. But there they were, chatting it up like BFFs.

Grrr, that crazy jealousy knifed through me again. Dana and McKenna laughed at something Clayton said. Dana in her bleached-blond glory, tossing her stupid, perfect curls back and laying her hand on *my* Clay's arm. Okay, I needed to check myself. He wasn't *my* Clay. He was only my friend, who I'd thought might kiss me earlier today. That didn't mean I had some sort of claim.

Despite my rationalizations, I was still beyond annoyed by the very obvious flirting happening on the other side of the bonfire. It was like watching a car wreck. My eyes were glued to the horror in front of me. After a few minutes, I was relieved that Kylie and the bimbettes moved back toward the house. Clayton stood there in the flickering shadow of the bonfire, looking like some sort of male model in his dark jeans and green Henley shirt. He was without his faded army jacket for once and he looked almost naked without it.

I nudged Rachel in the side and cocked my head in Clay's direction, letting her know I was heading over to him. "I'll be there in a sec," she told me.

I walked over to Clay and I knew the exact moment he saw me. It was like one of those supercheesy movie scenes when the boy and girl spot each other across a crowded room, and their eyes lock. Each moves slowly toward the other, as if pulled by an invisible force. Then they rush into each other's arms, kissing passionately and declaring their undying love.

Well, my scene didn't quite go that way. Clay and I met halfway and he kept his hands firmly in his jeans pockets and nodded in my direction. But he did give me an awfully nice smile.

"Hey, Mags. Raging party. Not exactly what I was expecting," he said jokingly as a junior stumbled past us to puke his guts out in the dirt not even ten feet behind me.

I cringed. "Yeah, I'm sorry, Clay, it's not usually like this. Apparently Melissa's parents are out of town, thus the massive kegger." Clayton shrugged, trying to act as if the crazy debauchery around us wasn't bothering him. I lightly touched his arm and he looked down at my fingers and then up into my eyes. "If this is too much for you, we can leave. You know, go get something to eat, go see a movie. Anything, really," I said, hoping he'd say yes and we could get out of there.

Clay looked around, tossing his dark hair out of his eyes. "No, that's cool. I mean, I'm already here, right?" I dropped my hand from his sleeve and it hung limply at my side. We fell into our normal silence as we watched kids from our school and the next town over partying like it was 1999.

"Hey, guys! Clay, it's so cool that you made it!" Rachel gave Clay a big hug. Clayton looked over her shoulder at me, his surprise obvious, because he and Rachel were definitely not at the hugging stage of their acquaintance. I tried not to laugh. There was no way she'd had more than one drink, but here she was, acting like she had been mainlining vodka all night. She was such a lightweight. I gestured to Clay that Rachel had already been gulping up the happy sauce.

Clay smirked and mouthed sarcastically, "No kidding." Rachel pulled away and then gave me the same boisterous hug. I couldn't help but laugh at her. She definitely put the *happy* in *happy drunk*. Well, until she was forced to interact with Daniel, who had a habit of setting her off when she was like this. I was plotting ways of keeping them apart for the remainder of the evening when I saw him walking toward us with Kylie firmly attached to his side.

I sighed and prayed that Rachel wasn't too tanked to keep a lid on the drama. "Mags! Rache! There you are! I've been looking everywhere for you!" Daniel gave me a Polo Sport–scented hug and I nearly gagged. He wore way too much and the smell got stuck in my nose. He then turned and kissed Rachel on the forehead. Rachel scowled at him.

"I seriously doubt you were looking for us, Danny. You seem busy enough." Kylie pulled herself up at Rachel's biting comment and interlaced her fingers with Daniel's in a territorial move.

Daniel frowned at Rachel but chose to ignore her words, which was probably smart on his part. He turned to Clay. "Hey, Clayton, good to see you made it out." I couldn't help but smile at Daniel's efforts to be nice. They engaged in that weird guy fist-bump/handshake/half-hug thing boys do.

Clay gave him a small smile. "Hey, Daniel. How's it going?" Daniel shrugged but gave a wary sideways glance at Rachel, who was now focused on anything besides him and Kylie. She was definitely failing in the subtlety department this evening.

"You know, same ol', same ol'." Rachel's head whipped around and gave him a hateful smile.

"Yeah, it *is* the same ol', same ol'. Isn't it, Danny? I can't figure out why you'd keep coming back for the same old and tired thing instead of finding something new." Kylie's face turned red and I knew I had to intervene before there was an outright catfight.

"Rachel, enough," I hissed under my breath. Daniel looked pissed.

"What the hell is your problem, Rachel? If I've done something to offend you, just tell me already." Poor, delusional Daniel. He was seriously about to open up Pandora's box and had no idea.

"Rachel's just had a few too many drinks. She'll be right as rain tomorrow. Don't listen to her . . ." Rachel shoved me in the chest so that she could move past me. She got right in Daniel's face, her expression murderous.

Clayton, thankfully, realized something was about to go down and moved deftly between them. "Rachel, could you help me find the keg? I'm pretty thirsty," he asked her, shouldering Daniel out of the way.

Rachel blinked a few times, but the change in topic worked and she gave Clay a bleary smile. "Of course, Clayton. I'd be happy to show you. I need to get away from all this bullshit, anyway." With a final look of death in Daniel's direction, she led Clay toward the house.

Clayton looked at me as he started to follow her. "Come find us when you're done here. I'll probably need the help." He looked at Rachel's rapidly retreating form.

"Sure, just give me a minute," I said. Clayton nodded before hurrying after Rachel.

"What the hell is that bitch's problem?" Kylie growled. My back stiffened. Yeah, Rachel was a little out of line, but no one could call my best friend a bitch but me.

"Watch your mouth, Kylie; don't say shit about her like that." My voice was hard and I gave the smaller junior girl a look of steel. Kylie shrank a bit under my stare.

I turned to Daniel. "Danny, can I talk to you a moment?" I looked pointedly at Kylie. "Alone, please." Kylie's face turned red again. It seemed to be her natural coloring tonight. She let out a dramatic "harrumph" and stomped off. Kylie wouldn't be joining the Maggie Young Fan Club anytime soon, that was for sure.

Daniel rubbed his hand across his face. "Seriously, Mags? I'm gonna get so much flak for this. I really didn't need all of this drama. I thought you girls were cooler than that." Daniel's shoulders sagged and for a moment I felt bad for him. He was my friend and I loved him.

"Sorry, Danny, but Kylie kind of grates on my nerves." I sat beside him on a large boulder along the edge of the bonfire. "Don't read too much into Rachel. She's just mouthing off." But Daniel knew as well as I did that Rachel didn't just "mouth off." When she spoke, she spoke her mind.

"I didn't realize you guys disliked Kylie so much," he muttered, hanging his head, his elbows propped on his knees.

"We don't dislike Kylie so much as we just don't like how she treats you."

Daniel just shook his head. He looked up at me and I felt bad that he was so miserable. He loathed any fighting among us as much as I did. "Is there more to this? Is there something you're not telling me?" he asked me, frowning.

When had Daniel become so perceptive? But there was no way I would tell him about Rachel's crush. That would be breaking her confidence, and if she had wanted him to know, she would have told him. So I just shrugged my shoulders.

"Not that I know of." But then I added, "Just be gentle with her, Danny. You know how sensitive Rachel can get. She gets her feelings hurt easily. Just be aware of the things you say and how they affect others, all right?" I put my arm around his shoulders and gave him an affectionate squeeze.

Daniel laid his cheek against mine. "I love you, Mags." He patted my knee and stood up. "Okay, enough of this girly crap. Let's go find Rachel and Clay so I can make this right."

I stood up, ready to follow him, but then paused. "What about Kylie?" I asked, surprised he didn't choose to go find his girlfriend first.

Daniel snorted. "I don't feel like hearing her particular brand of bullshit right now. Besides, Rachel comes first." I grinned. Daniel did have a good heart. Perhaps I'd never given him enough credit. "Let's go get a drink and find our friends." Daniel tugged on my hand and I laughed as he pulled me after him. My heart warmed when he included Clayton in our circle of friends, despite his wariness toward him. Daniel *was* a good guy.

We made our way through the backyard. It felt like trying to part the Red Sea: there were people everywhere. Melissa would have a nasty mess on her hands tomorrow morning. I would have been too paranoid to throw a party like this at my place, although, looking at her huge house, I figured she could afford to have cleaners come in and take care of it for her.

Daniel led the way and we went in through the kitchen. A few kids were mixing drinks with Melissa's parents' liquor, sloshing liquid all over the counter. "Hey, Daniel! Maggie! Want a Long Island Iced Tea?" Jake Fitzsimmons asked, pushing a full cup in our direction.

Daniel took the cup and sniffed. "Damn! What did you put in here? It smells like cat piss." He gagged and handed the drink back.

Jake laughed. "A little of this, a little of that. You know." I shook my head at the inebriated idiots.

"You want anything?" Daniel asked as we headed down the hallway toward the garage.

"Yeah, I'll grab a beer. But I'm DD tonight, so I can't drink much." We followed the wave of voices that drifted from the end of the hallway. This was obviously the way to the keg.

People crowded around the entrance to the garage. Daniel grabbed my hand and tugged me through the door. "You have got to be kidding me," Daniel muttered in apparent amusement. He had stopped just short of the keg and I ran into his back.

"Danny! What are you doing?" I called out.

"Get a load of your good buddy Clayton Reed," Daniel said, pointing in front of him. I moved around Daniel and was stunned to see Clay being held upside down by two football players, with his mouth underneath the keg tap.

It was then that I noticed the people circling him, chanting, "Go, go, go!" Rachel was jumping up and down, clapping her hands and cheering louder than anyone.

"What the hell?" I asked, not as amused as Danny had been. "We have to stop him, Daniel!" I pulled on his arm.

Daniel looked at me questioningly. "Why? It's not like you haven't done a few keg stands in your time, Miss Judgmental. Let the boy have some fun—he could use some loosening up."

I groaned. "You don't get it, Danny. Clay has a . . . uh . . . history with drinking and it's not a good one. This will end badly." I was becoming panicked as the keg stand seemed to never end. Daniel looked at me, frowning.

"If you say so. I think you might be overreacting. But whatever. You take care of Clay, I'll get Rachel." I smiled in relief, appreciating his help.

Daniel and I parted ways. He headed over to Rachel, who tried to push away from him as he put his arm around her shoulder and started leading her out of the garage. Daniel firmly held her by her upper arms and herded her outside.

I turned toward Clay, who was just now being put back on his feet. He stumbled, and one of the football guys put out a hand to steady him. "You all right, man?" he asked, laughing at my friend's drunken state. Clayton gave him a thumbs-up.

"I'm fantastic," he slurred. Good God, this was going to be just super.

Before I could get to Clay, Melissa, the hostess extraordinaire, rushed to his side and plastered herself against him like a second skin. "That was amazing, Clay," she cooed in his ear. Oh, gag. I grabbed hold of Clay's arm and squeezed.

"What the hell are you doing?" I asked quietly in his ear. Clayton looked over at me, only now realizing that I was standing there.

He grinned at me and pulled me into a hug. Melissa looked

miffed that she had been discarded. "Mags. I'm so happy you're here! Did you see that? That was epic!" he said, ridiculously pleased with himself. I pulled on him and we moved toward the door.

"Yeah, I saw you. I thought you said you didn't want to be doing that stuff," I replied, looking at him with concern.

A dark look crossed Clay's face and he yanked his arm from my grasp. "What are you? The party police? I'm having fun. I thought that's what you wanted. For me to meet people and, you know, socialize." I didn't say anything. Clearly, Clayton was not a friendly drunk.

"I did want that, but you were the one who said you had a history with this stuff. That drinking isn't good for you." I tried to grab his hand again.

Maybe if I could get him out of the garage I could get him to see reason. Well, that was wishful thinking. Clayton Reed was way past reason and had dipped precariously into Crazyland. He pushed my hand away. "Back off, Maggie! I don't need you telling me what I should and shouldn't be doing. I did just fine before you came along to mother me."

My mouth fell open to reply, but then I closed it. I wouldn't be this guy's punching bag. Drunk or not. Love of my life or not. I didn't put up with that kind of shit from anyone. So I shoved him in the center of his chest, making him stumble backward a few steps.

"Well, pardon me for giving a crap about you. I was just worried. But if you want to act like a drunken asshole, that's fine! I just won't be around to watch it!" I slammed out the door and into the cool night air.

I pressed my back into the cold metal of the garage door, trying to calm my breathing. That went well. I slid down the wall until I was sitting on the pavement. I leaned my forehead against my knees, wrapping my arms around my legs.

The door opened beside me and I lifted my head to see Clay step outside. He looked around and then noticed me sitting on the cold pavement alone in the dark. He sank to the ground beside me, keeping a cautious distance between us. I didn't say anything. I had nothing *to* say.

"I'm sorry. That was totally uncalled for," Clay said softly. Though his words were slurred, he at least seemed to possess some understanding of how horribly he was behaving. And he appeared genuinely contrite.

"Yeah, you kind of suck right now," I remarked, refusing to look at him. Clay's fingers touched my chin and he pulled my face around so that I was looking at him.

"Please don't be angry with me. I can't stand that. I need you way too much to have this between us." His words were desperate and I was shocked at what he had just said.

He needed me? Since when? And, while my heart thrilled, something inside me hesitated, unsure of how to respond. His fingers slipped into my hair and he started to pull me toward him. More specifically, my mouth toward his.

Before our lips touched I stopped him. I put my hands over his to still the movement. "What is this, Clay? What are you doing?" I murmured, the skin of our lips brushing against each other.

Clay gazed into my eyes and a pool of warmth flooded my belly. Why was I talking? Why didn't I just let him kiss me? How long had I wanted this, and I was making him stop? Was I freaking nuts?

But it just didn't feel right to have him do this when he was drunk. I wanted him in his right frame of mind when he kissed me. I didn't want it to be some sloppy event outside of Melissa James's garage. Clay backed up. "I thought you wanted this. You've been sending out signals like crazy." Clay seemed angry. Embarrassed, even. I had taken his guy card . . . again.

I touched his face, but he pulled away from me. Dear Lord, his moods were all over the place right now. "I do want to kiss you. Just not like this. I mean, you're kind of wasted right now. This isn't exactly romantic." I laughed nervously.

Clay shook his head. "Who said I'm looking for romance? Can't we just hook up and it not be all serious?" Whoa. Okay, that hurt. Glad to know that our kiss wouldn't mean quite the same thing to him as it would to me. Even though he had just told me he needed me. He had seemed absolutely wretched when he thought I was angry with him. He was so hot and cold, I just couldn't wrap my mind around it.

"All right, then. This is clearly not going to happen, so I'm going to go find Daniel and Rachel." I stood up. Clay got to his feet behind me. His face was unreadable but it was obvious from his body language that he *was not* happy.

"You go on. I'm just going to hang out. You know . . . socialize and all," he said nastily, and turned around and went back into the garage.

My stomach dropped and I blinked back tears. You have got to be kidding me. I had hoped tonight would be fun. But between Rachel's dramatics and Clay's drunken craziness, the night was quickly turning into a disaster.

I found Rachel and Daniel, who were swinging on the play set in Melissa's backyard. Rachel seemed to have sobered up and was actually smiling, which was a relief. "Hey, guys," I called out as I reached them.

They both looked up at me and smiled. "Hey. Where's Clay?" Danny asked, kicking his legs out in front of him to get the swing moving.

"Yeah . . . well, he's being a royal butt. I don't really feel like subjecting myself to that, if you know what I mean." I perched on the seesaw and pushed with my legs to make it bob up and down. Rachel blew the hair out of her face and slowed her swing down until she was swaying gently back and forth. She looked over at me sheepishly.

"I'm sorry about the amateur dramatics earlier. I think it's official that I can't exactly handle my alcohol." I gave her a look that said I agreed with her statement.

"Yeah, I guess we've learned that lesson. Next time *you're* the DD."

Rachel laughed. "Deal," she agreed.

"I had no idea that Clay had a problem with drinking, or I wouldn't have encouraged him to do the keg stand. But he never mentioned anything," Rachel said guiltily.

I pushed with my legs again and slammed back down on the seesaw. "It's not like you held a gun to his head, Rache. Clay is a big boy. He doesn't need us mothering him." I parroted his words, feeling hollow inside. I hated arguing with Clay. It felt crappy.

Daniel hopped off the swing and wiped grass from his pants. "Enough moping, you two. Let's go get our party on." Daniel pulled Rachel off the swing and grabbed my hand. We chuckled and followed him around the back of the house, toward the pool. It was nice having Daniel and Rachel be so normal with each other. Rachel looked at ease and none of their now-customary awkwardness seemed to be present between them.

The pool was obviously heated, evident as I watched steam drift upward from the surface of the water. People were swimming. Some without any suits. I looked away as Julianna Martin from my Spanish class climbed up the ladder in all her natural glory. Daniel's eyes nearly popped out of his head and Rachel smacked his leg, giggling.

Daniel went to join a group of his friends from the soccer team, while Rachel and I found a pair of deck chairs closer to the pool house to stretch out on. "Now, this is what I'm talking about." I groaned as I laid my head back on the cushion. Rachel did the same.

"I could get used to this," Rachel said, her arms dangling off the sides of the chair.

"This makes this crazy orgy all the easier to bear," I said, noting the paired-off couples making out around the pool. Rachel laughed and instantly sobered.

"How bad was I earlier? On a psycho scale of zero to ten." I looked over at my friend and saw how worried she was. I reached over and squeezed her hand.

"Very low, only like a two or a three. It could have been a lot worse."

Rachel sighed in relief. She rolled her head to the side to look at me again. "So, what happened to Clay?"

I started to answer when I was distracted by a noise coming from the pool gate. A big group of kids came through, led by none other than Clay himself. He had obviously had a lot more to drink since the last time I'd seen him and was the life of the party. The jocks were joking with him, the girls were flirting. He was the sun of the popularity solar system.

I realized that this was how life could easily be for him. With his looks, he could be that superpopular guy, with girls falling at his feet. But instead he had chosen to hang out with me. Not that I was unpopular, but I wasn't at the level Clay could clearly reach.

"What is up with him? He's being totally weird," Rachel said as she watched Clay jump into the pool with all his clothes on. He grabbed the ankle of Lydia Turner, a cheerleader, and yanked her in with him. She screamed as she fell into the water. Coming to the surface, she wrapped her arms around Clay's neck and nuzzled him.

I looked away, feeling sick. Clay somehow talked a bunch of other kids into jumping into the pool and soon they were horsing around and dunking one another. Daniel and his buddies joined them, while Rachel and I sat on the sidelines, unnoticed by the others.

I wrapped my arms around myself, feeling suddenly cold. I did not like this side of Clay. He acted as if he were amped up on amphetamines or something, like the Energizer Bunny. He spoke too loudly, acted erratically, but most of all just wouldn't stop. The people around him seemed to like this, but his behavior worried me. He was not acting like himself. Not like the boy I had spent almost every day with for the last few weeks. This was not my friend.

"What is he doing?" Rachel gasped from beside me. I had zoned out for a moment and missed Clay getting out of the water. He was currently climbing a tree that grew beside the pool. He climbed and climbed until he was almost at the top. He was easily twenty feet in the air. Balancing precariously, he edged out until he stood over the water below.

"He is not going to jump into the pool from up there, is he?" Rachel asked in horror. I just shook my head, my heart stopped in my chest. He was going to freaking kill himself.

"Dude, that doesn't seem too smart," one of the jocks yelled up at him. You know it had to be dangerous since one of his herd of followers had said something. No one was cheering him on this time. Everyone looked uncomfortable with what Clayton was obviously getting ready to do.

"You bunch of pussies! This is nothing!" Clay yelled down. He suddenly saw me, as he perched up on the branch. How he picked me out of the crowd and from that height, I have no idea. "Check it out, Mags! I can fly!" I started to stand up and rush over to the tree when he dropped from the branch. I held my breath as his body hurtled toward the pool.

The kids in the water quickly moved off to the side and he slapped onto the surface with a loud clap, dropping straight to the bottom. "Fucking hell!" Daniel yelled, diving under. Rachel and I hurried to the edge of the pool, peering into the water. I thought I would hyperventilate waiting for Daniel and Clay to surface. Why did he do that? That was just crazy! Not something a normal, sane person would do. I was so scared! What if he was hurt? Or dead?

Those seconds as we waited were the longest of my life. Finally Daniel and Clay surfaced. I could see blood streaming down Clayton's face from a cut at his hairline but, other than that, he appeared fine.

The pair swam to the shallow end and Daniel smacked Clay on the back of the head. "That was a pretty moronic thing to do, Clay. Get it together," Daniel told him angrily and swam away, clearly too pissed to say anything more.

No one else approached. Clearly Clay's stunt was too much even for this admiring crowd. Clay climbed up the stairs to where I stood with my arms crossed. His eyes were a bit unfocused and I wondered if he had a concussion.

He grimaced. "Not you too, Maggie. It was nothing." He got out of the pool and went to a chair to grab a towel. I followed him.

"You have got to be kidding me. That was totally insane. You could have killed yourself!" I called out. Clay dried his hair, shaking water out of his ears.

He reached up and touched the cut on his forehead and winced. "You might need stitches," I said, inching closer to have a look. Clay let me touch the abrasion.

"I'm fine," he said. He suddenly sounded tired. It was like a light switch flipped and now the energetic, over-the-top boy from fifteen minutes ago was gone. He sat down heavily on the chair and stared blankly ahead of him.

I sat beside him, not sure how to proceed. "Why did you do that? That was really scary."

Clay continued to look ahead of him. "Just wanted to know how it felt to fly," he said unemotionally.

What?

"Clay, I think we should get out of here. You're not yourself to-night. You're being really crazy," I said. Clay snorted as if my words amused him.

"What's so funny?" I asked him. Clay finally looked at me, a strange smirk dancing on his lips.

"Just an appropriate choice of words."

"Huh?" He made no sense, but apparently he thought he was being hysterical because he laughed again, louder this time. And, just like that, he bounced back up and his mood lightened.

"You want to leave? Let's go!" He grabbed my hand and pulled me to my feet. He started to pull me through the pool gate.

"Hang on a sec, Clay. I need to let Daniel and Rachel know I'm leaving." I tugged on his hand. Clay didn't let go. He looked at me over his shoulder.

"They'll figure you left with me. It'll be fine." And, like that, we were moving quickly through the party, toward the parked cars.

I was so confused by his sudden change in attitude. I had thought he was pissed at me, but now he wanted to leave the party with me. I didn't know what to think. We stopped in front of his car and he dug in his pockets for his keys.

"You're not driving anywhere," I told him. Clay pulled the lining of his pockets out and laughed. He had a strange glint in his eye.

"Well, I can't anyway; seems I've lost my keys." Clayton shrugged and pulled me in the direction of my car. "We'll just take yours."

Suddenly I wasn't sure I wanted to go anywhere with Clay right now. His behavior was freaking me out. I dug my feet into the dirt and refused to move a step farther. My sudden stop pulled Clay up short. He turned to look at me and frowned.

"What?" he asked.

"Where are we going? What's going on?"

Clay walked toward me and put his arm around my waist. He leaned in and whispered in my ear. "I thought you wanted to leave. So that's what we're doing. Let's go to my house. Ruby and Lisa are gone for the weekend."

His breath sent tingles down my spine. Shit, here we go again with the seesaw mood swings. Didn't we have this conversation not an hour and a half ago? I leaned into him slightly, Clay laid his lips on the side of my neck, and I shivered. Why did I have to develop a conscience all of a sudden?

I pulled away. "We talked about this already, Clay. That isn't going to happen." Clay reared back like I had struck him.

"Fine. Whatever. Just take me the fuck home." He stomped away like an angry child and waited by the passenger side of my car.

I unlocked the doors and Clay climbed in, leaning his wet head against the window, looking like he was about to pass out. I started the engine and pulled my phone out of the center console. I sent a quick text to Daniel and Rachel, letting them know I had left and that Rachel should get a ride with Daniel. And then I pulled out of the field.

Clay was completely silent, except to give me directions to his house. When I pulled up in front of a brick Cape Cod, I put the car into Neutral. Before I could say anything, Clayton wrenched open the door, slammed it shut, and bolted to his front door. I couldn't believe he didn't say anything to me. No apology for being a dick. No explanation for his whacked-out behavior. I knew he was drunk but that didn't excuse the way he was acting.

Maybe I was being supremely stupid, but I turned off the car and followed him into the house. Clay had left the front door wide open, a pair of shoes kicked off just inside the entryway. The house was dark and smelled faintly of patchouli.

I suddenly heard a crash from the second floor. I could see the stairs in front of me, so I slowly made my way up them. I could hear yelling and banging coming from the end of the hallway. What was Clay doing? And did I really want to follow him when it sounded like he was having a one-man boxing match in there?

But I couldn't leave things the way they were. I didn't understand why he was angry with me. Why he decided to drink, even after telling me that was a big no-no for him. He was a different person tonight and, if I was honest with myself, he scared me.

Yet I stupidly ignored the instinct that told me to get the hell out of there, and turned the knob on what I assumed was his bedroom door. My jaw fell to my feet as I watched him trash the place. He had pulled over his dresser, and clothes lay strewn all over the floor. He had pulled pictures off the walls. And there was a hole the size of a fist in the drywall. Okay, he was 100 percent freaking out.

I almost closed the door and left, wanting only to forget about this and the volatile boy who was currently destroying all of his possessions. That would have been the safe and sane thing to do. But if there was anything I had learned since meeting Clayton Reed, it was that I didn't feel necessarily sane feelings for him. These insane feelings made me experience things and act in ways that were completely out of character for me. So instead of bolting for the front door, I took a step inside and gently closed the bedroom door behind me.

The soft click seemed to break through the destruct-a-thon in progress, and Clay looked up. He seemed surprised to see me. A myriad of emotions crossed his face.

Surprise, anger, shame, and, finally, heartbreaking sadness.

"Why are you here?" His words were strangled and he pushed his hands through his hair, leaving it standing on end.

"I was worried about you; I couldn't just leave. Clearly I'm needed here." I indicated the mess around us.

And, suddenly, Clay crumpled to the floor. He brought his knees to his chest and began to rock. Um, okay. I had no idea how to handle this reaction from him. Screaming and yelling—I could deal with that. Clay in a near-fetal position on the floor as if he were trying to hold himself together . . . that was something else entirely.

I was really scared. Whatever was going on with this boy was beyond anything I had ever experienced. He needed something greater than I could offer. Yet I stayed. I didn't really have a choice. Again, those insane feelings of mine.

Maybe I was an idiot, or a glutton for punishment. Or maybe I naively subscribed to the foolish notion that my love could save him. Whatever the reason, I sank to the carpet beside that sad and broken boy.

I touched his arm and he flinched. "No, Maggie. I don't want you to see me like this." He hid his face in his arms while he continued to rock. His body shook with the force of his sobs. Each guttural noise ripped at my heart and I wanted to gather him to my chest and rock with him.

"I'm not sure what's going on with you. But I'm not going anywhere," I assured him, speaking softly as if to a wild animal that might bolt at any moment. I reached out and touched his arm again. This time he didn't pull away. I took that as an encouraging sign so I crawled closer to him.

"Clayton, look at me, please," I murmured. I gently lifted his face. His eyes were red and bloodshot, his cheeks flushed. The cut at his hairline had come open again and a small trickle of blood made its way down his forehead. He seemed to have sobered up a bit; his eyes were less bleary but there was something still there that worried me.

I hesitantly wiped the blood from his face and then left my

fingers on his cheek. Clay closed his eyes and took a deep breath. He seemed so tortured. What could be eating him up so? "What's going on with you?" I asked, not entirely sure he'd give me an answer.

Clay shook his head. "You should go. I don't wanna drag you into my shit. You deserve better than that. Than me." I slid my fingers down until they rested on the side of his neck. We were so close, our breath mingled together, each invading the other's personal space. But for once, Clayton wasn't pulling away. Instead he seemed to be desperate for my touch, for my contact, and I wanted to give it to him.

"Why don't you let me decide what I deserve? Now, tell me what's going on with you. Obviously you're going through something and I'd like to help if you'd let me."

Clay took a shaky breath. "I just wanted to be normal. For once, I wanted to feel normal. Is that so wrong?" he whispered. I had no idea what he was talking about. I gave him a small smile.

"Eh. Normal is overrated," I said lightly. I wanted to see Clay smile back at me. Instead my words seemed to cause him pain. He shuddered slightly and closed his eyes again.

"You just don't understand, Maggie. You really should go. Please," he said tightly, although I could tell he really didn't want me to leave. That he was just saying the words that should be said instead of actually meaning them.

"Nope, you're stuck with me. Friends don't leave when you need them." Clay looked at me with a stark hopelessness that freaked me out more than anything else had so far. What in the world could make him feel like that?

He slowly lay down on the floor, tucking his chin into his chest, and stared at the wall, closing in on himself. It was clear our talking was done. So I did the only thing I could. I grabbed a blanket off his bed and pulled it over us and I lay on the floor beside him. I carefully put my arm over his waist and snuggled into his back.

His clothes were still damp and they made me feel a little cold, but I held on anyway.

Clayton was rigid for a moment and then he relaxed into my arms, reaching up and lacing his fingers through mine. We lay like that for what felt like an eternity. Me wrapped around the boy I had grown to love as we drifted off into a fitful sleep.

chapter
eight

The beeping of my phone pulled me out of sleep the next morning. I awoke in an unfamiliar bed in an unfamiliar room. I spent a few moments extremely confused. I sat up, the blanket falling away from me. Then it all came flooding back. The party, Clay jumping out of the tree, his massive freakout after I brought him home. And, finally, us falling asleep together on the floor.

I was alone in Clayton's bedroom. The house was silent and I gave a quick thanks that my parents thought I was spending the night with Rachel. I pulled my phone out of my pocket and saw that I had fifteen new text messages.

Scrolling through them, I saw that most were from Rachel, who demanded to know where I was. There were a few from Daniel as well. The last one was from ten minutes ago. It was Rachel again, threatening to call my parents if I didn't call her back in fifteen minutes.

Shit! I hurriedly dialed her number and she picked up on the first ring. *"Where the hell are you?"* she screeched into the phone. I pulled the receiver away from my ear.

"Jeez, calm down, Rachel," I said.

"Calm down? *Calm down?* I have been worried sick! You disappeared from the party! I get a text saying you left with Clay! I tried calling you a bazillion times, and no answer! You never make it to my house! And I'm supposed to *calm down*?"

Wow, she was really angry. "I'm sorry. But Clay was going through some stuff. I ended up staying with him last night." There was dead silence on the other end.

"You stayed with Clay? At his house?" she asked, her tone changing to one that said she wanted the dirt and she wanted it pronto.

"Not like that. He just needed a friend." I ran my fingers through my hair and my tongue over my teeth. Gross. Morning breath.

"So you're telling me that you spent all night with Clayton Reed and *nothing* happened? I call bullshit." Rachel was like a dog after a bone and she wasn't about to give up. Thank God I was saved by Clay's sudden appearance in the doorway. He was already up and showered and he looked amazing for first thing in the morning. His eyes met mine and my heart thumped painfully.

"Uh, Rache, I've gotta go. I'll call you a little later."

"Uh-uh, you tell me—" I hung up on her. Yeah, I'd get chewed out for that later, but at that moment I didn't care. I swung my legs off the bed and stood up. I was suddenly very self-conscious of my less-than-fresh-faced morning appearance. I hoped my mascara hadn't smudged across my face in my sleep.

"Hey," I said. Clay just stood there, watching me.

"Hey," he said back softly. Okaaay. I picked up the blanket and folded it, laying it back at the foot of the bed.

"How did I end up in the bed?" I asked, after smoothing the sheets.

Clay still hadn't moved from the doorway; his eyes watched me intently. "I put you there not long after you fell asleep."

"And you slept . . . ?" My words trailed off. Did he sleep in the bed with me?

Clay gave me a small smile. I was so happy to see it after the drama of last night. "I slept on the couch."

"Oh," I said, not sure what else to say, kind of bummed that we hadn't been together all night.

I was disappointed to feel the renewal of the old awkwardness that had disappeared from our relationship over the past month. It was like putting on shoes that you had grown out of; not right. But our friendship had taken a drastic turn last night and I didn't know where we would go from here. Clay had some major demons and I had no idea what they meant for him or us.

"Bathroom?" I asked, my voice scratchy from too little sleep.

Clay continued to stare at me with his unreadable expression. "Down the hall on the right. There's an extra toothbrush and towels on the shelf." I scampered out of the room, sliding past Clayton, who had yet to move. I locked myself in the cheery bathroom. It was decorated in a bright nautical theme, with boats and fish painted on the walls. A little perky for my mood, if you asked me.

I really needed a shower. So I ran the water, stripped off my clothes, and stood under the hot spray. I stood there for an endless moment, letting the droplets drip down my body. I closed my eyes and replayed my night with Clay over and over in my head. What had happened to him? What was going on with him? Finally I turned off the shower and grabbed a fluffy yellow towel and dried off. I hated to put my dirty clothes back on but, considering my overnight bag was at Rachel's, I didn't have a choice. I found a comb and the extra toothbrush, still in its packaging, under the sink. I took my time working through the tangles in my hair and then put it back in the dreaded ponytail. Rachel would kill me if she saw it.

I brushed my teeth and started to feel semihuman again. Looking in the mirror, I barely recognized myself. I looked exhausted, with dark circles ringing my eyes and pasty skin. I took a deep breath and finally left the bathroom, slowly making my way back down the hall.

I entered Clay's room quietly and found him sitting on the bed, his hands hanging limply between his knees. He looked up when I moved toward him, his eyes as tired as I felt.

"I'm sorry," he said finally. I sat beside him on the bed and said nothing. Clayton's hands trembled and he clasped them in front of him. "I don't know what to say to you right now. Please tell me how I can make this better," he pleaded. I sat up straight, needing all of my strength to confront him.

"How about the truth? Enough with the evasive crap. Just tell me what's going on with you."

Clayton took a deep breath. "Yeah. I guess I owe you that."

"You think?" I snarked, feeling bad when I saw the hurt flash across his face.

"Mags. You are the best friend I have ever had. I don't know many people that would have stayed after all of that last night, particularly after the way I treated you at that party. You're way too good for me." He sounded so sad and I hated it. I took his left hand in mine and held it lightly, not wanting to frighten him off.

"I don't even know where to begin," Clay mumbled, turning his hand over until his fingers laced with mine. Just like they had last night as I held him.

"How about the beginning? That's usually a good place to start," I suggested, urging him on.

"Sure. The beginning." He stood up abruptly and moved to the window, looking outside.

"Well, I guess I should start by telling you the real reason I'm living here in Virginia and not in Florida with my parents. We had a rough relationship, to say the least. They are pretty well off. My dad is the district attorney for Miami–Dade County and my mom's a party-coordinating, pearl-earring–wearing, gin-and-tonic-at-nine-a.m. kind of socialite. They are on the inside of the social scene in Miami. I grew up with politicians and celebrities coming to my house for barbecues. But they have never been what you would call 'warm' parents. I was raised mostly by hired nannies who came and went out of my life, like a revolving door."

I tried to picture a little Clay all alone in a big house with no one who gave a damn about him. What a sad and lonely life. Clay turned to look at me and I could see tiny pieces of his perfectly erected wall start to crumble.

"When I was ten years old I started to have . . . issues. I became wild and angry. I would fly into these rages and destroy my bedroom, break windows, threaten my parents." His words instantly brought to mind his behavior last night. What he was describing was exactly what I had witnessed right here in his bedroom.

"I would go through periods where everything was fine. I was the picture-perfect son, getting straight A's. I would be on fire playing for the lacrosse team; everything was awesome. Then it would change and I would get angry, depressed." I shivered, imagining what he described. I had witnessed these erratic mood swings myself. One day Clay would be my best friend; the next, he would ignore me completely. Then there was the craziness of last night.

"I would lock myself in my room for days. And I would . . . hurt myself." His words made my stomach clench.

"Hurt yourself? Like, how?" I waited in dread for his answer, not sure I really wanted to hear it, but I couldn't stop him now that he was actually opening up.

"When I was thirteen I discovered that when I cut myself, or burned myself with a lighter . . . I felt, I don't know . . . better, somehow. That it stopped the craziness in my head and helped me focus. It became sort of like an addiction. I needed the pain to feel something close to normal, as weird as that sounds."

Clay slowly peeled his shirt over his head and he stood there, bare chested in front of his window. He took my breath away at the sheer beauty of what was before me. But then, upon closer inspection, I could see something else.

I stood up and walked over to him. I could see white scars crisscrossing his chest and running down his arms. How had I not noticed these before? I reached out and lightly touched my fingertip to a particularly large scar that ran from one side of his chest to the other.

"How did you do this?" I whispered, touching the raised skin.

Clay shivered under my touch but didn't move away. He closed his eyes as I continued to explore the map of scars on his body with my eyes and fingers. "That one was made with a piece of glass. I was high on cocaine and needed the pain to feel grounded. The cutting wasn't my only addiction. I already told you about that."

I dropped my hand and took a step backward. Dear God, how could he destroy himself like that? I just couldn't wrap my mind around someone driven to hurt themselves in that way. It was completely outside my realm of experience.

Clay put his shirt back on and turned away from me again. "By the time I was fourteen I was pretty heavy into drugs and drinking. There wasn't a day that went by that I wasn't loaded . . . and cutting. I was so deep into my self-destruction that nothing else mattered. My parents were never around. My so-called friends were only there for the drugs I could score with my parents' money. I really didn't have anyone that gave a shit about the fact that I was slowly killing myself. And I hated myself, Maggie. I mean *really hated* myself. I thought about suicide every day. I wanted to die, but was too much of a pussy to outright do it."

The agonizing pain in his voice was unbearable. Without thinking, I wrapped my arms around him and leaned my cheek against his back, feeling the steady rise and fall of his chest as he breathed. "You weren't a pussy for not killing yourself. I think it's much braver to keep on living, in spite of all that stuff," I said sincerely.

Clay covered my hands with his and held on. He stood rigidly against me. "So, how did you end up here, with Ruby?" I asked. Clay leaned his forehead against the windowpane.

"It all came to a head about six months ago. I had been partying pretty heavily. I was hanging out with my group of druggie friends and was so strung out on heroin and liquor that I never knew what the hell I was doing. I knew my parents were having a dinner party with some of my dad's constituents, but I just didn't give a shit. By that point, my parents had kicked me out of the main house. They were sick of seeing me drunk and high all the time, so I was living in the apartment over the garage."

"Your parents knew you were having problems? And they never tried to get you help?" I interrupted, aghast at the lack of love he'd received from the people who were supposed to give it to him unconditionally.

Clay laughed, a hurt and humorless sound, almost a snarl. "Oh, they cared about the fact that I was strung out . . . but only when it affected them. You know, like if I was supposed to go to some function with them but was too wasted to make an appearance. Then they'd get pissed. But, other than that, their solution was to get me out of their hair. I guess, in their minds, if they weren't seeing it, it wasn't happening."

"God, Clay, that's horrible." I couldn't help myself. I thought of my own parents and knew that if I was in a dark place like that, they would do everything in their power to help me. I felt a new appreciation for my mom and dad and all they did for me.

"Yeah, well, they won't be winning Parents of the Year anytime soon." He squeezed my hands and pulled my arms away from him, putting space between us once again.

"Well, I took this girl back to my apartment. Lacey." Oh, no, here came the jealousy again. I tamped it down with effort. "Lacey ran with my group of friends and was as drugged out as I was. We had just done lines of coke at a club in downtown Miami and we wanted to be . . . well, alone." He looked over at me, as if gauging my reaction. I simply nodded, encouraging him to continue.

"We had sex, did some more coke, and broke open the bottle of gin I had stored in my kitchen. I have no idea what happened, but the next thing I knew I was freaking out." Clay took another deep breath, running his hands through his dark curls over and over again.

"I remember smashing the mirror in my bathroom. And Lacey was just sitting there in her underwear, on my couch, doing lines as I'm tearing the apartment apart. Then the hurricane in my head just stopped. Next thing I knew, I had a piece of glass in my hand from the mirror and I was cutting my arm. Then my chest. Then my wrists." He turned his hands over and showed me two deep scars, one on each wrist.

"Lacey must have come into the bathroom and seen all the blood. I heard her start screaming, but I was way past caring. The next thing I remember was waking up in a hospital room, my hands strapped to a bed and my parents looking at me with absolute disgust. You see, my little *issue* ruined their dinner party. Was quite an embarrassment for them."

I was shaking by the time he finished. Whatever I had thought was going on with Clay, this was the furthest thing from it. This guy had been to hell and back.

Clay opened the drawer at his bedside table and pulled out a bottle of pills, tossing them to me. I caught them and read the label. LITHIUM. I shook the bottle.

"You take these?" I asked.

Clay nodded. "I was hospitalized in Miami General's psych unit for ninety days. After that, my parents shipped me up here to stay with my mom's sister, Ruby. I hadn't had much to do with her over the years. She's not close with my mom anymore, particularly after she came out and got together with her girlfriend, Lisa. But she is the complete opposite of my parents. She actually gave a shit and offered her home to me. She and Lisa are the closest things to parents that I've ever had."

I was relieved to hear that at least someone had cared about him.

"When I was in the hospital, the legion of psychiatrists diagnosed me with bipolar disorder and borderline personality disorder. They prescribed me lithium for the bipolar. It's supposed to help with the . . . swings. But therapy is supposed to be the only thing that helps with my other *problems*," Clay sneered, obviously unconvinced this was what he needed. I ignored that minefield and opted to focus on the other part of his statement.

"The swings?" Bipolar disorder? Borderline personality disorder? I had no idea what he was talking about.

"Yeah, my manic swings. I go through major extremes in my mood. You know, happy one minute, depressed and suicidal the next. I suffer from rapid cycling. My mood swings are severe and hard to control and come on really close together. But a lot of that also has to do with the borderline issue. The chemical imbalance in my brain is one thing, but the crazy behavior extremes are something else entirely. Which is why I turned to drugs, according to my shrink. I wanted some sort of control over what I was feeling all the time. That's also why I cut. It's so strange to know the textbook explanation of why I'm doing things while having no control over doing them."

I put the bottle of pills on his dresser and crossed my arms over my chest. This was a lot to absorb. I was in information overload. If I'd wanted to run the other way last night, that was nothing compared to the need to get the hell out of there that I was feeling now.

But what kind of friend would that make me if I bailed when he was finally sharing so much with me, even though it was scary and dark? If this were Rachel or Daniel, would I turn my back on them? I immediately knew that I wouldn't. And, as I looked at Clay, my heart filled with love for him. Because, despite all that he had just told me, it didn't change my feelings for him. Not one bit. I would stay, I would be there, and I wouldn't run like a coward.

"Does the lithium help?" I asked him, coming to sit beside him on the bed. Letting him know with my body language that I wasn't going to leave just because he'd unloaded some heavy shit in my lap. Besides, I had asked him for it.

"It does, I suppose, but I hate taking it. I feel like a fucking zombie on that stuff. Like I can't feel anything. I'm just numb. I guess I'd rather be crazy than not feel anything at all," he said. His answer scared me. So was he not taking his meds? Is that what had caused his psycho turn last night?

"But it's dangerous not to take your medication, right? I mean, is that why . . . you know . . . last night happened?" I didn't know how to word what I wanted to say. I was swimming in very deep waters here.

"I know that, Mags. I know I need to take them. But I just

wanted to feel normal for once. To be a normal teenager. To have fun. Hang out with people who didn't know anything about me or only wanted to use me for what I could give them. I wanted to feel what it was like to kiss you for the first time without being sucked into a medicated fog."

Oh.

"But you need them. Last night was bad. I can't stand seeing you do that to yourself," I said quietly. I turned my body on the bed until I was facing him. He looked at me and rested his forehead against mine. "And I want to kiss you too, more than anything. But not when you're like this." I watched Clay's shoulders sag with the rightness of what I was saying.

Because, as much as I wanted to take that step forward in our relationship, he needed me as a friend more. As much as that freaking sucked.

Clay cupped my cheek in his hand. "I am so tired of being this way. I just want it to stop. I want to be a guy you aren't afraid to be around."

I leaned my face into his hand and kissed his palm. "Then take your meds, Clay. I won't watch you destroy yourself over some ridiculous idea that those pills make you less than who you are. You need them. And I need you . . . as my friend."

That was really hard to say. Because it was such a lie. But he didn't need his life complicated by a new relationship. He needed my support without the added issue of the girlfriend-boyfriend thing. And I needed to wrap my head around all that he had just revealed, and what it potentially meant for any future between us.

Clay's mouth rose on one side in a half smile. "As a friend, huh?" he asked, his eyes questioning me.

I nodded, pulling away a bit. "Yes, as a friend. Because you've become one of my best friends, Clay." It really blew, being selfless.

"Okay, then." Clay got up and picked up the bottle. Shaking out two pills, he put them in his mouth and swallowed them without water. "There. Problem solved," he said nonchalantly, opening his mouth to show me he had indeed taken the pills.

I smiled halfheartedly. I seriously doubted a few tiny pills could solve all his problems. But it was a start.

chapter
nine

The week after Melissa James's party, on the whole, was pretty uneventful. My friends and I fell into a routine of school and hanging out. Daniel was off-again with Kylie, so he was around a lot more than he had been, much to Rachel's delight. I was also happy to see that the two of them seemed to have called a cease-fire. Since Rachel's drunken verbal vomit and my advice on caution and sensitivity, Daniel had been displaying just that. He was thoughtful and polite. In other words, nothing like himself.

I noticed the change in Clay almost instantly. The Monday after his Oscar-worthy freak-out, he was subdued and expressionless. He interacted some, but he had a perpetual stoned demeanor that was really hard to get used to.

In the following days, I felt guilty for thinking that I too liked Happy Clay, off meds. But then I just had to remember him crumpled on his bedroom floor, sobbing uncontrollably, and I put those thoughts firmly away.

The medication also made him really sleepy. He was having a hard time staying awake in his classes and at lunchtime. Instead of eating, he would often put his head down on the table and nap, pulling his army jacket up over himself.

During one such lunchtime nap session, Rachel poked him in the arm, eliciting no response. "I have never seen someone sleep like he does. What is his deal?" I glanced over at him. He hadn't touched his pizza. He never ate much anymore and I could see that he was losing weight.

"He's just tired. Leave him alone," I snapped at her.

Rachel looked hurt by my tone. "I was just asking. No need to bite my head off. Well, while we're on the subject: what is up with you lately?"

"Huh?" I asked, genuinely confused as to what she was talking about.

Rachel took a bite of her chicken-salad sandwich, then delicately patted her lips with a napkin. "Don't you 'huh?' me. I'm talking about your emergence as Superbitch. Well, at least where Danny and I are concerned. Clay, on the other hand, gets all the sunshine and roses." I looked at Daniel and he just shrugged a shoulder and went back to reading his sports magazine.

"I'm not grouchy *all* the time. Sorry if I've been less than my usual über-fun self," I joked. Rachel snorted in annoyance.

"Well, whatever—just stop taking your pissy moods out on the two of us. You know, if there's stuff going on, you can talk to us." Rachel looked pointedly at Clay, who was starting to stir. I ignored her remark, refusing to acknowledge, even to her, that there was any sort of problem.

Clayton sat up slowly, stretching his arms over his head, causing his shirt to ride up over his flat stomach. My insides did that funny little twist that often happened when I allowed myself to focus on how beautiful he was. Why did I have to be all "let's be friends"? Because watching Clayton rub his eyes and run his fingers through his hair made me really question my *own* sanity.

Clay wiped at his mouth. "I didn't drool, did I?" He smiled sleepily. I rubbed his bottom lip with my thumb, reveling in the feel of his mouth. God, I wanted to kiss him. Clay gave me a slow, sexy smile as if he were reading my mind, and I dropped my hand.

"Nope, drool-free," I told him, suddenly finding it hard to breathe.

"Here, guys. Don't forget to buy your tickets all this week after school." Lila, Rachel's friend, appeared at our table, dropping a brightly colored flyer among our lunch trays.

"What's this?" Clay asked, picking up the pink paper.

"It's the Fall Formal. We have it the last weekend of October. You should come; it's a lot of fun." Lila batted her eyelashes at Clay, who was oblivious to her flirting. He was studying the information on the flyer intently.

Lila, clearly disappointed by his lack of interest, gave us a despondent wave and headed to the next table. I leaned over Clay to have a closer look at the paper. I allowed my arm to brush his, feeling little prickles of awareness as our skin touched.

"You guys going?" Clay asked. Daniel and Rachel looked at each other and then back to us.

"Well, we usually go to the Fall Formal as a group. We save the whole date thing for prom. It's much more fun to go with friends. We go out to eat somewhere really cheesy like Pizza Hut, purposely wear horrible formal wear, and buy the ugliest corsages we can find. It's a lot of fun," Rachel told him, looking excited.

Clay looked at me. I realized how close our faces were and I backed away a bit. "You go to this? I can't see you doing the whole dressing-up thing," Clay said. I frowned, not liking that he seemed to have difficulty seeing me doing something girly. I was by no means a tomboy or anything. Maybe I wasn't as into the whole appearance thing as Rachel and other girls at the school, but that didn't mean I was lacking the required chromosome to enjoy it.

Clay realized he must have said something wrong and started backpedaling. "No, I just meant that it seems a little lame. I just can't see you doing something like that. You know, because you're too cool for a school dance." He squeezed my knee under the table in an unspoken apology. I covered his hand with mine and squeezed back.

"Nice save," I whispered, and he grinned.

"But I *do* go to the Fall Formal. Me, Danny, Rachel; Ray and Clare, when they decide to come to these things; and sometimes a few other people. We all go together; it's a good time. And there's usually a party somewhere after." I realized my mistake as soon as the words were out of my mouth.

Clay's mouth tightened at the word *party* and we both remembered his disastrous turn at Melissa's party.

"Or maybe not," I said quietly, letting him know that partying wouldn't be on the agenda. Clay smiled weakly.

"Well, can I come with you guys?" he asked shyly.

Rachel giggled. "Of course. You don't have to ask to come along."

Daniel nodded in agreement. "Yeah, man. The more guys, the better. These girls can get pretty crazy." He grinned at Rachel, who flushed.

Clay smiled at me, putting the flyer into his pocket. "Sounds cool." My stomach seized up at the thought of going to a dance with him. But I affected my best nonchalant smile.

"Yeah, cool," I replied.

✦

"So, do you want to see the dress I picked out for Formal?" I asked Clay two weeks later as we sat in my kitchen after school. Clay lazily flicked through my dad's *Library Journal* magazine. Riveting reading, I was sure.

He looked up at me and cocked that adorable eyebrow of his.

"Isn't that bad luck or something? To see the dress before the night?" he asked.

I laughed. "That's weddings, dork. The groom isn't supposed to see the bride in her wedding dress before the wedding. I don't think there are any superstitions tied to formal wear." He chuckled and closed the magazine, putting it back in the pile at the end of the counter.

I loved having him in my house. I had eventually succumbed to parental pressure a week and a half ago and invited Clay over for dinner. So that my parents could interrogate—I mean, *meet*—him. It had started out fine enough. Clay had shown up promptly at 6:30 for dinner. I had opened the door and struggled to stop my jaw from hitting the floor.

He had dressed in perfectly pressed khaki pants and a blue-striped button-down shirt. His black curls were slicked back, showing off his incredibly handsome face. He held a bundle of beautiful flowers that looked like they had cost as much as a small village.

"Hey, Maggie," he said quietly after I had let him in the front door. He seemed really nervous—not that I blamed him. This whole thing reeked of awkwardness.

"Those are beautiful," I commented, indicating the ridiculously large bouquet.

"They're for your mom. You know, to butter her up. Figured I needed all the help I could get. Lord knows I can't impress her with my amazing charm," Clay quipped in that self-deprecating way of his.

I had lightly punched his arm. "They'll love you as much as I do," I told him, and almost swallowed my tongue.

Had I seriously just admitted to loving him? Dear God, I wanted to run out of the house and far away from the humiliation of that moment. But luckily Clay was too nervous to catch my earth-ending slipup. He had only given me a shaky smile and followed me into the kitchen where my mom was finishing up the chili she had made.

My dad was getting plates and glasses out of the cabinets, but he looked up when we entered the room. "Mom, Dad, this is Clayton Reed. Clay, this is my mom and dad." I gently tugged Clay into the room by his shirtsleeve.

He wasn't exactly digging his heels in, but it took some strength to get him moving. My mom turned around and bestowed her dazzling smile on him. She wiped her hands on a towel and came over to greet him. "Nice to meet you, Clayton. We've heard a lot about you." Clay shook her hand and shot me a look.

"I don't talk about you that much, jeez," I muttered, embarrassed.

"Nice to meet you, Mrs. Young. Thanks for having me over for dinner." He handed her the bunch of flowers. "These are for you." My mom's eyes brightened. She was such a sucker for them. Clay had unknowingly made the perfect move.

"These are lovely, Clayton. Thank you so much. Let me put them in some water." My mom went in search of a vase, which left us with my normally mild-mannered father, who currently looked anything but mild. He was looking at Clay as if he were under a microscope.

"How are you, Clay?" my father asked, shaking his hand. Clay winced as he pulled back from his grasp. Had my dad seriously just squeezed Clay's knuckles together? Was he channeling Arnold Schwarzenegger?

Shit, this was going to be worse than I thought. "Fine, sir," Clay replied, tucking his hands into his pockets.

"So, Maggie tells us that you just moved here to live with your aunt. Where are your parents?" I wanted to smack my father. He couldn't build up to the big questions like a normal person. No, he had to go right for the jugular.

Clay shifted a bit uncomfortably on his feet. He hated talking about his parents, so he never did. But he looked my father in the eye and answered him honestly. "My parents and I don't get along, sir. So they had me come and live with my mother's sister, Ruby. I like it a lot better here in Virginia."

My father blinked in surprise at Clay's candor, and some of Dad's rigidity seemed to melt away. I wanted to smirk at his awkwardness. I could tell he didn't exactly know what to say to that. Well, take that, Dad.

"Well, I'm glad to hear you like Virginia. It's a lovely place to live. Uh, I think your mom is done with the chili. Why don't we have a seat at the table?" My dad gestured for us to sit down. Clay looked at me and grimaced in apology. I squeezed his hand, letting him know it was all right.

Mom came back with the vase of flowers and placed them on the table. She fussed over them and positioned them so that they were perfect. Clay and I sat down beside each other, Mom and Dad across from us. Mom served us our bowls of chili and homemade corn bread.

"This is delicious, Mrs. Young," Clay said between mouthfuls. My mom glowed at the compliment. For someone who claimed to not be charming, he was doing a number on my mother. My dad had let up on his cool attitude, but continued to watch Clay closely.

"Thank you, Clayton. Well, the reason we wanted to have you over was so we could meet you. We don't like Maggie May riding around with boys we don't know," my mom said, passing Clay the basket of bread.

My dad leaned forward on his elbows and stared at Clay. "We don't know anything about you, and parents can't be too careful about their children these days. There are too many crazies out there." I closed my eyes and bit down on a sigh. This was mortifying.

Clay swallowed his food and looked at my parents. "I totally understand. You can't be too careful about the crazies." His words were sarcastic and I shot him a look that clearly asked what the hell he was doing.

My mom cleared her throat. "Well, tell me, Clayton: you're from Florida, right?" she asked, trying to move the conversation in another direction. Clay stiffened beside me and his entire demeanor changed. I knew he was touchy about his past, though I hadn't anticipated such a strong reaction to such a simple question. His instant shutdown left me feeling panicked and eager to smooth over the sudden tension.

"Yeah, he's from Florida. But he loves Virginia. We had a blast at the outdoor market in Charlottesville last weekend. Remember that crazy vendor with the bird feeders made from gourds? They were too funny," I rambled desperately.

My mom looked at me questioningly, but my dad hadn't taken his eyes from Clay. I nudged Clay with my elbow, trying to get him to talk, but he remained stoically silent.

"I love that outdoor market! Your dad and I need to get back down there soon." My mom started telling me about some lady who made homemade jams and I tried to pay attention.

But I was too worried about Clay. He hadn't said anything else. The rest of dinner passed with my mother and me making ridiculous small talk while Clay stared at his bowl and my father stared at Clay. When Clay got up to help my mother clear away the dishes, I gave my dad the glare of death.

"What is your problem, Dad? You're making him uncomfortable!" I hissed. My father looked at me levelly.

"I'm just getting to know him" was all he said.

I cocked my eyebrow. "Getting to know him? You're staring holes into his head is what you are doing. Just stop it, okay? Clay is my friend and I want him to feel comfortable being here."

My dad frowned. "I'm just watching out for you, Maggie May. You're my only child. How much do you really know about this boy?" he asked me quietly. I looked at Clay as he helped my mom get dessert together. He still seemed closed off and distant, but at least he was talking to my mother.

"I know a lot about Clay. Probably more than most people. And I like him, so just let it go," I urged, giving my dad the pleading eyes he could never say no to. He softened a bit but didn't let the subject drop.

"There's something about him. I'm not sold, Maggie. Just keep your wits about you with that one," he advised as Clay and Mom returned to the table with a chocolate cake and plates.

Clay had left right after dinner, despite my asking him to stay and watch a movie. I think he wanted to get away from my dad's eagle-eyed stare. I walked him to his car and stood in the driveway with my arms wrapped around me. It was chilly and I could see my breath.

"Sorry if that was weird," I said as Clay got into his car.

Clay shrugged. "It was fine, Maggie. I'll talk to you later." And, with that, he left. And I hadn't heard from him for the rest of the weekend. I had tried calling him later that night, but his phone kept going straight to voice mail.

But the next morning Clay was at my locker as though nothing had happened. We never mentioned the dinner again. My mom had let me know that Clay was welcome at the house. My dad had stayed resolutely silent.

I made sure Clay came around only when I knew my dad was at work. Clay never asked why I was specific about the times he could come over. I don't think he wanted a repeat encounter, either.

In an effort to spend more time with Clay, I stopped driving myself to school. My dying car became the perfect excuse to ask him for a ride home. My oblivious parents would drop me at school in the morning, never realizing how I intended to spend my afternoons.

Clay would wait for me to get out of cross-country practice so that he could take me home when he wasn't working at Ruby's shop. Today he had brought over his calculus homework and was trying to get it done while I worked on dinner. My mom was going to be home late and Dad was still at the library.

Clay tried to stifle a huge yawn. He was looking haggard today. I reached over and ruffled his hair and he smiled at me.

"You look tired," I commented. Clay rubbed his eyes with the heels of his hands and sat up straight, trying to wake himself up.

"It's one of the side effects of my medication. *Extreme lethargy*. Sure, I'm out like a brick at night. But I could probably sleep all day as well." He looked at me as if to say, *See, this is why I hate being on medication*.

Wanting to change the subject, I put the vegetables I was chopping in the pot on the stove and set it to simmer. "Come up to my room. I want to show you this dress. It's hysterical!" Clay got to his feet. He curled his arm around my waist and pulled me into his side. My breath hitched in my throat. I always got this way when he decided to be touchy-feely. Which was a lot more frequently now, I noted with giddiness.

"Your bedroom, huh? You sure you want me up there?" His voice was husky and I had to stop myself from shivering. Damn straight I wanted him in my room. I wanted him in my room, naked, and in my bed, preferably.

I flushed at my R-rated thoughts. I gave him a playful shove. "Just come on." I tried to affect a playful tone and led him to the stairs. Clay had never been upstairs in my house. Maybe because having him in my bedroom felt too intimate. There was this tacit line between Clay and me that we were each hesitant to cross.

Sure, we were close; he had become one of my best friends. But that didn't stop me from lusting after him and wanting something so much more. I knew, deep down, he felt the same. Even though he could have had any girl in the school, he chose to spend his time with me.

But we were holding back. Clay was still trying to get a handle on his issues, trying to do what he needed to do to be healthy. There were days that he still fell into a depression, times he shut me out completely, even with the medicine. I had talked to him about going to see a therapist. I knew he needed more than the medicine to get a handle on things.

To say Clay was unwilling was a bit of an understatement. He had told me emphatically that he had had his fill of "head doctors" when he was hospitalized. I tried to not get frustrated with how stubborn he was about his mental health. But he was insistent, stating he knew what he needed and the meds were enough.

However, I didn't believe him, and I suspected there were days he didn't take them. I hated not trusting him about something so important but I knew he still hid so much.

"This is your room?" he asked in surprise.

"Yeah," I said defensively. Now I remembered the other reason I had never let him up here. The excessive amount of pink left over from my childhood was more than a little humiliating.

Clay went over to my window seat and picked up Mr. Prickles, my stuffed porcupine. "Cute," he said wryly. I grabbed Mr. Prickles from his hands and hugged him to my chest.

"Don't make fun of Mr. Prickles. He is priceless." I put the porcupine on my dresser and turned to my closet.

"I wouldn't dream of making fun of Mr. Prickles," he joked, moving to my bed. I hadn't bothered to make it today and I was just thankful I had picked my bras and panties up off the floor before leaving for school that morning.

"Have a seat," I told him, a lump forming in my throat at the sight of him on my bed. Yeah, that had been a central image in a number of my fantasies lately. But with a lot less clothing.

God, I was turning into a smut queen!

Focus, Maggie! Focus!

Clay leaned back on my pillows, his eyes already looking heavy. "Show me this dress of yours," he said drowsily.

"Well, I don't want to keep you awake," I said sarcastically.

Clay took his fingers and held his eyes open. "I'm awake, I swear!"

I laughed. "No need to be all *Clockwork Orange* about it."

I reached into my closet and pulled out the dress, which was sheathed in a plastic cover. "You ready for it?"

Clay gave me a thumbs-up. "I was born ready."

With a dramatic flourish, I pulled off the cover to reveal a bright-teal, knee-length dress with a huge bow in the back and one shoulder bared. The other shoulder was capped with a large white puff.

Clay covered his mouth, trying not to laugh. "Seriously? You're going to wear that?" He looked at me as if I were kidding.

I snickered. "We told you that the girls wear the most horrendous dresses they can find. We like to make the whole experience extremely ironic."

Clay gave in and laughed. "Well, I can't imagine anyone looking more . . . ironic . . . than you."

I took his comment as a compliment and quickly covered the dress again. "You should see Rachel's. It's hot pink with this slutty slit up to one thigh, covered in these horrible sequins. She bought these nasty velour high heels to go with them." Rachel and I were going to make quite a pair at the dance. The fact that we didn't take the whole thing seriously made it even more fun.

I went to sit at his feet on the bed. I shook his leg playfully. "That just means your suit had better be epic. Epically awful, that is."

Clay grinned. "I'm planning to go shopping over the weekend. Now that I've seen your masterpiece, I know what to go for." He let loose another mouth-splitting yawn.

He patted the bed beside him. "Come lay with me, Mags. Just for a little bit."

I looked over at my alarm clock. "My dad is going to be home soon, and he will flip if I have a boy in my room," I said uneasily. I think that was a bit of an understatement, given his less-than-jovial feelings about Clay. But, more than that, I was nervous about lying down with him, being that close. I felt like such a silly girl around him sometimes.

He patted the bed again. "Just for a minute. Please. Trust me, I don't want your dad catching me up here any more than you do. I just want to hold you for a bit," he said softly, his voice scratchy with tiredness. There he was again, tiptoeing on that line we had drawn in the sand. His brown eyes were heavy and he looked at me in that way that made my knees go weak. I never had any resistance where Clay was concerned. He was everything I craved and knew I shouldn't have. But none of that mattered—just the fact that he wanted me near him as much as I wanted it.

So I crawled up beside him and he slipped his arm underneath me, pulling me onto my side. I spooned up beside him, my head on his chest, my hand resting lightly on his stomach. My legs were suddenly tangled with his and I found myself extremely comfortable.

Clay pulled my arm off of his stomach and tightened it around his waist so that I was practically plastered to his side. He smoothed my hair off my forehead and rested his cheek on the top of my head. I wondered if he could feel the frantic beat of my heart as I lay nestled against him.

He let out a gigantic sigh and relaxed into me. "This is nice," he murmured, his other hand running slowly up and down my back. Whoa. Lying here like this with him made me forget all my reasons for not jumping in with both feet. I mean, I loved him. Completely. I thought he at least cared about me. So why wait?

Clay's hand slowed until it rested on my lower back, right underneath my shirt, against my bare skin. The warmth of his fingers seemed to shoot tingles into my flesh. I could hear his breathing deepen. I chanced a peek up at him and saw that he was almost asleep. I tried to move out from his embrace but his arms tightened around me.

"No, please stay. I like you close," he whispered sleepily. So I lay back down on his chest and quickly fell asleep.

chapter
ten

"What the hell is going on in here?"

I sat up suddenly, groggy from being pulled out of a deep sleep. I looked over and saw that Clay had opened his eyes, confused. I turned toward my doorway and felt the color drain from my face.

Dad.

I swung my legs over the side of the bed and stood up. "It's not what it looks like, Dad," I tried to explain. My father was furious. I don't think I had ever seen him this angry, at least not with me.

He held up his hand, shutting me up. "I don't want to hear it, Maggie. You know the rules." My dad turned his steely eyes on Clay, who was still trying to wake up.

Thank God he realized that we were in a bit of trouble, so he got off the bed as quickly as he could. He walked over to my dad and put out his hand.

"Hi, Mr. Young." My father looked at Clay's hand as if it were a snake and would bite him. He didn't shake it. I couldn't believe my dad was being so rude.

"Clay, we have rules in this house. A big one being, No boys are allowed in my daughter's bedroom when we aren't at home. And definitely not with the door closed." My dad pushed the door open as wide as it would go.

Clay dropped his hand to his side and cleared his throat. "I'm sorry, sir. Maggie was just showing me her dress for the Formal and we fell asleep. That's it." I was proud of how Clay stood his ground with my father. Many a guy would have simply hightailed it out of there. But Clay was being respectful and showing my dad he wasn't some horny teenage boy there to deflower his daughter.

Although that would be nice, too.

I intercepted my dad's cold stare. "Dad. Seriously, it's not like we're having crazy sex up here or anything. Chill out." Okay, bad choice of words. Clay turned bright red and looked as if he wanted to fall through the floor.

My dad's eyes nearly popped out of his head and he stuttered for a few seconds before finally saying, "Well, whatever it was, you know your mom and I don't allow this. You kids are to stay downstairs when we're not here. Is that clear?" Clay and I both nodded. "Now, Clay, I think it's time for you to go."

My dad turned and went back downstairs, and I was finally able to breathe again. Clay grabbed his book bag off my vanity stool. "Did you have to bring the word *sex* into it? I mean, seriously? I know your dad hates me as it is." Clay looked as if he wanted to throttle me. I did feel bad for embarrassing him like that.

"Sorry," I muttered, following him down the hallway.

Once downstairs, Clay respectfully told my father good-bye, and I threw a look of death in my father's direction after Clay's back was turned. My dad looked blandly back at me. I accompanied Clay to his car.

After throwing his bag into his car, he turned to face me. "Well, that was a rude awakening, huh?" I was relieved to see his small smile.

"Yeah. About gave me a heart attack," I joked. Clay chuckled and grabbed my arm, pulling me closer.

"And I was sleeping so well, too," he said, his voice deepening.

I swallowed thickly. Then I glanced up at the kitchen window and saw my father standing there like a voyeur or something and pulled away.

"Sorry about my dad. He's just being a little . . . um . . . over-protective."

Clay opened his car door. "I understand where he's coming from. If you were my daughter I'd want to most definitely protect you from guys like me." He seemed a little sad as he said that.

I touched his shoulder. "I don't need protecting from you, Clay," I said gently.

Clay wouldn't look at me; instead, he got in his car and started the engine. Not responding to my statement, he simply said, "I'll see you at school tomorrow." And, with that, he drove off. I was left feeling hollow and empty after feeling so good only an hour before. I could kill my father!

I stomped into the house, slamming the front door. My dad was still in the kitchen, although he had the decency to act like he had been reading a book the whole time and not spying on me.

"What the heck was that about?" I asked him angrily. My dad looked up at me in surprise. He wasn't used to me getting this sort of an attitude with him.

"Now, just wait a minute. I came home from work to find you in your room, the door closed, sleeping in your bed with a boy—who I don't know that well, I might add. What about this situation doesn't warrant the reaction I had?" my father asked reasonably. I hated when he did that—stayed all calm and logical. It made me feel stupid by comparison.

"We're just friends, Dad. Clay fell asleep and I fell asleep beside him. That's it. But you totally humiliated me." I hated the prickle of tears behind my eyes and quickly wiped them away. My dad's face softened a bit.

"I didn't mean to humiliate you, Maggie-Girl." I knew he was feeling guilty, because he was using my pet name. "But Clay is a boy and you are my little girl. And from the sound of your voice, I get the feeling there's a bit more than friendship going on there."

I started to protest, then stopped. What was the point in lying about it?

My dad nodded knowingly. "So I think my stipulations are very reasonable. Clay is not allowed in your room when you are home alone. Are we clear?"

I shrugged, not wanting to talk about it anymore. "Fine, whatever. It's not like I'm seventeen years old, about to turn eighteen in four months. I'm almost an adult, Dad, and you treat me like a child," I whined. I knew I sounded exactly like the child I tried to convince him I wasn't. I was not making a very good argument.

"I don't care if you're a hundred and two. When you are living at home, you follow your mom's and my rules. It's just how it is. Now, this has never been a problem before, so what's the issue now?" my father asked me pointedly, making it clear he *knew* what—or *who*—the problem was, and his name started with a *C* and ended in a *Y.*

I was nearly in tears. I had never really fought with my dad and it felt awful. But I knew something inside me was changing. I was sick of being treated like their little girl. I was finally becoming a woman, with the wants of a woman and the needs of a woman, and my parents were starting to cramp my style.

But I didn't argue anymore. I just left the kitchen, went up to my room, and closed the door. I was proud of myself for not slamming it, like I wanted to. I threw myself on my bed, gathering the pillow to my chest and pushing my face into the fabric.

I could still smell Clay's cologne and I felt a new wave of excitement. Those moments simply lying with him had been amazing.

And it made me rethink so many of the caveats in our relationship. Because I wanted him, desperately, and I was pretty sure I was done with waiting.

Sure, the issues were still there, but maybe loving him would be the best way to help him. Yep, my mind was made up. I wanted Clayton Reed as my boyfriend. I loved him and I wouldn't let my fears dictate my actions any longer. My parents and my inconsequential concerns be damned.

And if he went into the dark again, this time I would be there to find him—to follow him. Because I thought, perhaps quite immaturely, that my love could help him. Maybe *our* love could do even more than just help—maybe it could heal him. Fix him. Fix everything.

◆

"You look so amazingly awful!" Rachel squealed, making me turn around for the millionth time in my hideous Formal dress. I had teased my hair into an '80s 'do, complete with the poofy bangs and frizzy curls. I did look pretty funny. But I was pleased to note that the dress was actually very formfitting and gave the illusion of some amazing curves. So, despite the nasty puff sleeves and horrible color, I didn't look too bad.

Which was good, because I was ready to make my feelings for Clay known tonight. This was it—I was taking the plunge. Clay hadn't been back in my house for the weeks leading up to the dance. He made a million excuses whenever I suggested he come inside after school. I knew my dad had freaked him out and Clay was trying to be respectful of his wishes. But unfortunately that meant we hadn't been alone since falling asleep in my bed, and that sucked. Ruby had started taking the afternoons off at the shop, so we would end up hanging out in Clay's living room, watching TV and doing our homework while Ruby plied us with new herbal-tea concoctions she was trying out.

I really loved his aunt and her girlfriend. They immediately made me feel welcome (unlike what my father did to Clay) and were very clear about how happy they were that Clay and I were spending time together. I could see the worry in Ruby's eyes when she looked at her nephew. It was the same worry I felt underneath the anticipation that was building inside me whenever he and I were together.

The sexual tension was threatening to choke me, it had become so thick. Clay and I made every excuse to touch each other in seemingly platonic ways. Clay would brush the hair off my face. I would pick a piece of imaginary lint from his sleeve. It was a beautiful dance we were engaged in and the buildup was almost as delicious as what I imagined the real deal to be like.

"I can't wait to see what the boys are wearing," Rachel enthused. She looked fantastic in her bright-pink dress. She had pulled her dark-brown hair into a messy updo, with curls framing her face. If the way she looked tonight didn't have Daniel tripping over his tongue, I didn't know what would.

"Yeah, Clay was pretty cagey about his getup; it should be interesting," I said, touching up my makeup. I was wearing more than I normally did, but I was pleased with the result. My brown eyes were rimmed in kohl, for a smudged, smoky look. My usually thin lips were painted an almost garish red, but I liked the way it made them look fuller. All in all, I didn't look too bad.

"You look so pretty, Mags. Even in that eye-searing color," Rachel said, putting her arm around my shoulders so we could stand together in front of my full-length mirror.

"Let's do this. Daniel and Clay should be here any minute," I said as Rachel grabbed her beaded purse. I leaned over to pick up my messenger bag and Rachel stopped me.

"You *are not* taking that thing. It ruins the look." She went back to my closet and unearthed a black satin handbag that my mom had gotten me for prom last year. Rachel took my wallet, brush, and mints out of my bag and placed them in the much smaller purse.

"There, much better," she said after I slung it over my shoulder. I just shook my head, not wanting to argue with her about it. We had just reached the bottom of the stairs when the doorbell rang.

My mother was there instantly. She must have been lying in wait for the guys, armed with her heavy-duty Nokia camera. I rolled my eyes at the thought of the next ten minutes of picture-taking hell.

"Well, hello, Daniel, Clay," my mother said. She moved aside so they could come into the foyer. I covered my mouth with my hand trying not to crack up. They looked ridiculous. They had unknowingly worn similar suits, very dated formal wear. Daniel's was maroon and Clay's a horrendous plum. Each had a white tie and a robin's-egg-blue shirt. It was a horrible combination. But they somehow made it work.

I took a moment to muse on how different they were, yet equally good-looking. Daniel had started to let his blond hair grow out and it looked almost unkempt around his face. His toned arms barely fit into the tight sleeves of the jacket. I heard Rachel's barely-there sigh when she saw him.

Now, Clay was truly gorgeous. Even in the horrible suit, he looked handsome. His hair too was growing out into those curls I loved and they hung just above his eyes. He seemed excited; buoyant, even. His energy was apparent as he took my arm and placed my hand in the crook of his elbow.

"My lady. You are a vision," he said, looking me up and down.

I elbowed him and laughed. "And you, sir, look dazzling in your prune suit." He smoothed the jacket's front.

"This is not *prune*, it is a very lovely shade of puce, I believe."

"Well, whatever it is, you look pretty awesome," I said breathlessly. Clay smiled at me, catching the way my voice shook as he took my hand.

"Look at you guys! Aren't you a sight!" my mom said, pulling the four of us into the living room so she could take pictures. My dad looked up from the newspaper he was reading on the couch. His eyes darkened slightly at the sight of Clay holding my arm and I glared at him. Catching my look, my dad smoothed his expression and gave me a smile.

"You all look great," he said politely.

"Thank you, Mr. Young," Clay said judiciously, clearly trying to make this as painless as possible. Considering he hadn't seen my dad since their run-in, I thought it was pretty minimal in the awkwardness department.

After fifteen minutes of pictures, we finally got out the door. "One o'clock curfew," my dad yelled as we walked down the sidewalk. I knew what my curfew was, and was very aware that he was saying it more for Clay's benefit than mine.

"Yes, sir—not a minute later. I promise," Clay assured him, giving his best parent-pleasing smile.

Finally, we were in Clay's BMW and heading toward Red Lobster, where we'd be meeting Raymond and Clare. "You guys look awesome! Even in that horrible color!" Rachel said enthusiastically.

Daniel chuckled. "Yeah, you don't know how hard it is to find an *ugly* getup," he remarked, and I laughed.

"I'm just not sure if this color suits my complexion," Clay commented. The four of us laughed together. I felt on top of the world. Tonight was going to be wonderful. I just knew it.

Clay looked at me sideways and grinned. He was in a great mood tonight. Laughing and joking with everyone. He didn't seem tired or out of it. It was nice to see. Maybe the meds were finally working the way they were supposed to. Whatever it was, I wasn't going to focus too much on it. I was going to have a good time with my friends and my maybe-boyfriend.

Our dinner at Red Lobster was a blast. Daniel, Clay, and Ray insisted on wearing those silly plastic bibs and we all ordered piles of crab legs, trying not to get melted butter on our tacky formal wear. It was good to hang out with Clare. I hadn't seen much of her since school had started.

By the time we got to the high school, the dance was in full swing. The gym was decorated in fall colors and fake leaves. Twinkling lights hung from the rafters and a picture booth had been set up near the door to the boys' locker room.

Our group made its way to a table in the back of the gym. The DJ was playing some current pop hits and a bunch of kids were dancing in front of the stage. Clay took my jacket and went to check it with the chaperones out in the hallway.

Daniel and Ray had gone to get something to drink and Clare had spotted a group of her friends and had gone to join them. Rachel leaned over toward me. "So, I'm thinking you need to get your act together, girlfriend, and claim good ol' Clay before he's whisked out from under your nose."

I blinked in mock surprise, although I was more than a little shocked by her sudden approval of a relationship with Clay. "Whatever do you mean?"

Rachel rolled her eyes. "You guys have been circling around each other for way too long. Come on, put us all out of our misery and get together, already. Because if you don't jump at it, you may find that you're too late." Her eyes shot over to the entrance of the gym where Clay had been stopped by Kylie's friend Dana.

Dana just wouldn't give up. She stalked Clay almost as much as I did. Always putting herself in his way, making excuses to talk to him. I had to suppress the urge to body-check her. But I had to admit that she looked hot tonight. She wore a tight-fitting red dress with a plunging neckline, and her puppies looked about ready to spill out. Her blond hair was a mass of curls down her back, and most guys would have been drooling at the sight she made.

My face flushed red as I saw the way she moved in close to Clay, laughing at something he said. He was smiling down at her and I could see he was having a hard time keeping his eyes on her face. I suddenly felt very foolish in my stupid teal dress and teased hair.

I turned away from them, trying to keep my voice even. "Well, if that's what he's interested in, then why should I bother?" I wasn't fooling Rachel in the slightest.

She smacked my hand. "Don't be an idiot. Clay likes you. A lot. And even though I'm not entirely sold on him, I see how you guys feel about each other. And I'm not one to get in the way of young love. So I think you should stop being a moron and go for it."

I looked back toward Clay and Dana. She was pulling him out onto the dance floor. He was following her, laughing. He looked over at me suddenly and I cast my eyes down to my lap. The evil jealousy monster, rearing its ugly head. I blinked back the tears that had suddenly formed in my eyes.

Daniel had returned to the table and was trying to talk Rachel into dancing with him. "Come on, Rache. Let's get our groove on." He danced in front of her.

Rachel's eyes lit up and she got to her feet. "You okay?" she asked me, but not waiting for an answer before following Daniel onto the dance floor.

I looked over at Clay, who was dancing entirely too close to Dana for my taste. I wanted to have a good time and I would not mope over that stupid boy who I'd naively thought would be spending time with me.

But there I was, left sitting alone like a pathetic wallflower. The song ended and another started and still Clay didn't come back to the table. Once again, he was the life of the party. He was dancing with a group of kids in the middle of the dance floor, Dana beside him. I was relieved to see that he didn't make any move to touch her, not that she didn't touch him. Her hands were all over him.

Yuck. I pretended to be looking for something in my bag so I didn't feel like such a loser as I sat there alone. "Nobody puts Baby in a corner," a voice said beside me. I looked up at Daniel, who was standing there grinning.

I smiled back. "God, you are such a dork," I told him.

Daniel laughed and pulled me to my feet. "Come on, let's go do some dirty dancing." Thank God for my friends, or I would be running from the room sobbing right now.

We were soon dancing with Rachel, Ray, and Clare. I had lost sight of Clay, and that hurt. I'd really thought he'd be hanging out with us. I thought that was the point of us all coming as a group. Maybe I *had* waited too long. Maybe we had played friends to the point that that's all he thought I was. Mixed signals be damned. So I danced and tried to put my misery over him out of my mind.

After a few more fast songs, a slow one started. Daniel pulled Rachel into his arms and they started swaying together. I couldn't help but smile at the happy expression on her face. She met my eyes and I gave her a thumbs-up. She grinned and closed her eyes as she laid her cheek against Daniel's shoulder.

Left standing there all by myself, again, I made my way back to our table. "Oh, no, you don't," Clay said from behind me, putting his arm around my waist. I looked over my shoulder and there he stood, glistening with sweat from dancing. He smirked and turned me around.

"What, no one else would dance with you? Where's Dana?" I made a show of looking around the room. I couldn't help the blatant jealousy that came through in my words. Clayton put his arms around me and walked backward until we were in the middle of the throng of dancers.

"Don't be like that, Mags. There's no one I want to dance with but you," he whispered into my ear.

"Liar," I whispered back as I held my cheek to his chest and wrapped my arms around his shoulders.

Clay didn't say anything as we moved to the music. It was delicious the way his body pressed against mine. I felt completely alive. The music seemed to float over us and it felt like we were the only people in the room. Clay's fingers gently stroked my hair, and I sighed in contentment.

This was what it was supposed to be about. Tonight was about him and me. Together.

"Maggie," he murmured into my hair, and I pulled back and looked at him. He stared down at me as he slowly caressed my face. He had this way of turning me to mush. Did he have any idea what he did to me? We looked at each other for an endless moment. I was frozen in place.

We had stopped dancing and simply held each other as the song came to an end. And then, just when I thought our moment had come, when we wouldn't hold back anymore, it was over.

"Clay. I want the next dance. Come on." Dana was suddenly there, tugging on his arm. Clay didn't take his eyes from mine, a question there. Did he want me to stop him? What did he expect from me?

But that vicious emotion called jealousy made me mean. "Please, don't let me keep you," I said acidly, moving out of Clay's arms. I could have sworn I saw hurt flash in his eyes. But he dropped his hands from my waist and let Dana lead him away. Away from me and whatever had been there between us just a second before.

I couldn't help myself; I stomped off the dance floor and threw myself into the metal chair at our table. Rachel was sitting there by herself, looking as unhappy as I felt.

"Where's Daniel?" I asked her. Rachel jerked her thumb in the direction of the punch table where Daniel was involved in a very heated discussion with Kylie.

Great—we had both been ditched. So much for a fantastic evening. "Where's Clay?" she asked me in return. I jerked *my* thumb in the direction of the dance floor, where Dana had wrapped herself around him. I couldn't help but take sadistic pleasure in the fact that he didn't seem to be enjoying himself.

Rachel sighed heavily. "What is with these stupid boys?" she asked. I leaned on the table, propping my chin on my hands.

"They're boys, Rache. They're idiots." We sat there moping for a few more minutes until Rachel jumped to her feet.

"Enough of this crap. We are not going to cry over them. We are here to have fun and, damn it, that's exactly what we're going to do." She pulled me to my feet and I laughed as we stumbled toward the dance floor.

Rachel tapped a boy's shoulder. He turned around and looked at her in surprise. He was cute in a dorky kind of way, but he looked pleased with her attention.

She pointed at him and his friend beside him. "You two are dancing with us now." She took the boy's hand and pulled him toward her. The other boy looked unsure of what to do. I gave him a smile and that was all the encouragement he needed.

Soon he had pulled me into an overly close embrace as we danced rather awkwardly to the techno music. My partner tried too hard to play it cool and kept trying to grind against me. I attempted to give myself some space but he kept pulling me back toward him.

Luckily the song ended not long afterward and Rachel and I soon found ourselves dancing with two different guys. Thirty minutes later we had changed partners five times and were really enjoying ourselves again. And I didn't think about Clay and it was obvious Rachel wasn't thinking about Daniel.

Another slow song came on and the boy I was dancing with, Luke Tyler, who was on the football team, asked if I wanted to dance that one with him as well. I agreed and we started to move to the music. I didn't relax into him the way I had with Clay. But he was respectful and didn't move his hands anywhere he shouldn't.

We were halfway through the song when someone interrupted us.

"I'm cutting in."

I looked up and saw Clay standing there looking very, very pissed.

Luke frowned. "Dude, we're dancing here." Luke swung us away from Clay, who followed. What the hell?

"I said I'm cutting in." Clay's neck and face were turning an alarming shade of red.

Luke stood up straight and was clearly getting annoyed with Clay's aggressive attitude. "And I told you that we're dancing, so back the fuck off." Clay yanked Luke's arm off my waist and shoved him backward.

"Clay! Stop it!" I yelled.

Luke was angry. "What is your problem, man?"

Clay shoved him again, advancing on the other boy with an aggression that scared me. I gripped Clay's arm to stop him. "What are you doing? You're going to get thrown out!" I screamed.

Clay pulled his arm out of my grasp as he tried to lunge at Luke. He was shaking and he looked like he was going to explode. "Fuck this shit. I'm out of here," he said through gritted teeth, and pushed his way through the crowd that had formed around us.

I stood there completely floored by his behavior. I turned to Luke, who was trying to calm down. "Was that your boyfriend or something?" he asked. I shook my head. I didn't know who *that* was.

"Sorry," I muttered, leaving the dance floor.

Rachel intercepted me as I headed over to grab my purse. "What was that about? Clay just stormed out of here like his ass was on fire." I didn't know how to answer her, and I needed to find Clay.

"Which way did he go?" I asked her.

"No way. He seemed really pissed off. Give him time to cool down," Rachel reasoned. She looked worried.

I got my purse and headed toward the exit. "I'm going after him, Rache. I need to talk to him."

Rachel let me go, shaking her head. "I don't like this, Maggie. He didn't seem all there. I really think you need to leave it be." I didn't want to hear her advice. My single focus was on finding Clay.

I pushed past Rachel and went through the gym doors and looked down the darkened hallway. No Clay. I left the building and went out into the cool night air.

"Clay!" I yelled. I looked toward the parking lot and didn't see anything. Following some half-brained instinct, I went around the back of the school toward the football field and bleachers.

I heard a loud slam followed by a bellow of rage. Shit, I think I found him. Turning the corner, I saw Clay beneath the metal bleachers, holding his left hand against his chest, breathing heavily.

"Clay?" I called out. He looked up and then turned away from me.

"Go away, Maggie. Seriously. I can't be around you right now." He sounded so angry and I just didn't understand where it was coming from. Well, he couldn't tell me what to do, so I continued to walk toward him.

Seeing me coming, Clay yelled at the top of his lungs. "I said get the fuck out of here!"

I stopped short. Okay, he was freaking me out now. "Why are you mad at me? What did I do?" I asked him from fifteen feet away.

Clay shook his head and gave a gurgling cry as he slammed his hand into the bleacher. Shit. I rushed over to him and took his injured hand in mine. It looked as if he might have broken two of his knuckles. They were turning a nasty purple and there was the unmistakable yellow of marrow.

"What are you doing?" I cried.

The tremors in Clay's body were causing me to shake, too. "I just want to be alone. Please, just leave." The anger had left his voice and he sounded extremely tired. I pulled a tissue out of my purse and dabbed the back of his hand, where blood had started to ooze out of his skin.

"Not until you tell me why you're so angry," I insisted. Clay tried to pull his hand away but I refused to let go. "Stop shutting me out, Clay," I warned him. Clay hung his head, the fight leaving him.

"You stopped taking them, didn't you," I stated more than asked.

Clay sunk to the ground, not caring about the dust and dirt getting on his clothes. "Yes, all right. I stopped taking them three days ago. Happy?" he asked me with venom. Okay, now I was pissed.

"Happy? Happy!?!" I yelled at him. "Oh, I'm just ecstatic that you're not taking the medication that stops you from becoming a raging lunatic. I'm over the moon, here," I said. I turned to leave, sick and tired of his drama. My night had been ruined by him on multiple fronts and I was ready to go home.

I'd started to walk away when I heard him get to his feet and run after me. "Don't go, Maggie. Please. I need you here," he pleaded with me. There was that word again. *Need.* He needed me. And some annoying girly part of me thrilled at his words as much as the rational part of me was terrified of them.

"You just told me to go, Clay," I said tiredly, not letting him pull me back.

He sighed. "I know I said that. I just didn't want you to see me like this . . . again."

"Then take your medication, Clay. Then we won't have this issue," I said harshly. I tried to move away from him again but he grabbed my hand.

"Stay with me. Please." He sounded so broken and I hated how swayed I was by him, even when I knew I should get the hell out of there.

"Why did you do that back there? It was humiliating," I told him, still refusing to face him.

"Look at me," he begged, pulling on my shoulders until I was facing him. His eyes were frantic and he was breathing rapidly, as if he were about to have a panic attack. "I couldn't stand seeing you dance with that guy. He had his hands on you and I thought I would lose it. Well, I guess I *did* lose it." He chuckled humorlessly.

His words pissed me off. "Who the hell do you think you are? You had just spent the entire night dancing with other girls! But I'm not allowed to dance with other guys? What a bullshit double standard!" He flinched at my anger. Good. He had made me mad and he needed to see that.

"You're right. But I didn't want to dance with those other girls. You think I give a shit about Dana, or anyone else? Because I don't! I could never care about them because they aren't you! But you are constantly throwing me into the 'friend' pile. I thought you didn't want to be with me! Did I misread something here?" He sounded desperate. Where the heck did he get the idea that I wanted him to be with other girls? Hadn't I been making it very obvious that I was crazy about him? Maybe he was more delusional than I thought.

I shook my head; my thoughts were fuzzy, and my chest felt tight. This roller coaster we were on needed to stop. I wrenched backward, away from Clay's grip. He looked panicked and tried to reach for me again. I shook my head and he dropped his hands to his sides. He looked at me as if I were breaking his heart, which was nuts because I had no idea I even had that power.

"When you're in a room, Maggie, all I see is you. You make everything better. Clearer. You stop the crazy noise in my head. I can think—hell, I can *breathe*—when we're together. What you make me feel is the most unbelievable and scary thing I've ever felt." My eyes went wide at his confession. I didn't want to say anything, not wanting to break the spell we found ourselves under.

"I never thought I deserved to be happy. With all the shit that went down in Florida, it felt like my life was over. Moving here to Virginia might as well have been a death sentence. But then you literally ran into me." We both laughed at his choice of words, easing the tension a fraction.

Clay grabbed my hands and placed them over his heart. I could feel the erratic beat beneath my palm. "You ran into my life—this beautiful, amazing girl who changed everything. I finally saw what my world could be. What being *normal* and *happy* could look like. You've given me everything I never thought I could have! It scares me to think of life without you. Of not seeing your smile or hearing your voice. So when you didn't stop me from going off with Dana and then went and danced with that asshole, I thought you were telling me loud and clear that I didn't have a chance with you. And all I could see was my life without you in it. And it was a fucking dark and horrible place."

I closed my eyes, feeling the prick of tears behind my eyelids. How could I stay angry when he was saying everything I had wanted to hear since I had met him? Even in the midst of this whirlwind, he made me feel alive and adored. What girl could resist that combination?

And it was time that I revealed my own truths.

"That is so beyond ridiculous. I'm crazy about you, too. I've wanted to be with you since the day I ran into your life, literally. Even when you were being the biggest prick on the planet, I wanted you. But I thought being friends was all you could handle.

You know, with everything else going on." I looked at my feet, not wanting him to see my own vulnerability.

I heard Clay's sharp intake of breath and then felt his fingers on my chin. "Mags. I've wanted the same thing. You have no idea how much. But you said over and over that I was your freaking *friend*," he said in a desperate sort of way. I shook my head, my hair falling limply around my shoulders, the hairspray and teased styling long gone.

"You're sick, Clay. I didn't want to overly complicate things," I said in justification. Clay pulled me into his arms and I didn't fight him.

"No, Maggie! No, no, no! I can't stand just being your friend. It's driving me crazy, holding back on what I've really wanted to say. I need to be with you! It's the only thing that makes sense in my insane, fucked-up life."

I stood stiff in his arms, not sure what to do. He buried his face in my hair. "I'm a mess. If I were selfless, I'd make you leave. I know I'm a lot to deal with. I'm nowhere close to getting a handle on things. But I'm not lying when I say you make me feel like I can do it. If you're with me, I can do anything." He stopped for a moment and then the seriousness seemed to break and his mouth crinkled in a tiny smile.

"So, can we try? Even if it lasts an hour?"

I snorted. He was quoting one of my favorite songs to me after everything he had just put me through? First Japanese poetry, now indie rock. What next? Would he serenade me outside my window to Depeche Mode?

Yet if there was one thing I had learned about Clayton Reed, it was that I was powerless to resist him. He could charm the panties off a nun if he'd been inclined to do so.

Slowly I brought my arms up until we encircled each other. Even in the hazy glow of contentment, I worried that he would try to replace his need for medication with me. I didn't want to become his crutch. I wanted him to get healthy and do it for himself.

All of those concerns swirled around my head, making a decision difficult. And then he put his mouth to mine. The whisper-soft touch of his lips, and everything—my worries, my concerns, my doubts about our future—was lost in the amazing feeling of his mouth, his tongue, and the light nips of his teeth on my bottom lip.

We kissed for a while, his hands getting tangled in my hair, my fingers making their way underneath the back of his jacket, clutching his skin. I could barely breathe and I knew I was drowning. I was pulled down by the strong undertow. Down into what seemed to be a delicious darkness. And I was happy to lose myself in it.

chapter
eleven

It's amazing how something that had, in concept, seemed so insignificant to my life could now become my entire world. The weeks after the Fall Formal I was flying high. If I thought I couldn't get enough of Clay when we were just friends, it was nothing compared to the insatiable need I developed when he became my boyfriend.

Boyfriend.

Who'da thunk it?

"Ugh! Can you guys get a room, already?" Daniel made a gagging noise from across the table during lunch. I smiled as Clay kissed the soft spot below my ear. He nuzzled my neck and I leaned into his touch.

"Oh, shut it, Daniel. You're just jealous. Just because Kylie has cut you loose . . . *again*," Rachel said hatefully. My two best friends were the only dark spot in my state of Clay-induced euphoria. Ever since the night of the dance, after Daniel callously ditched Rachel in favor of trying to work things out with Kylie (who I supposed had dumped him already), they had been at each other's throats.

Personally, I was totally on Rachel's side with this one, although I typically tried to be Switzerland between them. But what Daniel had done was nasty and he deserved every ounce of Rachel's complete and utter bitchitude.

Daniel curled his lip at Rachel but didn't say anything back, angrily shoving his mashed potatoes around on his tray. The tension between the two of them was palpable. Clay cleared his throat, obviously uncomfortable.

"So, do you guys have any plans for Thanksgiving break?" Clay asked, trying to break the tense silence that had blanketed our table. Rachel shook her head and Daniel grumbled something unintelligible under his breath.

I leaned into Clay's chest. "I'd take that as a . . . maybe?" I posed the statement as a question, hoping to elicit some sort of response from my miserable friends.

"Well, I have an idea," Clay piped up, getting everyone's attention.

Daniel stopped swirling his potatoes and Rachel looked up from her *Cosmo*. "Oh, yeah? What's that?" I asked him. Clay grinned down at me and kissed the tip of my nose. I loved it when he did stuff like that. He had this way of making me feel like something infinitely valuable. Like I was the most precious thing in his universe.

"Well, Ruby's girlfriend, Lisa, has a cabin down by Franklin Lake. Maybe we could go down for the night. Like, say, the Saturday after Thanksgiving? I mean, it's really nice. With satellite TV and a huge Jacuzzi tub. It could be a lot of fun." Clayton sounded excited.

I was pleased to see this even-natured side of Clay. He had begun taking the lithium again, starting the night of the Formal. Despite my happiness about this, I continued to watch him closely, looking for any sign that he was lying about the meds and had again stopped taking them.

I knew deep down that this wariness of mine where he was concerned wasn't good for the long-term health of our relationship. But right now Clay was on his meds and they seemed to have evened him out. He was still tired a lot and his appetite was nonexistent but he seemed less zombie-fied than the last time he had been on the pills. Clay said his system must be acclimating to them now that he'd been on them for a longer period.

Well, whatever it was, I was happy to see it.

"So, what do you think?" Clay asked the table, pulling me out of my thoughts. I appreciated that Clay was trying to integrate himself into our circle. He had struggled with relaxing around my friends. He and I continued to exist in our isolated bubble most of the time. I knew opting to spend most of my time with him as opposed to my friends was having a negative effect on my other relationships. But I was in the blissful throes of the honeymoon period. I couldn't be faulted for that, right?

For the most part, Rachel had tried to be pleasant, although she watched the two of us warily. I knew that she worried after Clay's Hulk episode at the dance. And Daniel—well, he still maintained an arm's-length distance with Clay, though he tried, for my sake. So Clay inviting them along on an outing was huge. I hoped it was a positive step toward merging these parts of my life. I hated how being with Clay seemed at times to fragment my other friendships. Why did I have to have only one or the other?

I squeezed Clay's hand in appreciation for his gesture. He gave me a shy smile. I reached up and brushed a loose curl out of his eyes, letting my fingers linger on his skin. His gaze softened and I shivered in giddiness.

Daniel rolled his eyes at the two of us and I dropped my hand into my lap. I glared at my friend and he raised his eyebrows at me. "Sounds like fun to me," I said, giving Daniel a pointed look.

Rachel didn't look up and only shrugged. "I don't know. It all depends on what's going on with my family." I sighed in frustration. I knew Rachel didn't want to hang out with her extended family for any length of time. Her grandparents drove her nuts, and her aunts and uncles, for the most part, were a bunch of jerks. No, she was just being difficult.

"Well, I think it sounds cool," Daniel piped up, surprising me. Rachel stiffened beside him. I knew he was goading her.

Not to be outdone, Rachel sat up straight. "Well, I think it sounds cool, too. Count me in," she said through clenched teeth. Great. Maybe this wasn't such a good idea.

"Fantastic. So we'll all go," Daniel said tersely, shoving his fork through his peas. Clay looked at me questioningly. I lifted my shoulders in resignation.

"You two need to play nice or we'll leave your asses behind. Fair warning," I told the two of them, wagging my finger in their direction.

Rachel and Daniel briefly looked at each other and then away. Rachel gave Clay a tentative smile. "Thanks for inviting us."

"Sure," Clay replied, still feeling awkward, with the antagonistic vibe my friends were throwing out.

"I'm gonna go get a soda. Want anything?" Clay asked me.

"I'll have a soda, too." I dug a few coins out of my purse and tried to give them to him. Clay pushed my hand away and smiled.

"I've got it, baby," he said softly, and I beamed at the endearment.

Clay got up and went to get our drinks. I turned on my friends and leveled them with a glare of death. "You two need to get your acts together. Clay is making a big effort to be nice. The least you could do is give the battle royale between the two of you a rest for a while. You know, so you don't make the rest of us miserable."

Rachel and Daniel grumbled, but the chill between them thawed a bit.

"Hey, guys." I felt my bench dip as someone sat down beside me. I looked over to see Jake Fitzsimmons grinning as he snuck a piece of my brownie off of my plate.

"Get your own brownie, Jake. Hands off of mine." I swatted his hand away, giving him a small smile. The three of us had known Jake since kindergarten. He was sweet and cute and had never been subtle about the fact that he had a giant crush on me.

I chanced a look at Clay, but he was still waiting in line at the vending machine. "Daniel, Coach wanted me to let you know that practice was canceled today," Jake said, taking more of my brownie. I moved my tray out of his reach.

Jake and Daniel were on the basketball team together and on the soccer team in the spring. "Thanks for letting me know, man. That frees up my afternoon. Which is good because I have a shit-load of homework to catch up on."

"What are you getting into this afternoon, Maggie? Feel like getting into something with me?" Jake wiggled his eyebrows at me and I smirked. He was a horrible flirt.

He reached for my food again and I grabbed his hand. "One more bite and I will take your hand off," I warned him, locking my fingers around his wrist.

Jake laughed and pretended to lunge for my lunch again. I shoved him back, still holding on to his arm. So I guess it didn't look good when Clay finally reappeared.

"Get the hell out of my seat," I heard Clay say angrily from behind me. I saw Rachel's eyes get big as she looked over my shoulder.

I dropped Jake's hand like it was on fire. Jake's smile disappeared and he looked up at Clay with a frown. "Sorry, dude. I'm just saying hi. I was just leaving." Jake sounded nervous. When I saw Clay's dark face, I knew why. He looked murderous.

"Get your hands off my girl before I break your fucking fingers," Clay growled, moving forward aggressively. Jake got to his feet and put his hands out in front of him.

"Look, man. I'm not sure what your problem is, but I was just saying hey. No need to go postal." Clay's face turned a scary shade of red and I thought he was going to reach over and grab Jake.

I got between them, facing Clay. "Chill out, Clay. He was just leaving." I looked back at Jake and pointedly said, "Good-bye, Jake."

Jake looked between Clay and me with concern. "Are you sure everything's okay?" he asked me softly. Clay moved forward again and I wasn't sure I could stop him from escalating the situation if Jake didn't leave.

"I'm fine," I said, my eyes pleading with Jake to just get the hell out of there. Jake's face clouded as he looked at Clay.

"Okay. Well, see ya." He waved at Rachel and Daniel and then hightailed it out of there.

"What is your problem?" Daniel asked, clearly pissed by Clay's behavior toward his friend. Clay ignored the question, turning his rage on me.

"What the hell was that?" he hissed at me, his eyes full of anger and accusation.

"Nothing. He's just a friend. Calm down, all right? You're making a scene." I glanced at the tables around us and realized everyone was watching our exchange like it was the goddamn *Jerry Springer Show*.

I tried to put my hand on Clay's arm, hoping physical contact would break through this rage of his. He backed away from me as if I had a contagious disease.

"You let him touch you! You fucking let him touch you!" he yelled in my face. My skin flushed with embarrassment. You'd think I'd been caught having sex with another guy or something! Clay's reaction was ridiculous!

"Enough, Clay! Back off!" Rachel had come around the table and pulled me away from my boyfriend. Clay looked down at Rachel, his dark eyes simmering.

"Fine. I'm backing off. I'm backing the hell out of here." He grabbed his bag and stormed out of the cafeteria.

I was painfully aware of the silence around us. I wanted to curl into a tiny ball of mortification. "That was bullshit, Mags. I'm gonna kick his ass for treating you like that," Daniel fumed.

"No, Danny. He's just stressed. It'll be all right. Don't hold it against him. Please!" I begged. Daniel stared at me as if I were talking in another language.

Rachel looked at me with concern. "I don't like this, Maggie. The way Clay acted wasn't normal."

Normal. Ha! If Rachel even knew the half of it. I smiled weakly, hoping to placate them.

"No, everything will be fine. Come on, you guys would be pissed if you saw someone flirting with your boyfriend or girl-friend. He was just surprised, is all," I reasoned unconvincingly.

Daniel looked unswayed. "No, I can't say I've ever had that sort of reaction before. I swear, if he ever puts a hand on you . . ."

I cut him off. "That's enough, Danny. Clay would never hurt me."

"There are more ways to hurt someone than that, Mags," Rachel said quietly as the bell rang, signaling the end of lunch. I felt sick to my stomach because I knew she was right.

◆

I wasn't sure if Clay would wait for me after school to give me a ride home. I wished I had brought my car that morning. But I stupidly altered my entire routine to grasp at the tiny moments of time in his company. I was upset and angry and more than a little disgusted by the fact that I was becoming so dependent on our time together.

I hadn't seen him the rest of the day and my heart hurt when I thought about how angry he had been. Rachel had tried talking to me about it a few more times but I shut her down, refusing to dis-cuss it with her.

I knew she and Daniel only cared about me, but their worry irritated me. They had no idea what Clay went through every day. How hard it was for him to just get by. They didn't see how beautiful and perfect we were together.

They just didn't get it.

"You want me to give you a ride home?" Danny asked as he waited for me by my locker at the end of the day. I still hadn't seen Clay, but I didn't want to spend the next fifteen minutes rehashing the state of my relationship with either of my best friends.

"Nah. I'm sure Clay is just waiting by the car," I told him, slamming the locker door closed.

Daniel grabbed my hand and squeezed. "I'm not sure you should go anywhere with him. I knew I was right when I thought that guy was unstable. Maybe you need to just stay the hell away from him."

I snatched my hand back. "Shut up, Danny. He is *not* unstable. He got a little jealous. It's not a big deal! Don't you dare stand there and judge him! I've seen you do some pretty stupid things over Kylie. So just give him a break!" I said coldly. Daniel looked as if I had slapped him. I had gone from never raising my voice at him to snapping at him all the time.

I felt the strain in our friendship and I hated it. But I would be damned if I would stand there and justify my feelings for Clay to him or to anyone. "That's not fair. I have never blown my lid like that and you know it," Daniel reasoned.

I sighed, letting my shoulders drop. "Maybe you've just never cared enough about anyone to feel the way Clay does about me." I sounded like an idiot; even I knew that. But I knew that Clay cared about me pretty damn deeply, even if I also knew on some level that that didn't give him an excuse to act the way he had.

"Well, that's a shitty way of showing someone you care, if you ask me," Daniel quipped, following me out the door and onto the sidewalk outside of the school. I stopped and turned around, wrapping my arms around Danny in a hug.

"I appreciate your concern. I love you so much for it. But trust me when I tell you that everything will be fine. Clay and I will work it out and I can't have you being all big brother around me all the time. I want the two of you to get along. You're two of the most important people in my life. So, please, for me . . . just let it go," I pleaded.

Daniel looked torn. I knew this went against his protective instincts where I was concerned. We got out to the parking lot and I looked over to where Clay's car was parked. My heartbeat picked up when I saw him standing there, leaning against his BMW, his hands shoved into his jacket pockets, looking at me with apprehension.

Daniel followed my stare. "I don't like this, Mags. I'm serious. Just be careful." I nodded, making my way over to Clay. Danny followed me and we both stopped when we got to the car. Clay looked at me as if I would run away. His eyes were sad and I felt a twinge of guilt for my part in making him feel that way.

Why I felt any guilt was beyond me. But I felt it nonetheless. "Hey, Maggie," he said quietly, my name a breath on his lips.

"Hey," I said back, just as quietly.

"Look, Clay. I'm not sure what the hell your deal was at lunch. But I don't want to see that shit again. Maggie is special and I will break your legs if you hurt her," Daniel broke in harshly.

I wanted to elbow him. Hadn't I just told him to check the protective bit?

Clay didn't take his eyes from mine, even as he answered Daniel. "I understand. I was an ass. I'm sorry. If I hurt her, I would want you to break my legs, man. I swear it!" My throat felt tight.

Daniel grunted from beside me, but neither Clay nor I took our eyes off each other. "Well, as long as we understand each other, I'll see you guys later," Daniel said grudgingly. I looked at Danny quickly.

"Thanks, Danny. I'll call you later," I assured him.

Daniel gave me a smile. "Okay. Talk to you then." Daniel eyed Clay again and then walked away.

Clay reached out and took my hands in his. He pulled me close to him and I went willingly. "I'm so sorry, Maggie. You have no idea how much," he whispered, putting his arms around me and holding me to his chest. I laid my cheek on the rough fabric of his jacket and closed my eyes.

"I just don't understand. What did I do?" I asked softly. I felt Clay shudder.

"It's *not you*! It's me and my stupid insecurities. I saw you talking . . . touching another guy and I just lost it. I'm so scared of losing you that it makes me crazy!" he said hurriedly. His fingers kneaded the back of my neck and I felt him bury his face in my hair.

I pulled away and looked at him. He looked miserable and I hated it. "You can't act like that every time I talk to a guy, Clay. It's irrational and a little scary. I'm with you! Only you! I don't know how to make you see that!" I implored, cupping his face with my hands.

Clay closed his eyes and covered one of my hands with his own and pulled it to his mouth, kissing the palm. "I know that! I do! I never want you to be scared of me. Ever," he choked out. He seemed as if he were barely holding it together.

I hated to see him so broken. I leaned in and kissed him softly on the lips. "I love you, Clay," I murmured against his mouth. His eyes opened wide in surprise. Then a happy sort of contentment took the place of the angst on his face. He crushed his mouth to mine, his hands sweeping over my body with a desperate sort of possession.

"I love you, too, Maggie. God, I love you so much!" he strangled out. We clutched each other, trying to get as close as possible.

"I'm yours, Clay," I said softly as he kissed my cheeks, my neck, my hair.

"Mine," he growled before taking my mouth with his again.

chapter
twelve

To say that things were tense for the next few days was a bit of an understatement. The day after his meltdown over Jake, Clay had joined Rachel, Daniel, and me again at lunch, where he awkwardly apologized to my friends for his behavior.

Rachel had accepted his apology, mostly, I knew, out of consideration for me. Daniel was still cool toward Clay, but after a week he started to let up on his aloofness. A tentative sort of peace descended over our small circle and I was finally able to breathe a little easier.

Clay was going over the top to prove he was a kind and loving boyfriend. He left me beautiful drawings in my locker almost every day. Each one depicted a butterfly in varying degrees of detail. Each one was more unbelievable than the last.

When I asked him why he drew only butterflies, he had kissed me softly on the mouth. "Because you make me feel free," he had answered simply. My heart melted into a puddle at my feet. He could say and do the most romantic things.

Clay had broached the topic of Lisa's cabin again at the lunch table. I knew he was trying really hard to change Rachel's and

Daniel's idea of him. My friends seemed less enthusiastic about it than they had before. But, after some pleading on my part, they each agreed that it could be fun.

So we made plans to spend the night at Lisa's cabin over Thanksgiving break. I desperately hoped it could eradicate this division I felt deepening between my friends and me. I knew they didn't approve of my relationship with Clay. I knew they were worried we were in too deep, too fast. And I knew they hadn't forgotten for one minute the anger Clay was capable of.

And that upset me. Because I felt like no matter how much Clay tried to change their minds about him, their opinion was permanent. Despite how cordial they were to his face.

I became protective of my relationship with Clay. I didn't want anyone or anything to taint what we had. I felt like I was trying to hold on to a block of ice as it slowly melted under my fingers. I couldn't keep hold of the happiness I felt in those moments when things were good. Because the bad loomed not far off, just waiting to wipe everything else away.

But the trip to the cabin became the focus of all my hopes for changing that. Clay seemed excited about the trip and I loved seeing him look forward to something. To see the brooding darkness erased by a real and true happiness.

"Wow, you're really excited about this trip, aren't you?" I asked Clay after school. We were lying on my bed in my room. It had taken a lot of pleading to get Clay to return to my house. And, yes, I knew that I was breaking one of my parents' Ten Commandments, but I knew for a fact that they would be out for at least two more hours, giving Clay and me plenty of time alone together before he had to get the hell out of there. The truth was, not even my parents' wrath could stop me from being with him. I was so desperate to make things good between us that I was willing to risk anything.

Clay rolled onto his side, his feet wrapped around mine as we lay tangled together. He propped his head up on his hand and looked down at me. He rubbed his fingers over the skin of my stomach, making me squirm.

"Yeah. I'm really looking forward to it. I'm just glad everyone agreed to come," Clay said softly, and I felt a pang at the regret in his voice. He knew what my friends thought of him. He wasn't stupid. I hated it for him. For *us*. It didn't make things easy. But we had never done *easy*.

I sat up suddenly, surprising Clay with my movement. I straddled his hips and wiggled against him. He laid his head back against my pillows, his eyes changing instantly from sadness to molten desire.

"You start doing that, things are going to get out of control very quickly," he teased, running his hands up my sides.

"Stop it," I said, laughing. Clay chuckled and pulled my face down to kiss me.

"Mmm. You taste like cherries," he murmured against my mouth.

I smacked my lips together. "You can thank Lip Smackers." Clay laughed again, my heart thrilled at the sound, and he kissed me longer and more deeply.

"Thank you, Lip Smackers," he said huskily before putting his lips to the base of my throat. He sat up, my legs wrapped around his middle, and he held me tightly to his chest.

"Just think, Mags. An entire night together. I've wanted that for so long," he whispered breathlessly as he kissed a trail from my collarbone to my ear.

"Typical guy, only thinking with your penis," I said crudely.

Way to kill the moment, Maggie, I chastised myself.

Clay smirked, not put off by my choice of terminology. "Oh, no, I think with other things. Like my hands." He put them up my shirt and I gasped as his palms cupped my breasts.

"And my fingers," he whispered in my ear as his thumbs began to rub my nipples, causing a warmth to pool in my abdomen.

"And my lips." He sucked on my earlobe and I groaned. I swear, if he had wanted, he could have taken me right then and there.

"Oh, God. What am I going to do with you?" he said with amusement as I became frenzied under his mouth. I frantically began pulling at his clothes, trying to get him naked.

"Well, you could help me, you know." I pouted as I tried once again to get his shirt over his head. Clay only laughed and pulled away, placing a loud kiss on my mouth.

"Slow down, tiger. Not here, especially since, the last time I was in your room, your father almost had me lynched. And we were just sleeping that time."

I wasn't going to let him go that easily. I deftly undid the button on his jeans, sliding my hand just inside the waistband. "Are you sure about that, Clayton? You really want me to stop?" My hand drifted lower and I used my other hand to tug the zipper down.

Clay moaned deep in his throat, his head falling back as I found what I was looking for. My fingers touched him tentatively and he jerked against me. I couldn't help but smile at my victory. Then he grabbed my hand and pulled it out of his pants.

"You are an evil, evil woman, Maggie Young. Trying to tempt me like that," he said lightly as he gently lifted me off his lap and zipped up his jeans.

I rolled over on my bed and grabbed a pillow, tossing it at him. "You suck," I joked. Clay caught the pillow and threw it back at me.

"No, I just don't want to be *that* guy," he explained. I frowned in confusion.

"What guy?" I asked.

Clay sighed and sat up. "You know, the guy who waits for your parents to not be at home before deflowering their daughter in the bed she's had since childhood. You know, *that guy*—the one that looks for any and every opportunity to get you naked. I *was* that guy and I don't want to be him ever again."

Okay. So, logically, I appreciated what he was saying. I knew that he was telling me that he cared about me enough to not disrespect my parents and their house by having sex with me in it. But right then, all I heard was that he had done this very thing with girls before me. And he wasn't gonna do it with me. And it pissed me off. What was wrong with me? Was I not good enough to share that sort of intimacy with? I mean, it was obvious he had been less than discriminating in the past.

I turned my back to him and straightened my clothes, putting my bra back in place and gathering my hair in a ponytail.

"Mags," Clay said quietly from behind me. I leaned over and picked my Spanish book up off the floor and started to open it. Clay sat beside me. "Maggie. Don't be upset. Come on." He pulled the book off of my lap and I just sat there, staring at my hands.

I was embarrassed and, worst of all, I felt rejected.

"Look at me." I lifted my eyes to his very concerned ones. "What did I say to make you look like that?" he asked. Stupid, oblivious boy. My face flushed red.

"So, you've had sex a bunch before. You know, done stuff with girls. But you won't do that stuff with me—your girlfriend. Am I getting this right?" I asked tightly.

Clay brushed the hair from my face. "You silly, silly girl. Where does all this insecurity come from?"

I started to pull away, annoyed that he could throw insecurities in my face when he was the king of them! But he held me fast, holding on to my upper arms, forcing me to look at him.

"What I did before, that was another life. I was another person. I wasn't someone you would have ever wanted to be around, let alone be your boyfriend." I started to protest what he was saying, to argue that I would have loved him no matter what he was like. But he silenced me.

"No, listen, Maggie. I wasn't a good person. I was sick and addicted to the worst possible things. So, yes. I had sex. I fooled around with a lot of different girls. But none of it meant anything. Those girls, they used me. I used them, to try and feel *something*. But it was all a lie. Because I hated them. Hated myself. Nothing mattered until I met you." His eyes were intense as they looked into mine. I held my breath.

"Maggie. When we make love, I want it to be special. Not some quickie in your bedroom before your parents come home. I want more than that for us. I want to be able to hold you all night and feel you against me as I fall asleep. I want us to be perfect together." God, his words set me on fire. Had there *ever* been two people who loved each other as much as we did? I couldn't put into words the way we felt about each other.

"I love you," I breathed. Since saying it that first time, I found that I just couldn't stop. I wanted him to know every second of every day how much he meant to me.

"God, Maggie," he whispered, leaning forward, capturing my mouth with his. "I love you more than anything. With everything that I am," he answered me. Okay, I was done for. I crashed into him again. Our mouths melded, our breath coming fast.

"Just a little bit. Please, just give me something," I begged into his mouth. Clay's heart beat erratically beneath my hand as I pressed into him.

Helpless against my feminine wiles, Clay slipped his hands up my shirt and pressed them against my breasts. I groaned into his mouth, and that seemed to be his undoing. He reached around my back and unclasped my bra. Then, with an ease I didn't want to focus too much on, he peeled off my shirt, taking my bra with it. I felt a little uneasy being so quickly exposed. I tried to cover myself, not sure how to behave.

Clay stopped me and pulled my arms away from my chest. His eyes were bright. "You are so beautiful," he rasped, lowering his mouth to my breast, licking and kissing it slowly until I thought I would die from the pleasure of his touch.

With shaky fingers, I undid the buttons of his shirt and pulled it off of him. Clay's mouth returned to mine as we pressed our naked flesh against each other. "I want you so much, Clay. Please. I need this," I whispered hoarsely.

For a moment I thought I had won. Clay slowly unbuttoned my jeans and I raised my hips to give him easier access. He slid his hand inside, under the waistband of my underwear, and pressed his palm against my wet warmth. I had never been touched so intimately before. I was breathing in rapid pants and I worried I would hyperventilate.

His fingers began to move underneath the edge of my panties. So close to where I desperately needed him to be. His mouth was hard and wet against my lips as he seemed to fight with himself for control.

I then heard the worst possible sound. The front door slamming shut. Shit! My parents were home. I looked over at the clock, shocked to see that two hours had already passed.

"Christ! You've got to get out of here! My parents will spit-roast you if they find you in here." I hastily put my bra back on, inside out, I'm pretty sure, and I pulled my shirt over my head. Clay quickly buttoned up his shirt and slid his shoes on.

"How am I going to get out of here?" he asked in a near panic. I looked out my window. The only way would be to climb out onto the roof and down the old maple tree.

I pointed outside. "You have to go out that way!" I hissed, trying to shoo him in that direction.

Clay seemed frozen to the spot. I could hear my parents rummaging around in the kitchen, and my mom's laughter at something my dad had said. It would be only minutes before they came up here looking for me.

"Hurry!" I whispered frantically. Clay's eyes had gone as big as saucers. "What is it?" I asked him hurriedly. What was the holdup here?

"I'm deathly afraid of heights," he whispered back to me. I closed my eyes and tried not to groan in frustration. What happened to the fearless superman from Melissa's party?

"Didn't you climb a tree and jump into a pool?" I pointed out in annoyance.

"Yeah, and I wasn't exactly thinking clearly either," he hissed.

I walked back over to my desk and dropped into my chair. Clay looked at me as if I had gone certifiably insane.

"What are you doing? I have to get out of here! Your dad is going to kill me!" He was close to freaking out. I raised my hands in defeat.

"If you can't go out the window, there's no way I can sneak you past them to the front door. So we might as well look like we're doing something innocent up here and I'll take whatever they dish out." I picked up my Spanish book again and flipped open to the page I had for homework.

Catching a glimpse of my flushed face and too-bright eyes in the full-length mirror over my shoulder, I realized there would be no doubt about what we had been doing. But what else could I do?

Clay sat down heavily on the floor. "Your dad already hates me. Let's just give him another reason." He sounded so resigned and sad that I wanted to smack my father for making him feel that way. I gave him a reassuring smile.

"He doesn't hate you," I lied. Clay arched his eyebrow, letting me know he called bullshit. "Well, he might dislike you a bit. *Hate* is a strong word," I conceded. I wished I could say something else to make him feel better.

At that moment I heard footsteps coming up the stairs. "Maggie May? You up here?" I sighed in relief. At least it was my mom and not Dad.

"In here," I called back, throwing a look at Clay that told him to play it cool. He discreetly pulled a pillow over his lap and put his American history book on top of it. I had to hide my smile at how pleased I was that I had affected him like that.

"We've got Chinese food, if you want some . . ." My mom trailed off as she looked in my room and caught sight of Clay on the floor.

He looked up and gave her a sheepish smile and a small wave. "Hey, Mrs. Young."

"Hi, there, Clayton." Her tone was icy and she shot me a look that would kill a lesser person. She had been cool with Clay so far. But I knew from the expression on her face that her fuzzy feelings where my boyfriend was concerned were at an end. "I believe the two of you know the rules about being alone in here when we're not at home," she said, making it clear that a serious grounding was in my future.

There was a moment of silence that screamed *busted!* "Sorry, Mom. I know. I had to use my computer for my Spanish assignment. We have only been up here for a few minutes. No harm, no foul," I said lackadaisically. It kind of bothered me how easily I lied to my parents now. I had never been dishonest with them about anything. The guilt I felt low in my gut threatened to burn a hole straight through me.

But I looked my mother right in the eye and silently willed her to believe me. Clay was quiet on the floor, piping up with an apology only after I had finished my explanation.

My mom seemed torn. I could tell she wanted to believe what I had told her but needed to stick with her rules. "Well. I'm not happy about this. Clayton, I don't want you over here without either her father or me present. Is that clear?" she told him.

I could see Clay swallow and he nodded. "Yes, ma'am."

I wished the floor would just open up and swallow me. But my mom wasn't done yet. "I'm not sure what the rules are at your house. But in this one, we do not condone two young people, particularly when they are dating, being alone together in a bedroom. I remember what it was like to be your age. With the hormones flying and not always knowing when to put the brakes on things."

Oh, dear Lord! "Mom!" I yelped in mortification.

My mom turned her harsh gaze on me. "And you, young lady, will have consequences for blatantly disregarding our rules. Whatever your reason for doing so." She looked back at Clay and then at me. "Your father and I will be in the kitchen eating. I suggest you get Clayton out of here before your father sees him." I sagged in my chair with relief. My mom was bad enough, but I sure didn't want to be tag-teamed by both her and Dad.

"And then you come straight to the kitchen." The guilt flared up again as I heard the angry disappointment in her voice. With a final pointed look at Clay, she went back downstairs. Clay got to his feet and put his books back in his bag.

"That could have been a lot worse." I laughed, trying to lighten the mood.

Clay looked up at me through his hair. "Well, that was bad enough," he said gloomily. I hated when he got that tone. It tore at my heart. I went over to him and wrapped my arms around him, rubbing my nose with his.

"Don't worry about them. They disapprove of everything," I murmured, trying to make this better for him.

Clay hugged me back, kissing me lightly on the lips. "No, your mom hates me now. I get it. I keep screwing things up where they're concerned." He pulled back and slung his book bag over his shoulder. I touched his arm.

"Don't leave so upset, Clay. Come on. We were having a good time. Don't let them ruin it." I sounded a little desperate. But I hated these dark moods of his. They worried me.

Hearing the concern in my voice, he gave me a smile. A small one, but a smile nonetheless. "I just want to do everything right by you, Mags. I want to be the perfect boyfriend. I want your parents to like me and not blow a gasket when we spend time together." I wanted to cry at the despair in his words.

"I don't want perfect, Clay. I want *you.*"

Clay rested his forehead against mine, kissing me slowly. "I love you so much. I just want to be everything you deserve."

My stomach flopped over at his words. "You *are* everything. To me you're the world," I whispered against his mouth. At that moment, I knew it was the truth. I'd follow Clayton Reed to the edge of the earth if he asked me to. We stood that way for a moment, absorbing the comfort that only we could give each other.

But then, too soon, Clay pulled away. "Okay, sneak me out of here and I'll call you later." I took his hand and we quietly went down the stairs, my heart threatening to explode with every creak of the floorboards.

I could hear the indistinct murmur of my parents' voices in the kitchen and knew we were in the clear. I carefully opened the door and shepherded Clay outside. I blew him a kiss and he pretended to catch it. I giggled and closed the door after making sure he was out of the driveway. I then made my way to the kitchen. The walk down the hallway was like walking the gangplank.

chapter
thirteen

My parents looked up at me as I came into the kitchen. My dad gave me a warm smile. "Hi, there, my Maggie-Girl." I looked at Mom and tried not to shrivel under the dark stare she gave me. So she wasn't going to tell my dad about Clay being in my room, but I guessed that didn't mean I wouldn't be punished in other ways. Like being slowly tortured by her evil eye.

"Get a plate and get some cheese wontons before your mother eats them all," my dad joked, earning him a pinch in the arm from my mom.

"You make me sound like a gluttonous pig, Martin." She sounded annoyed. But I knew her bad mood had nothing to do with my dad and everything to do with me.

I opened the refrigerator and pulled out a soda. "Why don't you drink some milk or water instead of that syrupy junk?" my mom said sharply. I saw the look my dad shot her. He was confused by her apparent irritation with me. Normally I would have argued, but I recognized that would have been the wrong move. So I put the soda back and instead got a glass from the cabinet.

Filling it with water from the tap, I came and sat at the kitchen table. My dad moved the cartons of lo mein and sweet-and-sour chicken so I had room for my plate.

"So, how was school today?" my dad asked brightly. I shot a glance at my mother, but she was looking at her phone, checking e-mails.

"Good. I got an A-minus on my English-lit project," I reported, trying to ease the tension in the room. My dad patted my hand.

"Wonderful, Maggie. You take after your ol' dad, smart *and* beautiful." I couldn't help but smile at my dad's compliment and it made me feel even worse for being deceitful.

My mom looked up from her phone. "Yes. But book smarts don't replace common sense, wouldn't you say? Good decision making is important. Right, Maggie?" she asked me pointedly.

Great. I was going to have to suffer through a conversation laden with double meanings in the hopes my dad wouldn't catch on. I only nodded and stuffed my mouth with a piece of chicken. My dad scooped more lo mein onto his plate and tried to take the wontons from my mom. She moved them out of his way and smiled. She could never stay irritated with my father for long. They were kind of beautiful like that.

"Nice try, Martin," she said. My dad laughed and returned to his own food. We ate in silence for a while. It was awkward, but better than having to make fake small talk.

Finally, my dad asked me, "Do you have any cool plans for Thanksgiving break? You and the crew doing anything epic?"

I choked on my rice. "'Cool'? 'Crew'? 'Epic'? Have you been reading the Urban Dictionary again, Dad? Trying to get in touch with the youth, and all that?" I teased him.

My dad chuckled. "Hey. I'm hip. I'm down with the young folk." He tried throwing a really horrible hip-hop sign with his hands.

I was in hysterics. "Enough! I can't take it!"

My dad looked pleased that he had broken through the unbearable tension between us. My mom even laughed. Things relaxed a bit after that and I tentatively answered my father's question. I knew I could never tell them we all planned to go to Clay's cabin for the night. So I had to quickly come up with a story that would cover my tracks. One they would never question.

"Well, Rachel asked me to spend the night on Saturday. She wants a full-on girls' day. You know, get pedicures, go see that new Brad Pitt movie. We haven't spent a whole lot of time together lately."

My dad swallowed his food and nodded. "Sounds like fun. Can I come? I could use a new coat of polish on my toenails." I just shook my head, smiling at him.

My mom was quiet. "I haven't seen much of Rachel and Daniel lately. You've been spending so much time with Clayton. I miss seeing them." Oh, crap, here we go. My dad looked thoughtful, never a good sign.

"That's true, Maggie. You haven't gone out with any of your friends in a while. You know, it's not good to spend all of your time with Clay. It's just not healthy to isolate yourself like that," my dad commented.

I felt my blood pressure start to rise and I immediately became defensive. "I see them every day, Dad! It's not like Clay and I sequester ourselves off and never talk to anyone else. Jeez!" My voice was loud and I saw the surprised look on my father's face. But I was quickly getting tired of catching flak for my relationship with Clay.

"We're just worried, sweetie," my dad said gently. I threw my hands up in the air.

"What do you have to be worried about, for goodness' sake? My grades are still good; I've yet to break my curfew. I don't think I'm that bad of a kid." I looked straight at my mom when I said that, daring her to refute me.

She frowned. "No one's saying you're a bad kid, Maggie. Calm down." There's something about those words *calm down* that makes me anything but. My anger spiked.

"This is freaking ridiculous," I muttered, throwing my fork down.

"This is what we're talking about! You're completely irrational when it comes to that boy. You've become entirely too focused on him and less on other facets of your life," my mom barked, sending me to my feet.

"You have no idea what you're talking about. I love him. We are good together."

My dad's face turned a funny shade of purple. " 'Love him'? You are seventeen years old! You don't know what love is!" Great, now my dad was getting mad. I was making this worse. My mom put a hand on my dad's arm.

"This isn't love, Maggie May. This is obsession and it's not healthy. You are so worked up over a high-school relationship that most likely won't last but a few months. Don't be so immature," my mom said hurtfully. Wow, she was going for the jugular. I'd never known her to be this harsh.

"Thanks, Mom. You're making me feel all warm and fuzzy, here." I crossed my arms over my chest. My mom put her hands in her lap and leveled her gaze at me.

"I think you need to take a few steps back from this boy. Really look at what it's doing to you and how it's affecting your other relationships. I don't think this is good for *you*."

The funny thing about parental disapproval: it made me want to be with Clay all the more. My parents were really stupid when it came to teenage psychology.

"I need to get out of here." I ran out of the kitchen, making a beeline for my purse, which was hanging beside the door. My mother followed close on my heels.

"Where do you think you're going?" she asked. The anger had faded from her eyes and now she just looked worried.

I softened a bit and turned to give her a quick hug. "I know you and Dad love me and just want what's best. But there has to come a point where you trust *my judgment*." My mom rubbed her temples as if I were giving her a migraine.

"I have always trusted your judgment, Maggie. Until now. He's changed you. I feel like you're pulling away from everything but Clayton. It scares me to see this kind of intensity from you." I reached out and gave my mom another hug. She held me, stroking my hair.

I didn't say anything, just let her hold me like she'd always done. After a moment, I stepped out of her embrace. "Please don't worry about me. I promise that I'm fine. You can't start blaming Clay for everything. He's an important part of my life now. I want you to be okay with that. You *were* okay with that," I reminded her.

My mom frowned. "That was before I realized how willing you were to throw our rules and everything else out the window for him."

"Don't you think you're overreacting to the situation a bit?" I asked, hoping to reason with her.

My mom shook her head. "I tried to be okay with your relationship. I knew your dad was unhappy with it, but I wanted to be supportive. But I know what was going on upstairs before we got home. I'm not stupid." I flushed with embarrassment and my mother looked at me closely.

"Your father had told you not to have him up there. You have never disrespected us or our rules before. But now . . . you're doing it all the time. Blowing off family dinners, ignoring your friends, defying your dad when he asks you to not have Clayton in your room when we're not at home. Things are getting out of hand and I just want you to take stock of what it is you're jumping into." I hated to see the tears in my mother's eyes, but knew I couldn't give her the kind of assurance she really wanted.

"Please, Mom. Just trust me. Try to give me the benefit of the doubt. You always have before," I pleaded.

My mom sighed and tucked a bit of my hair behind my ear, like she'd always done when I was little. "I'll try. For your sake. But just don't go making rash decisions that could impact the rest of your life. Teenage pregnancy is a very real thing."

I cringed. "Mom, seriously. Can we not talk about that right now?"

My mom gave me her best stern expression. "Maggie May Young, I know that teenagers have sex. I've seen you with Clayton. I know sexual chemistry when I see it. Your dad and I had plenty of it when we first got together."

I made a gagging noise. "Yuck, Mom. Are you trying to kill me, here?"

My mother rubbed my cheek with her finger. "Just don't do anything stupid and I will try and trust you. Just don't make me regret it." Her words echoed ominously in my ears. Why did I feel the twinge of a premonition at her words?

I straightened my spine and gave her my best smile. "I won't. Now, I'm just going to go take a drive. Maybe stop by and see Daniel or something."

"Okay, but take your cell phone and don't be home any later than nine thirty. It's a school night."

I grabbed my purse and gave her a quick kiss on the cheek. "I'll be home soon. Love you," I told her.

I hurried to my car and got in. After driving around for ten minutes listening to my angsty indie rock at full volume, I ended up where I should have figured I was headed—Clay's house.

I knocked lightly on the door. I was startled when Clay's aunt Ruby swung it open. "Maggie!" she said brightly, pulling me into a lavender-scented hug. She was dressed in her normal gypsy/hippie wardrobe, a patchwork sheer blouse with bell sleeves and a long, leaf-patterned skirt that hung over her bare feet. Her bright red hair hung loose and her green eyes sparkled. She was one of the most sincerely kind people I had ever met, and I loved her for loving Clay so much.

"Come in, honey." She closed the door behind me and ushered me into the living room. Ruby's girlfriend, Lisa, sat at the computer, a pair of black glasses perched on her straight and severe nose. Lisa was what you would call "butch." She had short black hair and her clothes were very masculine. She was a little intimidating if you didn't know her. But the smile she gave me as I came in transformed her face into something lovely.

"We didn't know you were coming over, Maggie. Nice to see you," Lisa's rough voice said. I smiled back and dropped my purse on the armchair.

"I was just out for a drive and wanted to come and see Clay."

Ruby squeezed my shoulder. "Didn't he just leave your house an hour ago?" she teased.

I laughed. "Yeah," I said shyly.

Lisa chuckled. "Ah, young love. Remember what that was like, Ruby?"

Ruby crossed the room and leaned down to give her girl-friend a loving kiss on the mouth. "I still do, Lise," she murmured in her ear.

They were so sweet together, their love for each other apparent. Ruby straightened up. "Can I get you some tea? I've made some delicious raspberry wheat germ that is wonderful for cleansing your aura."

Lisa shook her head at me from behind Ruby's back. "No!" she mouthed, letting me know not to take Ruby up on the offer.

I tried not to giggle. "Um, I'm fine, Ruby. I think I'll just head up to Clay's room, if that's okay."

Ruby waved her hand. "Go ahead. Just follow the depressing goth rock." She laughed.

I gave her another hug before going upstairs. I loved how laid-back she and Lisa were. No stupid rules about girls in Clay's room, and they sure as hell didn't care if we were in there with the door closed. It was nice to be treated like an adult.

I could hear *30 Seconds to Mars* blaring from the room at the end of the hall. Clay listened to his music at an earsplitting volume. How he hadn't gone deaf was beyond me. I was eager to see him, make sure he was cool after the episode at my house. Mostly I just needed to kiss him and touch him.

I pushed open his bedroom door, my eyes adjusting to the darkness. The only light came from his dim table lamp. I could make out Clay over at his desk, his back to me.

He had no idea I was standing there. Not that he could hear anything with the music reverberating around him. I could see he was hunched over, his head down. Looking around his room, I felt it was so *Clay*. Stark, not revealing much about his personality. Basic gray walls and a dark-blue comforter on his bed. Television on an oak dresser. No photographs or knickknacks that would help someone know the person he was.

But there, on the other side of the room, tucked away from everything else, was a little strip of wall above his desk that was literally covered with sheets of paper. I knew they were different pictures that Clay had drawn. Some in pencil, others in ink, some in charcoal. Depictions of animals or random bridges. Some were things as small as a tiny flower, others were people he saw in town. Then there were the dozens he had drawn of me.

I had been embarrassed the first time I saw a drawing he had done of my profile. Because there was no way I could ever be as beautiful as the way he had depicted me. Yet I couldn't help but feel flattered that he saw me that way.

Each of those pictures was done in his passionate yet precise hand. They seemed to say more about who he was than any poster or piece of furniture ever could have. It was like he shoved everything that was *him* into that tiny space. As if he were scared to let too much out.

I walked over to his stereo and turned the volume down. Clay jumped and quickly rolled down his sleeves. He looked over his shoulder, a strange look of panic on his face. "Mags! What are you doing here?" He struggled to make his voice even. I watched as he grabbed a tissue and dabbed at something. I frowned, instantly suspicious.

"I just wanted to see you." I was very aware of the fact that Clay hadn't made any move toward me, which was unusual. The first thing he typically did was hurry over to me and kiss me senseless. I was definitely getting the impression that I had interrupted something I wasn't supposed to see.

"You just saw me an hour ago. You could have just called, you know," he said with a pseudo-nonchalance. His subsequent laugh was entirely too fake.

"Oh, I'm sorry. I wasn't aware that I needed to make an appointment to see you," I said blandly, moving toward him. Clay quickly got to his feet, closing the lid on a small wooden box on his desk. "Am I interrupting?" I asked him, trying to see around him to his desk.

Clay took hold of my wrist and pulled me over to the bed. "Of course not. I was just listening to music." He seemed nervous, which sent my suspicions through the roof. He clumsily buttoned the sleeves of his cotton shirt, something he never did.

What was he hiding?

"Do you want me to go?" I asked him, not liking his attitude. Clay's expression changed and he looked at me with tenderness.

"No, don't leave. I always want to see you," he said softly, reaching over and putting his arms around me.

I let him pull me to his chest as he nuzzled my hair. "You smell so good. Like apple pie." He buried his nose in the tender spot behind my ear, kissing the skin gently. My body responded instantly like it always did, but I resisted the urge to get lost in him.

"Yeah, it's my shampoo. So, you were just listening to music?" I let my question hang in the air. I pulled away from him and walked over to his desk, where he had been sitting. I tried to be subtle as I scanned the items lying there. All I could see were his schoolbooks and bits of paper. And that small wooden box. I put my hand on the lid and Clay was suddenly at my side.

He placed his hand on mine, putting an end to my snooping. He pulled my hands to his chest and laid them there. I could feel the beat of his heart beneath my palm. A tattoo on my skin.

"Yeah, I was taking a break from my calculus homework. It's been doing my head in," he told me, pulling my chin with his fingers. I held back, not letting him kiss me. He would not distract me with that tantalizing mouth of his.

"Well, you're acting kind of weird. Like you're hiding something," I said, getting to the point. I wasn't one to beat around the bush. I could feel him stiffen slightly and then forcibly relax himself. He pulled my hand toward his bed and he sat down, scooting back so he was leaning against his pillows. He crooked his finger at me and gave me his best come-hither smile.

"Come lay with me, Maggie," he purred. Oh, he was playing dirty. Going all sex-god on me so I'd stop asking questions. Well, he wasn't fooling me for a minute. I rolled my eyes, but moved to lie beside him anyway. I was so weak.

"Don't think I can't see right through your tactics, Mr. Reed," I said as he kissed the top of my head.

"I'm pretty transparent, huh? Excuse me if I can't think of anything else but getting that shirt back off of you," he said huskily as he played with the hem.

I smacked at his hands. "Stop it." I giggled as his fingers inched under my shirt.

I elbowed him in the arm playfully and froze when I saw him wince. He quickly wiped away the expression, but I saw it.

"You okay?" I asked, sitting up. Looking at him closely I could see that he was a little paler than usual and there was a definite strain in his eyes.

"I'm fine," he said breezily, reaching for me again.

It was then that I noticed a red spot on the underside of his sleeve. "What's that?" I asked, touching it with my fingertip. It was wet. Clay looked at it and pulled his arm away.

"Oh, it's nothing. Maybe some paint or something." He moved to the side of the bed. Paint? I didn't think so.

"That doesn't look like paint to me," I stated, trying to pull his arm back so I could get a look. Clay frowned and jerked his arm back again, roughly this time.

"What is this? The Spanish Inquisition? I said I was fine. You know, I've got a lot of homework, so why don't I just see you in the morning?" He sat down at his desk and pulled out his calculus book, effectively shutting down our conversation.

I pulled the book away from him and he looked up at me, anger apparent on his face. "What the hell? I've got shit to do, so why don't you just head home?"

I shook my head. He wouldn't chase me off with nastiness.

"No can do, Clay. You're going to tell me what you're hiding and you're going to do it now." My tone was hard and I could see it was only making him angrier.

"I'm not hiding anything. Don't be ridiculous," he said flippantly, trying to grab his book back. I saw a small movement in the dim light. Looking closer, I could see drops of blood dripping down his right hand.

I gasped. "You're freaking bleeding! Let me look!" Before he could react, I swung his desk lamp over so I could see and yanked up his shirtsleeve. I was horrified to see a steady stream of blood flowing down his arm.

"It's nothing, Maggie." He tried to pull the sleeve back down and I recognized the panic in his voice.

"That is a lot of blood, Clay. I need to see it. You may have to go to the hospital or something." I undid the buttons on his shirt and pulled it off him, manhandling him in the process.

I couldn't control my look of horror as I caught sight of the very deep and precise cuts along his right upper arm.

"Oh, my God," I breathed, grabbing several tissues and blotting the wounds. I went immediately into crisis mode, not pausing to think. I rushed down the hallway to the bathroom, grabbed some gauze, rubbing alcohol, and bandages, and returned to Clay's room.

He hadn't moved, as if rooted to the spot. The blood was coming thick now. "Shit, Clay, this looks bad. You might need stitches. I should go get Ruby." I started to head to the door.

"No, Maggie. Don't get her, please," he begged me.

I turned back to him. "You should see a doctor. Seriously." Clay picked up the gauze and pressed it to the cuts. Then, using the bandages, he covered it and held it in place.

"This will be fine. The blood will stop eventually," he said, as if from experience. I felt sick to my stomach.

"You did this to yourself, didn't you?" Clay didn't say anything; he wouldn't look at me. I raised my voice. "Answer me, damn it! You did this!"

Clay flinched. "Keep it down, would you?" He moved behind me and closed the door.

"What did you use, Clay?" My voice had gone cold. Clay sighed with resignation. He lifted the lid of the wooden box on his desk and pulled out a razor blade. I could see his blood on it. I shivered with revulsion. I snatched the blade from him, opened the window, and threw it out. I was so mad and upset and scared. How could he do this to himself?

Clay seemed remarkably calm, given that I was the one about to lose it. I stalked back over to him, putting my fingers to the skin of his chest. He hissed a quick breath as I touched the rigid scars crisscrossing his skin. The destruction he had caused himself was painful to look at.

"Why would you do this? I thought you were taking your meds," I whispered, backing away from him. Clay closed his eyes.

"I still hurt, Mags. All the time. Even with the medication. It's not a magic fix, you know," he told me sharply, opening his eyes.

"This is scary, Clay. I don't know what to do, here." I was at a complete loss and more than a little hurt, which was really selfish.

I thought he was happy, that *I* made him happy. But it was obvious I wasn't enough to help him. Not by a long shot. And that broke my heart.

"You need help," I said, feeling extremely tired.

Clay's answering laugh was a bitter one. "Been there, done that, got the certificate of completion." Clay roughly put his shirt back on. His fingers shook as he did up the buttons.

"Well, you need to do something. Do Ruby and Lisa know you're doing this again?" I asked him.

Clay's face grew dark. "No, and don't you dare tell them," he said, the threat clear in his voice.

I drew myself up straight. "Don't you take that tone with me, Clay. I'm just worried about you. Maybe they need to know."

Clay just shook his head. "There's nothing they can do," he muttered with that aching sadness.

He sounded so helpless. So utterly destroyed. How did I possibly think I could help him? That I could do this on my own? His issues, what he needed, were so beyond what I was capable of providing.

"I can't do this by myself. I don't know what to do, or what to say. I can't help you if you don't want to help yourself," I said matter-of-factly.

Clay looked at me for a second, then crossed the room toward me. "That's where you're wrong. You save me every single day. You are the one thing that makes me happy. You are the only thing I need." His words were so passionate and I felt myself being pulled along by his conviction.

"But you're still cutting," I argued, fighting the Clay haze that threatened to overshadow my better judgment.

"That was a onetime thing. I swear it. I was just upset about what happened with your parents. About not being the guy you need me to be. I just got depressed. But now that you're here, I'll be fine. *We're* fine. I promise." There were those words again.

I promise.

I had just said those same words to my mom as I assured her I would be *fine*. That Clay and I were *fine*. What a freaking lie.

And here was Clay, saying the exact same thing. Was he lying, too? What was the use of those words when they were so often untrue?

I knew I shouldn't let this go. Clay was sick. He needed to see someone. Ruby needed to know what he was going through. But I stupidly let him pull me into his arms, his breath teasing my lips as he leaned into me. I loved him so much. But was it enough?

"I love you, Maggie. You're all that I need," he murmured as his mouth captured mine and I forgot everything else.

Stupid, stupid girl.

chapter
fourteen

The time leading up to Thanksgiving break found me stuck in a weird balancing act. I continued spending every free moment with Clay, which then forced me to lie repeatedly to my parents about what I was doing and who I was doing it with. They continued to make their dislike of Clay very clear, and nothing I said seemed to change it.

I felt like I was living my life in the shadow of everyone's disapproval. My parents', Rachel's, and Daniel's. I saw it when they looked at me. Read it between the lines of their words. They could mask it with concern all they wanted, but it didn't change the fact that they wanted me to forget about Clay and our relationship. To find my way back to the person I was before.

Well, that wasn't going to happen. Because I was different now and I didn't want to be the girl I was before Clay. She was boring. Uninterested in life. That girl had never known what it was like to love someone more than herself.

I didn't like that girl anymore. She was my past.

And Clay, for all of his flaws, was my future. Whether my family and friends agreed or not.

But I couldn't ignore the gigantic elephant in the room. Clay's arms had healed after I had found him cutting. I tried not to touch the rough scabs when he held me. I avoided being reminded of that scary place I had found myself in with Clay by my side.

We never talked about it. Not once. There were times when it sat on the tip of my tongue, to ask him about the cutting. To find out more about what triggered him. I wanted to understand that dark part of him. Because if I loved him, I had to love every part of who he was. But I was a wimp. Instead, I refused to address it, choosing to bury my head in the proverbial sand like a damned ostrich.

I *had* decided to look up bipolar disorder and borderline personality disorder on the Internet one evening while I waited for Clay to call me. I didn't know much about mental illness, having never known anyone before Clay who suffered like that.

When he threw around words like *cycles* and *mania*, I had no idea what he was talking about. So I sat myself down, intent on solving at least part of the mystery that shrouded my boyfriend.

A few clicks later and the words started swimming in front of my eyes. *Manic and depressive episodes. Heightened mood. Hypomania.*

Okay, having had enough of the bipolar research, I had moved on to the borderline thing. That wasn't any better. I skipped over statements that read "pattern of instability and intensity within interpersonal relationships," "frantic efforts to avoid abandonment." "Inappropriate anger." "Suicidal behaviors."

I had closed my browser. I couldn't handle reading any more. It was that ostrich mentality again. The less I knew, the better.

Since then, I had staunchly avoided bringing up Clay's cutting and his mental health. But even though I wouldn't talk about it, it didn't stop me from thinking about it all the time. However, Clay wanted normal, so, damn it, I would give him normal. And that meant that I refused to address the blackness that threatened to engulf us.

Clay, for his part, was trying to keep things even-keeled. He took me to the movies, brought me my favorite coffee every morning. Beautiful drawings and heartfelt poems filled my locker. He was the picture of the considerate and thoughtful boyfriend. We became even more fixated on each other. The physical need to drown our fears in each other was overwhelming.

Our kisses had become almost desperate, our hands less than patient as we sought to erase the nagging doubts that tickled the backs of our minds in the hours we spent together. But nothing could erase the truth that had taken root in my brain: this would all blow up in my face in the most agonizing way possible. I felt like my life was a ticking time bomb, waiting to explode.

I started waking up in the middle of the night, startled out of sleep by horrible nightmares. I could never remember an entire dream. Only that Clay was leaving me and there was nothing I could do about it. I was wound as tight as a violin string. Those dark hours before seeing Clay again were the worst. I couldn't sleep for worrying about what he was doing.

I *knew* this was bad for me. I *knew* that perhaps my parents had been right. But I needed Clay as much as he needed me. We existed in this symbiotic relationship where our hearts beat and our lungs breathed only for each other.

Was all first love this intense? I remembered watching Daniel and Kylie as they stumbled through their relationship, sneering at how ridiculous they were. If only I had realized how hard it was to keep a level head when you were buried deep in these feelings.

I had convinced Rachel to cover for me so we could go to the cabin. She was not happy about lying to my parents. She felt guilt way too intensely and I worried she'd never be able to keep up the charade. But after days of begging, she finally agreed, even as I knew this was yet another tick in the anti-Clay column. But I needed to be with him, just the two of us. An entire night where we could be together. It sounded like bliss.

As the days to our getaway got closer, even my reluctant friends couldn't deny the excitement of getting out of town. Daniel had asked Clay if he could invite Ray and Clare, and Clay had agreed, much to my relief. I hoped their presence would help to neutralize the tension that I knew would otherwise be present. So everyone planned our crazy night away and I reveled in the new camaraderie that descended over Clay and my friends.

Thanksgiving came and went, and I enjoyed having a quiet meal with my parents. I even braved the mall to go shopping on Black Friday. I allowed my mom to talk me into some new clothes. I got some new pants and shirts, letting myself embrace my girly side with more feminine gear.

While my mom was busy picking out some new bras and underwear at Victoria's Secret, I took the opportunity to pick out some items for myself. I had to make sure that my mother didn't see me choosing several lacy pairs of panties and matching push-up bras. Holding up a pair of see-through underwear, I imagined Clay taking them off of me and my blood heated up. Yep, I was getting these for sure. I surreptitiously paid for the items and then hid the bright-pink bag in my purse.

Saturday morning, Rachel came over and helped me pack for our night away. She oohed and aahed over the new clothes I had gotten, calling dibs on the cute black off-the-shoulder top my mom had picked out. It was the first time in weeks that I had felt that old ease and normalcy in our relationship. I was convinced tonight would be just what I needed. Not only because I would have time with Clay, but because I could repair my relationships with my friends.

"Your mom has some serious style, Mags," Rachel commented, stuffing the black top into my overnight bag. I found my super-snug skinny jeans and put them in the bag as well.

"Yeah, she dresses way better than I do," I admitted, rummaging through my underwear drawer and pulling out several pairs of bras and panties that I had chosen yesterday.

"Wow, so, you and Clay. Alone. All night. Are you ready for that?" Rachel asked me, chewing on her bottom lip in a way that indicated she was nervous.

"Shh," I hissed, closing my bedroom door.

"Sorry," Rachel said, lowering her voice.

"I don't know, Rache. I do know that I love him and he loves me. And whatever happens, happens," I said determinedly. Rachel picked at her nails.

"Well, you don't have to do anything you don't want to do. Don't let a guy make you feel like you should, you know?" I knew what she was getting at. It didn't take a rocket scientist to figure out she was telling me that she worried I would be pressured to have sex. If she only knew how many times it was Clay who had called a halt to things.

"I know that. I'm not going to do anything I don't want to do," I assured her. Rachel nodded, apparently trying to take me at my word. Why did I get the feeling she didn't believe me?

"This is the real deal, Rache. I love him," I told her, sitting down on my bed. Rachel sat down beside me, put her arm around me, and laid her head on my shoulder.

"I know you do, Maggie. And I'm happy you've found that." Rachel sounded genuine and I felt my stomach unclench in relief.

I leaned into her. "Thanks," I said, and we were quiet a moment. "What about you and Daniel? Are you going to play nice this weekend?" I asked, nudging her with my shoulder.

Rachel grunted. "I'll play nice if he plays nice," she said tersely. I gave her arm a pinch.

"I know you're angry with him. He hurt you. I understand how hard it is to open that part of yourself to someone. But Daniel cares about you. And maybe the timing just wasn't right. Don't rule it out. You guys are made for each other."

Rachel shrugged. "I don't know. If he could forget about Kylie for more than two minutes, maybe you'd be right." I felt bad for her, because she was speaking the truth. "Besides, even though things are weird with us right now, he's still one of my best friends. And as much as I fantasize about us being something else, I really don't want to ruin our friendship," she said wistfully.

"I know. But the best relationships are built on friendship first," I said, zipping up my bag. Rachel shrugged again.

"I seriously doubt Daniel sees me as anything but a friend. Hell, he thought we had penises!"

I laughed, recalling that conversation clearly. But I, for one, knew that Daniel wasn't entirely unaffected by Rachel. I had seen his eyes when he saw her in that pink sparkly dress at Fall Formal. I saw how upset he got when she was mad at him. He had feelings for her, all right. Whether he was willing to act on them was the real question.

"I just think life's too short to get hung up on maybe's," I told her simply.

Rachel rolled her eyes at me. "Well, aren't you philosophical all of a sudden? Love has turned you into Gandhi." I laughed as I hoisted my bulging duffel bag to my shoulder and headed down the stairs.

We were still laughing as we rounded the corner into the kitchen. My mom was perched on a stool, tapping away at her laptop.

"What are you girls laughing about?" she asked, giving us a smile. I shook my head.

"Nothing, Mom," I said offhandedly.

"Hi, Rachel! Do you girls have lots of fun planned for your evening?" my mom asked, looking at Rachel.

Rachel swallowed thickly and nodded like a puppet. "Yeah,

we're going to see a movie at eight o'clock. You know, the new Brad Pitt one that's out. He is so hot. Even if he is a little old. I mean, who cares, when you look like that? And he and Angelina Jolie make the most perfect couple." I elbowed Rachel in the ribs so she would stop her nervous rambling. Rachel closed her mouth and gave my mom a pained smile. There was no way my mom was going to buy this! It was too obvious we were lying!

But the teenage gods were smiling on us. My mom simply gave Rachel an odd look and then nodded. "Okay, then, have fun. Do you have your cell phone, Maggie?" she asked me. I pulled it out of my jacket pocket and waved it in front of me.

"Love you. See you tomorrow," she said, returning her focus to whatever was on her laptop screen. Yes! Home free! I tried not to run out of the kitchen in my rush to get out of the house before she changed her mind.

Once we were in Rachel's car and heading down the road, she let out a loud breath. "Damn, I thought for a second we were so busted."

"I know. Especially after your fantastic monologue about the wonders of Brad Pitt. You are the worst liar!"

Rachel blew her bangs from her forehead. "Well, maybe you shouldn't have had me do it, then," she snipped at me.

It was time to lay it on a little thick. "Thank you, Rachel, for everything back there. You are seriously the best friend a gal could ever, ever have." I batted my eyelashes at her.

Rachel laughed grudgingly. "Oh, just shut up, will you?" She flipped on the radio, ending our conversation.

We arrived at Clay's house ten minutes later. Daniel, Ray, and Clare were already there. Ruby and Lisa were talking to them on the front porch. Clare waved at us as we pulled into the driveway. We parked and got out of the car.

"Everyone ready?" I asked, barely able to conceal my excitement. I moved to Clay's side and gave him a quick squeeze before greeting Ruby and Lisa.

Lisa dangled a key in front of her. "Here you go, guys. Have fun. There should be cut firewood up already, and there's a small grocery store about five minutes away. Have fun and be safe."

Clay took the key and gave Lisa a hug. "Thanks, Lise. You're the best."

We all called out our thank-you's as we piled into separate vehicles. Rachel, Clay, Daniel, and I loaded up into Rachel's car while Ray and Clare followed in his SUV.

I snuggled into Clay's side in the backseat, laying my head on his shoulder. He kissed the top of my head and laced his fingers through mine. I sighed in contentment. This was the most relaxed I had been in weeks.

Franklin Lake was only forty-five minutes away. Close enough that you didn't spend all day driving but far enough that you felt like you were getting away from it all. Things in the car were a little awkward at first. But finally, after a while, everyone started to get comfortable and we were able to engage in conversation that wasn't entirely stilted.

Rachel and Daniel were still tense around each other, but even they made an effort to enjoy themselves. I could have sworn I even saw Daniel smile at one point. Clay and Rachel talked about their creative-writing class. Daniel spoke endlessly about the basketball team. For the first time in weeks, I felt a sort of civility fall over my friends and me, and I realized with a pang how much I had missed them. I hadn't noticed how much I had pushed them away in my pursuit of my relationship with Clay. When was the last time I had talked to Daniel about something that wasn't in any way related to my roller-coaster love life? I couldn't remember. And that was sad. I was determined to rectify that this evening.

Clay wouldn't let go of my hand the entire ride. His thumb caressed the sensitive skin of my palm, shooting sparks straight to my belly. Running his nose up the side of my neck, he murmured in my ear, "I love you, baby." I squeezed his hand in return, my insides a twisty mess at his closeness.

Finally, Clay looked out the window and pointed to a turnoff just ahead of us. "You want to pull down this road," Clay told Rachel, pointing to the narrow dirt path to the right. "Are you sure my car will make it?" Rachel asked hesitantly.

Clay chuckled. "Your car will be fine. It's a little rough the first fifty yards but the rest is packed dirt; you'll be golden."

Rachel made the turn. "All right, but if I eat it, you're paying for the repairs," she grumbled.

"Stop worrying," I said, leaning forward and squeezing her shoulder. Of course, the first thing she did was hit a giant, cratersized pothole, tipping the car precariously.

"Fuck!" she screeched after getting back on the hard road.

Daniel was laughing in the front seat. "You should have seen your face, Rache! That was priceless."

Rachel smacked his arm. "Shut up, Daniel, or you're hoofing it to the cabin."

Daniel snorted. "Whatever," he muttered, but didn't make another comment. We drove for another two miles before the forest ended and we came to a clearing. Sitting up on a hill was the most fantastic house I'd ever seen.

"Shit, man, this wasn't at all what I was expecting when you said we'd be staying in a cabin," Daniel said, whistling. The wooden structure was built to resemble a Swiss chalet. The entire front was nothing but windows, and there were not one but two large stone chimneys jutting from the roof.

"Wait until you get inside. It's incredible," Clay promised as Rachel pulled into the two-car garage off the side of the cabin.

"I had no idea Lisa had the money for something like this," I told Clay, a little awestruck. Clay reached into the trunk and pulled our duffel bags out.

"It's actually Lisa's parents' place. Her family has the money but no one uses the cabin but Lisa. Most of her family has moved away, so she makes sure the property is maintained."

Ray and Clare had just gotten out of their car. "Damn . . . this is awesome!" Ray remarked. Clare seemed as amazed as the rest of us. I still couldn't believe that this was where we'd be spending the night.

Clay pulled out the keys and unlocked the door leading into the house from the garage. He quickly punched a code into an alarm panel on the wall, making it chirp. "Be careful—it's dark through here, so let's just get into the living room." Clay grabbed my hand as I trailed behind him through the dark hallway.

He pushed through a swinging door and flicked on some lights and I was totally dazzled. The living room, kitchen, and dining area were an open floor plan. A large sectional sofa sat in front of the huge windows overlooking the forest; a beautiful stone fireplace sat to the right. Just off to the left of the living area was an enormous kitchen with stainless-steel appliances, granite countertops, and a magnificent island topped with a gas range.

The dining area was truly spectacular. A magnificent cherry table sat in an alcove off the kitchen, and the wall was one large window overlooking the lake. A glass chandelier hung above the table. Wood floors, dotted with area rugs, ran throughout the first floor.

I walked to the window in the dining area and looked out. It was a sunny day and the lake glistened. I could see a gazebo down below with screens enclosing it. Clay came up behind me and wrapped his arms around my waist, resting his chin on my shoulder. He pointed to the gazebo. "That's where the Jacuzzi is. We *will* be enjoying that later." He nibbled my earlobe, making me giggle.

"So, who gets what rooms, dude?" Ray asked. Clay let me go and turned around. He pointed down a hallway leading from the kitchen.

"There are two bedrooms down there. Each has its own bathroom. You guys can decide who gets what." He tugged on my hand and I followed him to a spiral staircase hidden to the right of the dining nook.

He looked at me mischievously. "You and I get the room up here." I followed him up the stairs that led to a loft area. The room was the size of the entire first floor.

"Oh, my God, Clay!" I said breathlessly. Again, it was the windows. There was only one wall made of wood; the other three were nothing but glass. It was like being outside. An enormous California king–sized bed sat in the middle of the room. There were stairs off to the side that went down into a sunken area with a whirlpool tub and two pedestal sinks.

"We get to sleep in here? Are you kidding me?" I asked incredulously. I ran and jumped on the bed, laughing as I bounced. Clay stalked toward me and made a show of crawling on the bed until he was over me. I looked up into his face and smiled. I was so happy.

He pressed his mouth to mine, his tongue invading and conquering. I groaned as he licked my bottom lip, teasing it with his teeth. "Nothing but the best for you, Maggie," he said softly into the skin of my neck as he nuzzled me. I ran my fingers through his hair and molded my body against his. Clay left light kisses along the side of my face as he interlaced his fingers with mine.

"This place is seriously unbelievable. Thank you so much for inviting us," I told him as he pulled me tighter against him.

Running his fingertips down my face, Clay smiled. "I know things have been tense lately. I haven't given you many reasons to smile."

I started to protest, but he covered my mouth with his finger.

"I'm not blind. I know what being with me has done to your life. I see how your friends, your parents—hell, *everybody*—looks at you because you're with me. I haven't done much to give them a positive impression of me. I just wanted a chance to prove that I'm not such a bad guy. For your friends to see how much you mean to me and that I would literally do anything in the world for you. Then, maybe, they wouldn't look at us like we shouldn't be together."

I hated that this was where we found ourselves. That he was so aware of the fact that no one understood our relationship and what we meant to each other. I wasn't sure one night with my friends would erase the months of damage. But I wanted to be as positive about it as he was.

"I love you," I whispered before kissing him again, wanting to take away the sadness and pain that never seemed to leave Clay's face.

"Uh, guys, we have a problem, here," I heard Rachel call from downstairs. Clay sighed and rested his forehead on my chest.

"That doesn't sound good," he commented.

I chuckled and got up. "Come on. Let's go see what monumental crisis we have to avert." I straightened my rumpled shirt and smoothed my hair before following Clay downstairs.

Ray and Clare were gone when we entered the kitchen. Daniel was sitting on one of the stools at the island, his head propped on his hand, looking annoyed.

"What's up?" I asked, looking at Daniel, who I knew from experience was usually the source of Rachel's problems.

Daniel rolled his eyes. "You'd have to ask her. I don't see that there *is* any problem." I looked at Rachel, waiting for her to explain.

"I'll tell you what the problem is. There is only one extra room! And there's only one queen-sized bed in there! I told Daniel, if he were a gentleman he'd sleep on the couch, but he's refusing. He says I'm being ridiculous! Can you believe it? *Him* calling *me* ridiculous? That's just rich!" Rachel shot daggers at Daniel, who looked bored with the whole debate.

"Uh, Rache, it's not like you haven't shared a bed with Daniel before," I reminded her.

Rachel huffed. "We were, like, eight. That does not count, okay? Tell him he has to sleep on the couch, Clay." Rachel turned to my boyfriend, drawing him squarely into the middle of the argument. Clay looked flustered and his eyes found mine in a silent appeal. I knew he was worried about making Rachel any angrier. But I didn't know how to help him, so I just shrugged.

Clay put his hand through his hair in that flustered way he was known for. "Well, Rachel. I can't really say *who* gets the bedroom. I mean, that's really something the two of you have to decide." Rachel looked like she wanted to throw something.

"Well, I'm not sleeping on the couch. If the thought of sharing a bed with me disgusts you that much, *you* sleep on the couch," Daniel remarked grumpily. He hopped down from the stool and grabbed his overnight bag.

"Where do you think you're going?" Rachel asked him angrily.

He started walking down the hallway. "I'm taking my bag to *my* room. Later," he called over his shoulder.

Rachel whipped around and gave Clay and me a steely glare. "What the hell am I supposed to do? I shouldn't have to sleep on the couch because he's being a dick." I patted my best friend's back.

"I have a solution for you," I whispered conspiratorially.

Rachel looked at me, interested. "Yeah?" she asked.

"Why don't you stop being such a stubborn pain in the ass and take your stuff back to the bedroom? One night sharing a bed won't kill you."

Rachel harrumphed, picked up her bright-pink bag, and stomped down the hallway after Daniel. "You'd best stay on your side of the bed or I'll cut off your testicles while you sleep!" I heard her yelling. I couldn't hear Daniel's response.

Clay looked bewildered. "She's scary when she's mad. I'd hate to be Daniel right now," he said, going to the refrigerator and pulling out a beer. I cocked my eyebrow at him. He looked down at the can. "Okay, maybe not such a good idea." He gave me a smile and put it back, grabbing a bottle of water instead.

An hour later, Raymond and Clare emerged from their room, looking as if they had just woken up from a nap. Daniel and Rachel joined us in the living room not long after that, both looking less annoyed, though Rachel continued to bristle every time Daniel opened his mouth.

"Didn't Lisa say there was a grocery store five minutes from here?" Raymond asked.

"Yeah, if you go back down the driveway and head right, it's less than a mile on your left. It's just a little mom-and-pop place, but you can get the essentials," Clay told him.

"Cool. You want to come, Danny?"

Daniel jumped at the chance to get away from a still-fuming Rachel.

"Clay?" Raymond asked.

Clay looked at me and I nodded. "Go, have some guy time." Clay grinned and I could see how happy he was to be included.

◆

"Ugh! I seriously need to decompress. Didn't Clay say there was a Jacuzzi around here somewhere?" Rachel asked. I picked up our empty soda cans and threw them in the trash.

"Yeah, it's outside in the gazebo. You wanna check it out?" I asked.

Clare jumped off the couch. "Hell, yeah, let's go!"

Rachel, Clare, and I went to our respective rooms and changed into our swimsuits. It felt crazy to put one on when it was almost December. The three of us reconvened in the living room. I started to put my fuzzy robe on when Rachel let out a low whistle.

"What?" I asked her.

Rachel looked fantastic in her red one-piece, cut up high on the hips. She gave me the once-over. "When did you get *that*?" she asked, indicating my black bikini. I looked down at myself and blushed. Yeah, it was a little more revealing than my typical getup.

I covered myself, feeling self-conscious. "I got it last summer; just haven't worn it yet," I told her, slipping on a pair of flip-flops I had brought along.

"Well, you look hot. Where have you been hiding that killer body?" Rachel whistled again, making me blush. Clare giggled as she covered up her boy shorts and tank top. I grabbed some bottles of water from the fridge, tossing them at my friends, ignoring Rachel's comment.

"Come on, before the guys get back and we lose whatever chance we have at relaxing," I told them, leading the way outside.

As we stepped out the back door, the three of us began to shiver. "Damn. It's freezing out here." Rachel pulled her jacket tighter around her, but her bare legs were already breaking out into goose bumps.

It had easily dropped fifteen degrees since we'd gotten to the cabin. Looking at the sky, I wouldn't have been surprised if it snowed. Running as fast as we could, we headed to the gazebo. I opened the door and ushered them inside. "Hurry up, so I can close the door."

Inside, I was relieved to see baseboard heating running the length of two walls. I found the thermostat and cranked it. Rachel walked over to the Jacuzzi pump and turned it on. The water began to bubble and swirl.

We sat huddled together until it heated up. The gazebo had windows and I made sure they were all securely latched so as to not let in any cold air. Finally, it felt warm and comfortable so the three of us stripped off our outerwear, kicked off our shoes, and slowly slid into the water.

It was a huge Jacuzzi, easily fitting eight people. "Ah. Now, this is the life." Clare sighed in contentment, laying her head back. The water came up to our shoulders and fizzed against my skin deliciously.

"This is just what I needed," Rachel said after a long sigh. She had closed her eyes and sank down until the water lapped at her chin. Clare and I murmured our agreement. None of us said a word for a long time.

"So, Ray told me on the ride up here that Kylie was trying to get back with Daniel," Clare said, breaking the relaxing silence. I quickly looked over at Rachel to gauge her response. Rachel hadn't opened her eyes but I could see her jaw clench.

"Really? Danny hasn't said anything," I ventured, not sure I wanted to discuss Daniel and Kylie while Rachel was seeming pretty subdued.

Clare nodded. "Yeah. Apparently she's been hanging around a lot. I know I've seen her at their basketball practices after school. I guess she and that other guy she was screwing around with didn't work out so she's trying to get her hooks back into Danny."

Rachel suddenly got out of the Jacuzzi and wrapped herself in a towel. I watched her closely. I knew the topic of Kylie Good upset her.

I tried shooting Clare a look that said to drop the subject, but she apparently wasn't picking up on my cues. "Well, Ray said that Daniel turned her down flat. Seems he's finally seen the light and realized Kylie is a skank." My eyes widened in surprise.

If Daniel had a weakness, it had always been Kylie. He seemed to never be able to tell her no. So the fact that he wasn't running back to her as fast as he could was surprising. Rachel was vigorously drying her hair, trying to act unaffected by the news.

"Wow. That's awesome!" I enthused, truly happy that Daniel was taking a stand for once. Clare's eyes darted toward Rachel.

"Yeah, maybe he's ready to move on to someone else." Clare's eyebrows rose pointedly. I rolled my eyes at Clare's less-than-subtle tactics.

"Well, I doubt that, honestly. Daniel's head is too far up his own ass to notice anything. Let alone see someone standing right in front of him," Rachel fumed, her voice catching.

Clare and I glanced at each other. "Rache," I began just as the door to the gazebo swung open, bringing with it a gust of frigid air and three barely clothed teenage boys.

"Goddamn, it's freezing." Raymond latched the gazebo door behind them, as he, Daniel, and Clay scurried inside.

"Ahhh," Daniel sighed as he lowered himself into the Jacuzzi. "Move over, Clare." Daniel elbowed the petite girl out of the way as he situated himself over one of the jets. The water sloshed as Raymond and Clay followed Danny into the water.

"I'm heading inside. I'll see you guys in a bit," Rachel said coolly, letting herself out.

Daniel frowned. "Was it something I said?" he asked, confused. I gave him a look, then shrugged.

"She's just tired. Leave her be," I told him. Daniel seemed bothered by Rachel's sudden exit, but didn't say anything more about it.

"Hey, you," I said as Clay slid his hand up my naked thigh. Clay leaned over and gave me a lingering kiss on the mouth.

"Hey, miss me?" His eyes glazed over as he looked down at me in my bathing suit. They roamed over my barely covered chest.

"Always," I answered him. He kissed my shoulder and stretched his legs out in front of him.

"Can we move in, Clay? I don't think I ever want to leave." Clare moaned as she sank deeper into the warm water.

"Yeah, man, this is unbelievable. Thanks so much for letting us come," Daniel added sincerely.

Obviously the guy time had done wonders to change Daniel's attitude toward Clay. They seemed almost civil. It was a relief to see.

"I'm glad you guys are here," Clay said genuinely. I felt a warmth spread through my body that had nothing to do with the water. I could almost see those separated parts of my life slowly coming together. Finally!

Ray suddenly shoved his girlfriend under the water. Clare came back up to the surface sputtering and wiping her eyes.

"You are such an asshole, Ray!" she yelled, splashing him in the face. The two of them, followed by Daniel, started slopping water all over the place as they splashed each other.

After getting a face full of water, I decided it was time for me to leave. "Okay, I'm going," I said, getting out of the Jacuzzi. Clay was right behind me.

"We're heading back to the house. Just turn off the pump when you guys are done," Clay told the others before we left. I shoved my arms through my robe as Clay threw on his jacket. He took my hand. "Ready? On the count of three, let's make a run for it." He put his hand on the doorknob.

"One. Two. Three!" He pushed open the gazebo door and we ran as fast as we could to the cabin.

It had started to snow and it fell in pretty little tufts, landing in my hair and eyelashes as we tried to get back into the warmth. "Hurry, Mags!" Clay laughed, holding the kitchen door open. I sprinted through and Clay slammed the door closed behind us. I was out of breath and I had a stitch in my side but I couldn't get the silly smile off of my face.

My hair felt like it had frozen solid. "Ugh. I need a shower to warm up. I'm an icicle." I tightened the sash of my robe, still shivering even in the warmth of the cabin.

"I'm heading upstairs to change. I'll be back in a minute," I said to Clay as he sat down on the coach, flipping on ESPN.

"Okay, baby," he called as I left the room.

Upstairs, I located the shower, tucked behind a Japanese screen in the corner of the room. I was a little hesitant to strip naked when I again realized I was surrounded by windows. But I supposed no one could see me this high up, so I finally jumped into the warm spray.

After dressing in a pair of dark jeans and my new gray cashmere sweater that tied in the front, I dried my long brown hair and clipped it back, away from my face. Taking the time to put on a little makeup, I was actually pleased with the way I looked. Dare I say I looked pretty? I wanted tonight to be perfect. I just hoped it would be.

chapter
fifteen

Clay had come in just as I was finishing up. "Aw. You're already dressed," he pouted, pulling me up against him.

"Get away!" I squealed as his damp swimming trunks left wet marks on my jeans. He gave me a loud smack with his lips and rooted through his bag to find dry clothes.

"I'm gonna get a shower, too. Daniel, Ray, and Clare just came in."

"Have you seen Rachel?" I asked as he moved toward the shower.

Clay shook his head. "No, I'm guessing she's back in her room. She all right?" he asked.

"I'm not sure," I answered truthfully. Clay came back over and wrapped me in a warm hug, kissing the top of my head.

"I'll be down in a sec," he said, leaving me for the shower.

I joined the others downstairs. Clare was still wrapped up in her towel, sitting at the island while Daniel made her some sort of drink.

"Whatcha doin'?" I asked as Daniel poured cranberry juice into a glass and garnished it with a lemon slice.

"Clay said we could get into the liquor. So I'm making Clare here a cranberry splash. Cranberry juice, vodka, and a splash of club soda. You want one?"

My stomach clenched up. I did not think it was a good idea for Clay to be around people drinking, given his history.

I shook my head. "Just take it easy, guys. We're here to have a good time, not get loaded and throw up all night," I warned. Daniel rolled his eyes at me.

"When did you become the party Nazi?" he joked, handing the drink to Clare. She took a drink and made a face.

"God, Danny. How much vodka did you put in here?" She sniffed the glass.

Daniel shrugged. "Enough. Now, just drink up." He turned to make himself his own drink. I had a bad feeling about this. I wanted to find Rachel. I was worried about her. I headed down the hallway toward the bedroom she would be sharing with Daniel.

I tentatively knocked on the door. I heard a muffled "come in." I opened the door to find Rachel sitting on the bed, painting her toenails. I'll admit, I had expected Rachel to be curled into a ball, moping. So seeing her doing something as mundane as giving herself a pedicure was a nice surprise.

"Hey," I said, plopping down beside her.

"Hey," she said back, not looking up.

"Cool color," I commented, watching her coat her nails with a fire-engine red.

Rachel wiggled her toes. "Yeah, they'll look awesome with my strappy red dress."

Rachel put the cap back on the nail polish and placed it on the bedside table before stretching out her legs, waiting for her toes to dry. I lay down on the bed and pulled a pillow under my head. "Why are you hiding in here?" I asked her, point-blank.

Rachel leaned over to blow on her nails. "I'm not hiding." I looked at her archly. Who was she kidding? "Okay, so maybe I'm hiding. I just can't deal with *his* bullshit. Everything he says and does right now just pisses me off. He doesn't even mean to hurt me, which makes it all that much worse. I know I'm being a moody bitch. Just let me have my PMS moment in peace, please. I promise to put on the shiny-happy later. But now I feel like brooding." Rachel got up and hobbled over to the bathroom, making sure she didn't mess up her toenails.

"Fine. But I'm holding you to the whole shiny, happy thing. Because the gloomy, emo show you're putting on seriously sucks." I stuck my tongue out at her as she closed the door. But I was happy to see her small smile before she shut me out.

I went back into the living room. "So, is Her Majesty going to grace us with her presence?" Daniel asked, as I sat down beside Clay on the sofa.

"Shut up, Daniel! If you weren't such a self-centered prick, you'd figure out you're ninety-nine percent of her problem," I barked. That shut Danny up. Ray snickered from across the room and Clare's eyes widened at my outburst.

"Cool your heels, baby," Clay said, rubbing my arm. I sank into his touch, wanting to ignore the inevitable drama between my two best friends. When had things gotten so complicated? I hated this weirdness that existed between Rachel and Daniel. Even worse, I was focusing on their shit and not on what was happening between my boyfriend and me.

Rachel came out of the bedroom a short time later. "Check out the snow," she said, pointing at the window. The snow had picked up considerably since we had come inside and half an inch of white now lay on the ground.

"Oh, I hope we get stuck here!" Clare clapped her hands in excitement.

"Yeah," I said halfheartedly. That little scenario wouldn't be so great for me, considering my parents had no idea where I really was. I watched the flakes fall from the sky. Clay's arm rested warmly over my shoulders and I rested my head on his shoulder. For that one moment in time, everything was how I wanted it to be.

I must have dozed off, because the next thing I knew, Clay was nudging me awake. "Hey, sleepyhead. Time to get up. We need to start getting dinner together," he whispered in my ear, kissing it gently, sending shivers down my spine.

I stretched and tried to burrow back down into the couch cushions. "No, I want to sleep," I complained, closing my eyes again.

"Get up, Mags!" Daniel shouted, before jumping on top of me. He tickled my sides until I was gasping for breath.

"I'm up, I'm up!" I screeched, smacking his hands away. I shoved Daniel off me and stood up.

I met Clay's eyes as he watched me. His face was dark and I shivered involuntarily. I didn't like what I saw. There was no way he could be jealous of Daniel. That was just ridiculous. But, looking at him and how pissed off he seemed, I knew that's exactly how he was feeling.

I crossed the room to where Clay was standing at the island. I slid my arms around his waist. "Hey, you," I said softly, kissing his back through his T-shirt. I tried to let him know through body language alone that there was no one else I wanted.

"I've gotta get dinner ready. So just back off, all right?" Clay lifted my arms from around his middle and moved away from me. Wow, that hurt.

"Clay . . ." I began, but realized he wasn't listening to me. He had moved over to where Rachel was chopping vegetables. I watched as he began to laugh at something she said. He helped her get the salad together, completely ignoring me.

Rachel met my eyes in confusion over Clay's sudden chattiness. I gave her a small smile and turned away. If he wanted to pretend I wasn't there, then fine. I'd go in the other fucking room.

Screw this!

I grabbed a beer from the fridge and popped the top angrily. Throwing the bottle back, I drank half its contents in one gulp. I went back into the living room to sit with Clare, who was watching *Desperate Housewives*.

Dinner was awkward. The food was fantastic but I couldn't eat any of it, due to the huge lump that had taken up residence in my stomach. Daniel sat beside me as Clay brought in a platter of steaks. Seeing this, Clay dropped the plate on the table and walked around so that he was seated at the opposite end of the table from me.

He wouldn't look at me the entire time we ate. He laughed loudly with Ray and even flirted with Clare (which I thought was totally inappropriate). But it was as if I didn't exist.

"Problems in paradise?" Daniel asked between bites of salad.

I gave him a withering look and otherwise ignored the goad. Rachel sat across from me and gave me worried looks throughout dinner. This is not how I had envisioned this evening panning out. Rachel and Daniel were barely talking and Clay was refusing to acknowledge me. Could it get much worse?

After we finished, I decided to take the bull by the horns and deal with the ice that had formed between Clay and me. I grabbed a bunch of plates and followed him into the kitchen, where he began to load the dishwasher.

I dropped the dishes on the counter and pulled Clay by the arm. "Look at me!" I said loudly, trying to get his attention. He tried to shake me off but I wouldn't be swayed.

"Damn it, Clay! Just tell me what I've done to deserve the silent treatment!" I hated how wobbly my voice sounded. Clay must have heard it, too, because he finally looked at me.

Seeing how hurt I was, he sighed and the coldness melted away from his face. "It's nothing, Mags. I don't know. I'm just being irrational again." Clay filled the sink with water and started scrubbing the pans, apparently trying to avoid the conversation.

I dipped my hands into the soapy water and took his hands in mine. His fingers curled around to hold me. "I don't understand. I'm not a mind reader, Clay. You have to help me out a little, here," I implored, dropping my forehead to his chest. Clay wrapped his arms around me, his wet hands gripping my back.

"Please, can we just forget about it? It's nothing." He sounded tired and I wanted to push him. But I knew instinctively that it would only make things worse. So I went against my better judgment and let the matter drop. I decided moving back into Denial Land was my best option.

I went up on my tiptoes, placing a kiss on Clay's mouth. "I love you. You know that, right?"

Clay gave me a weak smile. "Sure," he said, turning back to the dishes in the sink. He didn't say anything else to me.

I stood beside him another moment, then left the kitchen, his arctic blast following me into the living room.

Ray was yelling at the television as he and Daniel played some sort of shooting game on the Xbox. Clare was drinking yet another alcohol-laden concoction and Rachel was curled up under a blanket. I plopped down beside Rachel. "So, what do you guys want to do?"

"Strip poker?" Ray asked, his eyes lighting up. Clare threw a pillow at him.

"Shut up, perv!" she yelled at him. The rest of us laughed. Clay came in the room and sat down beside Clare. Could he make it any more obvious he was giving me the brush-off?

"There are a bunch of board games in the cabinet over there. We could play one of them," he suggested.

"That sounds like fun; come help me find something," Clare said, jumping off the couch and pulling Clay by the hand.

I tried to subdue the jealousy that ripped through me. This was Clare! My friend! Her boyfriend was only three feet away. There was no reason to feel weird about their interaction. But watching Clay standing so close to another girl made me want to rip the hair out of my "friend's" head.

But, instead of going all territorial, I decided to stay where I was, marinating in my ugly emotions. Clay and Clare agreed on Trivial Pursuit. After Ray and Daniel finished with the Xbox, we set up the game on the coffee table. We decided to play boys against girls, but with a twist. Ray and Daniel wanted to turn it into a drinking game. So, for every wrong answer, that team had to take a drink.

I was nervous about this. I looked at Clay to make sure he was okay with it. He looked at me defiantly and took a drink of beer. He seemed to be making a point. Whatever; I wasn't going to nag at him about it. If he wanted to act like an idiot, so be it.

After a few turns, it became obvious that Clay was dominating the game. My worries about his drinking were unfounded because he missed very few questions.

"What is the fastest swimming marine mammal?" Rachel asked.

"The killer whale," Clay answered, without hesitation.

Rachel threw the card at him. "Have you memorized these cards or something? There is no way you know that much useless knowledge!" she griped.

Clay laughed. "Let's just say I used to have a lot of time on my hands and all I did was read," he admitted, handing the card back to her.

I answered my fair share of questions and Clay's frostiness had lessened considerably as the game wound down. "How many *Rocky* movies were made by 1990?" Clay asked when it was our turn.

"Oh! I know this one! There were five movies," I said, grinning because I knew I was right. Clay turned over the card.

"Yep, the answer is five. See, I'm not the only one with a head full of useless knowledge. Nicely done." He smiled at me, handing me the pink wedge for our wheel.

My body buzzed when his fingers brushed mine to hand me the game piece. Our eyes locked and I felt like maybe he was finally over our earlier misunderstanding. I hated to admit that I was getting very, very drunk. Clare and Rachel were giggling beside me and Ray was all but passed out on the couch.

After a few more rounds, the boys declared victory and we girls had to down the rest of our drinks. My head felt fuzzy and Rachel was laughing about nothing in particular. After that, we decided to play Scattergories. Daniel and Rachel decided to team up for this one. Ray and Clare were another team, leaving Clay and me together.

Suddenly, Daniel's phone began to ring. He looked down at the screen and got up quickly to answer it. "Hello?" he said quietly, leaving the room.

"Who was that?" I asked.

"I bet it was Kylie. She's been calling him all day," Ray said nonchalantly, waking up a bit so he could get his hands up Clare's shirt.

"Kylie? I thought they were broken up," Rachel said quietly.

"Yeah, they are, but that didn't stop them from hooking up last week. I think she just wants another go." Ray could be such a pig.

Clare smacked her boyfriend. "Shut up, Ray!" she hissed at him.

Rachel looked at me and I knew she was hurt. "See, Mags. This is why I won't ever say or do anything. Because *she* will always be in the picture." Rachel threw down the cards in her hand and got to her feet a little unsteadily.

Daniel came back into the room just then and looked at Rachel in confusion. "Where are you going? We've got a game to win." He had tucked his phone back into his pocket. Rachel was wobbling on her feet, the alcohol making itself known.

"You know what, Daniel? I'm fucking done."

I got to my feet, ready to intervene. "Come on, Rachel. Maybe it's just time to go to bed," I said quietly, moving to stand beside her. I took her arm and tried to lead her away but Daniel stopped us.

"No, Maggie. Let her say what she wants to say. Obviously I've pissed her off, *again*," he spit out nastily. We were all wasted; this was not going to end up well.

Rachel's face turned red. "Damn straight you pissed me off! I'm so sick of watching you go back and forth with that skank!" she shrieked. Clay had come up on Rachel's other side and the two of us were trying to lead her down the hallway.

She yanked her arms away from our grasp and turned back to Daniel. Danny looked livid. "What the hell is it to you?" he growled, moving toward Rachel.

I put my hand on Daniel's chest. "Back off, Danny. You know how she gets when she drinks. Just let her sleep it off." I looked over to Ray and Clare, hoping for some more help, but they had passed out.

"No, Maggie! I'm sick of him walking all over me!" Rachel yelled. Daniel frowned, the veins in his neck bulging.

"Walk all over you? What *are* you talking about? We're friends, Rachel! We've been friends for a long time and lately all we do is fight. The fucked-up thing is I can't think of one damn thing I've done to you!" he yelled, his face an inch from Rachel's.

"Man, just let it go," Clay said, trying to pull Daniel back. Rachel had started to cry.

"Yes, we're friends! But damn you, Daniel! I love you! I'm tired of you hurting me!" she sobbed. I pulled her into the crook of my arm and let her cry into my shirt.

Daniel was dumbstruck. He looked at me in confusion. "She loves me? What the hell is she talking about?" I just shook my head. Rachel pulled out of my arms and ran down the hallway, slamming the door to their room.

"What the fuck?!" Daniel yelled, and turned to punch the wall.

"Stop that shit, Daniel!" Clay roared, pulling the other boy back. Daniel pushed past Clay and me and slammed out the kitchen door.

"Well, crap," I said tiredly. I looked out the window, trying to find Daniel in the darkened yard. "I should probably go find him," I said, pulling on my coat and putting on my shoes.

"Just let him be. He'll calm down," Clay said, pulling me back from the door. I turned on him and gave him a dark look.

"Look, Clay. Daniel is my friend. He's pissed off and drunk. He needs me right now." I found my gloves in my coat pocket and tugged them on.

Clay grabbed my arms. "Well, I need you too. Doesn't that count for something?" he asked me angrily. Was he serious? How could he make this all about him?

I wrenched away from him. "Stop being a selfish prick. My friends need me right now. I would hope you'd understand that. But if you don't, well—fuck you," I ground out, before leaving him to find Daniel.

chapter
sixteen

I found Daniel down by the lake, sitting on a bench as the snow fell around him. He hadn't put on a coat, so he was shivering from the cold. "You'll freeze out here, you idiot," I said, coming to sit beside him.

Daniel was still a little wobbly, but he moved over to make room for me on the bench. "What the hell was that? Was she serious? Because I had no clue she felt that way," he bit out angrily.

I touched my shoulder to his in support and took his hand. "Danny, Rachel loves you. I mean *loves you* loves you. I'm not sure I should even be telling you this, but I can't stand aside and watch the two of you hurt each other over and over again. So, now you know how she feels. What are you going to do about it?" I asked him.

Daniel hung his head. "I don't know. This is insane. I've known Rachel since we were babies. I just never thought she felt that way about me." He shook his head.

"Well, I guess the question is, Do you feel that way about her? I know she's your friend. The three of us have been attached at the hip for a long time. But there sometimes comes a point when things change. And that can be a really good thing, Daniel." I wrapped my arm around his shoulders and hugged him close.

"I'm really messed up right now. I can't think." He gripped his head with his hands like he had a headache. "Our friendship is really important to me. I don't know if I can ruin that." He sounded vulnerable and I leaned over to kiss his cheek.

"Well, maybe for now, you just need to go in there and talk to her. Sort through your shit. Because I can't play middleman between the two of you much longer. It's exhausting." I rubbed the back of his neck, trying to soothe him.

"You're pretty damn fantastic, Mags," Daniel said, smiling his sad, drunk smile.

"Yeah, I know," I quipped, letting him pull me into a tight embrace, his hand coming up to stroke my hair. We stayed like that for a while, hugging each other. Daniel seemed to cling to me like a lifeline. He pulled back finally and patted my cheek.

"You're right. I should go talk to her. This has gotten out of control."

I grabbed his other hand and squeezed. I gave him a nudge. "Okay, well, go on," I urged.

Daniel got to his feet. "Wish me luck. If you hear my screams, know she's trying to kill me and come help. Okay?" Daniel was joking, of course, but I could see how nervous he was.

"Sure," I said, smiling.

After Daniel left, I sat on the bench a while longer. It was then I felt a strange prickle at the back of my neck. Turning around, I could see Clay's dark form in the shadow of the trees.

"Clay?" I called out. He didn't answer me, just stood there watching me. I got up and walked toward him, my stomach dropping at the look on his face.

Great, he was mad again.

"How long have you been out here?" I asked, shoving my hands into my pockets. His eyes met mine.

"Long enough to see your touching little interlude there," he spat out with disgust. I lifted my hands in the air and huffed.

"Of course you'd say that. Because apparently all I do is go behind your back with other guys. I mean, that *is* what you're accusing me of, right?" I said bitterly, moving around him to go back in the house.

Clay grabbed my arm. "Well, if the shoe fits," he said coldly. I whipped around and got in his face.

"Well, I'm not the one out here like a damn stalker! Daniel is my friend, you moron! I'm through explaining myself to you!"

I ran back into the cabin and went straight upstairs.

Clay was right on my heels. "Maggie, stop. Please." I could hear the change in his voice. He sounded worried; panicked, even.

"If it wasn't snowing, I'd tell you to take me home. This is ridiculous! You've been an asshole all evening. I've had enough of your irrational insecurities!" I yelled at him as I ripped off my coat and threw it on the floor.

"Maggie! God! You know how I am. How hard it is . . ."

I cut him off. "Stop with the goddamn excuses! I have been nothing but loving and supportive of you. But your shit will ruin us. You need to get it under control!" I could tell that was the wrong thing to say as Clay's eyes lit with a sudden anger.

"Nice, just throw my issues in my face, why don't you?! I'm trying, here! Which is more than I can say for you. I think you're just looking for an excuse to get rid of me. Well, I'll make it easy for you. Get the fuck out!" he screamed at me.

"You bastard," I breathed, hardly able to believe he had just said that. After everything we'd been through. After all the times I had shown him how much I loved him. Well, if he wanted to act like a baby, I was getting off this roller coaster.

Clay's eyes flashed at me. I shoved him solidly in the chest. He wasn't expecting it so he stumbled back a bit in surprise. "Fine. To hell with you!" I was out of breath as I shoved past him.

The rage drained from Clay's face and he looked stricken, the realization that I was leaving him sinking in hard and fast. I knew in that moment he hadn't meant what he said, that he was just trying to hurt me. But who does crap like that? I would not stand there and be his whipping post a moment longer.

"Mags, I'm sorry. I don't know what I was saying." He tried to reach out for me and I slapped him. Hard.

His face swung with the force of my assault and a red splotch blossomed on his cheek. He put his hand to his face, stunned by my action.

"You do *not* get to speak to me like that!" I stormed to the bed and yanked off the top blanket, took a pillow, and moved toward the staircase.

Clay followed me. "What are you doing? Maggie, stop! I'm sorry!" he begged me, trying to stop me from leaving.

I swung back around. "I'm sleeping on the couch. I'd rather sleep alone than share a bed with someone who has no respect for me!"

Clay's face crumpled as he tried to grab my arm. "Please, Maggie. I *do* respect you! So much! I was being stupid. I'm just so scared of you leaving me. I guess I push and push just to see if I'm right and that eventually you'll walk away. I say these horrible things just to know if you'll take it. If you'll stick by me no matter what. But I was wrong! I shouldn't treat you like that just to prove some sick, twisted theory in my head. Please, don't leave me! I can't live without you!" That was the closest to honest he had been about his feelings in weeks. But at that moment, it was too little, too late. I was beyond hurt and angry and I just needed some space.

"Then I guess you should have thought about that before treating me like your emotional punching bag, huh?" I left him standing there alone and went downstairs. The house was quiet and I quickly made my nest on the couch. I lay down, trying to calm the rapid beat of my heart. I waited to see if Clay would follow me, but he didn't.

I was relieved but also disappointed by that, which annoyed me beyond reason. His emotional ups and downs were becoming more and more painful. It didn't change the fact that I loved him more than was rational. But when did I stop this constant upheaval and protect myself? I began to sob into my pillow, remembering the way he had looked at me so coldly as he told me to leave. Was this how it was always going to be? Perfect one minute and then screaming and yelling the next? I didn't think I could handle that.

As it was now, I was in a constant state of anxiety. Always waiting for that other shoe to drop.

But thinking about my life without him in it was inconceivable. I couldn't stomach the prospect of my every day without knowing I'd see him. I was between a rock and a hard place. Scared to death of what our relationship was doing to me, but even more terrified to end it. My love for him was a powerful, overwhelming thing. But where did I draw the line?

My nose was stuffy from crying and I wiped the tears from my face. I was so sick of crying. I hated it. So I tried to go to sleep, but my mind wouldn't stop. The house was too quiet and it was driving me nuts. I tossed and turned. As pretty as the couch was, it was not comfortable to sleep on. I finally drifted off around 1:00 in the morning, only to be startled awake an hour later.

"Maggie, please come to bed," Clay coaxed in my ear. I rolled over and saw him kneeling beside me. I turned away again, refusing to speak to him. I was still more than a little angry, and really, really hurt. And if I heard *please, Maggie* one more time I would scream.

I could feel Clay rest his forehead on my back. "I can't sleep. I need to make this right," he begged me. His voice broke and I could hear the rasping that came from him crying. Without realizing I did it, I rolled over to face him. He looked a mess. His hair stood on end as if he had been raking his fingers through it over and over again. His eyes were bloodshot in the glow of the dying fire and he looked horribly pale.

Damn it, I felt myself weakening at the sight of him. I propped myself up on my pillow. "I'm fine here. Just go to bed," I told him, wiping sleep from my eyes.

Clay looked desperate. "No. I won't sleep in that bed without you. I'll stay down here on the couch, too." He went to the other end of the sectional and lay down.

He fidgeted around, having as hard a time as I did getting comfortable. He curled up and fluffed the pillow under his head. After a few minutes I sat up.

"This is ridiculous. Just go upstairs, Clay. You are not sleeping on the couch with me."

Clay looked at me. "I can't be away from you. I know I fucked up. I deserve your anger, but I need you, Maggie. You know that. Everything is so dark without you." I understood that despair in his voice, because it was so close to how I was feeling. I also recognized what he was conveying between the lines. He felt like cutting.

My stomach dropped. "You didn't, did you?" I asked in a horrified whisper.

Clay shook his head. "No, but I wanted to," he admitted. I was relieved that he hadn't hurt himself.

"You were completely out of line, Clay. What you said to me was really hurtful." I could hear myself wavering as the tears started again.

Clay was by my side in an instant. He rubbed the wetness with his thumb. "Don't cry, baby. I can't stand knowing that I've hurt you." I pulled away from him, not ready for him to touch me. He dropped his hands to his sides.

"You can't go all Neanderthal on me. You can't hit me over the head with your club and drag me back to your cave when you get upset at something I do. And stop trying to push me away in some bizarre test of my devotion. Because you *will* push me away, Clay. For good, next time," I threatened.

Clay hung his head in shame. "I know. I am so, so sorry. I can't tell you how much," he whispered as his own tears fell. I was upset. That rigid part of myself didn't want to let this go. I was afraid that if I did, I would be opening a door I couldn't shut.

But as I watched my poor, broken boy cry over hurting me, I felt incredibly torn. I wanted to forgive him in the worst way possible. But I wasn't sure I should.

I gently shoved Clay's shoulders, so that he looked up at me. "Don't you see how messed up this is, Clay?"

He frowned at me. "I know what I did was wrong. I hate myself for it," he said, trying to grab my hand.

I pulled back and refused to let him hold me. "But what if this becomes, I don't know . . . a pattern or something? How you behaved earlier was nuts. I don't have time for your mind fucks," I said harshly, wanting to make my position on this clear.

Clay nodded. "I know that. It was so stupid. I can't excuse my behavior. I have this horrible way of taking my insecure bullshit out on the people I love the most." Clay pushed his hair out of his eyes and looked at me intensely. My stomach flipped over as it always did when he looked at me like that. Like I was the center of his universe.

"And I love you more than anyone. Which means you are the one person I shouldn't be treating like that. But I've told you, I'm insecure, Maggie. Ridiculously insecure," he admitted.

"You're gorgeous, Clay. You could have anyone you wanted. You have nothing to be insecure about," I scoffed, though I knew why he felt the way he did. His mental-health issues made it hard for him to see things as they really were. He lived in this dark world where he had nothing to give anyone but pain. I tried so hard to change the way he saw himself. But I didn't think I could ever do enough.

Clay laughed in a humorless way. "I'm a mess. You know better than anyone everything I've done. I try so hard to change. To make sure that guy never shows himself again. But the struggle is really hard sometimes. And then I meet you. And I feel stuff that I've never felt before. Things that I never thought I would be lucky enough to experience. And I feel so out of control in the way I am with you. Like I'm stripped bare and for once someone sees everything inside of me . . . the good and the really, really ugly." He sounded so vulnerable. I wanted to hug him but I wasn't sure I could bridge the gap just yet.

"I'm afraid that the ugly will scare you away. Because I know I'm high maintenance. That I can't get a handle on the crazy, conflicting shit going on inside of me." He took a deep breath. "But Maggie, I want to try. And I *am* trying. But there are times that I'm reminded of why you are so much better off without me. Seeing you with that guy Jake, Daniel, or any other guy kills me. Because each and every one of them can give you something I can't. Normal." I started to protest the idiocy of that, but he held up his hand.

"I know that there is absolutely nothing going on with you and Daniel, or you and Jake, or you and the fucking mailman. What I'm trying to say is, *who* it was is inconsequential. It's the fact that it could be anyone. That any other guy out there would be a hell of a lot better for you than me."

His eyes were bleak as he looked away from me. His low self-esteem was ridiculous. How could he not see himself the way I did? How could he not understand how full he made my life by just being in it? Sure, what we had was hard and complicated, but it was also passionate and amazing. There would never be anyone in my life that affected me the way he did. I was sure of it.

The thing was, I was petrified that the bad was starting to outweigh the good. What would we be left with when I could no longer make Clay see everything that was wonderful about him and what we had? What happened then? And, just like that, my anger withered away until it was replaced with only sadness.

And that was way harder to stomach.

"I don't know what to say. I don't want you to feel that way. I love you. So much. But I can't make you feel better about yourself, about us. Because that's entirely on you." I lifted my hands in tired defeat.

Clay hung his head. "I'm really trying," he said softly. Sure, it was messed up and there was no way I'd forget about what he had done, but seeing him so depressed tugged at that gnawing nurturing side of me that had developed since meeting Clay.

Maybe I shouldn't forgive him so easily for treating me the way he had. For not trusting me. For doubting my love for him. And maybe I would feel angry about it again later. But now I just wanted to erase that despair from his beautiful face. Despair that was caused by something so much deeper than our argument.

We sat there in silence, the tension palpable. I was wound tight and I didn't know what to do to make any of this better. Before I could come up with a solution, Clay got to his feet.

"I'll leave you alone. I'm sorry, Mags," Clay whispered. I watched him walk away, back toward the staircase, and I said nothing to stop him.

I lay there in the darkness for a while. There was no way I would go back to sleep. I ruminated over our conversation ad nauseam. Clay's neediness was a little hard to swallow. I got that he loved me. But was this a love I could deal with? Was this love going to tear me apart?

I couldn't stop thinking about what he had said about his insecurities and how much he was trying to change. And while I believed him, there was a niggling of doubt. Doubt that he was trying hard enough. And then I had to think that maybe I shouldn't come down so hard on Clay, when I was riddled with my own doubts where he was concerned.

I rolled onto my side and hugged the pillow to my chest. I ached in the worst way. Tonight was supposed to be special. I had dreamed of it for so long. My mind drifted to Clay, who I knew was as wide awake as I was.

Do I go to him? Do I let this whole thing go and try to find some semblance of happiness in what we have together? Or do I take a stand and not back down?

I hemmed and hawed, not sure what to do. I scraped my hair back from my face in agitation. My heart felt heavy and I missed him. I wanted him to hold me and make me believe that everything would be all right. I needed that fantasy, even if it was just that. A fantasy.

Suddenly I was on my feet, with my pillow and blanket under my arm, and found myself walking up the spiral staircase to the loft. My footsteps were soft, barely making a sound as I made my way up to Clay.

I stopped just inside the doorway and stared at him in the murky darkness. I could make out his form under the blankets. I dropped my stuff on the floor and lifted the covers on the bed, sliding in beside him.

Clay turned over and I could see his eyes shining in the blackness. "What are you doing?" he breathed, his body taut beside me.

I rolled onto my side and reached out to stroke his face. "I'm mad at you, all right. I'm mad and hurting." My voice trembled. Clay put his hand on top of mine and pressed it to his cheek.

"Maggie . . ." he began, but I put my fingers over his mouth to stop him.

"Just shut up, okay?" Clay closed his mouth and let me continue. "I'm upset. What you said, how you acted—it wasn't cool. This wasn't the first time you did this to me. But I had hoped you wouldn't do it again. But you did. Part of me wants to pack my stuff and leave. Forget this drama . . . forget you." The tears started to leak from my eyes, but I kept my gaze on him. His breathing became labored and I knew my words were affecting him.

"But I can't do that, Clay. Because I believe that you are trying to change. That you do love me. But you need to know that what happened here earlier . . . that has to stop. I wasn't kidding when I said it would ruin us. What we have, what we feel for each other, is too special to kill that way," I bit out.

Clay shook his head and pulled my hand from his lips. "It will *never* happen again. I swear to you!" he pleaded, pulling on my arms so that I was pressed against him. Our noses brushed and I closed my eyes, resting my forehead on his.

"This night was supposed to be our night. I wanted it to be about us, together. Now I feel mixed up and confused and I just want to stop feeling that way." I recognized the neediness in my tone. I wasn't sure what I was asking him to do. I could see that Clay didn't know, either.

But then I just plunged ahead, without thought of consequences or what it would mean to do this right now after the emotional turmoil of the last few hours. I kissed him, pressing my mouth to his, running my tongue along his bottom lip.

Clay pulled back to stare at me. I knew I was confusing the hell out of him. Damn, I was confusing myself. But I just needed to lose myself in him. To feel that sense of peace that came only when we were close.

I needed to feel his love, not his jealousy or his anger and insecurity.

My body woke up at his close proximity. The physical attraction I felt muddled my brain and made it difficult to think of anything else. I could feel my heart beating against my rib cage and I had a hard time catching my breath as we lay so close together, our legs brushing against each other. Our chests a whisper apart.

I wrapped my hand around the back of his neck and tugged him toward me again. This time he resisted. "I don't know, Maggie. I don't like doing this when it feels like we still have so much to resolve." He sighed as I kissed his chin, nibbling his skin.

"Clay. I know you love me. I love you, too. Let's just forget the drama. Please," I murmured. I wasn't entirely sure what possessed me. But I wanted the conflict to be over. I wanted to see the beautiful sparkle in my boyfriend's eyes. And, yeah, maybe I was using my body to manipulate the situation a bit. But at that moment I didn't care.

I threw myself into kissing him. Into tasting his mouth and his neck. My hands ran up and down his back as I pressed my chest into his. I felt the slow, dizzying warmth of arousal as he kissed me back with equal ardor.

I pulled his shirt over his head and ran my hands down his bare chest, scraping my nails so that he shivered. I pressed kisses to the flesh below his throat, teasing with my tongue.

Slowly, as if he were waiting for me to stop him, Clay lifted the hem of my shirt and brought it over my head. Clay stared at me, his eyes smoldering with desire and an aching tenderness that made my breath hitch.

"You are so beautiful," he whispered, letting his fingers barely brush the soft fabric that still covered my breasts.

Not waiting for him to do it, I reached up and unsnapped my bra, shrugging out of it and throwing it onto the floor. Clay's eyes grew large, and then, with agonizing slowness, he lowered his mouth to my waiting nipples. His tongue danced and teased over me.

In that moment, I realized that despite his hang-ups, despite the crazy drama he created, I would love him always. Clay was mine just as surely as I was his. My life and his were inextricably intertwined and there was no denying the intense connection we shared. I wanted to give everything to him, to make him feel whole, and loved, and worthy.

He pressed me to him, our naked skin melding perfectly as he took my mouth again. His hands caressed my flesh and I thought I would burn up inside.

After a forever of this, I unbuttoned his jeans and released the zipper. Clay hissed in a breath and moaned deep in his throat as I put my hands inside and found him. He groaned into my mouth as I rubbed him with unsure fingers. I didn't really know what I was doing but, given his reaction, I must have been doing it right. My hand slid up and down the length of him, feeling him shudder beneath my grip.

"My God, Maggie!" he moaned into my mouth as my hand's movements became more confident. I smiled against his lips as his hands palmed my breasts, the pad of his thumbs running over my nipples roughly, making me shiver.

Clay pulled my hand from his hot flesh and grinned at me. "You need to stop doing that, or we'll be done before we've even started." He began to unbutton my pants. With deft fingers, Clay peeled my jeans back and pushed them down to my ankles, leaving me only in my panties. He rolled on top of me, the feel of his weight sending delightful shivers throughout my body. He rubbed his hand down my side, sliding down to kiss my stomach, my inner thighs, my breasts, and then my mouth again.

"You are the most gorgeous woman I have ever seen. I love you so much." His words were quiet as he adored me with his mouth.

I flushed with the compliment. "I love you too, Clay." I gripped his hair as he traced a line upward from my knee with his tongue. I swallowed hard as I waited for him to kiss me . . . you know, there. And I was really disappointed when he stopped and suddenly leaned over me.

"Are you sure you want this?" he asked me. He seemed unsure, though I could feel how much he wanted me as his body pressed against mine. I initially wanted to grab hold of his hair and shove him back between my thighs. I was about to get primal, as the intense waves of euphoria brought on by his fingers and tongue cascaded over me. But then I sobered a bit and really thought about what he was asking me.

Was this really the right time to make this leap into intimacy? After everything that had happened this evening? I stared into his brown eyes and the unbelievable depth of emotion I saw there made my heart pitter-patter.

I wanted to do this. Okay, so maybe I couldn't exactly think beyond the throbbing between my legs. The aching in my body took away any hesitancy I might otherwise feel. So, in that instant, my decision was made.

"Make love to me, Clay," I whispered, dipping my hands back into his boxers and sliding them down his hips.

He didn't need any more encouragement after that. He hooked my panties with his thumbs and drew them down, pulling them over my feet and dropping them on the floor. We were naked and I was suddenly exceptionally nervous.

Clay, sensing this, kissed the sensitive skin behind my ear, while his hand caressed the warmth between my legs. I gasped as he slid a finger inside me. The tingles of pleasure coursed through me again as he rubbed, moving his finger in and out in a perfect rhythm. I forgot to worry about my inexperience. I just let myself flow along with this tidal wave that threatened to take me under.

Finally, Clay reached over and pulled a condom out of his bag. He tore open the package and slipped it on, positioning himself at my opening. He put his hands beneath my knees and drew my legs up so they were wrapped around his waist. He kissed me deeply again and I could feel him pressed against me, waiting.

"Maggie," he said huskily. I opened my eyes and looked at him.

"I love you." He swallowed and pushed himself into me. My breath hitched at the sharp pain. "Forever," he choked as he surged forward.

I arched my back off the bed, my muscles straining and stretching to fit around him. Clay sucked in a sharp breath with the sudden sensations. He was still a moment. He looked down at me.

"Are you okay?" he asked, kissing my eyebrow, my cheek, my nose. I nodded, squeezing my legs around his hips, pulling him deeper inside me.

And then he started moving and I thought I would die from the pleasure of it. I could feel him sliding in and out of my body and it was the single most intense experience of my life. I began to move with him in a sensual dance.

Clay surged over and over again, each thrust taking him deeper into my body. His hands touched me everywhere. I was acutely aware of the way our breaths mingled as he stroked the innermost part of me. The feel of his hips beneath my thighs. The stubble on his chin as he kissed me.

I threw my head back and Clay suckled my neck, making noises in the back of his throat as his movements became more frenzied. I felt a strange searing heat build in the pit of my belly. I dug my fingers into his shoulder blades and he yelled my name as we exploded together.

Clay collapsed on my chest, his sweat-slicked hair sticking to my skin. I smoothed the strands back from his forehead. Clay kissed the hollow of my throat, his lips lingering on the frantic pulse that beat there. We didn't speak, each of us too spent, too emotional. I felt tears prick my eyes and I was completely overwhelmed by what we had just shared.

Clay would always be a part of me now. No one could ever replace this first time for me and, despite everything, I was so glad it had been with him. He traced his fingertips over my stomach, tickling it and making me giggle. He pulled out of me slowly and went to the bathroom.

I pulled the sheet up under my chin, suddenly feeling shy about lying there without anything on. Clay came back, clearly not as modest. He smiled at me. He gently pulled the sheet away.

"Don't cover yourself, baby. You're amazing." He lay down beside me, pulling me against his front.

We lay together, entangled. He nuzzled my hair. "This is what I wanted, Mags. To fall asleep holding you. I don't know what I would have done if you hadn't forgiven me. I am so, so sorry." I snuggled as close to him as I could get. Clay pulled the blankets over us and I felt warm and safe in our cocoon, our earlier fight not forgotten, but less pertinent.

My eyelids began to droop and just as I was about to fall off to sleep, Clay whispered in my ear. "This is forever, Maggie. I would follow you into hell if I had to." His breath tickled my skin. He kissed my temple. "You are all I want for the rest of my life."

I was so tired that I couldn't be sure I'd heard him correctly. But I knew his love was an intense, hungry thing. I worried for a moment, as I fell asleep, that his love would eat me alive.

chapter
seventeen

I woke up the next morning, blinking in the pale morning light. It was still early; I could tell by the lingering darkness that clung to the corners of the room and the edges of the sky. Clay was wrapped tightly around me and I could barely move. His face was buried in the back of my neck and his arms pinned me to his side. I felt hot and sweaty from the warmth of his body.

I needed to go to the bathroom. Badly. I tried to wriggle out from underneath him, but that only caused him to tighten his hold on me. Okay, I was starting to feel claustrophobic. I lay there until I felt his hold slacken, and I slowly lifted his arm from around my chest and placed it gently beside him.

I was then able to disengage my legs from his and roll out of the bed. I landed on my feet, feeling like a gymnast with the crazy maneuvers I'd had to use. I looked over at Clay and saw that he was still asleep. I tiptoed behind the Japanese screen and tried to pee as quietly as possible. I wasn't entirely comfortable relieving myself with him so close by. There were just some things I wasn't ready to share with him.

I quickly brushed my teeth and pulled my hair back into a ponytail. I looked in the mirror over the sink and stared at myself. I didn't look any different, but my body *felt* different. I could feel soreness when I moved certain muscles I had never used before. I felt more like a woman and less like a little girl.

I thought back to the previous night. Staring at my reflection in the mirror, I wondered whether I had made the right decision. It had all seemed to make sense in the moment. The fight had been a distant memory. But now, in the cold light of morning, I was reminded of how awful things had gotten. Had I rushed into sex to attempt to block out how much he had hurt me?

Shaking my head, I tried to ignore the nagging concerns that threatened to ruin my good mood.

I found a clean pair of underwear and put them on and then slipped into my favorite pair of yoga pants and a white cami. I looked outside and was taken aback by all the white stuff.

It had probably snowed five inches during the night and it was beautiful. But I hoped we could get out of here today, or I would have some major explaining to do to my parents. I cringed even thinking about it.

I heard Clay stirring in the bed and I looked over my shoulder. He blinked sleepily. "Come back to bed, baby. I'm missing you." His voice was raspy and I smiled at how amazing he looked first thing in the morning.

I crossed the room slowly, feeling strangely shy with him. I crawled back into bed, not knowing what to do. Things were different now, on so many levels. Clay smiled at me. "I like waking up with you," he said huskily, watching me with sleepy eyes.

My insides clenched as his fingers inched toward me and gently rubbed my arm. "What's wrong?" he asked me. I rolled my head to the side to look at him. He seemed more awake and I could see the worry on his face.

"Do you regret it?" he asked, the horror evident in his tone.

Did I regret it? His fingers stopped their dance on my skin and I looked at my boyfriend. His love for me was startlingly clear and I could see how much the idea of my regretting our intimacy would crush him.

I couldn't tell him that I was worried that I had simply swept our bigger problems under the rug. That we weren't really addressing his ongoing issues. For all our closeness, there was still so much that he kept from me. Things that I didn't feel comfortable voicing *to him*. What did that really say about our relationship?

"Maggie," he breathed, scooting closer. He laid his arm across my stomach. His face was close to mine. I could feel his breath on my cheek. I realized I had been silent for quite a while. But damn if my body didn't start to heat up as his fingers went under my shirt to rest against my bare skin.

Did I regret it? I closed my eyes as he rubbed his nose against my cheek.

No. I didn't. Because even with all of our shit, I still loved him. More than I probably should.

"No, Clay. I could never regret being with you," I told him truthfully. As if taking that as an invitation, Clay rolled on top of me and kissed my chin. I couldn't help but laugh at the sudden change in him. From sad and worried to delighted and giddy in the span of seconds.

"You were scaring me, love," he murmured as he nipped at my bottom lip. I ran my hands up his back, enjoying the feel of his flesh beneath my fingers.

"You don't ever need to be scared of little ol' me," I joked as I wrapped my legs around his hips. I was instantly aware of the fact that he was still very naked. And *very* happy to see me.

Clay pulled back. "You scare me more than anything," he told me quietly, looking into my eyes in that intense way of his, as if I were the air that he breathed. "If you leave me, I would be destroyed. I don't know that I could come back from that." His vulnerability broke my heart. How could needing me this much be good for him?

Suddenly, Clay leaned over the side of the bed and started rooting around in his duffel bag. After a few seconds, he righted himself and held his hand firmly fisted before me. He looked a little shy, his hair flopping in his eyes as he looked at me.

"What do you have there?" I teased, trying to pry his fingers apart. Clay smiled endearingly and pulled back, falling onto his side beside me. He leaned up on his elbow, his hand cradling his head as he looked down at me. Slowly, he opened his hand and dropped a silver chain into a shimmery puddle on my stomach.

I sat up and scooped the piece of jewelry into my hand before it got lost in the sheets. It was a necklace. The delicate silver chain fell between my fingers as I held it up. Hanging from it was a beautiful butterfly, made of thin silver and tiny slivers of what looked like diamonds.

It was the most amazing thing I had ever seen. My breath stopped as I stared at it. I looked at Clay, who was watching me nervously.

"I wanted to give this to you last night. I had planned to, anyway. But then after everything that happened, I just didn't feel like it was the right time."

I swallowed thickly around the lump that had formed in my throat. I didn't say anything; I was too overcome with the depth of emotion I had for the boy lying beside me. Taking my silence as disapproval, Clay continued on quickly. "I've had it for a while, actually. I had it made for you by this lady Ruby knows who makes her own jewelry."

His thoughtfulness overwhelmed me. What was it about the butterflies? He had said once that it was because I made him feel free. Wanting more of an answer, I asked him.

"I was this sad and lonely creature before you came along. And then, just being with you, knowing you love me, has transformed me. My entire life has become this metamorphosis into something beautiful, something happy. I told you before that you've freed me. You've reminded me of what it means to *believe* and *hope*."

Tears gathered in my eyes and threatened to spill. Seeing this, Clay rubbed his thumb beneath my eyes, gathering the wetness there.

"Don't cry. I'm sorry if it upset you. I just wanted to give you something as beautiful as everything you've given me. I'll take it back. Forget about it," he said, totally misreading my silence. I could hear the hurt in his voice as he tried to take the necklace from my hand.

I closed my fingers and moved it away. "No, Clay. I love it. I'm just . . . I don't know what to . . ." Words failed me completely, so instead I seized his mouth with mine, kissing him deeply. I let my tongue invade his mouth, tasting him. I couldn't stop the moan that I made deep in my throat.

"God, I love you so much," Clay whispered against my lips as I ran my fingers up through his hair.

"I love you too. More than anything," I said softly back to him as he tugged my tank top over my head. And we lost ourselves in each other all over again.

It felt like hours later that we finally emerged from the loft, Clay's necklace lying against my chest. Clay wore a contented smile and I knew I was glowing. I was riding a blissful wave of euphoria. Our earlier argument, all the misunderstandings and doubts, had been erased by the reminder of why I was so intensely in love with my boyfriend. Clay watched me touch the butterfly at my throat and he gave me that smile that said I was the only thing in his world that mattered.

"Good morning," I said to Ray and Clare, who were drinking coffee and looking a little bleary eyed.

"Too loud, Maggie. Shh." Ray put his finger to his lips.

"Oops, sorry," I apologized, filling a mug for myself.

"You guys look rough," Clay commented, opening a packet of croissants.

Clare grimaced. "Thanks, Clay."

He looked sheepish. "I just meant you don't look like you slept much."

Clare became irritated. "Well, my charming boyfriend, here, spent most of the night throwing up."

"Yuck. Sorry, Clare." I gave Ray a look before turning to the refrigerator to get the milk for my coffee. "Are Daniel and Rachel up yet?" I asked.

Ray shook his head. "Don't think so, haven't seen them."

I was worried about how things went between my two best friends last night. I was dying to talk to Rachel and get the scoop.

Clay came up behind me and wrapped his arms around my waist, placing a soft kiss on the side of my neck. He pushed a plate of buttered pastries toward me. I picked one up and started eating it.

Ray watched me for a moment, then turned an alarming shade of green. "I'm gonna be sick," he said, before running down the hallway.

Clare sighed before getting off of her stool to go after him. Clay and I grinned. "Sucks to be them," Clay remarked, turning me around in his arms so he could kiss me properly. He pressed my back into the island as his hands held my hips tightly.

Someone cleared their throat behind us, causing me to break away. Looking over my shoulder, I saw Rachel and Daniel come into the kitchen.

"Good morning, you two," I said, pulling away from Clay so I could get my friends some coffee.

I watched the two of them closely, trying to gauge the current state of their relationship. They didn't touch or do anything else that indicated a change in the way things were between them. But

I just knew. There was a difference in the way they looked at each other. The air around them seemed to crackle with an electricity that I had never noticed before.

I handed Rachel a cup of coffee and raised my eyebrows at her. She looked back at me blandly. "So, how was the rest of your night?" I asked them pointedly.

Daniel propped himself up on a stool and grabbed a croissant. "Fine. Slept like a brick" was all he said.

I looked over at Clay, but he had gone into the other room to straighten up the couch from the night before. Okay, I was going to have to get Rachel alone if I was going to get any answers. "I've got to finish packing up my stuff. Rachel, can you come with?" I asked, pulling her by the arm.

Daniel looked over at her for just a moment and it was then that I saw it. The way his gaze rested on Rachel told me everything I needed to know. They had clearly moved through their impasse. And I wanted details!

"I guess," Rachel said less than enthusiastically. She must have sensed my inner cobra preparing to strike. I led the way up the stairs and I heard Rachel's gasp as she came into the gigantic room. "This is where you slept? Dear Jesus," she said, taking it in.

She walked down the stairs into the sunken area with the whirlpool. "I'm feeling a bit gypped," she joked, before sitting on the edge of the tub. She looked at me and arched her eyebrows.

"Hmm. There's something different about you," she told me coyly.

I blushed a deep and furious red. Crap. She was so going to turn this whole chitchat around on me. Damn her! Rachel tapped her chin with her finger thoughtfully.

"Yes, something is definitely different. But I can't quite put my finger on it." Rachel cocked her head to the side and then grinned at me deviously.

"You and Clay totally did it!" Rachel squealed.

I rolled my eyes, trying to hide my embarrassment. "Uh, yeah," I said. My face was on fire! Of course I wanted to share that important piece of information with my best friend. But I felt a little strange talking about it.

"And . . . how was it?" she prompted. Rachel was notorious for needing the dirty details and I fully intended to disappoint her.

"Well, he had me hanging naked from the rafters for a little while . . . and then I decided to use the end of my hairbrush and . . ."

"You're so ridiculous, Maggie," Rachel retorted as she cut me off. She pinched my arm. "You aren't going to tell me anything, are you?" My friend knew me too well.

I shook my head. "Not a thing." I grinned, crossing my arms over my chest.

Turning the conversation around, I gave her a look. "So, you and Daniel . . ." I trailed off, hoping she'd fill in the blanks.

Rachel flushed red and turned away from me, which surprised me. Rachel wasn't one to skimp on information, so her sudden hesitancy to talk threw me. "What happened last night? Did you guys talk?"

Rachel covered her face with her hands and groaned. "Ugh. I don't know. I guess we worked through some things. We talked," she said through her fingers.

I reached out and pulled her hands down. "Why are you so embarrassed? That's not like you. I mean, is everything okay?" I asked, getting a little worried.

And then I saw the huge grin spread across Rachel's face and I relaxed. She closed her eyes a moment and touched my arm. "We're more than okay." Well, that was good. But she still wasn't explaining much. Rachel must have seen the frustration on my face, because she suddenly laughed.

"Annoying, isn't it? Wanting to know something and your best friend not giving an inch?" She raised her eyebrows at me knowingly.

"Yeah, yeah. I get your point. Now, just spill it already before I have a litter of kittens, here." I smacked her hand playfully.

Rachel flopped back on the bed, pulling me down with her so that we lay side by side. She stared up at the vaulted ceiling for a minute before finally answering me. "Well, I was pissed. No, I take that back. I was bordering on a murderous rage when Daniel came in after talking to you." I snorted, knowing how true her words were. No one could do vengefully angry like Rachel.

"And . . ." I said, prodding her.

"And . . . he apologized and I yelled at him some more and he apologized again. And somewhere in the middle of all that he kissed me." I sat up and looked down at my friend, questioning whether I'd heard her right. I wasn't expecting Daniel to take that plunge. At least not yet.

"He kissed you? For real?" I asked her, still in disbelief.

Rachel nodded. "Yeah. And it was beautiful, all right? I know what you're thinking, that I'll just get hurt. And I told him as much. But we sort of hashed everything out."

"Including where Kylie fits into this happy little picture?" I asked, a little more harshly than I meant to. I was just worried that Daniel would hurt Rachel and then our threesome would be irrevocably damaged. But I had wanted this. Had wanted them to get their acts together and acknowledge that there was more than friendship between them. But now that it was finally happening, I was scared of the change. And selfishly I worried about what all of this meant for me.

Rachel looked momentarily hurt by the mention of Danny's ex. "Yeah. We talked about Kylie. And Daniel admitted she has been more of a bad habit he just hasn't been able to shake. But that he wants to give us a try. And, in spite of all the doubts and worries I have, I want that, too."

I flopped back down beside Rachel and took her hand in mine. "If he hurts you, Rachel, I will rip off his nut sack and shove it in his ear. I love him, I really, really do. But us girls need to stick together," I swore to her as she laughed.

"He knows that, Maggie. Trust me. Your reaction was a source of some serious angst on his part last night." I snorted at that, knowing that Daniel would be freaking out over how I would take all of this. Fine, let him sweat.

"Well, as long as it's what you want. Just try not to let your friendship become collateral damage. Promise me that," I implored, squeezing her hand.

Rachel rolled her head to the side so she was looking at me. "I promise. I won't let that happen."

Promises were easy to make but even easier to break, I thought as we lay there silently together.

We were still like that when Clay came into the room. He saw us and started to back out. "Sorry. I was just seeing what was taking you so long. But if you're still talking, I'll give you some space."

Rachel sat up and got to her feet. "No, Clay. You're fine. Thanks, Maggie." She leaned over and gave me a loud kiss on the cheek.

She gave Clay a grin before disappearing down the stairs. Clay came over and kissed me, sitting down on the bed beside me. "Was everything okay?" he asked, putting his arm around me, pulling me up against his side.

I snuggled close, burying my nose in the soft fabric of his shirt, and spent a few seconds just enjoying the scent of him. "She's great. I guess she and Daniel finally got their crap together," I told him as he rested his chin on the top of my head.

"That's great" was all he said, leaning down to kiss the skin behind my ear. I felt heat erupt inside of me and I let out a tiny sigh.

"I wish we could stay here. You know, in our own little bubble," I said mournfully as Clay placed small, shiver-inducing kisses on the underside of my jaw.

He nuzzled my neck as he spoke. I could feel his warm breath on my skin and the tickle of his lips.

"We'll just have to move the bubble back to Davidson, is all," Clay said confidently.

"But bubbles have a nasty way of popping." I was being really gloomy, but I couldn't help it. Nothing good ever lasted.

"Then we'll just make a new bubble," Clay murmured as he pulled me into another mind-blowing kiss. And I let my pessimistic thoughts go as I thought that my forever was starting right now.

chapter
eighteen

but I was right. The bubble did pop, and it was loud and painful. It started with my epic grounding, courtesy of some very pissed-off parents. I was so deliriously happy over my night with Clay that I was oblivious to the twenty-some texts I had received over the past twenty-four hours from my mom and dad.

Turns out my mom had called Rachel's house looking for me when I hadn't returned her phone calls or texts. She wanted to confer with me on pancake recipes or something equally asinine. Of course, I wasn't there. And Ms. Bradfield (whom Rachel had, to my annoyance, told the truth to) filled her in on our lovely evening away in the woods. To say my parents were angry was an understatement. I'm surprised I lived through the epic screaming that followed my arrival home.

My father confined me to my room until Monday morning, allowing me to leave it only to use the bathroom and to eat. I was grounded for a month, and I was not allowed, under any condition, to see Clay outside of school.

Of course, they blamed him almost entirely for encouraging

me to lie to them and to go away overnight with him. (The fact that my friends were also there was inconsequential to them.) Even when I—very maturely, I might add—tried to take responsibility for my choices, my parents insisted on viewing Clay as the villain.

I was able to send Clay a few quick texts before they confiscated my phone.

Busted. Grounded until I'm fifty. Love you.

I received his reply less than thirty seconds later. *I'm so sorry, baby. Any way I can bust you out of Alcatraz? Should I send a file in a cake through your bedroom window? :-) I love you!*

I smiled and furiously typed back, trying to be sneaky so my parents didn't flip again.

I'll see you tomorrow. I'll meet you at school. Dad will be driving me. No file necessary, though I may be forced to resort to cyanide tablets from the sheer boredom.

I quickly turned off my cell. My dad took the phone, unhooked the Internet in my room, and confiscated my car keys. Yep, I was a prisoner. And I was also receiving the silent treatment. My mother barely acknowledged my presence and my father just shot me looks of hurt and disappointment. Disappointment was a hundred times worse.

They were champions of the guilt trip. So I sat in my room all of Sunday evening, alternating between catching up on my homework and staring blankly at my wall. And all I could think about was the night before and everything that had happened between Clay and me.

I hadn't taken off the butterfly necklace he had given me. I felt it lying warmly above my breasts. It was almost like having his fingers touch me. I was still so blown away by his thoughtfulness. And the words he had said to me, the way he had opened up and revealed things about himself that were painful, only made me love him more.

I tried not to let the memories of our earlier fight taint our night together. But no matter how much I pushed them away, they simply bounced back, bringing with them the recollection of his anger and my hurt.

But, despite the painful start, the night had ended in the most romantic and toe-curling way possible. I hugged my pillow to my chest and let the delicious memories of us together fill me. I shivered as I remembered his hands touching me and the feel of him as he sank inside me. I rolled onto my back and groaned. Hell if I knew when we'd have a chance to be together intimately again. I might be under lock and key until I started collecting Social Security.

I thought about Clay whispering how much he loved me and how he wanted to be with me forever. And I, in my naive, young-adult mind, thought it would happen. That of course Clay and I could overcome anything and we would walk off together into the sunset.

I ignored the nagging voice in my head that whispered doubts and concern over Clay's intense need to be with me. How he used me as a bandage for all his other problems. I pushed aside the annoying realization that *perhaps* that wasn't a healthy way to be . . . that I *couldn't* make everything better for him, as much as he told me that I was all he needed.

Instead, I focused on my memories of making love to him and holding him the entire night. Of feeling safe and secure as his arms wrapped around me, purposely ignoring any and all thoughts of what had occurred *before* that. The point was that I couldn't imagine *ever* loving someone the way I loved him. And I swore I never would.

◆

"Wow, grounded with no cell phone or car! You might as well be dead, Mags," Rachel said sympathetically as we sat around the lunch table commiserating over my horrible fate the following day. Clay squeezed my hand tightly, pressing close to my side. It felt like a week since I had last seen him, when it had been less than a day.

I turned my head and met his mouth, kissing him deeply, not caring who saw it. Pulling my lips from Clay's with a groan that made him smile, I returned my attention to Rachel . . . who was sitting closer to Daniel than usual. Daniel, when he thought no one was looking, would lightly rub her back and then drop his hand to his side. I hadn't had a chance to talk to Daniel about everything (you know, with the whole grounded-until-I-die thing), but you'd have had to be blind not to see the change in their relationship. I couldn't help but smile at them, feeling happy for my two best friends.

"I know. But they went nuclear." I crunched on my carrot stick. Clay rested his hand on my lower back.

"We'll find a way around it. Maybe I should start sneaking into your room after your parents go to bed," Clay teased—although, looking into his eyes, I knew he was being serious.

"I thought you hated heights," I reminded him, lightly pinching his leg.

Clay shrugged. "If that's what it takes to see you alone, then I'd climb Mount fucking Everest." I appreciated the sentiment. I really did. But I knew that his doing something like that, given the precarious state of my relationship with my parents, could spell only disaster.

"Yeah, I don't think you sneaking into my bedroom is the greatest idea," I said, trying to dissuade him.

Clay frowned at me. "Well, if you don't want me to come over, then I won't bother." His mercurial mood changed in an instant and he turned away from me, pulling his arm from my waist, and started eating his lunch.

Rachel cocked her eyebrow at him, and then looked at me. I rolled my eyes, trying to make light of it, though I hated when he did this—when he would become upset or angry and then shut down. I watched Clay out of the corner of my eye and saw he was doing just that. His body was stiff and he wouldn't make eye contact with anyone. Rachel and Daniel talked quietly to each other, making a point to ignore the scene that was brewing between Clay and me.

I couldn't take this stupid wall that had suddenly gone up between us, so I scooted over to him on the bench and put my hand on his upper thigh. I leaned in and rubbed my nose on his chin.

"Don't be like that, Clay. Please," I whispered. I felt him pull away slightly, but I didn't give up. "You know I want to be with you all the time," I insisted, kissing the corner of his downturned mouth.

I felt him soften and he covered my hand with his. "I just can't take not seeing you or talking to you at night. I need you," he told me urgently. His eyes met mine.

"We'll figure something out. I need you, too," I reassured him, kissing him gently.

That seemed to settle him down and I could feel his body relax beside mine. "I told my parents I was staying after school so I could get some extra help in chemistry. Why don't I blow off my study group and we go to your house?" I suggested, kissing him again.

Clay put his hands on my face, rubbing his nose with mine in a way that made my heart melt. I saw his eyes smolder as he contemplated what I was suggesting. "Mmmm. I like that idea," he murmured, wrapping his arms around me again and pressing his face into my hair.

At that moment the assistant principal, Mr. Kane, decided to make an appearance. "Enough, you two. We have school rules about PDA. Do you need to come down to the office to review them?" He crossed his hairy arms over his chest and looked stern.

Clay and I broke apart as I gathered my messenger bag and tray. Last thing I needed was for Mr. Kane to call my parents because I couldn't keep my hands off my boyfriend at school. That would make them love Clay even more.

"No, sir. We're sorry," I stuttered, unable to look at the administrator. I could hear Daniel and Rachel trying to keep from laughing as Mr. Kane walked away, off to find other teens to terrorize.

"Well, that was just freaking great." I got up and went to dump my tray, my face stinging with mortification. Clay came up behind me.

"Don't get so worked up, Mags. What's the big deal?" Clay was laughing and it irritated the hell out of me.

"Well, I don't like getting called out by the assistant principal for making out with my boyfriend, all right? It's embarrassing. I don't need to give my parents any more ammunition right now." Clay tried to grab me by the waist to pull me close again.

I shoved him back. "Stop it, Clay. Give it a rest. I don't want to get into trouble."

Clay's face turned dark. "Fine. I'll see you after school." And, with that, he turned and left the cafeteria. I sighed and didn't bother to call after him, feeling sapped of all my energy.

Clay was at my locker after school, wearing an expression of contrition that I was becoming all too familiar with. "I'm sorry," he said, as I opened my locker to drop off my books. I wanted to bang my head into the wall. I was so sick of hearing *I'm sorry*!

I took a deep breath. "Do you ever get tired of apologizing?" I asked Clay coldly.

Clay frowned. "What's that supposed to mean? I just wanted you to know that I understand I was a dick and that I'm sorry, because I love you. Why do you have to be so dramatic about it?" he asked me with obvious irritation.

I barked out a laugh and slammed my locker door shut. "Me,

dramatic? From you, that's rich," I huffed, starting down the hall-way.

Clay caught up with me and grabbed my arm, pulling me to a stop. "Are you seriously that pissed? I mean, I get that I was kind of an asshole, but I don't think it warrants this sort of reaction." Wow, he really didn't get how our relationship, even as much as I wanted to deny it, was falling into this crazy pattern of him being a jerk and then apologizing for it. Of me getting upset but then relieved when he came around.

"Don't you see that fifty percent of our interactions have become you spouting your apologies for something you've said or done? That we spend most of our time upset at each other? This is getting ridiculous."

Clay tugged on my hand and wrapped his arms around my stiff body. "I know, baby. But I'm trying. I really am. Please be patient with me," he urged, leaning down to place his lips on mine. I wanted to tell him that "trying" was quickly becoming not good enough. That I was emotionally spent and I wanted us to get back to being that boy and girl who swam in the river together.

But I could feel the desperation in his embrace, in his sadness-tinged kiss. I knew he loved me. And I wanted so badly for that to be all that I needed to be happy.

"Can we go to my house? I think we need some time alone. Just the two of us. With everything going on, we're both stressed out," Clay said. I felt myself weaken and cave to him.

"Yeah. Let's go." Clay gave me the most dazzling smile and lifted me off my feet and swung me around.

"I have the most beautiful and amazing girlfriend *ever!*" he yelled, as he covered my face with kisses after putting me back on the ground. I hid my face in embarrassment at his display of affection. I could feel Clay's laughter under my cheek as he led me to his car.

As I got in, I had a moment of guilt that here I was again, lying to my parents. However, as Clay leaned over and kissed me lovingly on the mouth, warmth settled into my belly, ensuring those feelings were fleeting.

Clay peeled out of the parking lot, his tires screeching in his hurry to get away from the school. "Slow down, Clay, or we'll never make it to your house."

Clay grinned his crazy, happy smile and reached over to take my hand. He kissed my fingers, one at a time, as he came to a stoplight.

"I love you, Maggie."

I smiled. I couldn't help but forget everything else when he said those words to me.

I ducked down in the seat as we passed the library where my father worked. Clay just laughed at me again, telling me how silly I was being. "Yeah, well, if I want to see the light of day, I can't let them catch me with you, okay?" I grumbled.

That sobered Clay. "They hate me that much?" He sounded gutted and I instantly felt horrible for not choosing my words more carefully.

"It's not that they hate you; they just worry we're too serious. That I'm spending too much time with you," I said.

Clay gave me a smirk. "That we're having sex?" he asked.

I smacked his arm. "Well, obviously their concerns are founded in that department, huh?" I joked. Clay pulled into his driveway and cut off the engine. And, just like that, he was over the center console and kissing me like mad.

"Clay! Don't you think we should go inside?" I laughed as his hands started up my shirt. Clay moaned something unintelligible. "Clay! Come on, you have neighbors," I gasped as his fingers found my breasts and began gently rubbing them.

He kissed me again and pulled away with a sexy smile. "Well, come on, then." He jumped out of the car. I smiled back, shaking my head as I got out. Clay wrapped himself around me again as we started walking toward his front door.

It was then that I noticed the black Mercedes parked on the street in front of the house. I stopped walking. Clay looked at me in confusion. "What?"

I pointed to the car. "It looks like you have a visitor."

The blood left his face and he looked like he was going to throw up. His teeth clenched. "You have got to be fucking kidding me," he growled. His sudden and extreme anger scared me.

I grabbed his arm. "What is it, Clay? Whose car is that?"

Clay didn't respond and just started walking toward the front door, fury evident in his every step. I had to hurry to catch up with him. I wrenched his hand before he could go inside.

"You're freaking me out, Clay. Who's here?" I could hear the trembling in my voice as I tried to reach the boy who had suddenly disappeared inside himself.

He wouldn't look at me, his body rigid. "I guess you're going to get to meet my parents," he said coldly. I felt like I had been plunged into ice water. His parents? Oh, shit. Clay swung open the front door and let it slam back against the wall.

I stood on the front stoop, not knowing what to do. He was seething with anger and I wasn't sure I wanted to witness whatever was about to go down. But I couldn't leave him. He needed me now more than ever. So I tentatively walked into the house.

I was relieved when Lisa came from the living room and gave Clay a stern look. "Don't you come into this house like an elephant. Close the door like you have some sense." She looked at me. I knew I was pale and she must have sensed the tension radiating from Clay. "Hey, Maggie. Nice to see you." Her smile was kind and I tried to give one back. I'm sure it was shaky.

Clay slammed the door shut and dropped his book bag. "So, where are they?" he barked.

Lisa frowned. "Get it together, Clay. They just got here thirty minutes ago. Ruby ran out to get some stuff for dinner." Clay turned his angry gaze on Lisa, who didn't flinch but stood steady. I would have withered under that glare.

"Did you know they were coming?" he demanded accusingly.

Lisa put her finger in his chest. "Now, look here, Clayton Reed. Don't give me your damn attitude. Their visit was as much a surprise to Ruby and me as it is to you. But don't go in there like a bull in a china shop. Like it or not, they're still your parents and they have a say in what happens to you. Remember that."

Her warning was rational, but Clay was a bit beyond rational at this point. Lisa looked at me to help her. I tried taking Clay's hand again. He let me interlace my fingers with his, but he didn't squeeze mine back.

"Clay. Come on. Acting like this will only make things worse. Please." I moved so that I stood in front of him and pulled his face down to look at me.

His eyes darted around so they wouldn't make contact with mine. "Damn it, Clay!" I implored.

Finally, he looked at me and he softened as he saw my worry. "Christ! I'm doing it again. I'm sorry," he whispered and I was glad to see some of the tension leave his shoulders. But he still looked mad.

"Well, let's go see Mommy and Daddy Dearest," he said sarcastically. Lisa nodded and stepped aside as we started down the hallway. She didn't follow, apparently wanting to give Clay some privacy. I stood beside him, trying to show him my support.

It was eerily quiet. Walking into the kitchen, I got my first look at Mr. and Mrs. Reed. Mr. Reed sat at the small kitchen table, typing away on his laptop. He was dressed casually in black slacks and a blue button-down shirt, although his clothes probably cost more than my entire wardrobe.

Clay was the spitting image of his father. Looking at Mr. Reed was like getting a glimpse of Clay thirty years into the future. Mr. Reed was a good-looking man, with dark hair dusted with gray. The skin around his eyes was just now starting to show signs of crow's-feet. He appeared very stiff, his face a complete blank as he read the screen in front of him.

Clay's mother was trying to work the ancient coffeemaker on the counter. She was decked out in a gray pencil skirt, ruffled blouse, and heels. Her red hair, the exact same shade as that of her sister, Ruby, was swept back from her face in a severe bun.

Clay cleared his throat. His dad didn't acknowledge him, but his mother turned to look, with what seemed to be a fake smile on her perfect lips. Her eyes were a bright blue and icy cold.

"Well, there's my baby boy," she cooed, but made no move to hug or kiss him. Clay's eyes were fixed on his father, who still hadn't looked up from his computer.

God, Clay had been right when he described them as cold and loveless. I couldn't imagine growing up with this couple as my parents. And I felt the guilt again as I thought of my own warm and loving mother and father who, in all of their overprotectiveness, just wanted what was best for me.

"Coffee?" Mrs. Reed asked, after finding the filters and grounds.

Clay and I shook our heads. "Why are you here?" Clay demanded, getting straight to the point. I cringed, not feeling comfortable being privy to this familial exchange. His fingers clenched mine so tightly they were cutting off my circulation.

"We wanted to see you, Clay. To make sure everything was the way it should be," his mother said frostily. Her eyes moved to our joined hands and she looked me over appraisingly.

"And this is . . . ?" Mrs. Reed looked at me pointedly.

Clay stood up straight. "This is my girlfriend, Maggie Young," he told her, his voice hard. I stuck my free hand out in an attempt at civility, though Mrs. Reed had made no such motion toward me.

"Nice to meet you, Mrs. Reed."

She looked down at my outstretched hand and then back at my face. She looked at me with suspicion for a moment, but the expression vanished and was replaced with her practiced fake politeness.

She took my hand in hers and gave it a firm shake. "And you, Maggie. This is Clayton's father, Nicholas. Nick, say hello," she commanded, as if her husband were a child.

Nick Reed finally lifted his eyes from his laptop. His gaze slid over me, head to toe, as if assessing a horse, never making eye contact, then returning to his work.

"Hello," he said without interest. Clay stiffened beside me at his father's rudeness.

This was becoming increasingly awkward as the silence stretched on. "Girlfriend? Well, isn't that . . . nice," Mrs. Reed commented, though her tone registered distaste.

"So, you're just stopping by, right? I mean, you can see everything's *fine* here," Clay said. He was becoming increasingly more agitated, if that was possible. I squeezed his hand to try to help him calm down.

His mother looked at him, making it clear that she didn't believe his assertion that everything was okay. "*Is* everything fine, Clayton? I think that has yet to be determined." What a bitch! It was as if she wanted something to be wrong with Clay. Mrs. Reed poured herself a cup of coffee and sat down at the kitchen table, crossing her legs.

Watching Clay and me levelly with icy eyes, she sipped her drink. I felt like a bug under a magnifying glass. I tried not to squirm beneath her steely gaze.

"I'm not sure how long we'll be staying. We're at the Hyatt in Rockbridge County. Your father is assisting on a case in Charlottesville. A high-profile case that's getting a lot of national attention.

I decided to come along to visit and to make sure you *are* fine," she said condescendingly.

Clay's lip curled upward in a sneer. "I assure you, *Mother*, that I've managed all right without you. Wouldn't want you to put yourself out or anything." The bitterness in his voice made me sad for him. I could see how much he really wanted these people to love him. And I could see just as clearly how completely unable his parents were to truly love him the way he needed. Or at all.

No wonder he clung to me the way he did. The poor, lost boy beside me had never known unconditional love and support. He had been reared by the coldest individuals I had ever met. His mother didn't respond to his blatant jab.

"Well, I think it would be best if we stayed for a while. Moreover, your father's case could take weeks. Months, perhaps." Her words seemed almost threatening as she looked at her son with no emotion in her voice or face.

Months? From the way Clay had begun to tremble, I knew that would be very bad for him. These people triggered something dark in him and their presence could spell disaster for his precarious mental health. Clay made a strangled noise in the back of his throat. I looked at him in surprise as he snatched his hand from mine and fled the kitchen. He left me all alone in the lion's den. I could almost hear Mrs. Reed sharpening her claws as I stood there, uncomfortable and dumbfounded.

Finally, I made my feet move as I turned to follow my boyfriend. "Maggie," Mrs. Reed called out, stopping me. I turned back to face her, trying not to be intimidated by Clay's beautiful yet cold mother.

"Why don't you have a seat. I'd like a moment with you." She wasn't asking me, she was telling me. She indicated the seat beside her. I looked at Mr. Reed again, but he was oblivious to what was going on outside of his computer screen.

Mrs. Reed watched me as I slowly approached the chair and sat down. I folded my hands in my lap and looked at her politely.

"How long have you and my son been dating?" she asked me, sipping her coffee. I cleared my throat, feeling strange sharing anything with her.

"A few weeks, ma'am." I fidgeted in my seat under her unyielding stare.

"And is it serious between the two of you?" she asked nonchalantly. Why was she asking this? What business was it of hers? This just felt creepy.

"I guess so," I answered reluctantly.

Mrs. Reed leaned forward, attempting to appear as if we were two girls sharing confidences. It made my skin crawl. "And are you aware of Clayton's . . . issues?" She said it as if he had a contagious disease. Her lips curled and I could see how repulsive her son's mental health was to her.

"I'm very aware of all his qualities, good and bad, Mrs. Reed. Clay has been very honest about his struggles with his mental health," I said, sticking my chin out defiantly. I saw a flicker of disappointment, almost as if she wanted to be the one to tell me this. Maybe she wanted the information to drive a wedge between Clay and me. But why?

"My son is a very sick boy. He has been on a self-destructive path for a long time now. He hurts those around him, lacking regard for anything but his own feelings. His doctors in Florida are very concerned that he will relapse. They've encouraged us to have him readmitted for prolonged inpatient treatment. He is a danger to himself and others." Her eyes flashed at me as she watched me absorb her words.

They wanted to put him back in the hospital? They couldn't do that to him! What Clay needed was love and support, not to be shoved inside an institution with no way out. I knew then that I hated this woman and her complete disregard for Clay and what was truly best for him.

"I haven't seen him being a danger to himself or others, Mrs. Reed," I lied, effortlessly. I couldn't tell her how worried I'd been for Clay, and how I often wondered if he needed more intense help than I was capable of giving him. But she didn't need to know any of that. She didn't deserve to know, this woman who had thrown her son away because his *issues* had become an inconvenience in her life.

Mrs. Reed watched me closely and I swore she saw straight through my lie. "Well, that's good," she said in that fake, syrup-sweet voice of hers. "But to be on the safe side, Clay's father and I will be staying for a while. We have serious concerns about him. So if you notice anything troublesome about Clay, please let me know so we can get him the help he so desperately needs."

I wanted to gag. No, she just wanted to shut Clay away, like an ugly family secret. I saw right through her and she knew that.

"No offense, Mrs. Reed, but I don't feel comfortable discussing Clay like this behind his back. He and I are very open and honest with each other." I started to stand up. I couldn't take sitting here with this woman any longer.

Mrs. Reed's eyes went cold. "Honesty is wonderful. But are you sure he's been entirely truthful with you?" she asked, making it clear she didn't expect me to answer her. She wanted her words to creep into my brain like a parasite, feeding on any doubt I had about him—about us. She was an evil and manipulative person.

Talk about trying to sabotage Clay's happiness. This woman couldn't give a shit about what was good for her son; that much was painfully clear. Without saying another word, I turned my back on Clay's horrible parents and left.

I looked for Clay in the living room and found Lisa at her computer. She glanced up at me when I walked in. "I think he went up to his room," she said. I nodded and turned to follow.

"Maggie," she called out. "Please keep an eye on him. I'm worried, with them here. This won't be good for him. If you had seen him when he came to us . . ." Her words trailed off and I could see how much she truly cared for her girlfriend's nephew. Clay was lucky to have her and Ruby in his corner.

"He loves you, and I think he probably listens to you more than anyone else. Ruby and I know how hard things are for him. We've tried to get him to see someone here in town. But he's stubborn. And Ruby and I are hesitant to step on any toes. It's not that we don't care, but the relationship between Clay and his parents and Ruby and her sister is extremely complicated," she said sadly. Her words shocked me. I had no idea Ruby and Lisa had tried to intervene. Clay had always made them out to be clueless.

"Clay acted as though you and Ruby didn't know," I said quietly.

Lisa shook her head. "We know, Maggie. We see the cuts and the crazy mood swings. We hear him shattering things up in his room. Ruby is scared for him but she's even more scared to involve his parents. Because they still have full guardianship, Ruby has zero say in any treatment he has, even though he's living here. His father made sure of that," Lisa spit out in disgust.

"He's tough to be around; we get that. But he *has* been better since the two of you got together. So just love and support him the best you can. And if you ever worry about what's going on with him, do not go to *them*." Lisa's eyes darted in the direction of the kitchen in frustration. "Come to Ruby or me. We'll try to figure something out."

I smiled at her, though it didn't reach my eyes. I knew she was trying to be supportive but her words only made me feel cold inside. Because the truth was, his parents seemed to control everything. And, not for the first time, I felt even more alone.

I made my way up to Clay's bedroom. My stomach was in knots. I wasn't sure what to expect when I opened the door. I didn't knock, I just walked in.

Clay sat on his bed, his elbows resting on his knees, his head hanging down. His right hand was clenched in a tight fist. I sat beside him, hesitant to touch him.

"You okay?" I asked, realizing how stupid the question was. Of course he wasn't okay. Nothing about his body language said he was all right. His hands were shaking and he slowly opened his tightened fist.

"Here," he rasped, dropping a razor blade in my hand.

I trembled as I took the small piece of metal and quickly wrapped it in a piece of tissue before putting it in my pocket. I didn't say anything, scared that I would make everything worse for him.

"I don't know if I can do this, Maggie. Not with them here. It makes me want to take that fucking razor blade across my skin, just to stop the way I feel in *here*!" Clay pulled at his T-shirt over his chest. His breath came in rapid pants and I knew he was struggling for control.

I clasped my hands tightly together, trying to stop their shaking.

"I can *feel* myself losing it! I can't hold it together knowing they can show up and walk into my house whenever they want! I wish I could just end all of this shit!" His voice rose in anguish and he started pulling at his hair. Then he started rocking, like he had that first night I found him freaking out after the bonfire. He made a horrible keening noise in the back of his throat. His tenuous hold on sanity was quickly slipping away.

I grabbed his shoulders, forcing him to stop his incessant movements. "Stop it, Clay. Now!" I told him firmly.

Clay shook his head. "No. You don't understand. I hate them! And what's worse is they make me hate myself! They remind me of every horrible and stupid thing I've ever done! They never waste an opportunity to shove the fact that I'm an embarrassment and a failure in my face!" he ground out, his words like knives.

I snapped. He was scaring me. It was like he was giving up already. And I wouldn't allow that to happen. I grabbed his face and held it between my hands. I gave him a little shake.

"Enough! You are giving them all of the power here! That's exactly what they want. They want to see you broken, a shell of a person. And you're playing right into their hands!" I hissed.

"But they have all the power. I have nothing," he whispered, and I could see him fragment. I gave him a gentle tap on the cheek.

"How can you say that, Clay? You have Ruby and Lisa. You have me! You have my heart and soul inside you every second of every day," I said, kissing him on the mouth, trying to vanquish the darkness that had taken hold of him.

His expression was shattered. "I don't deserve your heart, Maggie. I should never have dragged you into this hell I live in. It's not fair to you. What kind of future can I give you when I don't even know if I have one?" he despaired, closing his eyes. I felt tears rise up and pour from my eyes as I took in his pain.

"I love you, Clay. I love every single part of you. I need you to hold it together! Please! Do it for me, if not for yourself." I was playing dirty. Using his love for me as leverage.

Clay's eyes pleaded with me. "I don't know if I can. I hate this lost feeling." His voice shook. I gently rubbed his cheek; my fingers brushed his hair back from his face.

"If you're feeling lost . . . well, I'll just have to find you," I said, with more conviction than I felt.

Clay leaned forward and rested his forehead against mine, our noses brushing. "I can't do this without you," he murmured. I closed my eyes at the raw yearning I heard. Was I enough to hold him together?

"I'm here, Clay. Always," I said as our lips found each other in a desperate need. As we tried to drown all our fears in the feel of our mouths and the love we had for each other.

chapter
nineteen

Things went from bad to worse. The arrival of Clay's parents created a ripple that encompassed everything. I was still grounded, so I wasn't able to be with Clay after school. And then he started disappearing. He would leave immediately after the last bell, often not even waiting for me after class like he usually did.

We typically tried to spend a few moments together before I had to be sequestered at home. But soon he started to bail on me almost every day. I didn't know where he went or what he did. Not being able to keep an eye on him, particularly when things were so bad for him, was maddening. And I was hurt. Really hurt. I knew he was shutting me out. Hiding things from me. And when I questioned his behavior he became angry and defensive, refusing to speak to me.

Clay's moods fluctuated like crazy. I asked him, on more than one occasion, if he was still taking his medication but he would simply ignore me, as if I hadn't asked anything. It was almost as if he were self-destructing on purpose. As if he were trying to give his parents a reason to lock him away.

Is that what he wanted? Because he sure as hell was acting like it.

When Clay showed up at my locker one morning, a week after his parents had breezed into town, I noticed the fresh cut on his wrist.

"What is this?" I hissed, grabbing his hand and pulling up his sleeve. Clay ripped his arm away from me and put his forehead against my locker over my head, leaning into my face.

"It's nothing. Leave it alone," he said in a low tone. The look in his eyes frightened me. He wasn't teasing. He was telling me to back off.

"No," I pushed, not letting him close me out. "I *will* tell Lisa and Ruby if you keep this up," I threatened, holding my English book tight to my chest.

Clay's face flushed and he reeled back as if I had struck him. He hit the metal beside my head, making me flinch. "Don't threaten me, Maggie. That's a stupid thing to do." He hit the locker again and stormed off, leaving me shaken and confused.

His behavior and mood were becoming more and more erratic. I felt any control I had had over the situation fading every day. It was as if he was putting that wall back up, one angry brick at a time.

And I couldn't find my way over it, under it, or through it. He was on one side and I was firmly on the other. Soon, Clay started ditching school earlier and earlier.

And that was just the beginning. I had asked him about cutting school and Clay had given me that angry look again and told me to stop acting like I was his mother. His words were like a knife to my gut. I had been unable to stop the tears from forming in my eyes. He was so short and terse with me all the time lately. I felt us drifting further and further apart.

I hated crying and that's all I did anymore. I was one big pile of misery. And that misery had the name Clayton Reed.

I seriously considered going to Ruby and Lisa. I wanted to tell them what was going on with Clay. I needed someone's help desperately. But what would they really be able to do? Lisa had made it clear that his parents held all the cards. So I watched as he moved further away from me and I was powerless to stop it. My words meant nothing to him anymore. The fact that he hurt me every single day didn't matter.

I was losing him. And it terrified me.

After being completely ignored for several days, I had finally lost it during lunch. I had yelled at Clay and, then, to my utter humiliation, I began to sob. Rachel and Daniel were frozen, completely paralyzed by my sudden crazy emotions. This was not the Maggie May Young they were accustomed to seeing.

Clay had started off angry but when I had begun to cry, it was like the flick of a light switch. He had softened, seeing how badly he had hurt me. He had hugged me and told me he loved me, apologizing for his attitude. I melted into his arms like I always did, desperate for things to be as they had been.

But they weren't. Not by a long shot. Clay was mad all the time and I had no idea how to help him. Eventually he stopped coming to lunch, leaving school around midday. I didn't know where he went. He would never say. He would tell me only not to worry so much. But of course I worried. That's all I did anymore: Worry. And cry. Then worry some more.

I had defied my parents' grounding after a few more days of this miserable existence. I decided to head to Clay's house after school. My heart sank when I saw his parents' car in the driveway. My palms started to sweat as I made my way to the front door.

I knocked and waited. No one came to the door. I knocked again. Finally Clay answered. He looked like hell. There were dark circles under his eyes, his skin was pasty, and his clothes were rumpled as if he had slept in them.

What was worse was that he looked less than thrilled to see me.

"What are you doing here?" he bit out, looking over his shoulder. I tried to peer behind him to see what had made him so skittish, but he blocked my view.

"I was worried about you. I wanted to make sure you were all right," I said softly. I tried to reach out and touch him but he moved away from me.

"Well, I'm just fucking dandy. You can leave now." He tried to shut the door in my face but I stuck my foot out to stop it from closing.

"Clay. Stop shoving me away! How can you treat me like this after everything we've been through?" I pleaded, feeling those annoying tears slide down my face yet again.

I saw a momentary crack in his cold facade. His eyes softened and I thought just maybe I had reached him. But he slammed the wall back up and his face hardened. "I'm tired of everyone's *support*," he spat out, looking at me with disdain. "Stop worrying about me. I don't need your pity or your concern."

I opened my mouth to argue with him some more. I couldn't let him push me away like that. But then I saw Mrs. Reed come down the hallway. She came up behind Clay and put her hand on his shoulder. He tensed, as if waiting for a blow.

"Aren't you going to ask your friend inside, Clayton? It's Marcia, isn't it?" she said condescendingly. She knew my name; she was just being a bitch.

I didn't have a chance to correct her before Clay nudged my foot out of the doorway. "No, she's just leaving. In fact, I think we're done here." He looked at me then and I couldn't swallow around the lump in my throat.

We were done? Did that mean what I thought it meant?

"Clay. What are you saying?" My voice had left me. All I could do was whisper as the pain lanced through my body. I hated that we were having this discussion with his evil harpy of a mother two feet away. She watched us the whole time and I couldn't miss the malicious triumph on her face.

"Just what I said, Maggie. I'm done. So don't come around here again!" he told me forcefully. Had he really just broken up with me? In front of his fucking mother? I got angry then.

"You asshole!" I breathed, clenching my fists at my sides.

"Clay, it's time for dinner. Hurry up with Marcia so you can eat." Mrs. Reed flashed me a cold smile and went back down the hallway.

Clay glared at me. "You just couldn't leave well enough alone. Are you happy now?" he seethed.

"Fuck you, Clay! I've done nothing but love you! But you really are a selfish prick. Screw my feelings, right? It's the Clayton Reed Self-destruct Show. And you're right. We are done. I don't need any more of your abuse!" I turned on my heel and left, feeling like my heart had just been ripped out of my chest.

The anger got me home but then it transformed into gut-wrenching depression. Clay and I were over and I had no real idea why. The reality of what had happened sank in and I cried myself to sleep.

After that I became a shell of the person I used to be. I barely ate. I hardly slept. I never talked to my friends. I never joined in discussions with Rachel and Daniel of things to do once my grounding was lifted. I half-listened to their conversations at lunchtime. I stopped waiting for them after school, instead choosing to get to my car as fast as possible so I could get home and lock myself in my room.

"You are going to tell me what is going on with you and you are doing it now!" Rachel said angrily, grabbing my arm as I tried to slink down the hallway unnoticed, to my locker. It had been days since I had gone to Clay's house. It felt like forever since I had spoken to or seen him. I didn't even know if he had shown up to school. And I felt like living was becoming increasingly difficult. How could someone endure this much pain and survive?

"Nothing's going on," I mumbled, trying to pull out of her grasp.

"Yeah, right! You've become the walking dead! So, unless your brains have been eaten by zombies, something sure as hell *is* going on and you're going to spill it!" Daniel said, at my other side. The two of them took me by the arms and half-dragged me to the library.

I heard the bell ring, signaling the end of lunch. I had eaten in the girls' bathroom, wanting to avoid this very conversation. I should have known they would find me. I couldn't even appreciate how much they cared about me. Because right then I was unable to think beyond the gaping hole in my chest.

"We've got to get to class. We'll be late," I argued feebly. Daniel dragged me into the library, moving toward the back of the stacks, where we'd have some privacy.

"Screw class. Our best friend is in full-on meltdown. That trumps geography any day," Rachel replied, sitting me down in a chair and taking her place beside me.

Daniel sat across the table and looked at me. "We know this has to do with Clay. He's MIA all the time now and you look like someone ran over your cat. Just tell me if I have to kick his ass. I've been wanting to for a while, anyway." I closed my eyes and struggled to hold it all in.

"We broke up," I admitted, putting my head down on the table.

"Aw, sweetheart. Why didn't you tell us?" Rachel asked soothingly, rubbing my back as I started to shake. I couldn't answer her, so they just let me try to get myself together. I couldn't cry, having no tears left. I sat there trying to breathe around the pain in my chest. Finally I calmed down.

"What happened?" Rachel asked, still rubbing my back in gentle circles.

"He changed. We changed. He didn't want me in his business. There's not much else to say about it," I answered cagily. I didn't want to get into the root of our relationship's problems. There were too many to list.

"You're better off, Mags. Trust me. You don't need that shit," Daniel said as he reached over to squeeze my hand.

I pulled away. "You don't understand! I'm not better off! I miss him!"

Rachel and Daniel were quiet a moment as I started to cry. So much for not having any more tears. When would I be done with this crap? After a few minutes of enduring my misery, Rachel wiped my cheeks and snapped her fingers in front of my face.

"Wake up, Maggie! He makes you miserable! Do not wallow over someone who you're better off without. Have more self-respect than that!" she said sternly.

Daniel nodded in agreement. "This is not the Maggie Young we know and love. I'm not sure who this whiny, pathetic chick is, but I kind of hate her," Daniel quipped, raising his eyebrows at me.

"I know you're right. But it's hard to ignore my feelings like that. I love him so much," I lamented, feeling the beginnings of a headache.

"Love? Really? I'm not sure if that's a love I'd want to have, Maggie," Rachel commented. I didn't respond to her statement. I didn't want to try to justify the relationship I had had with Clay. Because it would sound needy and sad and only further her argument.

But I needed to get myself together. I needed to try to move past the heartache. I had to try to forget about the fact that no matter how much I hurt, I knew deep down that Clay was in his own personal hell. I wanted to save him so badly, and that was an instinct that was hard to turn off.

"Come on, let's get to class. And after school I'll come back to your house. I bet you I can get your parents to let up on this ridiculous grounding of yours," Rachel said confidently.

I gave her a wobbly smile. "Thanks, guys. You really are the best," I said quietly, feeling absolutely no energy. I had cried it all out.

So I made the decision to let go of Clayton Reed. But he had become so deeply entrenched in my heart and my life that removing him was like removing a limb. How do you try to forget about someone you had loved like the other half of you?

It helped that I never saw Clay anymore. It was like he had disappeared. Or died.

My parents had finally agreed to end my stupid grounding. It probably helped that the reason for my punishment was no longer in the picture. I knew Rachel had talked to my mom about what was going on between Clay and me. Because the frosty climate in my house thawed considerably.

I tried to be happy with the renewal of the relationship I had with my parents. They stopped looking at me like I was a mutant that had taken over their precious daughter's body. And I really worked on overcoming the urge to curl up into a ball and stay that way. I forced myself to do my homework. I made myself go out with Rachel and Daniel after school, though I refused to set foot into Bubbles when Rachel suggested a banana split. Every time I drove by the place, I thought I would throw up.

I found myself fighting the need to call Clay. Even though two weeks had passed since we had broken up, it did nothing to deaden the pain. I wanted to see him so badly that I finally made Rachel erase his number from my phone.

Because the heartbreaking truth was, if Clay wanted to see me, he would have. The fact that he had made zero effort confirmed all of my deepest fears. That he didn't love me as much as he said he did. Otherwise, how could he stay away from me like this?

Then there were the days I worried that something had happened to him. What if he had hurt himself? I would have to talk myself off the ledge of a full-blown freak-out by convincing myself that Ruby or Lisa would have notified me if that had happened. Despite the fact that Clay had cut me out of his life completely, they had to know that I would want them to do that.

Okay, so I eventually caved and drove by Clay's house one Friday. I just wanted to make sure he was all right. I was relieved when I saw his car in the driveway as well as by the fact that it was the only one there. He must be home alone.

I slowed down as I passed by, my eyes flickering up to his window on the second floor. Of course I couldn't see anything, but I couldn't stop myself from wondering what he was doing. I had to push aside the scary thoughts of him cutting himself or worse.

I had pressed my foot down on the accelerator and driven away as fast as I could.

And I had thought that was it. I had decided from that point on that I needed to put Clay and our destructive relationship behind me. I felt firm in my resolve.

And then it all crumbled around me.

chapter
twenty

my days all started to blur together. The pre-Clay boredom came back with a numbing quickness. My old routines started all over again and the excitement at beginning my day every morning had dwindled into non-existence.

I tried not to think about him. But it was hard. Everything seemed to carry with it a memory of our time together. We hadn't been a couple for long. The time from when I had met Clay Reed until the moment of our separation had been a blip in the grand scheme of my life. Or at least I tried to tell myself so.

But the truth was, he had bulldozed his way into my life and there was no going back. Although I had worked hard to convince myself that ending things with him (okay, so I didn't have much say in any of that, but it's amazing how you can warp things in your mind to make them palatable) was the right thing to do, I couldn't erase how incomplete I felt without him.

I thought I had done a semi-decent job of pretending I was okay until I opened my locker after school on the third Monday after the breakup, and a piece of paper fluttered to my feet. My heart seized up, my stomach dropped to the floor. I was hit by a wave of déjà vu.

With trembling hands, I lifted the paper from the floor and unfolded it. Butterflies. Of course. What else would it be? And, along the bottom, in Clay's frantic scrawl, were the words *I have learned that sometimes "sorry" is not enough. Sometimes you actually have to change.*

I recognized the quotation, although I couldn't place where I had read it before.

Gah. What was I supposed to do with this? My eyes darted around the empty hallway, looking for him. But he was nowhere to be seen. Should I call him? Should I crumple up the drawing and forget about it? I was stuck with uncertainty.

Instead, I folded it carefully and put it in my book bag. When I got home, I couldn't resist taking out the picture and tacking it to my mirror. I stared at it for a long time. The ice around my heart melted a bit. But I didn't call him. I just couldn't.

The next day, I found another picture in my locker. This one was of my face. I had no idea when he had drawn it. It wasn't one I recognized. My hair was swept over one shoulder and I was staring off into the distance with a dreamy look on my face. The beauty of it took my breath away. There was nothing written on this one. I felt sad and torn.

Each day that week brought a different drawing. Some had sayings on the bottom, some did not. But each one conveyed Clay's longing in a heart-stopping way. On Friday I found a picture of what could only be the swimming hole, where we had gone the second week of school.

Clay had written, *The most perfect memories are the ones too painful to forget.*

I didn't hear Rachel come up behind me. She grabbed the paper from my hand before I could hide it. I swallowed thickly as she looked at it, her brows furrowed.

"Is this from him?" she asked, before handing it back.

I nodded. "Yeah," I answered, shoving it into my book bag.

"What's that all about?" she asked me as we left the school. I shrugged, not bothering with a verbal response. "Mags, it looks like he's trying to win you back. You aren't going there, are you?" she asked me angrily.

I stopped in the middle of the sidewalk and faced my best friend. "I don't know, Rachel! All I do know is I feel like I can't breathe! I'm miserable without him!" I said, trying to get her to see what he meant to me.

Rachel sighed. "I know. But you can't forget how miserable you were *with* him, either," she said. I knew she was right. But that didn't stop my heart from swelling up at the thought of him wanting me again.

Yeah, I was an idiot.

I was about to suggest to Rachel that we go see a movie, anything to get my mind off my drama, when my cell phone chirped in my pocket. I pulled it out. Even though I had erased his number, I recognized it instantly.

The text read, *Will you meet me at the swimming hole? I need to see you.*

Fuck. What do I do?

"Who was that?" Rachel asked suspiciously. I tucked my phone back into my pocket and gave her the fakest smile I could muster.

"My mom. She just wanted to know what I'd like for dinner," I lied.

Rachel gave me a look that said *you are a liar.* "Then why didn't you text her back?" she asked me.

I gave the most insincere laugh possible. "Oh, yeah. Duh!" I pulled out my phone and pretended to send a reply.

"Mmm. Chinese," I said lamely. Rachel frowned but didn't push the issue.

"So, I'm guessing you have plans with your *parents* this evening, then?" Yeah, I wasn't fooling her in the least.

I cleared my throat. "Uh, yeah, looks that way. I'll call you later," I said, heading toward my car. My heart was thudding in my chest.

"Hey, Mags," Rachel called out as I got into my car.

I turned around, plastering a smile to my face. "Yeah?" I yelled back.

"Just be careful. You know, with your *parents,*" she said, and then turned to get into her own car.

I got into the driver's seat and sat there for a moment, taking deep, calming breaths. When that didn't work, I turned on the radio to try to settle my jangled nerves. I took out my phone and punched in a quick reply to Clay's question.

Sure. Be there in ten.

I waited for a moment to see if Clay would text anything back, but my phone stayed silent. Okay. Well, I guess he'd just meet me there. I pulled out of the parking lot and made my way to the swimming hole. What did Clay want? A million different scenarios went through my head. I wasn't sure I was emotionally strong enough to resist him if he told me he wanted me back.

I had missed him so much. I literally craved him like I craved caffeine in the morning. But I forced myself to remember the way he had treated me the last time I'd seen him. I also thought about how he had effectively shut me out when I had wanted nothing more than to help him.

Rachel had said she'd never want a love like that. But did I?

I pulled into the field by the swimming hole and parked beside Clay's BMW. He was already here. Of course he was. I got out of the car and took a deep breath. Well, here goes nothing.

I stomped through the tall grass and went into the woods. After a few more minutes, I got to the river. I saw Clay sitting on a rock by the water. He looked up when I arrived and I had to stifle a gasp at his appearance.

He looked horrible. He seemed to have lost weight and his complexion was ashy. Here was a man who had been to hell and back. I didn't know what to say. Everything I had imagined telling him slipped from my mind and I was at a loss.

"Maggie," he said quietly, getting to his feet. I didn't move toward him. I started to feel the telltale signs of weakening and I tried to stay firm. So I didn't go to him, even as I fantasized about throwing myself into his arms. This boy had hurt me. Badly. I had to retain some control. Some . . . what do you call it? Oh, yeah. Self-respect.

"Hi, Clay," I said, and was proud of how cold my voice sounded. Clay winced at the chilly reception. He put his hand through his hair. It had grown out in the three weeks since I had seen him, the curls brushing his collar.

"You look beautiful," he said softly, giving me a hint of the smile that I loved. I refrained from straightening my hair like a moron and instead stared coolly back at him.

"And you look like shit," I told him harshly. Wow, that was hateful. The bitch was out in force!

"Direct, as always," he remarked, scratching the side of his neck in nervousness.

"What do you want, Clay? 'Cause I've got to get home soon," I stated, getting to the point. Clay sighed and started toward me. But then, as if he picked up on my need for physical space, he stopped.

"I just needed to see you. I've missed you. So much," he told me, his eyes meeting mine.

"Yeah. Well, you made your feelings on seeing me pretty obvious," I bit out. I hated the wobble in my voice and worked hard to clamp down on the tears that threatened to well up.

Clay scrubbed his hands over his face in agitation. "I was an idiot. I've been a mess without you."

Then, without giving me time to react, he was in front of me, a breath away from touching. He reached out to caress my cheek and I flinched backward. Clay dropped his hand as if I were on fire. I saw the hurt flash across his face and I wanted to scream at him.

He had no right to feel hurt! He was the one who had rejected *me*!

"Clay, you pushed me away. I tried to be there for you, but you wouldn't let me! I can't go on feeling like I don't know if I'm coming or going! Stop screwing with my head!" I couldn't stop myself from pleading.

Clay closed his eyes. When he opened them again, they were bright with unshed tears. Shit. Clay's tears were my kryptonite! I needed to get out of there, and fast, or I'd never stay strong enough to resist him.

"I never meant to screw with your head, Maggie! You are the only thing that has ever kept me grounded. I was a complete and total ass. My parents came to town and it threw me. I started backsliding into my old destructive patterns. I was terrified of having you see me like that, so I pushed you away."

He stopped and took a deep breath. I stood perfectly still, not wanting to move away but too scared to go to him. "I was so, so wrong. I've been in the worst kind of hell these last three weeks. I need you so much! I can't survive without you! Please, Maggie! Please tell me you'll give me another chance!" he implored, finally taking my hand and putting it to his cheek. He closed his eyes again at the touch of my skin against his. As if that were all he needed for things to be okay.

God, I wished that were true.

"You destroyed me, Clay. I've been miserable without you," I admitted quietly. Clay opened his eyes and I saw the hope there. "But, Clay. I can't keep doing this. I'm so tired of worrying about you. Of going to sleep scared that you will do something to yourself. You're killing me." The words were wrung out of me and I could feel my exhaustion.

Clay pulled me closer until our chests were touching and I had to look up to see him. He reached down and pushed the bangs off my face. I melted as his fingers glided over my skin.

"I will never hurt you like that. As long as we're together, I have something to fight for," he whispered.

I wanted to yell at him that he had hurt me like that a million times already. That he hadn't fought for us, or himself, despite the fact that I gave him all the love that I had. But he made me weak. I hated myself for not being able to verbalize the thoughts and doubts that swam through my head. Why couldn't I just say how I felt? Why did I allow myself to get sucked under by him time and time again?

"I love you. You are my life." He placed my hand over his heart. I could feel it beating erratically beneath my palm. "Feel that? It's yours. For now and always!" he said emphatically, before wrapping his arms around me.

He leaned down and placed a soft kiss on my shoulder as we held each other.

"I love you," he whispered again before burying his face in my neck. I let him hold me for a while before I pulled away. He looked at me with confusion as I stepped back, trying to give myself some space.

"Clay. I love you, too—" I started but he cut me off.

"And that's all that matters! We love each other! That's all we need!" He seemed so sure. But, then again, he always had. This time, I wasn't.

"No, Clay. That's not all we need. You need help!" I told him.

I watched as Clay's face darkened. "Not this again. We've talked about it. You are everything! If we're together, I'm fine!"

I held up my hand to stop him. "This is a lot to take in. I need time. I need to think. Please, just stop," I begged him, backing up even farther. I didn't bother to argue with his ridiculous statement. I just needed to halt this conversation before I caved completely.

Clay came toward me again, looking broken. "Maggie, I was wrong! Please, don't leave me!" he cried, reaching for my hand again. I moved away from his grasp.

"I have to go," I said, and turned to leave.

I started to run through the trees. I didn't get far before Clay's hands grabbed me from behind. I tripped as he pulled me to a stop. He crushed his chest against my back and pressed his face to my neck.

"I can't lose you again! I'll do anything! Just don't walk away from me!" he pleaded. I could feel his body shaking as he gripped me. His hot tears burned my flesh as they slid down my neck. I reached down and tried to unwrap his arms from around my middle.

"Then let me leave. Just give me time to think. I can't do that when we're together," I urged, not turning around to look at him. I knew that if I saw his grief-stricken face I would be a goner. And I needed to decide whether a life with him was what I wanted. If a life without him was something I could stand.

Clay was quiet for a few minutes. I could feel the ragged draw of his breaths against my back, the warmth of his tears on my shoulder as he pressed against me like his life depended on it. Then, without another word, he moved his arms and I felt the cold air of our separation as he moved away from me.

Letting me go.

✦

I was shaken by my time with Clay. I went home practically in tears and more confused than ever. My mind was churning and I struggled against the need to run straight back to him. I hadn't been lying when I said I needed time. But something told me that time wasn't going to solve anything.

How did I reconcile myself to the fact that I had just walked away from the love of my life? Particularly when he needed me most. What kind of person did that make me? I had acted on a desperate sort of self-preservation when I left him standing alone in the woods. I was scared and mixed up. But I couldn't think past the fact that he loved me and wanted us to be together.

Why couldn't that be enough?

I was a complicated mixture of scared and angry. I felt like punching the wall or pulling my hair out. It was unfortunate for my mother that she happened to walk into my room in the midst of my very real freak-out.

I sat at my desk, twirling my chair in circles, wishing I could grow a pair of wings and leap out of my second-story window. I had chewed my nails to the quick and was currently gnawing on my cuticles.

I heard a light knock on my door and, without waiting for permission, my mom pushed it open with an armful of laundry. She wore an annoyingly perky smile and was still dressed in her office clothes. She must have just gotten home from work.

She dropped the pile of clean clothes on my bed. "How was school?" she asked me. I shrugged, not looking at her. I just wanted her to leave. I still blamed her and Dad for a lot of my current situation. Maybe if they had been more accepting of Clay, things would have been different. Or maybe it would snow in July. Well, whatever—I needed to blame someone and they filled the bill.

"Is that a good shrug or a bad shrug?" she asked lightly.

I shrugged again. My mom was quiet and then I heard the squeak of my bedsprings and suppressed a sigh. Great, she wanted to *talk*. I swung my desk chair back around and gave her my best stink eye.

"Yes?" I asked in irritation.

My mom frowned at me. "What's with the attitude? I just wanted to know how my only child is doing. Is it wrong for a mother to care about her daughter's well-being?" Okay, that was it. I was sick of their concern. Sick to death of their overprotective mama-and papa-bear bullshit.

I glared at my mother, the woman who had been my best friend and biggest support for most of my life. But in that moment I forgot all about that. Instead, all I saw when I looked at her was my enemy.

"You know what, Mom? If you cared about my *well-being* you'd back off and let me live my life with whomever I choose to live it with," I spat at her. My mother's eyes widened in shock at my outburst.

Yes, this was not the little girl she knew. This was some crazy woman who was wearing Maggie Young's skin. My mom drew herself upright and a stern look took over her face. "Don't you dare speak to me that way! Your father and I have always done what was best for you."

I cut her off with a maniacal laugh. "What's best for me? Are you kidding? You have pretty much forbidden me from seeing the only guy I'll ever love! How is that good for me?" I shrieked at her.

My mom sighed and gave me a less-than-patient look. "Stop being so dramatic. I tried to like Clayton, if you'll remember. It doesn't change the fact that while you were with him you made terrible decisions and behaved reprehensibly. You started lying, sneaking around, shutting out your friends. Love doesn't make you act like that, Maggie. No matter what you choose to believe."

"You don't know the first thing about Clay and me. You never will!" I yelled, grinding the heels of my hands into my eyes. I felt like I was about to bust out of my skin. I was so wound up about Clay and everything else, I just couldn't deal with my parents right now.

Her face took on a concerned expression. "What's going on, Maggie? You've always been able to tell me things. You know I'd listen." For a moment, I softened. I wanted to tell her everything. I wanted to go back to the time when I felt like my mother would listen to me without condemnation and judgment.

Maybe, just maybe, I could share with her everything that was going on with Clay and she'd have some advice, a suggestion or two. And I wouldn't feel so freaking alone in all this mess.

But her next statement blew my little fantasy out of the water.

"But you have to stop getting so worked up over that *boy*. He is nothing but trouble. Look at yourself, Maggie May. Look at who you've become. I think you need to really think about the way he has completely taken over your life. Is this thing you have with him really worth saving?" Her psychobabble made me want to gouge my eyes out. Or hers. Whichever came first.

I covered my face with my hands and screamed in frustration. "Are you serious?" I screeched. I leapt to my feet. "This is total bullshit! Nobody has taken over my life. Your Clay paranoia is ridiculous! Have you ever thought that maybe I'm just changing? God forbid that I'm not your perfect little girl anymore. That I have feelings that have absolutely *nothing* to do with you and Dad?! My life is mine! And I'm sick of your insane need to control it!" My mom opened her mouth to say something, probably to scold me for cursing, but I kept on going.

"You are the ones driving me crazy and creating all of this drama. So, please, just give it a rest." My anger dissipated and only exhaustion remained. If there was one thing this little powwow had accomplished, it was making a decision about Clay crystal-fucking-clear.

I wouldn't turn my back on him the way everyone else always had. He needed me and that was more important than my parents' anger and disappointment. But I couldn't argue about this with them anymore. I was done. This would no longer be a topic of conversation between us.

My mom's mouth hung open and she was for once at a loss for words. She took a deep breath and looked at me as if I had morphed into a mutant. She stood up, still looking at me, as if trying to see the daughter she used to know inside me somewhere.

"I don't even know the person you've become, Maggie May. This person"—she waved her hand toward me—"is angry and bitter and way too invested in some high-school romance that in no way defines the rest of your life. Wake up! Get yourself together," my mother said coldly. I knew this was her idea of tough love, but I was having none of it.

I sagged to the floor, my legs not supporting my weight any longer. I didn't have anything else to say. I was all out of words. I couldn't convince someone who was way past convincing. My mom walked to the door and turned back to look at me again. Her expression had changed to one of worry. And I could see how much she ached for my pain. But I also saw her grim resolve and that, in her mind, she truly knew what was best for me.

"Clay *is not* what's best for you, Maggie. I know he's not a bad kid. In fact, I can see a lot of what you love about him. But he is leading you down a very bad path, one that you may not be able to turn away from. Sometimes love can't make everything better, and the best thing for everyone is to walk away. No matter how much it may hurt."

My heart constricted at her words. They resonated inside me and I had a hard time catching my breath. But then my anger surged forth again and I looked at her with all the rage I had been feeling.

"What do *you* know about Clay and me?! You know *nothing*!" I spat hatefully.

My mom actually flinched at the venom I threw at her. I was being an ungrateful little bitch and I knew it. But my priorities in life had significantly changed, and my parents and their need to keep me safe was not one of them.

Without another word, my mom left, looking heartbroken. But I was done feeling guilty about all of this. I flopped back on my bed, wanting desperately to sleep. Rest evaded me and I lay there, staring at my ceiling, and wondered how my life had gotten so messed up.

chapter
twenty-one

I didn't go down for dinner, refusing to leave my room even after my dad came up and offered to bring me something to eat. I wouldn't go downstairs and pretend life was hunky-dory when it was all a lie. So I holed up in my room, playing depressing indie rock and staring at the drawings Clay had given me over the past few months.

The words he had written burned into my brain and I felt the sting of tears in my eyes. I thought over and over again about the look on his face when I'd left him that afternoon. He looked like I was killing him.

Why did things have to get so out of control? I replayed things in a continuous loop in my head. The first time I met Clay. The Fall Formal. The way he held me the first time we said *I love you.* Falling asleep in his arms at the cabin.

But then those warm memories became tainted by the dark ones. The night of Melissa's party. His breakdown on his bedroom floor. His constant anger and jealousy. Finding him cutting.

However, none of that changed what I felt deep down. I loved him with every fiber of my being. And I felt like I had failed him.

He had warned me that he pushed and pushed to see if I would stick. And I hadn't. I had allowed him to shove me right out of his life without fighting.

And what Clay needed was someone to fight for him.

I waited until I knew my parents had gone to bed before leaving my room to wash my face. I wanted to avoid any further confrontations. Back in my room, I changed into my favorite flannel pajamas and turned on Pink Floyd. I needed something to soothe my frazzled nerves.

I lay down on my bed and within five minutes I was asleep.

I wasn't sure exactly what woke me up. One minute I was in a dead sleep, the next I was startled awake. My room was pitch black, except for the soft glow of the streetlight outside. My music had been turned off and everything was eerily silent.

My eyes adjusted to the blackness and my heart stopped in my chest. Clay sat on the end of my bed. I rubbed my eyes and looked again. I had to make sure they weren't playing tricks on me. "Clay?" I whispered, still not believing he was there.

"Hi, Maggie," he said softly. I could barely see his face in the shadows. I sat up and scooted over until I was beside him. I looked at him closely and could see his eyes were bloodshot and tired.

"What are you doing here?" I asked him, careful to keep my voice low so as not to wake my parents. Clay didn't say anything. He sat there, staring at me as if he were trying to memorize my face. Like he was scared to forget me.

"What's going on? You're freaking me out," I told him with a nervous giggle.

Clay reached out and wrapped a piece of my hair around his finger and then dropped it. "I just had to see you one last time," he whispered. One last time? My stomach flipped over.

"What do you mean? Are you going somewhere?" I asked him, watching as he took one of my hands in his and laced our fingers together.

Clay ignored my question and looked into my eyes again. "I love you. So much. I'm so sorry for everything I've put you through. You never deserved any of that. I just wanted you to know how much I hate myself for all of the shit I threw at you. You did nothing but love and support me. God, I just love you. More than anything! I told you before that you were my forever. And I will love you that long. I promise." His words sounded suspiciously like a good-bye.

I was confused and more than a little numb. Clay leaned forward and I felt his lips on mine. He tangled his hands into my hair and pulled me against him with a force that surprised me. His kiss was hungry, as if he would devour me.

Our tongues slid together and Clay's hands were hot on my back. Finally, he pulled away and cupped my face in his palm.

"I have to go," he murmured, leaning in again to kiss the corner of my mouth.

My eyes fluttered closed as he kissed my neck and shoulder. "Go? Go where?" I asked breathlessly. Clay stopped kissing me and rested his forehead at the base of my throat.

"After you left me this evening, I went home," he began. I could hear the pain in his voice and I felt compelled to wrap my arms around him.

Clay took a shaky breath and continued. "*They* were there. They're *always* there. But tonight, it was too much. I just couldn't deal with their shit. Ruby and Lisa were there, too, but that didn't matter. They started in on me as soon as I got in the door. Talking about how they had gotten a call from the school about all of my unexcused absences. That I was in danger of failing three of my classes. Then *she* started screaming at me that I was an embarrassment and a burden." I heard the catch in Clay's throat.

I wanted to kill his parents. His mother was a heartless bitch. How could she tear her son down so callously? All of his problems, all of his issues, every single one of them was be-cause of them. They were to blame and no one else.

Clay sat back and the hopelessness in his eyes frightened me. He gripped my hands as if he would fall away. "What did Lisa and Ruby do? Did they let them yell at you like that?" I asked. I felt suddenly pissed at his aunt and her girlfriend. They continued to allow those horrible people to treat Clay like he was garbage. Why the hell didn't they intervene?

Clay shook his head as if reading my thoughts. "Ruby tried to stop her. She really did. Lisa argued with them. Ruby threatened to call the police to have them removed from their house. Yeah, that's a joke. My mother just said she'd take me with them. That shut Ruby up pretty quickly." Clay sighed.

"Then my mom told me to pack my bags," he said, all emotion leaving his voice.

I stilled. "Pack your bags? Why?" I asked. Clay looked at me with a heartbreaking sadness.

"Because she has been in contact with my doctor back in Florida and they had decided I needed to be checked back into the treatment facility. They want to lock me away again. But this time it won't be for a ninety-day program. Nope. This will be a long-term deal. They had planned to make me leave tonight."

I thought I was going to throw up in his lap. He was leaving. For good. Suddenly my need for time and space seemed stupid. I was losing him.

"Oh, my God," I said in a hushed voice. Clay held my face again and pulled me closer. He kissed my mouth again with aching tenderness.

"I'm not going," he said adamantly.

I blinked in confusion. "You're not? But I thought your parents had control over that stuff. I mean, what choice do you have?" I asked him.

Clay threaded his fingers through my hair. "I'm not going. I won't let them shut me away like a damn dog. I'm leaving. To-night," he said.

"Where will you go?" I asked, feeling the panic of our situation grip me tightly.

"I don't know. I just know that I have to get out of here. But I wanted to see you again. I needed you to know that I love you. There was no way I could take off without seeing your face and letting you know that my heart is yours. Always."

He was leaving. This was it. Everything we had was coming to an end in my bedroom. Who knew when I'd see him again? If ever.

Clay gently touched the butterfly I still wore around my neck. "You are my butterfly," he whispered before pulling me back into his arms. I could feel his tension as he held me. I was taken over by an all-consuming panic at the thought of him leaving me behind. How could I go on with my life without him? That just didn't seem possible.

So I made a spur-of-the-moment decision.

"I'm going with you," I told him, pulling away.

Clay frowned and shook his head. "No way, Maggie. You have friends and a family that love you. You cannot give up your life for me. I've already taken so much from you. Don't do this! I'd never forgive myself." Clay caressed my face with his fingers. I reached up and held his hand to my face.

"I can't live here without you! I'm not giving up anything, be-cause *you are* my life! You are not allowed to make this choice for me. I choose to be with you. You will *always* be my choice!" I said emphatically, trying to get him to see reason.

Clay shook his head again. "No! You aren't coming with me." He started to get to his feet. I jumped up after him and grabbed his arms.

"If you leave me here, Clay, I will never forgive you! You will only be showing me that everything you've said is a lie. You told me I was your forever! Now, prove it!" I implored desperately.

Clay looked torn. I knew he wanted to do what was best for me. But I also knew how badly he needed me. "It doesn't really matter what you say; I'm coming," I said, when he hadn't responded. I went to my closet and pulled out my duffel bag. Going to my drawers, I grabbed handfuls of panties and bras. Shirts, jeans, pajamas.

When I was finished, I pulled on a pair of jeans and a heavy sweatshirt, grabbing my fleece jacket off the chair. After I was dressed, I turned to look at Clay.

"How can I let you give up everything for me like this? It's not right!" He sounded sadly resigned. I went over and wrapped my arms around him.

I looked up into his gorgeous face and knew that my life began with him. And that it would end with him. "I *am not* giving up anything. I'm getting what I've wanted since I ran into you on your first day of school." Clay's mouth cracked into a smile at the memory. "I'm getting a life *with you*. That's what I want. Nothing else," I assured him.

Clay hugged me tightly. "I love you," he whispered into my hair. I untangled myself from him and tugged on his arm.

"We should get going," I said, and Clay hesitated.

"Will you leave a note? I mean, your parents are going to be really worried."

I felt a pang of guilt thinking about my parents finding my empty bed in the morning. It gutted me to hurt them like this. I looked at my beautiful boy and all doubts left my mind. He needed me and that was all that mattered.

"I'll call them." Clay arched his eyebrow at me. "I will. I promise." I grabbed my cell phone to make the point.

Clay let out a deep breath and took my hand. "Okay, let's do this." We quietly crept out of my bedroom and made our way down the stairs.

Once we were outside the house, I stopped and looked at him questioningly. "How did you get in my room, by the way?" I asked.

Clay looked at me sheepishly. "I, um . . . well, I climbed the tree." I looked at the side of the house to the enormous maple that grew beside my window.

"But you hate heights," I said, a little in awe.

Clay shrugged as we walked down the street toward my car. "Well, let's just say it took me a while to get up there. But it was worth it." He looked at me sideways and my heart thudded against my chest.

"Yeah, totally worth it," I agreed, smiling.

✦

I thought about sending a text to Rachel and Daniel. I felt like maybe I should tell them what was going on. They would be furious with me. But I couldn't change things now. I was quiet as Clay drove down the darkened interstate. He said we'd drive just over the border into North Carolina and then stop somewhere to sleep.

The further we drove from home, the more ugly doubts crept into my mind. I looked down at our hands joined together and felt the electric tingle where our skin touched. No, I'd made the right decision. This boy was my world.

"Are you going to text Rachel or Danny?" Clay asked me suddenly. I looked up with a start, having been lost in my fairy-tale thoughts of a happily-ever-after with him.

"Um . . . I don't know," I answered, a little unsure.

Clay grunted and suddenly pulled off the road and put the car in Park.

"What are you doing?" I asked him in confusion. Clay unbuckled his seat belt and climbed over into my seat. He pulled me into his arms and kissed my entire face before stopping on my mouth.

"I know what you're giving up to do this. And I love you so much, Maggie. You have the biggest heart of anyone I've ever met and I thank God every day that he brought you into my life." His lips lingered on mine, tasting me.

"But please don't give up on everything else because of me. I've made my choices. I'm okay with them. But your friends deserve to know you're okay. I don't want you to wake up tomorrow morning thinking this is the worst mistake you could have made."

"Aren't you glad I came with you?" I asked quietly, worried he regretted bringing me along. Clay kissed my mouth, his lips lingering on mine.

"God, of course I'm glad you came. But I just don't want you to think you have to cut everyone out of your life because of it. I want you to be happy," he told me. His eyes never left mine and I could tell he really meant what he was saying.

Clay reached into my jacket pocket and pulled out my phone. He put it in my hand. "Text Rachel and Daniel. Please." I looked at him and nodded.

I leaned over and kissed his cheek. "I love you," I told him again before scrolling through my contacts until I found Rachel's number.

I sent her a quick text telling her that I had left with Clay. That things had gotten bad with his family and he needed a little breather—a break. I asked her to tell my parents that I was sorry, but that I was okay and I would contact them soon. I knew she wouldn't get the text for a while, since it was 2:30 in the morning. Just hitting the send button made me feel better, made my chest not feel as tight.

Clay pulled back onto the interstate after I put the phone away. "Thanks for making me do that," I said.

Clay shook his head. "You don't have to thank me for that. You do what you have to do, Maggie. I'll support you the way you've always supported me. We're in this forever," he stated, with such certainty that I believed it—all of it.

I knew he loved me, and maybe, just maybe, that would be enough.

We drove for another two and a half hours before we pulled off at a small town just over the North Carolina border. Clay had seen a sign for a Motel 6 off the highway. We were both exhausted and I desperately wanted a bed and a good eight hours of sleep.

Clay pulled into a darkened parking lot. The Vacancy sign was flickering, making it all look like something out of a cheesy horror movie. There was only one other car outside the motel.

"You sure know how to wine and dine a gal," I teased as we got out of the car. I was happy to stretch my legs.

Clay smiled. "Next time, we'll find something a little nicer. Promise." I put my arms around his waist.

"It doesn't matter, Clay. As long as we're together." He kissed me sweetly before we went into the lobby to get a room.

The guy behind the front desk seemed unfazed by the fact that two teenagers wanted a motel room at 5:00 in the morning. He never once made eye contact as Clay paid him in cash and collected the room key.

"There's ice and vending machines outside," the front-desk guy said mechanically. We nodded our thanks and walked out of the dingy lobby.

We found our room and I tried not to shudder as I took in the shabby stained carpet that might have been green when it was new. There was one queen-sized bed with a comforter that had obvious cigarette burns all over it and two flat pillows.

Clay put his bag down on a chair that looked as if it had been rescued from a Dumpster. "Sorry, baby. I know this ain't the Ritz."

I smiled. "I'll just keep my clothes on; it'll be all good."

Clay pouted. "Well, that's not exactly what I had in mind."

I playfully shoved him. "You are such a guy, Clayton Reed."

He kissed me loudly and patted my behind as I went into the bathroom to wash up. I was relieved that it was actually clean. The tub was stained but there were towels and a small, half-full bottle of Suave shampoo. I rummaged through my bag to find my flannel pj's. Yeah, they weren't the sexiest thing I owned, but I hoped wearing them might make me feel better.

I ran the water as hot as I could stand and stood under the spray. I used the shampoo to wash my hair and body. When I got out, skin pink from the steamy water, I felt a little better. I then remembered that in my hurry to leave, I hadn't brought any toiletries. No hairbrush, no toothpaste. For some reason, after everything, that tiny detail made me want to burst into tears.

I gripped the edge of the sink and took deep, gulping breaths, trying to get myself together. After a few minutes I was able to calm myself down. Using my fingers, I combed through my wet hair and then rinsed my mouth with water. I put on my warm pajamas and left the bathroom.

Clay was leaning back against the headboard, flipping through channels on the ancient television. He looked up when I came out and his eyes softened at the sight of me ready for bed.

"Feel better?" he asked, watching me as I put my clothes in the corner of the room.

"Yeah. But we'll need to get toothpaste and stuff in the morning. I forgot to bring some." I went to stand by the side of the bed, not sure I wanted to sleep underneath the gross-looking comforter. Clay, understanding my hesitation, peeled the cover back.

"The sheets look clean, at least," he remarked.

"We're not going to get eaten alive by bedbugs, are we?" I asked hesitantly before getting into the bed.

Clay looked under the covers. "Well, I sure hope not."

I threw a pillow at him. "That's not comforting," I said blandly.

Clay grinned at me. "Come on, get in here, this room is freezing." I climbed into the bed, sighing in contentment as I snuggled down between the sheets. At that moment, I didn't care if I was eaten alive as I slept, I was that bone-achingly tired.

Clay turned off the television and stood up. He slowly undressed, his clothes forming a pile beside the bed. In nothing but his boxers, he got into the bed beside me. We lay on our sides for a while, just looking at each other.

"Cute." Clay smirked, fingering the collar of my pajama top.

I rolled my eyes. "Sorry, I left my Frederick's of Hollywood stuff at home. I'll remember next time we decide to run away in the middle of the night," I replied sarcastically. At the mention of what we had done, Clay and I both became quiet.

The only sound in the dark room was that of our breathing. Ever so slowly, as if scared I might stop him, Clay reached out to touch my face. He gently traced my eyebrows with his fingertip, touched my eyelids, then ran his fingers down to my lips. His eyes came alive with a sudden hunger and desire, but most of all love. My heartbeat picked up as his hand dropped to my collarbone and he traced the curve from one side to the other.

It was so quiet, I swear he could hear my heart beating. He dipped his hand down farther, beneath the top edge of my shirt, and cupped my breast. He closed his eyes as his thumb rubbed my taut nipple. He hissed a breath in through his lips as he felt my smooth skin and I moaned a bit in response.

Clay opened his eyes. "Maggie?" He said my name as a question and I knew he was making sure I was okay with this. I nodded and leaned in to kiss him. The first touch of his tongue as it mated with mine was all I needed to get lost in the heady feeling he unleashed inside of me.

With sure fingers, Clay unbuttoned my top and carefully removed it. He continued to touch my breasts reverently, his breathing shallow as I arched toward him. Clay bent his head to take my nipple in his mouth, his tongue dancing over the sensitive flesh. I gripped the back of his head as he moved to my other breast.

Clay's hand made its way to the waist of my drawstring pants. He slid his fingers under the elastic, making me shake inside. Gently, he pushed my pants down, moving them lovingly over my hips. His mouth trailed down my body as he removed the clothing.

Starting at my ankle, Clay kissed a path up the inside of my leg, licking with his tongue as he savored me. He made tiny moans in the back of his throat as he continued his tortuous ascent. As he kissed the inside of my thighs, my fingers found themselves wrapped in his hair.

"Oh, God, Clay!" I rasped as he moved his mouth until he was breathing against my hot core. With slow precision, he licked the length of me, suckling to the point that I forgot my own name.

"You taste amazing," he murmured against my flesh as his tongue moved inside me. I had never experienced anything like this before. The burn deep in my belly laced fire throughout my body. Clay's mouth never stopped as I started to buck beneath him. With a violence that surprised me, I exploded against his tongue.

As I lay on the bed, spent, Clay kissed his way back up my body until he found my lips again. I could taste myself on his mouth and it was weirdly erotic. I thought I'd be grossed out by something like that. But I felt instead a strange sense of possession. Like I had marked him as mine.

Clay's hands dipped between my legs. He rubbed and caressed the sensitive folds until I was panting once again. He slid two of his fingers inside me and curved them until they were stoking a fire that threatened to consume me. Clay's tongue danced inside my mouth, tasting every inch as his fingers elicited another earth-shattering orgasm from my already trembling body. In the aftermath, Clay rolled me over until I was on top, my legs straddling him as I felt his hardness against me.

Digging into the pocket of his pants on the floor, he pulled out a condom and handed it to me. I arched an eyebrow at him and he gave me a sultry smile. I ripped open the package with my teeth, making Clay laugh. Then, slowly, with careful precision, I rolled it down over him. Clay moaned and laid his head back, closing his eyes as my fingers touched and caressed him.

When I was finished, Clay carefully lifted me up, and I angled myself so that I could slide down onto him. Clay pulled my mouth back down to his as I held him inside me. Not breaking our kiss, Clay moved his hands until he held my hips and I started to move up and down, enjoying the control I had.

"I love how I feel inside you," he whispered against my lips as I pressed into him, taking him as deep as he could go. "You're mine. Forever." He groaned as I started to pick up the pace. I broke off our kiss so that I could throw my head back, bracing myself against his chest.

Suddenly, Clay grabbed hold of me and flipped me on my back, pushing into me as he laid me down. I moaned loudly as I wrapped my legs around his waist in an effort to keep him buried inside me. "I love you so much," I panted as we moved our bodies together. After weeks of madness and separation, we came together in one beautiful cacophony of need and desire.

Together, like this, I felt we could take on anything. Clay moaned as I clenched myself around him and he kissed me deeply as he went as far as he could into my body. I opened my eyes to find him watching me with such tender sadness that it took my breath away.

I reached up to run my fingers over his face. "What is it?" I asked breathlessly, never stopping my perfect rhythmic movements with him.

Clay smiled, a truly gorgeous smile. "I just love you so much. Sometimes it hurts."

"I don't want it to hurt, Clay. Our love should make you feel wonderful," I told him, even as I almost wanted to laugh at how cheesy I sounded.

Clay didn't say anything more as we each began to build toward a burning explosion. Clay wrapped his arms around me, burying his face in my hair as I shattered around him. Finally, he surged into my body one last time as he came, and we lay against each other, too tired to move. Clay pushed up on his elbow and brushed my sweat-soaked hair off my forehead. He kissed my eyelids before rubbing my nose with his. I laughed at his affectionate gesture.

He took my hand and placed it over his heart, its frantic beat strong against my palm. "This is all I need. You, me, together," he said, still a little breathless. I picked up his hand and kissed his palm. Clay pulled out of me and rolled us both onto our sides, so that he held my back against his chest.

"Get some sleep, baby," he said quietly in my ear, kissing the back of my neck. So we fell asleep wrapped up in each other, unwilling to think anymore of the reality we would find ourselves thrown back into when we woke.

chapter
twenty-two

I awoke later in the day to the sound of my cell phone beeping. I had a moment of disorientation as I tried to figure out where I was. Then it all came back to me. I rolled over to find Clay sound asleep beside me, his hand reaching out as if he had been searching for me in his sleep.

I got out of bed and looked down, realizing I was naked. I went into the bathroom and changed into a clean pair of jeans and a T-shirt. I debated rinsing my mouth out with shampoo but decided against it. Instead, I swished around some water and spit it out. I still had demon breath, but it would have to do until we bought some toothpaste.

My cell phone beeped again. I looked at Clay; he hadn't stirred. He looked so young as he slept. The tension on his face melted in relaxation. I smiled at how good he looked lying there in the bed. I found my phone on the bedside table and turned it on.

A new text was waiting. It was from Rachel. *Where are you?!?! Your parents are freaking out! You better call me ASAP!*

I sighed. I quietly left the motel room. Once outside, I dialed Rachel's number. She answered on the first ring.

"*What is going on, Maggie?!*" she shrieked into the phone. I pulled the receiver away from my ear.

"Chill out, Rache. You're going to bust my eardrum," I said lightly.

"Don't give me your blasé crap. Why did you and Clay take off? Your parents called me at five o'clock this morning and they are absolutely a-hundred-percent flipping out! You had better have a good reason for all of this." I could tell she was angry. I would have felt the same way had our roles been reversed. I knew I owed her an explanation.

I sat down on the curb outside our room. "Clay is going through some major stuff right now and my parents were being unreasonable. He needed me."

She huffed on the other end. "Not good enough, Mags. Now, cut with the bullshit and 'fess up. Because I swear if you feed me some stupid song and dance about young love I'll bash your head in the next time I see you!" Rachel seethed.

"Fine, you want to know the truth? Clay has bipolar disorder as well as something called borderline personality disorder. Don't ask me what it all means, because I really don't know. Anyway, he had just gotten out of the hospital before he moved up here and now his parents are in town and threatening to lock him back up. And his crazy moods and temper are all because he's been on and off his meds. Plus, he really needs therapy, but so far has refused it. We're just trying to figure everything out, okay? He needs me! And I need him to be healthy." I finished my rambling explanation and waited for my friend's response.

"Rachel?" I said into the void.

"I'm here," she said quietly. I didn't like the tone of her voice. "I had no idea all this was going on. Why didn't you say something sooner?"

"It wasn't really my story to tell," I said simply. I heard Rachel cluck her tongue.

"But you know you can't save him. He needs serious help. Help from people who know what they're doing when it comes to that kind of stuff. If he's not taking his meds, like you said, then there's nothing you can do." She paused. "Maybe his parents are right. Maybe he needs to go somewhere where he can get some major treatment."

I was shocked and deeply hurt by her reaction. How could she side with those horrible people? She was supposed to be my best friend. "No. I can't let them do that to him," I bit out coldly.

Rachel sighed. I could almost see the exasperated expression on her face. "How could you do this to your parents? Don't you think they would have understood if you just told them? They love you and they're worried sick."

I felt the guilt flip in my gut. I hated that she reminded me of what I was doing to the other people I loved. "You just don't get it," I sulked.

"Oh, I get it, all right. You're on a one-woman mission to save Clay Reed from himself. I get that you love him. But there are times when love ain't enough, sweetheart, and I have a very bad feeling he's just going to take you down with him. Not that he means to. But that's just what happens." She seemed to be speaking from experience.

"What do you know about any of this? What do you know about Clay and what he's going through?" I asked hatefully.

"Listen. My grandmother suffered from bipolar disorder as well as a slough of other mental illnesses, if you must know. I saw firsthand the nightmare she put my grandfather and my mother through. It wasn't pretty. She refused to get help, too. And you know what happened?" she barked at me. I was shocked to hear this. I had no idea that her grandmother had suffered from any kind of mental illness. Rachel had never mentioned it.

"What?" I asked quietly.

"She killed herself when I was ten years old. That's what happened. And all because she swore she was fine and my grandfather believed her." Rachel's voice broke. I felt cold at her words.

"So, don't you see? You aren't helping Clay by enabling him! You need to get your ass back here, and let the people whose job it is to help him do it. Yeah, his parents sound shitty, but they just may ultimately know what's best for him—not you." She was being harsh and I wanted to ignore what she was telling me. But there was a small part of me that heard her and knew the advice she was giving me was good.

"And you should call your parents. Hearing from me that you're all right isn't the same as hearing it from you. You have great parents. Don't ruin your relationship with them for some ill-conceived Florence Nightingale complex."

I heard the motel door behind me open. "Maggie? Why are you out here?" Clay asked from the doorway. I looked over my shoulder at him. He had put on his pants but hadn't bothered with a shirt. His hair was rumpled as he squinted in the morning light.

"I've gotta go, Rache. I'll call you when I know where we're going," I assured her.

"Maggie. Seriously. Come home. This is nuts!" she pleaded. I didn't answer her; instead I disconnected the call.

Standing up, I shoved my phone in my pocket. "Rachel?" he asked.

I nodded, following him into the room and shutting the door behind us.

"What did you tell her?" He eyed me warily.

"I told her you had some stuff going on and we needed to get away for a while," I lied. No way could I tell him that I had spilled his entire mental history to her. I seriously doubted he'd want her to know about all of that ugliness.

Clay pulled me closer and kissed me. "I was scared when I woke up and you weren't here. I thought . . . that maybe you had left." He looked at me with a vulnerability that frightened me.

I hugged him tightly. "Never, Clay. I'm not going anywhere without you," I told him, and he relaxed in my arms.

Clay got in the shower and I looked on my phone for a place to get some provisions. There was a Target two towns over. So we got in Clay's car and went to Brookerton. We loaded up on shampoo, soap, toothbrushes, and toothpaste. I splurged a bit and got myself a curling iron and hair dryer. I was glad that I had thought to grab my cash card before leaving Davidson.

We went back to the motel room and I brushed my teeth for at least fifteen minutes. I had never been so thankful for toothpaste in my life. I spent some time and curled my hair, letting it rest in pretty waves around my shoulders. Just because we were on the run didn't mean I couldn't look nice. When I was finished, I sat beside Clay on the bed. He was going through messages on his phone. He looked up at me and smiled tenderly.

He touched a strand of my hair. "You look beautiful," he said softly. I leaned over and kissed him, feeling so full of love in that moment.

His attention was pulled back to his phone. "What is it?" I asked, peering over his shoulder.

"Ruby texted me last night," he said, turning the screen off.

"What did she say?" I asked him.

"She wanted to know where I was."

"Did you answer her?"

Clay shook his head. "Not yet. I'm not really sure what to tell her."

We were quiet for a while, the weight of our decision playing heavily on our minds. "What *are* we going to do? I mean, we can't stay in this motel room forever," I reasoned.

Clay smirked. "Why not? This is high-class living," he joked. I lightly punched his arm.

He sobered. "I know you're right. I just can't go back there. My life is over if I go back. Maybe we could find some quiet town to live in. We could get jobs, a place to live. Really start a life together." Clay seemed so hopeful. I, of course, knew that sort of wishful thinking would never happen. I still needed to finish high school.

And what about college? Yeah, I hadn't thought things through very clearly in my rush to run away with Clay.

In the harsh light of day, things seemed a lot less simple and more like a big ol' mess. I didn't respond to his statement, not sure I could agree with his rose-colored view of the future.

"Why don't we just stay here a day or two? We have enough money for that, and then we can figure things out," Clay said, taking my hand in his.

A day or two seemed okay. Maybe just some time to relax and put things in perspective was what Clay needed to make a sensible decision. I could give him that.

"Okay," I agreed, snuggling into his side. Clay wrapped his arms around me and kissed the top of my head.

"This is all I need, Mags. Just you and me, together," he murmured as I listened to his heartbeat under my ear. He made it sound so perfect. But I knew the life we were creating for ourselves was anything but.

✦

"Did you bring your medication, Clay?" I asked after I woke up from our afternoon nap. Clay stiffened for a minute before pulling away. He got off the bed and walked into the bathroom. I followed him and watched him from the doorway as he filled a cup with water and took a drink.

"You didn't bring them, did you," I stated instead of asking.

Clay gave me his best charming smile. "I'll be fine without them. I haven't really been taking them for a while, anyway. You'll see. Now that we're away from all that stress, it won't be like it was before. I promise." I couldn't believe he had been lying to me for weeks. I thought he had still been taking the lithium. His crazy behavior started to make more sense.

"What's 'a while'?" I asked him.

Clay frowned. "I don't know. A few weeks I guess. Don't worry about it."

Early November! I know my mouth hung open. I couldn't believe he had been so sneaky about it.

I felt like such a fool. Here I had been trying to rationalize everything, thinking he was just jealous or under a lot of stress. But no, it was because he hadn't been doing what he needed to do to regulate himself—to take care of himself. I wanted to punch him or scream at him. But I knew that would just make it worse.

Damn it! Rachel was right. I couldn't do this. I needed to get Clay back to Davidson. This was a tightrope walk, and I knew it was just a matter of time before he fell off and took me with him. My face must have paled because Clay grabbed me by my upper arms.

"Stop it, Maggie! Don't start worrying about me. I will be all right. Things will be perfect. Just how we wanted them to be. I don't need those stupid pills as long as I have you." His words chilled me. He really did seem to believe that.

When had I become his new medication? And when had I started enabling him? I loved Clay so much, but this was *not* right. He couldn't replace his medication with me and think things would be okay. He was seriously deluding himself.

"Clay, you need your meds," I whispered, trying to hide how appalled I was at his lack of responsibility and maturity.

Clay's face darkened. "Don't start with me, Maggie. I told you, I'm fine." He brushed past me into the room.

I had to figure something out. But I wasn't sure how I could convince Clay to go back home. He was certain that being away from Davidson and his parents would make everything okay. He was so, so wrong.

"I'm scared for you," I said, watching him as he pulled a new shirt out of his bag and put it on. His shoulders tensed.

"Well, don't be. You're overthinking things again," he said flippantly. I wanted to be angry with him for putting us in this position. For doing this to himself. But I caught a glimpse at the healing cuts on his chest and arms as he pulled his shirt over his head and I just felt sad. I wanted him to be happy and healthy. Maybe I could just give him the few days he'd asked for. And then convince him to go home. He would listen to me, right? I mean, he loved me.

I came up behind him and put my arms around his chest and buried my face in his back, breathing in his amazing smell. "I love you. You know that?"

Clay turned in my arms and held me. "Of course I know that, Mags. I love you too." I reached up on my tiptoes and locked my mouth to his, the taste of him causing the same butterflies in my stomach that it always did.

Clay broke the kiss and grinned at me. "Let's get out of this depressing room. I want to take you out to dinner. A proper date."

I laughed at the giddiness in his voice. "A date, huh?" I raised my eyebrows at him.

"Yeah. Let's go paint the town red, baby." He pulled on my hand, tugging me toward the door. Clay tucked his wallet in his pocket and pulled out his car keys. I let him lead me outside.

Soon we were making our way through the tiny town of Glass Lake. There wasn't a whole lot to it. But there was a restaurant on the north end of town called Elk's Ridge Bar and Grill. Funny name, considering there were no elk in North Carolina.

I ordered a steak and potatoes and he got the chicken Alfredo. We ate until we were completely stuffed. We laughed and talked. I loved being with him like this. This was the Clay I loved more than anything.

As I waited at the table for Clay to come back from the bathroom, my cell phone made a ding in my pocket. I was hesitant to check it. I didn't want anything to ruin the great evening I was having. But curiosity won out.

Looking in the direction of the bathrooms to watch for Clay, I quickly took out my phone. There was a text waiting from Rachel.

You guys are in some serious shit. Did Clay tell you what went down when he left his house last night?

Feeling immediately edgy, I quickly typed out, *What do you mean?* I tapped my foot in impatience as I waited for the responding message. A minute later the phone dinged again. Looking at what my friend had written, I thought I would be sick.

He threatened his parents with a knife. Destroyed stuff, stole a bunch of money from his dad's wallet and took off. The police are looking for you guys. His parents are threatening to press charges against him. You really need to come home. Otherwise it'll just get worse.

Why hadn't Clay told me about what had happened? Again, he was keeping secrets from me! The one person he swore he'd be honest with! I shoved the phone back in my pocket and plastered a smile on my face as he came back to the table.

"Ready?" he asked. I nodded, not trusting my voice. Clay put some cash on the table (his parents' money, I was sure) and held out his hand for me to take. I wrapped my fingers in his and let him pull me to my feet. He hugged me and kissed my nose.

"Thank you for being my date," he said with a grin.

I couldn't help but smile back, despite what I had just learned. "Thank you for asking me to be your date," I replied, squeezing his waist. We walked out of the restaurant, our arms wrapped around each other.

Out in the cold night air, I felt unsure. I needed to talk to Clay about what I had just learned. But how did I broach the subject? His parents were a sore spot, to say the least, and I knew it would just lead to an argument.

But I had to know why he had kept it a secret. Why he hadn't told me the truth when he'd come to my room the night before. Though part of me wanted nothing more than to pretend it was all a mistake. That what Rachel had told me couldn't possibly be true.

We walked down the street a ways and came upon a small park. We found ourselves at a tiny bench in a shady grove of trees. The air was crisp and chilly and I wrapped my jacket tighter around me. Clay put his arm around my shoulders and held me tight against his side. He kissed the top of my head and I tried to relax into him.

I didn't fool Clay for a second. He knew me too well. "What's wrong, baby?" he asked me softly, curling my hair around his finger. I pulled back a bit so that I could look at him.

"I got a text from Rachel while you were in the bathroom," I started.

Clay frowned. "Okay. Did she say something to upset you?" he asked, rubbing his thumb across my bottom lip.

I cleared my throat, trying to ignore the burn of desire that ignited at his touch. "Well, she told me the police are looking for us."

Clay stiffened, his thumb stopping its slow caress across my skin. "Well, I kind of expected that," he admitted, dropping his hand into his lap.

"Well, they're after us because of what happened. You know. At your house." I looked at him pointedly and I watched his face grow cold.

"At my house," he stated.

I nodded. I felt myself getting angry with him. "Is there something you need to tell me? About what went down with your parents?" I prompted, scooting back, putting distance between us.

Clay gave an angry sigh and got to his feet. He started pacing. "I told you everything," he insisted harshly. I jumped to my feet and grabbed hold of his arm.

I wrenched him around to look at me. "No, you didn't! You sure as hell didn't tell me that you pulled a knife! On your parents! Are you fucking crazy?" I shrieked at him.

Okay, bad choice of words. Clay pulled my hand off his arm. "Yes, Maggie! I am *fucking crazy*! Everyone thinks it, so it must be true!" he yelled back at me. I blanched at his words and started backing away from him. His face dropped and he raked his fingers through his hair in agitation.

"I want to go home, Clay. This is all so messed up! We can't do this!" I implored him, collapsing on the park bench and covering my face with my hands.

Clay came to sit beside me and pulled my hands down. He held them tightly in his and looked at me with the most desolate expression I had ever seen.

"I can't go home. Not now. I know I screwed up. I let things get out of control. But they weren't listening to me! They *never* listen to me! Because none of this was ever about me. It was all about my parents and how much of an embarrassment I am." His voice cracked.

I softened at seeing him like this. I reached out and touched his cheek, lingering. "What about Ruby and Lisa? Can't they help?" I asked desperately.

Clay barked out a laugh that sounded almost maniacal. "Uh, no. My parents threatened to have Ruby charged with contributing to the delinquency or something. I'm not sure how they could charge her with anything. But if anyone knows how to bend the law to get what they want, it's my parents."

God, I hated those people. Clay clung to my hand. "They just wouldn't stop. They told me I was useless and a liability. That I was . . . deranged. That I wasn't fit to be in normal society." Clay's voice cut off on a ragged breath. His parents had broken him. How could they say such horrible things to their son, when he deserved so much more?

"So, yeah. I was angry. I felt trapped and needed to get out of there. So I grabbed a knife off of the counter and pointed it at them and told them I was leaving." I gasped. Clay arched his eyebrow. "A butter knife, Maggie. It was a fucking butter knife."

A butter knife? Really? They were pressing charges over a butter knife? This was ludicrous!

I couldn't stop the laugh that crept up out of my throat. And suddenly I was laughing. An insane sort of laughter. I couldn't stop. After a startled moment, Clay joined me and we were both laughing at the absurdity of it all.

Finally we were able to calm down and Clay sobered instantly. "Do you see why I can't go back there? They won't leave me alone! I'll never have a life. They want me out of the way. And now they've involved the police, I'll be locked away for sure. There's nothing you, or me, or anyone, can do about it. I just have to disappear." He seemed so sure and I was tempted to be swayed by his logic.

Clay kissed the corner of my mouth. "I understand if this is too much for you. If you want to go home, I won't stop you. You have to do what's right for *you*. Not for me," he said softly, his eyes full of sadness and love for me.

He was giving me an out. I appreciated that he was trying to be selfless. But after everything, all that I had sacrificed to be with him, there was no way in hell I'd let anyone take him from me. Despite my misgivings and the red flags that continued to go up all over the place, I was firm in my resolve to stand by him.

"I can't leave you. Not now, not ever," I whispered, my eyes never leaving his. One way or the other I had to make things right for him. I didn't have any sort of a plan. The only one I had was to ride things out here. Just a few more days and I'd figure something out.

"God, I need you so much." Clay's voice broke and he pulled me to him and sat on the bench, taking me with him so that I was straddling him. His mouth pressed against mine and he nibbled mercilessly at my bottom lip. I groaned into his mouth as I wiggled closer to him.

"Fuck, Maggie," he whispered, wrenching my shirt out of my pants and moving his hands up the front of my body. I wrapped my legs around his waist and kissed him with all the pain and desire I felt. His hands cupped my breasts and kneaded the skin roughly.

The cold night air whipped around us but all I could feel was the heat being generated between us, the feel of him hard underneath his jeans.

"I need to be inside you. Now!" he gasped as he rubbed my nipples between his fingers.

"But we're outside, in a park. I don't know . . ." I suddenly felt self-conscious. Anyone could come up on us like this. Yet the park seemed to be deserted. And we *were* shielded from view by the trees.

"No one will see. Please," he begged, unbuttoning my pants and pulling down the zipper, his fingers slipping underneath the edge of my panties, finding me wet and ready.

"Clay," I groaned as his fingers slipped inside me, a tantalizing tease. I frantically unzipped his jeans, rolling them down so that they released him. Clay sucked in a breath and shoved my pants down my hips.

He was being rough and desperate. Not at all like the gentle lovemaking we had had before. His lips were hot and pressed hard against my neck as I shrugged out of my pants. The chill around us made goose bumps break out all over my bare legs.

I barely registered the sound of ripping foil, and then Clay lifted me up and shoved my underwear aside, settling me down on top of him, plunging deep into my body. I gasped at the suddenness of it.

"More. I need more of you," Clay pleaded as he jerked his hips upward, while pulling me down against him as he held my hips tightly. His fingers dug into my flesh as he moved me up and down over him, piercing me deeply.

"Oh, my God!" I groaned as I wrapped my legs tighter, pushing us as close together as we could go. Clay pulled me hard against him, his lips leaving wet trails along my neck and shoulders. He bit down on my skin as I ground against him, the feel of him deep inside me causing the familiar burn to build up in my belly.

"Don't leave me! Ever!" he rasped in my ear, sucking the lobe as we rocked into each other with a frantic pace that both scared and thrilled me. My knees slammed into the metal of the bench and I barely registered the pain as I fell apart around him. After a few more moments of punishing thrusts, I felt Clay release inside me.

It was at that moment that I realized what we had done. I couldn't believe I had let us have sex in a park. In the middle of town. That was right up there as one of the stupidest and riskiest things I had ever done.

I collapsed against Clay and he held me tightly, running his fingers through my hair as we tried to get control over our breathing again.

The cold wind finally broke through the postcoital haze and I moved off of Clay's lap, feeling his wetness between my legs. I scooped up my discarded pants and hastily put them back on.

"Well, that was a first," I joked, still a little out of breath. Clay smirked at me as he buttoned himself back up.

He pulled me back onto his lap. "I just needed to be close to you. Sorry the setting wasn't more romantic," Clay apologized, kissing my temple as I snuggled into his chest.

I sighed and laid my head down over his heart. The steady beat both calmed and soothed me. Clay rubbed my back and traced the length of my shoulder blades with his fingertip. "You're all that I have," he said quietly, kissing the top of my head. I let him hold me and tried to convince myself that everything would be all right. But I knew I was just living another lie.

chapter
twenty-three

funny how two days can change everything. Even my staunch refusal to let anything come between me and the boy I loved. My picture of the world had been flipped on its head and I lived in a constant state of confusion and near-paranoia.

We went to bed at night curled around each other. We never said anything; no words were needed. Clay clung to me as if I would disappear. We made love frantically and desperately, as if we were trying to hold on to something that would be snatched from our grasp at any moment. But I couldn't pretend any longer that things were going to work out. It was only a matter of time until we were discovered.

Rachel had been texting me nonstop, urging me to come home. She worried that things would only get worse the longer we were gone. And I knew she was right. I didn't want to think about what would be waiting for Clay back in Davidson. But with every hour that went by, I saw Clay deteriorating. He was paranoid and hypervigilant. He wouldn't let me out of his sight. He had unplugged the phone in our room and put a chair against the doorknob when we slept.

He was edgy and angry, snapping at me for no reason and then immediately pleading with me to forgive him. He was also cutting again. I saw the marks on his skin, even as he tried to hide them. I thought about confronting him but thought better of it, knowing he was dangerously close to losing what small semblance of sanity he had left.

Things were spiraling out of control, not just for Clay, but for me as well. I was scared all the time. I could barely sleep and I couldn't handle sitting by and watching the boy that I loved slowly slip away into the darkness of his mind.

I needed my parents and my friends. I wanted their support and the safety of home so badly that I ached for it. I wanted Clay to get some help, because now I couldn't deny that that was exactly what he needed. He didn't need me pretending that we would gallop off into the sunset like some fairy tale.

Because that wasn't our story. Not by a long shot.

After seeing the newscast, I knew I had to call my parents. They were probably going out of their minds if they thought Clay had kidnapped me. Who knew what bullshit Clay's parents had fed them?

I waited until I knew Clay was asleep, and I quietly got dressed and went outside. I gripped my cell phone and with shaking fingers dialed my mom's number. I realized how late it was, almost 11:30 at night. But I needed to hear her voice.

"Hello?" I heard my mother's shaking voice on the other end.

I almost hung up, scared as hell to say anything. "Maggie! Is that you?" my mom pleaded. I took a deep breath.

"Yes, Mom, it's me," I whispered. I heard her choking back a sob.

"Oh, my God, are you all right? Where are you?" she asked me.

"I'm fine, Mom. Clay and I are in North Carolina . . ."

"North Carolina! What are you doing there?" I didn't answer her—not sure what to tell her. My mom seemed to make an effort to pull herself together. "Please tell me he isn't keeping you there against your will," my mother asked, as calmly as she was able.

"No, I left willingly," I assured her.

My mom sighed in relief. "Okay. Well, that's something, I suppose. Clay's parents have shared some things about Clay that have your father and me worried sick. He isn't hurting you, is he?" my mom asked, and I could tell she was crying.

"God, no, Mom. Clay would never hurt me! What have Clay's parents told you?" I asked coldly.

"That Clay has a history of violent and suicidal behaviors. His mother said he needs to be back in treatment but he refuses to go. Then she told us that he . . . that he tried to stab them."

I blew out a breath. "It wasn't like that, Mom. Please don't believe everything they tell you," I urged.

"So you're saying there's nothing to these stories they told us? That they're making everything up?" my mother asked in disbelief.

Here was the moment of truth. Did I lie, like I'd been doing for months? Or did I finally come clean?

I was silent for a while, prompting my mother to say my name again. "Maggie? What is it?" she asked.

I felt the tears slide down my cheeks and suddenly I was sobbing. I cried and cried until there was nothing left. And then I told my mom everything. Every last bit of Clay's story. This was the second time in as many days that I had shared what was going on. And it felt good to do so. I had been holding on to this stuff for too long and I couldn't shoulder it alone any longer.

"My God, Maggie May. Why in the world didn't you say something?" she asked, her voice quiet and hurting. I sighed after I had calmed down.

"You would have just told me to stay away from him. I know how you feel about Clay. You haven't tried to hide it. And he needed me. I couldn't turn my back on him like everyone else had.

I love him!" I struggled to keep my voice down, not wanting to wake Clay.

My mom was quiet for some time. "You're right. We would have judged him. I would have told you to never talk to him again. And that's wrong. I'm sorry." My mom's words surprised me.

"You're sorry?" I asked, needing clarification.

"Yes, Maggie. Because maybe if your father and I hadn't been so narrow-minded, you would have felt you could talk to us. Because we know Clay isn't a bad kid. But he needs help. And we'd like to help you both. If you'll let us."

She said exactly what I needed to hear. I wanted my parents. I needed their help to figure out what to do for Clay. "I want to come home, too. I'm worried about him. But what about his parents? The charges? I can't walk him back into all that." I looked back at the motel door, making sure I was still alone.

My mom sighed again. "I know, sweetie. I don't know what will happen. But I do know being on your own, trying to deal with all of this by yourself, is not the way to handle it. Clay needs help; serious help. I'm scared for you. And him. I know you love him, but there's no way out of this but coming home and facing things. And I swear, darling, your father and I will help you both in any way that we can."

My mom had officially broken through all of my arguments. And I was tired of fighting them and everything else. My heart hurt to think of what would become of Clay. But what would happen if we stayed on the run? And if he continued to fade away. What would happen to him then? Or me? It was a damned-if-you-do/damned-if-you-don't situation. But one thing was for sure: I needed my family. Maybe more than I needed Clay at that moment. Because I was in way over my head and I was scared to death of making the wrong choice.

"Okay, Mom. I know you're right. Clay needs help. I'll get him home. One way or another. I'll let you know when we're on our way," I said.

I heard my mom's relief. "Oh, thank God! Please be careful! And call us!" I told her that I loved her and hung up.

"I'm not going back there!" Clay growled from behind me.

I whipped around to see him standing in the doorway. How much had he heard? How had I not heard him open the door? He looked livid.

"How could you do this to me? I trusted you!" he yelled at me, the betrayal on his face stinging me.

"Clay, please. Just listen!" I begged. Clay's eyes flashed at me and I saw how hurt he was underneath the anger.

"After everything I've told you. You know what they'll do to me if I go back. And you're trying to hand me over like a god-damn birthday present! They'll lock me up! I thought you loved me! What a fucking lie!" His voice became dangerously quiet.

I tried to reach for him but he yanked his arm away. "I do love you, Clay! I'm just so worried about you! I just think you need help . . ."

Clay's bitter laugh cut me off. "Help? Help?" His voice rose. "You don't know a damn thing about what I need! You're just as bad as *them*. No, actually you're worse, because at least my par-ents never pretended to love me. I knew what I was getting with them." My mouth dropped open, and I couldn't believe the hate-fulness spewing from my boyfriend's lips.

Clay gripped his hair in his hands as if he were going to pull it out. It was clear something in him had snapped. That I had pushed him over the edge.

"But you! I thought I was safe with you! But you were just biding your time, weren't you, Maggie? Until you could get rid of me, just like the rest of them. Well, I hope you're happy, because you're about to get your fucking wish!" Clay bellowed at me, making me flinch.

He was being completely irrational. How could he possibly be-lieve the things he was saying to me? Hadn't I proven over and over again how willing I was to sacrifice just about anything for him? If I wasn't so scared for him, I'd probably be seriously pissed off.

I didn't respond, choosing to silently let him vent his crap at me. When he wasn't getting the reaction he obviously wanted, he turned away from me. I tried grabbing him again but he threw my hands off him with enough force to knock me back on my butt. The pain in my backside was instantaneous and took my breath away.

"Clay!" I gasped.

He paused a moment but didn't turn around. Did he realize what he had just done? Well, if he did, he was beyond caring, because he disappeared into the room, slamming the door behind him.

Shit! I scrambled to my feet and tried to open the door but he had locked it.

I banged on the door. "Let me in, Clay! Please! Will you just listen?" I pleaded as I slammed my hand against the hard wood.

"Go away! You're a fucking liar and we are done! You've destroyed everything!" he screamed from the other side. I heard a smash and I started beating the door frantically.

"Clay!!! Open this door now!" The reply was the sound of more destruction on the other side of the door. I heard Clay yell and the sound of breaking glass. The horrible noises of his tirade seemed to last forever. I kept banging on the door with my hands until they were bruised and raw. And then it all stopped and everything went eerily quiet.

"Clay!" I screamed into the thick wood that separated us. But I heard nothing.

Then I felt the fear.

I ran down the sidewalk and into the lobby. I forced myself to slow down and act nonchalant. The same kid that had checked Clay and me in was manning the desk.

"Hey. I locked myself out of my room. Can I get a spare key card?" The pimply faced guy barely looked at me.

"Room number?" he asked.

"Room forty-three," I told him. He lazily punched some stuff into the computer.

I stood there for fifteen minutes as the guy moved through the required motions with the speed of a snail. I tried to control the urge to reach across the counter and do it myself. Jesus! How long does it take to get a new room key? My skin was crawling with the urge to get back to Clay.

"Here. You need another one; it'll cost ya twenty-five dollars," the guy said, already dismissing me as he turned back to the small, fuzzy-screened TV behind him.

I grabbed the key card and took off back toward our room. I had already been away too long. I quickly put the key in the door and pushed. It took all my strength because something was blocking the door from the other side.

After four or five good shoves, I got through the door and I gasped in horror. It looked like a bomb had gone off. Clay had pulled over the television set and the screen had shattered all over the floor. He had pushed the mattress off the bed and ripped and shredded almost all of our clothing.

The item that had been blocking the door was the ancient-looking armchair. Clay had broken one of the wooden legs and it lay on its side. How could one person do so much damage?

"Clay?" I called out, praying for an answer. But of course there was none.

The bathroom door was closed but I could see light filtering out around the edges. My stomach felt heavy with dread. The icy fingers of fear spread through my entire body. I turned the handle of the bathroom door, slowly opening it.

And then I screamed.

Clay had broken the mirror, and glass lay all over the sink and floor. But what made me scream was the sight of Clay curled on his side in a fetal position on the grubby tile floor, a slowly expanding pool of blood blossoming out around his prostrate body.

I hurried to his side, slipping in his blood and falling hard to my knees. I rolled him onto his back. His eyes were open but glassy and unfocused. His skin was ashen and I had to swallow the vomit rising up in my throat as I took in the sight of his wrists.

He had used glass from the shattered mirror and slashed deep into the skin above each palm in a vertical line, almost all the way up to his elbow. Blood flowed from the injuries at a rate that terrified me.

"No, Clay! No, no, no!" I wept as I ripped towels from the rack on the wall and wrapped his arms. My tears mingled with his blood on the floor. I pulled my cell phone out of my pocket and dialed 911. The dispatcher answered and asked me to state my emergency.

"Please! My boyfriend has tried to kill himself! We're at the Motel 6 outside of Glass Lake, near the highway. Room forty-three," I gasped out as I tried to stanch the blood that just would not stop flowing out of him.

"Ma'am. How did he try to kill himself?" The lady on the other end was to the point, yet calm. I picked up the jagged piece of glass from the bathroom floor. It was coated in Clay's blood.

"He slit his wrists. With a piece of glass."

The dispatcher began to reel off advice on how to slow down the blood loss. To put pressure on the wounds and to try to keep him alert and lucid by talking to him. She assured me the paramedics were on their way.

"Clay! Please. Talk to me." His eyes slowly moved to my face, but I wasn't sure he even recognized me. Their expression was dull and practically lifeless. I pressed my hands over his injured wrists, trying to ignore the fact that the towels were slowly soaking in his blood. I wrapped his arms with another towel.

"Don't you dare leave me, Clayton Reed! Not after everything we've been through! How could you do this to me?" I sobbed as I cradled his body to my chest. My hair fell into his face, like a curtain.

I felt his mouth move against my cheek as he struggled to speak. I leaned down and put my ear to his lips. "Sorry. So, so sorry," he said, over and over again.

His words just made the tears come faster. So I sat there, on the nasty bathroom floor in the middle of nowhere, holding my dying boyfriend as I told him repeatedly how much I loved him and needed him.

chapter
twenty-four

finally the ambulance arrived, and everything moved way too fast after that. I was pretty much shoved out of the bathroom as the EMTs took over. They made me leave the motel room and wait outside while they treated Clay. I gnawed at the skin of my lips and paced back and forth in front of the door.

After five minutes or so, the three EMTs brought Clay out on a stretcher. I noticed they had bandaged his wrists with gauze. I could tell he had lost consciousness. Two of the paramedics loaded Clay into the back of the ambulance while the third turned to me.

"You're the girlfriend?" he asked. He was a large guy with kind eyes. I nodded.

"You can get in the back with him. I need to get some information on our way to the hospital." I jumped up into the ambulance and took a seat beside Clay's motionless form. He was so pale and still that he looked dead already.

"Will he be all right?" I asked the EMTs as they hooked Clay up to a million monitors and read out numbers that were meaningless to me.

I heard the siren start up and we sped away at a lightning pace. The paramedic with the kind eyes looked at me sympathetically. "It's too soon to say. He lost a lot of blood. How did this happen?"

And I just unloaded it all. I told the two EMTs about Clay's history. His previous hospitalizations as well as his unwillingness to stay on medication. I told them about his erratic moods and even about his family life. I wanted them to have a complete history. Hell, I'd tell them about his childhood fear of the dark and the fact he hated brussels sprouts if I thought it would help. The male and female paramedics alternated asking several questions pertaining to Clay's medication and how long he had been off it but, other than that, they just listened.

Once we got to the emergency room at the local hospital, everything was a blur. Doctors and nurses came as soon as we arrived and whisked Clay away. I tried to follow but, because I wasn't family, I wasn't permitted to go in with him. A nurse brought me some soap and a towel and showed me where the bathrooms were. I thought that was quite odd until I got a full-on look at myself in the mirror. Oh, my God—I looked like I had just survived *The Texas Chainsaw Massacre*.

Blood was caked on my face and neck. My jeans were almost black with dried blood from the knees down. My hands were coated with the sticky, flaky stuff, and I had to dig it out from under my fingernails. I used the soap to wash my skin, and then I tried sticking my head under the faucet so I could rinse my hair. I felt sick at the sight of the pink water as it swirled down the drain.

Thinking that was Clay's life gurgling down into the pipes.

When I was finished, I went back to the front desk, where I was directed to the waiting room. I joined twenty other people as I sat in my own personal hell. I alternated between pacing the floor and hounding the nurses about Clay's status. They never had much to tell me.

Finally, at around 5:30 in the morning, a nurse came out and called my name. I had been crunched up in the most uncomfortable chair on the planet for the past hour, and I thought my back would break from the crazy position I had put myself in. I jumped to my feet and rushed over to her.

"I'm Maggie Young," I said a little breathlessly. The nurse gave me a once-over.

"You're Clayton Reed's girlfriend?" she asked.

"Yes. That's me." The nurse put her hand on my shoulder and pulled me off to the side.

"We need to get in contact with Clay's parents. They have to be notified. Do you have a way to reach them?" I started to protest, knowing Clay would hate that. But the nurse, whose name badge read KELLY BURKE, RPN, cut me off.

"Maggie. He is a minor. We have to notify his family of his condition." I felt the tears spill down my cheeks.

"Can you please just tell me how he's doing? I'll give you the number. I just need to know what's going on. Please tell me if he's gonna be okay," I pleaded with her.

I saw Nurse Burke waver. "I'm not permitted to share medical information regarding a minor with anyone but his family. But . . ." She looked around and then back at me. "You saved his life," she said quietly.

I put my hand to my mouth and tried to stifle the sob that rose up in my throat. Kelly Burke patted my back. "Clay is in ICU and is listed in critical condition. He lost a lot of blood. We had to give him three pints. He's still unconscious but we anticipate he'll be waking soon. We're not sure of the impact his blood loss has had on the rest of his organs and won't know until he wakes up." She cleared her throat and dropped her voice even lower.

"Aside from the physical ramifications, there are the psychological impacts that factor as well. The staff psychiatrist has been notified and will be in to see him once he regains consciousness. I don't anticipate him being released for a while."

I tried to stay on my feet, but I felt myself wobbling. I was exhausted. I hadn't eaten in almost twelve hours. I just couldn't take anything in anymore.

Nurse Burke must have seen the look on my face, because she gripped my arm and walked me to a chair. "Let me get you some juice. You look like you're about to pass out."

Nurse Burke returned a few minutes later with a foil-topped juice cup and paper-wrapped straw and placed them in my hand. I opened the cup and took a few sips and felt a little better. I pulled out Clay's phone, which I had grabbed before leaving the motel, and went through the contacts until I found his parents' number. I gave it to the nurse. She thanked me and then left to make the call.

I sat there, numb. I felt completely empty. After another hour had passed, Nurse Burke came back out to let me know that Clay's parents were on their way. I simply nodded and thanked her. I pulled out my own phone and called my mom.

"Maggie? Are you on your way home?" she asked as soon as she picked up. I took in a shaky breath and felt the tears start again, completely unbidden.

"No, Mom. We're at the hospital."

"Oh, my God! Are you okay?" she demanded in a panicked voice.

"I'm fine, Mom. It's Clay. He tried to kill himself."

"Oh, Maggie! Where are you? We're coming to get you!" I gave her the name of the hospital and she assured me that she and my father would be there as soon as possible.

I hung up and dropped the phone onto the table beside me. Unable to move, I stared blankly at the TV mounted on the wall. How did things get this bad so quickly? How could I have allowed it to get so out of hand? I blamed myself entirely for Clay being here.

I should have stopped him from leaving town. I should have forced him to face what was going on with his parents. But most of all, I should never have ignored how badly he needed help. I was the biggest culprit in the enabling category.

My "love" had only made things worse for him. Because I had refused to see what was right in front of me. My denial had failed Clay. I put my face in my hands and cried.

A while later, I felt a hand touch my shoulder and I sat up with a start. Nurse Burke stood over me with a kind look on her face. "He's awake and asking for you. I shouldn't let you back to see him, but he's been very agitated, demanding to see you. We've had to give him a sedative. But I can only give you a few minutes."

I got to my feet. "Thank you so much," I whispered as she led me back through a set of locked doors. The hospital smell made me feel light-headed and I tried to keep my breathing even and stay steady on my feet. Nurse Burke and I continued to walk until we were outside of the ICU. She led me to his room and quickly waved me inside, watching the corridor as I hurried through the door.

Clay lay in a bed, a bunch of wires hooked up to his body, the beeping of machines echoing much too loudly in the small space. "You can only have a few minutes. I'll be back," Nurse Burke said, before leaving to give us some privacy.

Clay noticed I was there and watched me as I came to his side. His eyes were heavy and clouded with the sedative. The white of his bandaged wrists stood out against the blue hospital blanket. He was deathly pale and he looked at me with an unreadable emotion as I gently took his hand in mine.

"Maggie," he said. His voice sounded as if he had been chewing broken glass. My name rolled roughly off his tongue. I carefully sat down on the edge of the bed.

"Hey," I replied, trying hard to smile.

Clay closed his eyes. "I'm so sorry. I can't believe I did this to you. I'm just so, so sorry." I didn't say anything, just leaned over and pressed my mouth to his cheek. His skin was cold on my lips.

"Your parents are on their way here," I told him, and he only nodded. The nurse must have already told him.

"They're going to put me away," he said matter-of-factly.

"I know" was all I could reply. Clay opened his eyes and I could see a spark of the old Clay there, hidden in their depths.

"They're going to take me away from you. That's exactly what I didn't want to happen," he told me flatly. I could see him struggling under the weight of his sedation.

He reached out to touch my face, but his fingers fell back to the bed before they could make contact. "You look so sad. I did this to you. I hate myself for making you feel this way. I ruin everything. I always have," he said, his voice deadened by the drugs.

I shook my head. "No! Don't say that. It's not true." Clay closed his eyes and leaned back against the pillows, almost as if it were too painful to look at me.

"I can't keep doing this to you," he whispered, covering his face with his hands. I needed to put an end to his bitter self-loathing. I just didn't know how.

"Just stop this, Clay. You need to worry about getting better. Nothing else," I said with more conviction than I felt. I reached up and pulled his hands down. "Please, just get better," I begged.

He covered my hand with his and held it to his face. "I love you, Maggie. Forever. I was being selfish, only thinking about myself. I should have put you first, always," he agonized, showing more feeling than he had since I'd walked in. I didn't say anything more. I pulled myself up onto his bed and spooned my body against his and held him until Nurse Burke returned.

As I was forced to leave his side, I turned back to look at him one more time. Who knew when I'd get to see him again? His eyes met mine and he looked completely and utterly shattered—broken. His expression was haunting.

And was burned into my mind.

Once back out in the waiting room I was greeted by a very angry Mrs. Reed. Mr. Reed stood behind her, looking bland and uninterested as if he'd rather be in a meeting at work than a hospital waiting room. Regardless of the fact that his son had been admitted there for trying to take his own life.

Mrs. Reed took two steps and leaned in uncomfortably close to my face. "What did you do to him?" she hissed.

I reeled back in surprise. Was she for real? I almost laughed at the absolute absurdity of her question. To think this self-important bitch could actually stand there and place the blame for Clay's condition squarely on my shoulders, especially when the root of so many of his problems rested solely with the two narcissistic people standing in front of me.

"Does this amuse you? And here I thought you and my son were *in love*. When in reality you're that little gold-digging mooch I knew you were. Did you talk him into leaving town with you? Have him take you on some whirlwind vacation with *our* money?" she spat at me with all the venom she could muster.

This time I did laugh. "Oh, yeah, because the Motel Six is livin' large," I said sarcastically. Mrs. Reed looked as if she wanted to slap me as her hand tensed by her side.

"My son is a very sick boy. He doesn't need to be led astray by a selfish little bitch like you." The hatred in her voice startled me. What in the world had I done to garner such strong dislike from this woman?

Yet if I thought about it, I knew Mrs. Reed's problem was that she wanted to place blame anywhere and everywhere but where it belonged—with herself and her husband. She couldn't see her own failings as a parent, so instead I became the bad guy.

Well, screw that!

So I got right back in her nasty, smug face and poked my finger in the middle of her chest. "Back off, Mrs. Reed. Your son is lying in a hospital bed after slitting his wrists because the *two of you* have been more concerned with how this could make you look than involving yourselves with what's going on with *your son*." Mrs. Reed's face turned crimson and her jaw clenched. And I wasn't even close to being done speaking my mind.

"Maybe if you spent more time being actual parents, he wouldn't be where he is now. In an ICU! After attempting suicide! I love your son. More than anything. And because I love him, I can recognize that the best thing for him is to get help, even though that means he will go away. I love him enough to realize my desire to be with him is *not* necessarily what's best for him. And I hope you can remember that he is *your* son. Your own flesh and blood! And that what he needs, more than anything, is love and support. *Not* judgment and condemnation. And he sure as hell doesn't need you pressing bogus charges against him! So, *for once,* maybe you can do what *he* needs rather that what *you* want."

My anger fizzled and all I felt was bone-weary sadness. I wanted to keep throwing my rage at these two horrible people, but I just felt depressed. Being pissed off wouldn't change what had happened or help Clay.

Mrs. Reed pulled herself up as straight as her spine would let her. Her red face and icy eyes looked like she was about to rip into me again when Nurse Burke interrupted.

"Are you Mr. and Mrs. Reed?"

"Yes, I'm Samantha Reed and this is Clayton's father, Nicholas. Where is my son?" she demanded. Nurse Burke's no-nonsense expression never faltered. She was probably used to dealing with pain-in-the-ass people all day long.

"I'll take you to see him. But I have to let you know that it is extremely important that he not be agitated. He is in a very delicate state right now, and needs nothing but calm. The staff psychiatrist, Dr. Lang, is waiting for you to discuss possible options for continued treatment. So, if you'll follow me . . ."

Mrs. Reed picked up her purse and, with a final scathing look at me, she followed Nurse Burke, who offered me a slight, sympathetic nod. I smiled halfheartedly in return, hoping she understood my appreciation for her intervention.

After Clay's parents disappeared I collapsed into a chair. I must have dozed off, because the next thing I knew, Rachel was shaking me.

"Maggie! Oh, my God, Maggie!" I opened my eyes to see Rachel, Daniel, and my parents crowded around me. Daniel pulled me to my feet as he and Rachel hugged me.

"You scared me to death! I could smack you," Daniel said with a frown, but not once did he let go of me. Rachel just started crying and clung to me as if we had been apart for months rather than days.

I pulled away from my friends and launched myself at my parents. They held me tightly to them, each telling me over and over that they loved me. I was so appreciative of them, especially after being subjected to Clay's cold and self-centered family.

"I'm so sorry," I whispered repeatedly.

"Shh. Don't worry. It's all over now. Let's just go home."

I hesitated. I felt torn about leaving Clay. How could I just go back to Davidson and leave him here at the mercy of his parents?

As if on cue, Mrs. Reed came back through the ICU doors, talking to a tall, bearded man with a hospital badge that identified him as Dr. Lang, the staff psychiatrist.

Knowing it was futile, I approached her after she finished speaking with the doctor. "Is Clay all right? Are you taking him home?"

Mrs. Reed looked at me with cold, unfeeling eyes. "We're taking him back to Florida where we can get him the help he needs" was all she said as she started to turn away from me to fill out the paperwork Dr. Lang had handed her.

I peeked at the form she was signing and saw that it was transfer paperwork. My throat tightened. They really were taking him away.

My mother came up behind me. "Mrs. Reed, I'm Elizabeth Young, Maggie's mother. I know my daughter will be very worried about Clayton. Is there any way you can let her know about his progress? Maybe let them communicate while he's in treatment?"

I tried to control my shocked expression. I couldn't believe my mom was actually advocating for me to be able to maintain communication with Clay. I squeezed her hand in thanks. Mrs. Reed didn't even bother to look up at my mother. Rude bitch.

"I *don't* think that would be appropriate. Your daughter has been the source of a lot of my son's problems during his stay in Virginia. I think the best thing for Clayton will be to get as far away from here, *and her,* as possible." I felt my mom tense beside me, and I waited in anticipation for her to unleash the mama superpowers.

"Excuse me, Mrs. Reed, but I think you are quite mistaken." Mrs. Reed looked up at my mother, seeming bored with their conversation. My mom continued. "Maggie has been nothing but supportive of your son, even when he treated her badly. Perhaps you need to take a long look in the mirror and see why your son is so troubled."

Mrs. Reed simply raised her eyebrow, which was so much like Clay, and didn't bother to respond. She turned on her heel and walked back into the ICU.

And, just like that, the door to my relationship with Clay slammed firmly in my face. I was crushed and my body literally sagged in defeat, as I felt an immeasurable weight pressing down on me.

"Thank you for trying, Mom," I said, as she gathered me to her.

"What a horrible woman. Poor Clayton. No wonder he struggled so." That was the nicest thing my mother had ever said about Clay. She held me close against her as we left the hospital, my father on my other side, and my two best friends following close behind. We all piled into my family's minivan, and I tried to stop the tears as I watched the hospital, and Clay, disappear behind me.

"I need to go back to the motel and get my and Clay's things," I said as my dad pulled out onto the road.

"I don't know if that's a good idea." My mom sounded concerned. I leaned forward and gripped the seat.

"Please, Mom. I need to do this." My mom and dad didn't pose any more arguments. And when we pulled up to the Motel 6, my parents and friends accompanied me into the tiny room that held my last good memories of Clay and me together.

I felt like he had died, because I knew I wouldn't be allowed to see or talk to him for a very long time. At least not until Clay was able to make those decisions for himself. I wanted to be confident in the belief that he would contact me as soon as he was able. But I couldn't be sure and that made the hollow feeling that was building in my chest nearly intolerable. Clay had looked so broken when I left. I wasn't positive he would ever be a part of my life again.

"Shit," Rachel breathed as she took in the destroyed room. No one said anything as I pulled out Clay's duffel bag and started gathering the clothes that he hadn't shredded and stuffed them inside.

I went into the bathroom and almost lost it at the sight of the dried blood on the floor. I closed the door and fell to my knees and let loose my pain. I cried for Clay, for myself, for the future together that we would never have. I put a clean towel under the tap and then got on my knees and scrubbed. I wanted to wipe up every last drop of his blood; as if that would erase the horrible memories of him lying motionless in my arms as I struggled to keep him with me—to keep him alive.

I must have been in there for quite a while, until my mom came in and found me still furiously wiping the floor.

"Honey, you can leave that. That's enough," she said gently, yet I couldn't stop. I wet the towel again and got back on my knees and scrubbed some more.

"Maggie. Please, just leave it." She got down on the floor with me and put her hands over mine. I looked up into her eyes that were filled with love and concern. "You don't have to do this. Leave it here." I knew that she meant more than the blood. I dropped the towel and let her lead me out of the bathroom. Daniel picked up the duffel bag and we closed the door to the motel room. I left the key card outside on the stoop.

Rachel rode beside me on the way home, squeezing my hand every so often. I let my head drop to her shoulder and my best friend stroked my hair as we finally made our way back home.

epilogue

"Maggie, can you bring me the bag of salt from the garage?" my mother called from the front door. I got up off the couch and made my way to the foyer.

My mom was covered in fresh snow and I could see it falling from the late-January sky behind her. "I think your dad put it up on the shelf. Hurry up; this snow won't shovel itself." I pulled on my boots and thick wool coat. I stuffed my hands into a pair of gloves and went outside, then around to the side of the house toward the garage.

Over a month had passed and I was still trying to feel normal, like I still fit inside this life that I had once called mine. My parents kept me busy. My weekends were now filled with shopping trips and movies. My parents had decided to try their hand at some home improvements and enlisted my help in figuring out how to hang drywall and use my mother's ancient sewing machine to make curtains.

Christmas had been hard. I had expected to hear something from Clay, but the holiday came and went. Nothing. Just silence. I tried to hide the hurt I felt, but I wasn't fooling anyone. Rachel and Daniel had been glued to my side for the entire winter break. Even though it was a little suffocating, I appreciated their presence.

Now that we were back in class, Rachel had talked me into signing up for the school musical. I was helping out with the set design and that was eating up a lot of my downtime in the evenings. Time I would have otherwise been moping in my room.

Everyone else was trying, so why couldn't I? Most of the time, I put on a good show. I had become practiced at pretending I wasn't broken inside. Pretending that part of me didn't still linger in that tiny room in the ICU where Clay and I had last been together.

"Do you need help with that?" my dad asked, as I struggled to get the bag of salt from the shelf. I gave up and let him lift it down for me. "Wow, that's heavier than I thought. You want me to take it to your mom?"

I laughed at him. "You are so out of shape, Dad. We're getting you on an exercise plan as soon as it's warm," I threatened.

My dad feigned indignation. "I'm plenty in shape."

"Sure you are, Mr. I-eat-four-doughnuts-for-breakfast-and-a-bag-of-Doritos-for-lunch. Go on inside and let us younger, fitter people handle the heavy lifting," I joked. My dad chuckled, but left me to my chore.

It felt good to have my relationship with my parents on the mend. Sure, they still watched me closely. But I really couldn't blame them. I had dragged them through hell and back. I deserved their vigilance, despite how much it smothered me at times.

I wasn't entirely sure what they were watching for, though. Clay was gone. I hadn't heard from him or his parents since that day in the hospital waiting room. Not that I was surprised. His mother had made it very clear she wanted me to have absolutely nothing to do with her son. I had spoken to Ruby several times but she never had any information to give me. So I struggled with the betrayal that pierced my chest when I wondered why Clay hadn't tried harder to get ahold of me. I had honestly thought his love for me was stronger than that. If the tables had been turned, I knew I would have stopped at nothing to talk to him again.

But I tried to focus on the marginal happiness I felt in knowing that, despite my not hearing from him, he was getting help somewhere. Even if it was away from me. Yeah, I didn't wear selflessness very well.

And every time I thought of him, I ached inside and I found it hard to breathe.

I had wondered a million times how I could possibly go on living when my heart was gone. How was it possible that it still beat in my chest when it felt so empty?

"Here you go, Mom," I said, as I let the heavy bag fall to the ground. My mom stopped shoveling and bent over to rip it open.

"Thanks, Maggie May," she said, before scattering some salt on the sidewalk.

"I don't know why you bother. Just wait until it stops snowing. You realize it'll just have to be redone in the morning," I told her, watching her freshly shoveled path disappearing under a blanket of white.

"Because it'll be much worse in the morning if I don't do some of it now," she said, returning to her task.

I just shook my head and turned to go back into the house. I stopped for a moment, possessed by some childish impulse. I turned my face upward toward the sky and stuck out my tongue, letting the cold flakes melt in my mouth. I loved the snow, and it, like almost everything else, reminded me of Clay. I remembered our time at the cabin, lying together in the loft as snow fell outside and me thinking that I could never be happier than I was at that moment.

I sighed. Those memories were a blessing and a curse. I was thankful that I had them, but they hurt so much. It had to get better eventually, right? I asked myself this every single day. I slowly trudged forward, my steps feeling heavier than they had before.

I tried hard to pull it all together. I wanted to be the daughter my parents deserved, and the friend I knew Rachel and Danny needed. But it was hard to be that girl some days. Maybe it was the lack of closure. Not knowing what Clay was doing, or *how* he was doing, made it torturous.

Then there were the doubts that festered like a disease in my mind. Sometimes I found myself thinking that maybe he realized he *was* better off without me. That what we had wasn't as life-altering for him as it had been for me. That maybe I was alone in the love I still felt as deeply as I had from its onset. I tried to put my dismal thoughts away. Every day I tried. I couldn't let myself get mired in them, or I'd likely find myself in the same depression I had been drowning in for too long after leaving Clay lying there in the hospital. I determined that I must go on, move forward, live my life, and be as happy as I was capable of without him. Despite how daunting and impossible the task seemed.

I caught sight of the mail truck as it skidded to a stop in front of the house. I don't know why it made me pause, but it did. I walked out to meet the mailman. "Here, I'll get that," I said, forcing a smile and taking the pile of envelopes.

"Drive safely," I told him as he got back into his truck. He thanked me and left.

My hands began to shake as I sorted through the stack of bills and junk mail. My reaction was always the same when the mail arrived. I always wished—actually, yearned—for, just once, a letter addressed to me to be in there. I hated that I repeatedly got my hopes up, but I did anyway.

But this time, I found what I was looking for. There at the

bottom of the pile was a small envelope. As I pulled it out, my heart stuttered at the sight of my name written in a familiar, sloping hand. Funny how just the sight of his handwriting had the power to shred my guts.

Standing there, with snow up to my ankles, I didn't know what to do. Part of me wanted to rip the letter to pieces, frightened by the crippling pain that would inevitably accompany his words. But that was such a small part of the hurricane of emotions I was feeling that I hastily shoved it away. Of course I would read it. I had to. I felt compelled to, never mind the emotional wreckage it could create. It wasn't really even an option. I most definitely would read it. Just not right now.

I folded up the letter and put it in my jeans pocket and went about the rest of my day, even as the envelope weighed me down like a stone around my neck.

I spent the rest of the morning channel surfing, enjoying the snow day. Rachel and Daniel trekked over in the afternoon and Rachel insisted on giving me a haircut. Normally I wouldn't let scissors anywhere near me but, with Clay's words deep in my pocket, I felt a sudden overwhelming need for a change.

Daniel flopped down on my bed and leafed through a magazine as Rachel snipped and layered and snipped some more. "I can't believe you read this junk," Daniel snorted.

Rachel held my head straight as I tried to see the article he was reading on how to get a boy to notice you. "If you don't want to have to buzz your head later, hold still." I immediately sat up straight.

When Rachel was finished she held up a mirror. "So, whatcha think?" she asked. I turned my head from side to side and grinned. She had done an awesome job. My normally long brown hair had been chopped off above my shoulders. Rachel had given me chunky layers around my face and it looked amazingly sleek and stylish. I fluffed it.

"You have a gift, my friend," I complimented her, very pleased with the result.

Daniel looked up and gave me a low whistle. "You look hot, Mags." Rachel and I grinned.

"So, Maggie . . ." Daniel began. I was instantly suspicious, because he *never* used my full name. I looked at him archly.

"Yes?" I prompted.

"I was talking to Jake Fitzsimmons the other day and he was asking about you." I looked away from my best friend. I knew he was trying to be helpful, wanting me to move on with my life. Attempting to reacclimate me to the life I had led before Clay had appeared in it. But Jake Fitzsimmons—actually, any guy—didn't have a chance as long as Clay still held my heart.

"Don't think so, Danny," I said lightly, trying to hide the misery the thought of dating other guys created.

"Jake's hot. I mean, what would it hurt to go out on a date with him? We could all go together if that would make it easier. It's not as though you're cheating. I mean . . . you know, I don't think Clay's . . . ummm . . . well . . . you know." Rachel didn't finish her thought, letting her sentence trail off into what became an awkward silence.

Her well-intentioned encouragement made me snap and I flushed with anger. "Well, I can't do that, okay? I love Clay and it wouldn't be right. So just drop it, please," I told them shortly. I didn't miss the look that passed between them. But the subject was dropped.

Daniel and Rachel didn't stay much longer and, sadly, I was relieved when they left. Trying to put on my happy face was proving difficult today. Not when I was just waiting to read Clay's letter.

Finally, after dinner, I excused myself and went to my room. My parents didn't question it, as this had become my normal routine. I closed the door behind me and sat on my bed. I slowly pulled out the crumpled letter from my pocket and held it, feeling its warmth from being tucked against me all day.

I inspected the envelope and saw that there was no return address. That seemed to indicate pretty firmly that whatever Clayton Reed had to say to me required no response. I couldn't help but feel equal parts angry and hurt by that.

Tearing open the envelope, I carefully unfolded the paper. My name jumped out at me. I noticed the indentations where Clay had pressed his pen down hard. I could almost feel his anxiety. His fear. His grief. Undoubtedly because that was exactly how I was feeling. I closed my eyes, bracing myself and gearing up my nerve. Then I began to read. His love for me immediately leaped from the page. I was almost crippled with intense relief. I realized then how scared I had been that he would stop loving me. That he would go on and live his life and forget all about me. But I guess I should have given him more credit than that.

Maggie,
I'm not sure I should be writing this. I feel like it's incredibly
selfish of me to need to write these words and to need you to
read them—to need you to know they are true. As if I am
more entitled to these feelings than you are. But I'm not.
Your thoughts, the way you feel, every single thing about
you, means everything to me.

I guess that's why I'm writing. There isn't a second of
every day that passes that I don't think about you. You are
everywhere. I can still smell your hair, hear you cursing me
when I drive too fast, and feel your breath as I fall asleep.

It hurts to remember you. But it scares me to try and
forget. I remember you telling me that my love for you
shouldn't hurt, that it should be something wonderful.
And it is. It is the most wonderful thing I've ever had. But
the truth is, it does hurt. My love for you destroyed

everything around us and almost destroyed you, and I hate myself for that.

You deserve so much more than me. You always have. I hope you do find what you deserve one day. Someone who can love you selflessly and unconditionally without baggage and strings. Someone who doesn't let you leave your family behind. Someone you don't have to follow into hell.

I am a selfish person, Mags. Because I still love you and I know that I will until I die. And even as I tell you to move on with your life and live it—to find someone else, I pray you don't. Because I can't handle the thought of anyone else holding you, anyone else touching you, anyone else experiencing your love the way I did.

I don't know exactly what I'm trying to tell you here. I can see the frown on your face as you're reading this and hear you telling me to spit it out and get on with it.

I smiled through my tear-filled eyes at that comment. Clay knew me too well.

I suppose what I'm really trying to say is thank you. Thank you for giving me the most beautiful and amazing months of my life. Thank you for loving me in spite of me. Thank you for giving me hope and light, even if it was only for a little while. And I want to tell you again, I'm sorry. I should have been stronger and let you lean on me, instead of forcing you to shoulder the burden for both of us.

I realize my love for you crippled both of us.

But your love saved me.

Which is why this has to be good-bye. I can't stomach the thought of you waiting for me, for a person that I may never be. I'm trying to get better. But it's a hard and bitter road and I don't know when, or even if, I will ever be completely okay.

I want you to move on. To live your life, even if it rips me apart to not live it with you. I can't even give you the hope that there is a maybe at the end of all this. Because I would hate to kill that hope again.

Just know that you are and always will be my world. You found me in the dark and saved me from myself. You have shown me the type of person I want to be and I strive to be him. For you and for me.

I will love you forever.

Always,

Clay

Wow. I dropped the letter at my feet and made no effort to wipe away the tears that streamed down my face. Whatever I had been expecting, that wasn't it.

Damn Clay Reed and his stupid back-and-forth crap! How perfectly typical of him. Telling me how much he loved me and in the next breath pushing me away. He had effectively shut me out of his life. Again. He wanted me to move on. To live my life. He told me not to wait for him, that he wouldn't be coming back to me.

I found it hard to breathe as I faced the finality of his words. We were over. There was no more *us*. I couldn't help but feel anger and betrayal at how he had given up. How he had just let go of all that we had.

I picked the letter up from the floor and balled it in my fist, planning to throw it away. But I stopped myself. I placed the paper on my desk and smoothed it out. I couldn't get rid of it. It was my last link to him, and I needed that.

So I put it in the very bottom of my desk drawer. I didn't want to see it again, but I couldn't let go of it, either. I couldn't read his good-bye again, but I had to know that it was still there. That his love was a real thing. That I hadn't imagined it.

I felt older, and maybe just a little bit wiser. I had my own baggage and strings and it would take time for me to lighten my load. But I would.

Because I was Maggie Young. And from now on I vowed to stay out of the dark.

important resources

Depression, suicide, and cutting are serious issues. Statistics show that 2 to 3 million people in the United States and 13 percent of fifteen- to sixteen-year-olds in the United Kingdom cut every year. Self-injurious behavior is often a way for people to cope with larger issues.

If you or someone you know is dealing with cutting or depression, it is important to talk about it, to get help, and to find a way to stop it!

There are so many great resources out there. Seeking help is the place to start.

Depression and Bipolar Support Alliance (DBSA)
www.dbsalliance.org

Teen Self-Injury Hotline
1-800-DONT-CUT

Teen Suicide Hotline
1-800-SUICIDE

This is a great source of information about self-injury:
www.selfinjury.com

acknowledgments

Thank you so much to my fantastic husband, who endured weeks of being left alone in the evenings so that I could get this book done. Your support has been unwavering.

Thank you to my beautiful and amazing daughter, who never fails to make me smile.

Thank you to my fantastic friend and editor, Julie, who helps me wade through all the crap to get to the story underneath. You are great at what you do!

Thank you to my friends, who played guinea pig and gave me great feedback.

And, most of all, thank you to my readers. Without you, I wouldn't be doing this at all!

Don't miss the *New York Times* and *USA Today*
bestselling sequel to

find you
in the dark

Maggie and Clay's emotional love story continues in

light in the shadows

BY A. MEREDITH WALTERS

Available July 2014 from Gallery Books

Turn the page for a preview of *Light in the Shadows*. . . .

chapter
one

clay

"You're cheating! There is no freaking way you can win six rounds of poker!" the scrawny boy across the table from me said, throwing his cards down in frustration. I chuckled as I scooped up the pile of red and blue chips, adding them to my pile.

"I warned you that there was no way you could beat me, Tyler. Not my fault that you didn't take my advice," I said. Tyler grumbled under his breath, but grabbed the pile of cards and started to shuffle them again.

I leaned back in the wing chair, waiting for my roommate to deal. I had been at the Grayson Center, a private facility for teenagers experiencing mental illness, for almost three months. I was enrolled in a ninety-day program and my time was almost up. Looking around the recreation room, I realized I would actually be kind of sad when I had to leave.

Which is weird, considering how much I had fought coming here in the first place. Once I had gotten over my anger and resistance to treatment, though, I almost came to enjoy my time here.

I found that the staff and the other patients did something I never thought was possible.

They showed me how to heal.

And that's what I was doing. Slowly. Not that I expected a perfect fix in three months. I realized my healing would take years. And there were days I thought I would never be able to leave and live a decent life outside the support of the center and the safety of its walls. But then there were good days, like today, when I felt like I could take on the world.

Like I could find my way back to Maggie.

"What's with the goofy smile, bro? You look like an idiot," Tyler said good-naturedly as he tossed out cards. I blinked, taken away from my happy thoughts, and picked up my cards.

"Nothin', man. Just having a good day."

Tyler smiled. Other guys would probably have given me shit for acting like an emo pussy. But not the people here. We were all here because we *needed* to have those good days. So we understood the importance of happy days for those who had them.

"Cool, Clay. Glad to hear it. Now, focus on the damn game. I want to win some of my chips back," Tyler retorted, concentrating on his hand.

I grinned before beating him soundly—yet again.

◆

The group sat on the floor, kids relaxing on oversized cushions. Looking around, I could almost imagine that this was just a bunch of friends hanging out together. Except for the two adults who sat in the middle asking them questions like "Tell me about your relationship with your family" and "How does that make you feel?"

Yep, group therapy was a blast.

The girl to my right, a dark-haired chick named Maria, was here to deal with her severe depression and her promiscuity brought on by serious Daddy issues. She was trying to figure out how to answer the question that Sabrina, the female counselor, had just asked her.

"Just think about your happiest memory with your mother. It can be something simple like talking to her about your day, or a time that she smiled at you," Sabrina prompted gently. Maria's problems, like those of most of the kids' in the room, were rooted firmly in her relationship with her parents.

Today's group topic was trying to acknowledge the positive aspects of our familial relationships. To say this was hard for most of us was an understatement.

I dreaded the sessions when we had to talk about our parents in a more positive light. It was so much easier to vent about how crappy they were than to find something nice to say.

"Um, well, I guess there was this time . . . I was probably, like, six. And my mom took me to the park and pushed me on the swings," Maria volunteered, looking at Sabrina and Matt, the other counselor, for approval.

They each nodded. "Good. And how did you feel then?" Matt urged.

Maria smiled a bit. "It felt good. Like she . . . I don't know . . . loved me." The smile on her face was sad and my heart hurt for her. I understood her need to feel loved by her mother all too well.

There was some more processing to help Maria identify and handle her feelings, followed by a period of silence while everyone allowed Maria time to get herself together. Then it was my turn. Matt looked at me expectantly. "Clay. What about you? What is a happy memory you have about your parents?" The group looked at me, waiting for my answer. Over the last two-and-a-half months, this disclosure thing had proven difficult for me.

I didn't reveal personal details very easily. It had taken Maggie, the person I loved most in this world, a long time to get me to open up. And if it was hard for me to talk to Maggie, then it was nearly impossible to get me to open up to a group of strangers.

But, over time, after lots of individual and group-therapy sessions, I was able to loosen up and talk more about what I had experienced. The things I felt, my fears, my pain, and what I wanted most in my life. And I found that the more I talked, the better I felt.

I began to recognize that these people weren't here to judge me or make me feel bad when I talked about wanting to kill myself or how hard it was for me not to cut. Cutting had always been my form of coping. Comforting and familiar, it was easier to make myself bleed than to face the truth of my issues. And these people didn't look at me like I was crazy when I would break down after a particularly gut-wrenching session. This was the most support I had felt from anyone besides Maggie, Ruby, and Lisa in my entire life.

And it felt unbelievable.

So, with all eyes on me, I really thought about my answer to Matt's question. And then, just like that, I had it. A memory that was actually good and not tainted by anger and bitterness. "My dad taking me fishing." Sabrina smiled at me. "Yeah. It was before things got really bad. My dad wasn't the district attorney yet, so he had more time for me. He picked me up from school early one day and drove us out to a lake. I can't really remember where. Anyway, we spent all day fishing and talking. It was nice."

I smiled as I remembered when I could be with my dad without wanting to rip his face off. Matt nodded. "That sounds awesome, Clay. Thanks for sharing that with us." And he was moving on to the next person.

The memory of that time with my dad made me feel pretty good. I was feeling that way a lot more lately. Less of the crazy depression and anger, and more of the happy-go-lucky thing that I never thought I was capable of experiencing.

I'm sure it had a lot to do with my new medication. After I came to the Grayson Center, my new doctor, Dr. Todd, as we kids called him, put me on a new pill. Tegretol helped control my manic mood swings without turning me into a zombie.

It was pretty great. And even though I had moments where, strangely, I missed those energetic highs—which Dr. Todd told me was normal—I sure as hell didn't miss the crippling lows. The psychotherapy that I attended three times a week was also helping a lot. It was nice to not have to worry about hurting myself or someone else. To think that maybe I would be able to get my shit together and find a way back to where I belonged.

With Maggie.

I shook my head. I couldn't think about her here in group. That was something I saved for when I was alone. Because if I started thinking of her now, I would invariably remember how much I'd hurt her and how I'd fucked things up so royally. And then my good mood would evaporate in a flash. *Snap.* Just like that.

I must have zoned out for a while, because I suddenly realized that the other kids were getting to their feet. Maria grinned at me. "Earth to Clay!" She reached for my hand to help me up. I looked at her for a moment as I stood. Maria had a nice smile and really pretty eyes. But she wasn't Maggie. I dropped her hand quickly. I tried to pretend that I didn't see the disappointment flash across her face.

We walked together out of the common room and headed down the hallway to the cafeteria. "That was pretty tough today," Maria said as we caught up with the others, who were getting in line for lunch.

I nodded. "Yeah. It's kinda hard finding something nice to say about my parents. You know, considering they're a bunch of self-absorbed asses," I joked, picking up a tray. Maria giggled behind me.

"I know what you mean. My mom is a cracked-out deadbeat who refused to protect me from my dad because it got in the way of her next high. Thinking of the ooey-gooey times together is hard."

I took a plate of pasta and a salad and moved to drinks, getting myself a bottle of water. Maria followed me to our regular table near the large window overlooking the gardens. Tyler and our other friends, Susan and Greg, were already seated.

"Hey, guys," I said as I sat down. Greg scooted over to make room and Maria sat on my other side.

"How was group?" Tyler asked around a mouthful of sandwich. Maria and I shrugged in unison and we laughed.

"It was group. How about you guys?" Maria said. The other three were in a group for substance abuse while Maria and I were in ours. Susan Biddle, a short girl with brown hair and big brown eyes who reminded me a lot of Maggie's friend Rachel, snorted.

"It would have been better if loudmouth Austin hadn't decided to be a total dick to Jean." Jean was the substance-abuse counselor at the center. And Austin was this place's Paul Delawder, the dick who had destroyed my MP3 player my first day at Jackson High School back in Virginia. The guy Maggie had jumped to defend me from. I smiled at the memory of my brave girl.

Maria elbowed me in the side to bring me back to the conversation. "Fuck Austin. He sucks," I said, smiling. Greg, Susan, and Tyler agreed and the conversation then focused on the movie the center was showing that night.

Every week, if we had earned enough merits and were doing well in our therapy, we were rewarded with a movie night. We earned merits for completing various chores that the behavioral aides and therapists assigned us. This week my job was to keep the common room clean. I shared the job with three other kids. I had earned all of my merits for the week, which was pretty cool. I had lost a lot of them my first two weeks here. So getting to join in the fun stuff was about the most exciting thing that happened to me anymore.

It wasn't like we left the facility or anything. But it was cool to hang out with everyone in a nontherapeutic way and watch a movie without having to talk about our feelings. Everyone could just relax and remember for a little while that yeah, we were still teenagers.

Maria, Tyler, and I walked back to my room after lunch. We had an hour until afternoon sessions started. I had a one-on-one with Jean. The others had sessions either with their counselors or in groups. That was the thing about this place. It was one big session after another.

Maria flopped onto my bed, making herself at home. I had become pretty close to Maria since I had arrived (in a purely platonic way, of course), and she often came back to the room to hang with me and Tyler. But it still felt weird to have her on my bed, even if she was just sitting on it. Because I didn't want to see any girl but Maggie May Young on my bed.

Even though I had written Maggie a letter a month ago, telling her to move on, it didn't mean that I had moved on. I couldn't stomach the thought of being with anyone but her. No one else mattered. I had a feeling that Maria was starting to like me as more than a friend. And even though I hadn't done anything to encourage it, I felt like I was going to have to say something to her soon.

No way was I going to hurt another girl I cared about.

Tyler got on his computer and started typing out e-mails. I pulled up my desk chair and straddled it backward, resting my arms on the back. Maria leaned over and picked up the framed picture on my bedside table.

"She's really pretty," Maria commented with a twinge of something in her voice that I couldn't identify. Maria had picked up the only picture I had in the room. It was of Maggie and me from the

Fall Formal. We were sitting beside each other at Red Lobster and we were both making faces at the camera. I didn't need to look at the picture to remember how things used to be between us. It was all I could think about. Every second of every day. All I did was think. About the good times. And the bad times. And all the messed-up stuff in between.

Maria gave a small sigh and placed the frame back in its spot. "Do you ever talk to her?" she asked me. I always felt strange talking about Maggie. Even though things had gotten ugly between us, my love for her was the one pure thing in my life. I wanted to keep it all to myself and not share it with anyone. She was the last thing I thought about before I went to sleep and the first thing my mind went to when I woke up.

I constantly wondered what she was doing, if she was happy, if she had started dating anyone. That thought hurt. A lot. Because I really did want her to live her life, even if that meant moving on from me. But that didn't mean I had to like it.

"No. I don't think that would do either of us any good," I admitted, repositioning the picture frame so that I could see it.

Maria frowned. "Why? If you love her so much, don't you think talking to her would be a good thing?" I gritted my teeth. Explaining anything regarding my relationship with Maggie made me defensive. But I forced myself to calm down, using those breathing techniques the counselors had been drilling into our brains for months.

"Because, Maria, the fact that I love her is the reason I can't go turning her life upside down anymore. I won't fuck with her like that again. She's been through enough because of me." I sounded so pathetic. Maggie's hold on me was as unyielding as ever.

Maria's face softened, her eyes getting that dewy look that girls get when a guy says something sweet (Maggie used to get that same look every time I told her I loved her). "She's lucky to have your love, Clay. I hope she realizes that."

I swallowed, getting a little uncomfortable talking about this with Maria, particularly with Tyler playing with his computer five feet away. Maria reached out and squeezed my arm, her fingers, I noticed, lingering on my skin. "Just keep doing what you're doing and maybe one day you'll feel like you can call her."

I smiled. Yeah. Maybe . . . one day.